REVERB

TWISTED WISHES
BOOK 3

ANNA ZABO

This is a work of fiction. Names, characters, places, and any incidents are either the product of the authors' imagination or are used fictitiously. Any resemblance to actual persons, living or dead, to business establishments, events, or locales is entirely coincidental.

Reverb

Second Edition

First edition published by Carina Press, 2019-2025

Edited by Mackenzie Walton

Cover design by L. C. Chase

Print ISBN: 978-1-947550-22-3

CONTENT NOTES

This book contains:

- consensual light kink
- on-page consensual sex, including where they might be caught in public
- sex with strap-ons / dildos
- mention of death of parent from cancer
- mention of previous hospitalization of other character
- scenes in hospitals
- mention of another character almost dying
- mention of deaths due to war combat (but not described).
- mention of scars from war
- stalking, both physical and on-line
- paparazzi following characters, and photos shared online, including in swimwear.
- Top surgery scars are mentioned, but by trans fan of band looking for advice / support.
- mention of sex work, including stripping
- alcohol consumption by characters

- harassing emails
- misogyny from villain
- theft of items, including one with personal significance
- trans and queer microaggressions (not from main characters or supporting characters)
- stabbing
- past near sexual assault of a minor lightly described

This one is for my trans siblings, and for me, too.
We deserve happily-ever-afters.

CHAPTER ONE

Mish Sullivan hated hospitals. The harsh light, the antiseptic smell, the curtains and lack of privacy, and all the bad memories being in one dredged up. All those times back when she'd been a teen, sitting at her mom's side, waiting for the inevitable to happen. More recently, she'd sat at Ray's hospital bed, her heart in her throat for the leader and singer/songwriter of their little band when he'd had a horrendous allergic reaction after being roofied by their former shitbag of a manager.

Twisted Wishes wasn't so little now. They had a reasonable new manager, and they were about to go on their own headlining tour across the US. This time, it was Ray sitting by her bed, pale and upset while the rest of the band, plus their social media coordinator, lingered behind him, all looking shaken.

She really needed Ray to calm the fuck down before that expression of horror on his face spread to the rest of the guys. Last thing she needed was *four* nervous wrecks. The guys were all too strung out most of the time as it was.

"I'm fine, sweetheart, really." Mish patted Ray's hand. She was, too. Mostly. Yes, her right hand was sprained and in a brace, her knees were bloodied and bruised, and fighting off that shithead had ended with her ripping her brand-new patterned stockings. And she'd fucking loved those things. She had a few other scrapes here and there, but nothing major. "None the worse for wear."

Ray made a sound that was a weird combination of a laugh, a sob, and a grunt. "The fuck you are. He nearly broke your hand!"

Not quite true. She'd slugged that guy in the jaw *before* she'd lost her footing and landed weirdly on it. Bad piece of luck. The crowd at their pop-up concert had been so thick and the venue security too thin. She'd been knocked around and dragged in the rush to get the band out of there, and that certainly hadn't helped her hand any.

She'd had worse in bar fights. Nothing was broken this time, there was hardly any blood, and she hadn't needed stitches.

Zavier, their drummer and Ray's husband, put a hand on Ray's shoulder. His blue eyes locked on Mish's and the look he gave her, while sympathetic, was also worried. Fucking Zav. He was going to take Ray's side in this. Coddle her. He was usually the most levelheaded of the lot.

She cut him off even as he opened his mouth. "I fell wrong, that's all. I'm fine. They're gonna spring me from here soon, and we can all go home."

Though she wouldn't be playing until her hand healed. No way she could move her fingers on the strings of her bass when everything was *this* swollen. Thankfully, they had a couple of weeks before their tour. She'd exercise the hand as it healed. Keep it limber. They planned to marathon some practices before the tour started anyway. She'd be healed up by then.

"He came at you with scissors." Soft words from Dom, their guitarist. He was still in most of his makeup and all of his studded leather, but he'd turned back into the quiet, thoughtful version of himself.

"He just wanted some hair, the weirdo." She waved his concern away.

Behind Dom, Adrian—their social media/tech guy and Dom's boy toy—crossed his arms. He didn't say anything. Didn't need to. He was the oldest out of all of them and as even-keeled as Zav. His thoughtful frown wasn't a good sign.

"Adrian..." Last thing they needed was *him* to go mushy-brained about this.

He shook his head. "It's not an isolated thing, Mish. You don't see the emails."

But he did. Mish flinched when her stomach tumbled. "I want out of here." Though it galled her that Adrian might be keeping secrets from her, she didn't want to hear that she had a stalker, or obsessive fans, or whatever it was that he was going to tell her. "Can one of you find a doc or a nurse?"

Before any of the boys could do what she'd asked, their band manager, Marcella, strode into the room. Thank god. Someone who'd understand that none of this was that big a deal. Just...the normal stuff of being a rock star.

Mish turned to her. "Will you please talk some sense into these boys and tell them everything's fine?"

Marcella sighed. "You have a badly sprained wrist that will keep you from playing for several weeks, plus cuts and abrasions. The tabloids have photos of you bloodied up out there on the scandal sites, and people are speculating that the tour will be canceled. Everything is *not* fine."

"See?" Ray pointed at Marcella, as if to underscore the point.

"Fuck that. I'll be fine by then, and I'm not porcelain, Ray. I got a little banged up because of some dork—that's it. If I were Zav, would you be this upset?"

Probably the wrong person to pick. "If that had happened

to Zav, to my *husband,* I'd be hiring a security guard for his ass."

Zavier frowned. "The hell you would."

"See?" Mish pointed at Zavier. "He doesn't need protection, and neither do I."

Ray stepped closer to Zavier, fire in his eyes. "The hell I *wouldn't,* Zavier..."

Marcella cleared her throat. "Actually, you need protection. *All* of you. Hiring a guard for the band is a fantastic idea. You're too big now not to have someone working for you, especially with the more...exuberant fans."

Like the one who'd come after her. "I don't need a damn bodyguard," Mish said, even as her arms and knees started to ache from the fall. "Besides, I bet that guy looks worse. That'll stop people."

"That guy is in a holding cell at the police station," Marcella said. "And the booking photos are on the internet, too, with comments about your temperament. Frankly, you all need someone watching over you. This isn't a you thing, Mish." She waved her hand around the room. "It's an *all of you* thing."

Ray nodded, and Zavier had a resigned look in his eyes. Shit.

Mish pushed her hair back. "Ray, *no.* I can take care of myself. Fuck it, I take care of you lot. And I don't give two shits what the press says."

The fucking press. They were all over her no matter what she did or didn't do. Too foul-mouthed, too sexy, wore too much makeup, never mind she wore less than Domino most of the time. Not a lady. Too much the whore.

Dom peered up at the ceiling, then back at Mish. "I don't want a bodyguard any more than you. I like it *just us,* but Marcella's right."

Adrian nodded and Zavier scratched the back of his head,

looking younger than he usually let himself, and a tiny bit scared, too.

Marcella blew out a breath and turned to Ray. "So that's a yes?"

"Yeah," Ray said. "See who you can find, and we'll interview them."

Great. This was exactly what she didn't want. Mish rose from the bed, thankful they hadn't hooked her up to an IV or made her change into a gown. "I'm gonna find a goddamned person to check me out of this fucking hellish place."

Even after she'd tracked down the nurse on duty, it still took another hour and a half to get released from the hospital. All that time, the band stayed with her. It was both endearing and absolutely frustrating. She loved every last one of them like her own flesh and blood, but damn it, she needed to process what had happened. Alone. Her insides were as ugly as a badly tossed salad and her nerves skittered and pinched, but the moment she let anything show, the guys would be all over her with even more worry and concern.

Didn't stop the thoughts swirling in her head. The warning signs she'd missed before the guy came at her, how she could have turned, moved, or lunged differently. Maybe if she'd put her hair up after the show...

God, she didn't know. Her hand throbbed now, and a dull ache pounded behind her eyes, that pain she hated, that telltale sign that both her body and mind were *done* and her emotions were about to spill into reality.

She wasn't about to shed any tears in front of the guys, though. If they caught *her* tearing up, they'd lose it. Plus, she fucking *hated* crying, that betrayal of her body over her mind.

She was so grateful when they finally piled into the SUV Marcella had hired. Right after she belted herself in, she closed her eyes and tried to pretend that she was tired, not—overwhelmed. Hurting. Thank god there were no paparazzi with cameras here. Had there been, she might've punched them out, too, and that would've driven everyone bonkers.

Like it or not, the press—even the bloodsucking, shit-stirring scandal sites—had an impact on the band and they had to play nice. The guys got crapped on, though not as hard as she did. But *they* held it together. She could, too.

"Hey, Mish?" Adrian's deep voice sounded next to her, barely audible over the rumble of the car. Though he was the newest member of their little musical family, he'd woven himself seamlessly into their group, his relationship with Dom notwithstanding.

She opened her eyes and turned toward him. "Yeah?"

"Don't be too hard on Ray. He wants you all safe." He paused. "Us all."

The late addition made her smile. "Finally figuring out you're part of us?"

He chuckled, but sobered. "Seriously, though."

"I don't need anyone taking care of me, hon."

His gaze was so solemn. "We all do, sometimes."

Mish grunted and rolled her head back. Maybe they did, but not her. Every time she'd let anyone try, it always went to shit, because "taking care" meant the other person taking over, and fuck that to hell. First her deadbeat father, then a string of her mom's boyfriends, then her jerk bosses. When she'd joined Ray's band, she'd made a stipulation: Ray could make suggestions, but he needed to listen to the band, too. They'd decide things together. And they had.

Ray's heart was in the right place, and Marcella's, too. Didn't mean Mish wanted a fucking bodyguard watching over her because *she* was a liability.

"I'm the one watching out for you boys. I don't need a caretaker."

"You can't punch out every too-rabid fan," he murmured.

Yeah, she could. And would. To keep them safe, to keep herself safe. Even if she already knew what was coming.

Because once Ray Van Zeller got an idea in his head, it was nearly impossible to shake it loose. Which meant, sooner or later, she'd be saddled with security and she'd probably end up taking care of whoever that was, too.

CHAPTER TWO

David Altet heard the argument floating down the stairwell as he made his way up to the third floor of the converted warehouse. At first, only tones filtered down, two strong voices straying over each other, one higher pitched than the other, both mirrors of intensity. As he neared the third floor landing, those tones sharpened into words.

"But nothing has happened in weeks!" Mish Sullivan had a lovely voice. Vibrant, with a sharp edge and gritty finish. The kind of voice he wouldn't mind whispering into his ear in bed.

"We haven't been in public in weeks. And Adrian's gotten some weird emails and comments on the accounts about you." That was Ray Van Zeller. He'd met Ray several times while interviewing, then hashing out the details of his contract while they both got a feel for each other to see if David could provide what Ray wanted and if David wanted to work with Ray and his band.

"I don't fucking need anyone protecting me." More grit there, and a rumble that was sexy and tantalizing.

Ray had warned David that the firebrand bass player

who'd leveled her attacker with one punch wasn't taking kindly to the idea of a security detail. At least not for *her*.

From all the press he'd seen of the band, Sullivan was no-nonsense and sharp. Reminded him of several of the women he'd known in the army. Strong. Independent. Fierce. Yeah, a woman like that would not take kindly to having her back watched by someone she didn't know. On the other hand, that was exactly his job.

Twisted Wishes needed Mish Sullivan—and the rest of the band—safe.

He pulled open the door to the third floor, keeping the noise to a minimum. Part of securing the band was learning how they interacted with each other. All signs pointed to them being a united front. They'd weathered quite a lot in their short and meteoric rise to stardom, including Ray nearly dying by the hand of their former manager.

What a shit show that must have been, and all the more reason for Sullivan and the band not to trust an outsider. However, public fronts and what happened behind closed doors could be vastly different, even if Ray'd said they were like one big family.

Families fought. Like now, apparently. David slipped down the hall, too aware that he was an interloper.

"It's the whole band," Ray said. "Not just you."

"Yeah, right. 'Cause you have Zav, and Dom has Adrian, so who're you sticking this dude with, huh?" Silence, then a sigh from Mish. "Kiddo, I know you're trying to do the right thing."

David continued toward the open studio door, the scent of concrete, brick, and moisture lingering in the hall on this humid, late spring day. New York was soupy as fuck. Would only get worse in the summer.

"Then let me do the right thing." Ray's voice was pained. "You haven't read the stuff Adrian has."

"You haven't let me."

David had read them, though. Most of the mail, comments, and replies Twisted Wishes got on their various social media accounts were benign. Excited and appreciative fans, especially queer ones. Notes to specific band members that were gushing or of the "I love you!" variety, but harmless in nature. Lovely and endearing stuff. Twisted Wishes had a stellar fanbase, one that they seemed to enjoy and interact well with.

But there were the few pieces that *weren't* like that. Those were about Mish and seemed to be from one sender, going by syntax and style. Details about her hair and skin, and what he wanted from her. A date. To talk. A kiss on the cheek. To hold her hand. Run his hands up those legs of hers. Creepy, creepy stuff.

Even if there hadn't been the attack a couple of weeks ago, the band sure as shit needed to be taking this seriously. Especially considering the guy who had gone after Mish wasn't the one who'd sent those messages. That guy was in jail and couldn't have sent the latest batch, though David was certain Internet Dude had some connection to that event.

Mish Sullivan had an obsessive fan, and he was *dangerous*.

"You shouldn't have to see that shit." Ray's voice sounded pained.

"I don't need you or Adrian protecting me. You've both got enough on your plate."

And that was David's cue to step into the doorway and rap his knuckles on the frame.

Five heads turned to stare at him, and David got his first personal look at the core of Twisted Wishes. Ray Van Zeller he'd met during his interview, and he knew Zavier Demos, Mish Sullivan, and Dominic Bradley—known as Domino Grinder—from the music videos, publicity, and news stories. The other guy had to be Adrian Doran, Dominic's lover and their social media guru.

Ray looked relieved. "You found the place."

David gave a shrug. "GPS is a wonderful thing." Ray'd given him the address, but he'd also checked the fan spaces online and found the same location, which explained the gaggle of people outside, all with cell phones and some with cameras. David had walked around the building and found a door that'd been propped open by workers doing a reno job on the second floor. No one had bothered him when he'd made his way up the fire stairs, despite this being a secure building.

He wasn't about to lead with that, though, so he smiled at the band members and their media guru.

Ray turned to the rest of the group. "This is David Altet. He's the guy I hired to be our security."

There were murmurs of hellos as David made his way into the room, all except from Mish. She was glaring at Ray. When that same gaze was leveled at David, she crossed her arms, defensive and wary.

He didn't blame her. Couldn't. He understood the desire, the absolute need to be who you were. And Mish Sullivan was a woman who was equal parts protector and individual. No doubt she'd chew David out if he gave any of her bandmates flak.

"I suggested to Ray that meeting you all before the tour would be a better plan than showing up at your first gig, barking orders." He found an old stool that had a few paint splashes on it, and propped his ass on the edge. "Though I don't bark all that often."

"Well, that's good, since I don't take orders." Mish shoved a hand into her red curls and peered at Ray. "Please don't tell me this is the guy I'm gonna have to take care of."

David couldn't help the quirk in his lips, which of course Mish caught. She raised an eyebrow at Ray, then focused on David. All six foot one inch of fire, strength, and beauty strode right up, and those sweet hazel eyes, tinged green in the light of the studio, bore down on David. "You're tiny."

David cocked his head and looked up. "I'm five-nine."

"Hey! *I'm* five-nine." Domino stood up straighter. "I'm not tiny."

"Babe, you are kinda shorter than the rest of us when you're not wearing your boots." Adrian slung an arm around Dom and pulled him close. "But it's not the size that matters, it's how you use it." There was almost a purr in his voice.

Ray rolled his eyes, Zavier coughed into a fist, and David couldn't help his own laugh. Yeah, this group was okay. Well, except for the firebrand towering above him. She was more than okay...she was *glorious*. What he needed, though, was someone he could work with, and who could work with him.

Mish's stern visage had softened into humor. "Damn it, Adrian! I'm trying to be imposing, and you're throwing around double entendres!"

"Sweetheart," he said with a very New York accent, "there ain't nothing but double entendres around you."

"And that," Zavier said, "is Twisted Wishes. You still want to work with us?"

David nodded. "You guys seem like tons of fun."

Mish put her hands on her hips. "I could stick you in my pocket!"

"You could *try*." He grinned up at her. "But I'm well versed in taking tall people down, I have a couple of black belts, and was in the army for twelve years. So you might not succeed."

This time, it was her mouth that twitched up. "*Might* not?"

"I'm confident in my abilities, but never say never, you know?" He rocked back on the stool. "Besides, I saw the photos of your assailant. You're *tough*, Sullivan."

"Call me Mish." Her hands were still on her hips, but her smile was wide. "Sounds like I might not need to take care of you."

He shrugged. "I'm pretty self-sufficient."

"But never say never?" She winked at him.

He snorted. Yeah, Mish Sullivan was something else. Beautiful. Sexy. Talented. Intelligent. Too bad she was also the job, 'cause that kind of woman made his blood heat. "Life is full of surprises."

With that, Mish stepped back and seemed to loosen up. "All right. He can stay." She directed that bit at Ray. "But I want to see the shit you've been getting about me."

Ray looked at Adrian, and Adrian raised a brow at David.

Time to earn his keep. "You should share them. Mish deserves to know what's going on. It's her life, and she's right —she can take care of herself."

"But you're going to be guarding me."

"Technically, I'm running security for all of you." Technically. The threat was to Mish, so he'd be paying the most attention to keeping her safe. Still, he would look out for the whole band.

She shook her head, sending cascades of red curls around her face. "So no personal hot bodyguard just for me?"

Hot? That sent a bolt of awareness straight through him and he shifted on the seat. Flirting wasn't a good idea, especially with Ray and the rest of the guys *right there,* but he couldn't help himself. "Princess, if you need a *personal* bodyguard, I'm sure we can work something out." He kept his tone light and humorous.

Mish laughed, and it was deep and loud and perfect. "So what do you go by anyway? Dave? David? Altet? Some other nickname?"

"I prefer David." He almost included *and he/him pronouns,* but he'd been read as male for years at this point. Being asked whether he preferred David over Dave was new, though. An unexpected kindness, one that made him aware of who he was, and how comfortable his skin felt now.

"Well, David." Mish was close again, towering over him once more, and a huge part of him really fucking liked that, which was a problem. "Here's something you should know: I ain't no one's fucking *princess*." She had a razor-sharp smile and her eyes were nearly green.

"Rock queen. Got it." He held her gaze.

Her eyes widened. "Fuck. I think I like you." She spun around on her heel and headed back to her instrument.

Ray blew out a breath. "Yeah, I guess we better get back to work."

The rest of the band grabbed their instruments, and Adrian gestured toward the hallway. "Got a minute?"

So either Adrian was going to chew David out for flirting with Mish...or something else. Adrian seemed wary, but not in an angry or protective way. David pushed himself off the stool and followed him out.

The closed door muffled most of the sounds of the band tuning, plunging the hall into relative quiet. Adrian rubbed the back of his neck and looked downright worried when he turned to face David. "I—um." He dropped his hand. "Look, are you sure about showing Mish the emails?"

Okay, he was not getting chewed out. David nodded. "She should see them. She has every right to know what's going on, and that her attack wasn't as random as it seemed. Plus, I think it'll smooth over my presence here if she understands why Ray and you all are taking this seriously. At this point, she's the only one who hasn't seen those messages, right?"

Adrian's neck was on the red side. "I don't think Zavier's seen them. Dominic hasn't either, but we talk about it sometimes."

"You really ought to show her, before she kicks all of your asses."

Adrian's chuckle was largely embarrassment. "You've got our number already."

He did—and didn't. "It's gonna take time. But I'm glad that—" he nodded at the studio door "—went well."

Adrian gazed at the studio. "I don't want any of them hurt, you know? I wasn't there when shit happened to Ray, but Dominic talks about it." He shook his head. "Anyway. Do you want to show them to Mish, or should I?"

That was a good question. "Maybe I should. I'm more removed both from the situation and the band. If she needs to yell at someone, better it be me."

"Don't think she's going to yell at you." Adrian glanced at the door again. "But her reaction's not going to be all that great."

Well, they'd find out.

They headed back into the studio and listened while the band practiced. Given the intensity and energy, this tour would be even better than their last—which was saying something. They'd already been labeled a must-see touring band. Fans crowded the venues and VIP tickets had sold out *fast*.

Listening to them now, David could see why that was true. He settled into his seat and flipped through the emails and messages Adrian had forwarded to him. One in particular caught his eye—a candid photo of Mish walking along a sidewalk somewhere in Manhattan. She had sunglasses on. No coat. A black skirt that rode above her knees and bright pink tights paired with a top made up of every color close to red and purple quilted together in a mishmash of shapes. Mish was smiling into the brilliance of the sunny day. Long strides on heels that added two inches to her height.

Yeah, the camera loved her. Loved every member of Twisted Wishes. Beautiful people, all of them.

The text that had accompanied the photo had been chilling, though.

Those tights are too garish for a lady like you. I do not want to see you in them again. I'll be watching.

Personal. Direct. Whoever this guy was, he was talking directly to Mish.

Yeah, Mish needed to know. From their short interaction, David had a decent idea how she'd react—with a slew of curses. Pretty much what he'd do in the same situation.

He'd never liked anyone dictating what he could wear, who he could be, or how he chose to express himself. That had been a fight all through his youth.

David had swum the waters Mish navigated, knew the danger there. He closed his eyes. This wasn't going to be an easy job, but then the best ones never were.

So David Altet was going to watch over her. Between rehearsing songs with the band, Mish stole a few looks at him. She'd teased him about his height, but damn if that wasn't perfect. He was *built,* proportioned just right. Muscular without being bulked out. His long face sported a trim beard. Short, dark hair. Lovely brown eyes. Sunglasses hung from a blue T-shirt he'd paired with black jeans.

God only knew how old he was, though. Couldn't get a sense of that.

But if she was going to be stuck with David, at least he was easy on the eyes. Smart, too. Good for banter.

Still, worry wormed around the back of her mind. The guys, *her* guys, were keeping her out of the loop on this email and social media nonsense. They weren't overprotective of her—usually it was the other way around. So this shit must be *something*. Which...damn. And fuck, too. Her insides twisted in between sets.

The first thing she'd be demanding of David would be a full accounting of what the *fuck* was going on. Better she know than be kept in the dark, despite her well-meaning bandmates. David seemed like the type to be honest with her, and he'd said she *should* know. Bonus points in her book.

When lunchtime rolled around, they took a break to eat.

There were enough sandwiches for *all* of them, which meant Ray had planned for David being here. Made sense, but she hated that Ray hadn't included the entire band on this hiring decision. Worse, she wasn't sure if he was leaving Dom out, too, or just her.

Yes, they'd all discussed the plans to hire someone, but once upon a time, they'd all have been in on the process. She toyed with the edge of her sub wrapper. The whole thing bothered her enough to say something.

"Hey, kiddo?"

Ray looked up—she only ever used that for him, after all. "Yeah?"

"I'm not liking this 'being left out of the loop' thing you've got going on."

Everyone in the room stilled.

A creep of a blush appeared on Ray's cheeks. He opened his mouth, but paused as if considering his words. He did that more often now—a good thing. Nice to see him grow, even if she was miffed at him.

"What do you mean?" His expression was honest and open, though the lines of worry were there, too. Next to him, Zavier looked curious but unfazed.

"Well, you kind of hired David just like that." She snapped her fingers. "Used to be we did things all together."

Ray's brow creased. "We talked about it, in the hospital. You were okay with the idea."

For some value of okay, sure. But she didn't say that. "I know. It's not that."

"Then...?" A hint of annoyance. Zavier bumped his arm. Ray startled, glanced at him, then back to Mish. "I'm sorry, I don't think I'm getting what you're saying."

That was also nice to watch. Zavier tempered Ray, kept him clearheaded while letting him lead.

"Who interviewed him?" She nodded to David, who

didn't seem upset by the conversation. In fact, he nodded back as if understanding what she was asking.

"Me and Marcella—oh." Ray let out a breath. "Yeah. It was only the two of us."

"Used to be the band," Dom said. "I mean, I don't mind with this, but Mish's got a point."

Ray studied his hands. "Yeah." He looked up and around the table. "Sorry, guys. This *was* something we should've done together."

David stirred. "If you want to go through the interview process again, check out other people, that's fine. For this to work, I need everyone to be happy with hiring me." All business. All class.

He was sure pretty to look at, too.

"No, no. You're fine." Too damn fine. She turned to Ray. "David's *fine*. I trust your judgment, it's just..."

"I fucked up, 'cause I'm already keeping stuff from you?" There was chagrined Ray, which she hated seeing, but needed to in this case.

"Basically." She picked up her sub. "I love ya, sweetheart, you know that. But I can't deal with not being fully invested."

"I know." Ray sat back and spoke to David. "You okay with all that?"

David caught her eye, then focused on Ray. "Yup. I like that you guys talk shit out, rather than letting it fester." He gestured at the table. "It's a good dynamic. Says a lot. You care about each other."

They did. Mish loved each member of Twisted Wishes, and Adrian, too. Even Marcella, though she wasn't around as much as Adrian. Then again, he was more or less engaged to Dom, even if they hadn't said anything outside the band. Mish tucked into her sandwich. They were her *family*. Her really weird, queer-as-fuck, musical family. She'd only ever had her mom before this—and not very long at all.

Now David was here. Compact, intelligent, handsome David, with his bell-like voice. Seemed pretty damn mature.

"How old are you, anyway?"

She'd asked right as he'd taken a bite of his Italian sub. David rolled his eyes and chewed, taking his time. She chuckled and went back to eating her own food.

When he finished, he took a gulp of water and met her gaze. "I'm forty-three."

She nearly choked on her sandwich. No fucking way he was *ten years* older than her. She couldn't say anything because her mouth was full. Payback.

David's eyes danced with amusement. "I know. I look younger."

She finally swallowed, and with a rough voice answered, "Much."

He made one of those amused sexy grunts guys could do. Damn him. But he slipped into serious with an apologetic shrug. "You shouldn't be kept out of the loop. I can show you the stuff Adrian's been getting and explain the situation, if you'd like."

Fucking at last. "This gonna throw me off practice?"

"Yes," Ray said. "Mish...don't. Not now."

David inspected his food, then met her gaze. "It'll probably piss you the fuck off, so I'd recommend later. And maybe a beer or something stronger after that."

Well, fuck. "You do realize that I've been an opinionated woman on the internet, right?" She'd kept a low profile after joining Twisted Wishes, but before that—well. She'd had some choice words thrown at her. Different name back then, though, so nothing to connect her to Twisted Wishes unless you knew where to look.

His brows furrowed. "It's not rape threats or someone yelling *whore* or *cunt* or trying to doxx you." He took another bite—a small one—and chewed. Stalling technique? Probably.

"So after practice, then. Go out for drinks?"

He shook his head. "Somewhere private."

Well, there was only one place that would fit the bill. "Hey, David, wanna go home with me?"

He had the decency to blush. Granted, it was faint, a hint of color on his cheeks and under his beard, but a victory nonetheless. "Sure," he answered. "I'll even walk you."

Her very own bodyguard. "Suddenly I feel like I'm in a Whitney Houston musical."

David's lips twitched. "I do like karaoke."

"Oh no," Dom said. "She's gonna drag us out again."

"Not if she has a willing victim." Zavier leaned back in his chair. "This will be fun to watch."

"Zav." Ray had his aghast look on, and Zavier answered with one of his big fucking grins.

David pulled a slice of pastrami out of his sub and addressed her. "You that good or that bad?"

Before Mish could reply, Ray spoke. "That good. She's..." He huffed a laugh and turned to her. "I really should write you a song."

"We really should collaborate," she countered.

Ray nodded and there were murmurs of agreement from the others. Finally. Maybe it was because he'd been such a dork earlier, but Ray was definitely pulling her back into the fold, where she fucking *belonged*.

As for David—She wiped her hands with the napkin and stood. "Well, honey, we've got some practicing to do, but after that, you can walk me home from school."

Once more, he grinned up at her with those sinful lips. "Can't wait, darling."

Well, fuck. This one might be more trouble than Zavier had been. The excitement in her belly at *that* thought didn't mean a damn thing.

CHAPTER THREE

A side benefit to David's new job was finally hearing Twisted Wishes play live. He wasn't a superfan by any means, but he did have their albums and enjoyed their music. Watching them practice was an absolute *treat*. The passion they had for the notes, the words, and each other shined through in the way they moved and played. The love of their music was layered into Ray's voice and woven into Mish's hip shimmies and thrums of her bass. It wrapped every roll of Zavier's drumming, and Domino's outlandish riffs.

Wasn't an act—this *was* Twisted Wishes.

David's heart ticked up as they worked through song after song and he found himself catching his breath whenever Ray interrupted one to go back over a piece of it.

Adrian must have noticed. During one pause he leaned over. "Kinda intense, isn't it?" His voice was a low murmur.

David nodded. "If this is how they are in private..."

"...just wait." Adrian's grin was toothy. It slipped into profound when he gazed at the band. "They own the stage when they're on it."

David believed that.

Mish...she was a force of nature. The way she played and

danced on those shoes of hers...even with all his training, David wouldn't want to go toe to toe with someone that agile. Her legs were stellar, too.

He grunted and looked down at the floor. *Don't get interested. Don't get attached. Stay objective.* He'd heard of so many jobs going sideways when emotions got involved. Didn't want it to ever happen to him.

Wasn't going to be easy. He *liked* these people already, which was unusual for a loner like him. Found himself warming to Mish...and fuck, was she an amazing woman. Maybe it was fine to enjoy the sights and sounds. Safe to let down his guard a bit here, even with the lax building security. Only one door in and out, and that was in his line of sight.

Everything was fine.

When Twisted Wishes finished and were putting away their instruments for the night, David rose and joined Ray. "You know, your manager might want to talk to the building security tomorrow." He tried to keep his tone light.

Ray's head whipped up. "Why?"

Well, maybe David had missed the mark with trying to play that down. The others paused, seemingly sensing Ray's apprehension. They were tuned in to each other. Had to be.

David gave a small shrug. "Fans know you're here. Plus they're doing some work on the floor below this one. I got in through an open door and no one stopped me. Security never saw me." There hadn't been any cameras in the stairs or halls.

"Well, shit," Ray said. "That's not good."

"It's fucking stupid." Mish marched over. "Last thing we need is a riot when someone else figures that out." She turned her sights on David. "And you didn't bother mentioning this before now?"

"I was keeping an eye on the door. Besides, the sites say you've been playing here for five days. If they were gonna come in, they would have. Your fans seem decent about boundaries."

"Unlike the paparazzi," Dom said. He rolled his shoulders. "I hate those guys."

"I doubt the paps would risk trespassing." David paused. "Well, maybe they would, but I'm guessing you guys wouldn't be too kind if they showed up."

Ray grunted. "I'll talk to Marcella. She'll get it cleared up."

"What about my stalker?"

Mish's words froze David. They hadn't applied that term to the guy, but it was accurate. "I don't think he'd come up here, since he's not shown his face to you." He waved off any other questions. "Let me give you what we have, then we can talk theories."

Mish huffed. "Okay, fine. But I want all of it, David."

"All that I have," he said. "And like I said, I *was* watching the door."

A small smile formed on Mish's lips. "Not all the time, you weren't."

For the second time that day, David felt the heat of embarrassment touch his cheeks.

"Still wanna walk me home, honey?"

His voice was as dry as his mouth. "Would be a delight, darling." He held out his arm for her. "Shall we?"

Laughter danced in her eyes, and her smile did nothing to quell the warmth in his gut or the stiffness of his cock. *Fuck.* She took his arm. "Lead on, Mr. Altet."

They walked out of the studio to the smiles and amused looks of the rest of Twisted Wishes.

When they got into the elevator, Mish patted his arm. "You realize if we walk out into the street like this, your face will be all over the internet within thirty seconds?"

"My face is gonna be all over the internet anyway, given how much time I'll be spending with the band." They reached the ground floor and stepped out, still arm in arm. He pulled her to a stop before they got within view of the outside world.

"Question is, do you want them to think I'm your latest boy toy?"

She made a sour face. "I have a feeling you're no one's toy."

David couldn't help the chuckle. "Oh, I *can* be. But only in private, and off the job."

Her penetrating stare pinned him. "That's *interesting* to know." Her lips slid into a smile. "Too bad you're on the job."

Yeah, but the job was a hell of a lot safer than being a rock star's boy toy. "You think *I'm* trouble?"

That got him a laugh before she disentangled from him. "You know, I was dreading this, but you're fun, David."

"I try," he said. "And I know perfectly well you can handle yourself, but it doesn't hurt to have someone watching your back."

Oh, the wickedness in her grin. "I don't think it's just my back you're watching." She headed toward the front doors.

He was trying very hard not to watch her ass and legs. Failing, too. He grunted to himself and followed her into the street. As he expected, there were some shouts and several fans headed in Mish's direction. He slipped on his sunglasses and caught up with her. "You planning on signing for the fans?"

"Yeah, I always do," she said.

Which left her exposed to the cameras that appeared around her. He held back the sigh, though. Given all he knew about Twisted Wishes, suggesting Mish bypass the fans wouldn't be taken well. So he crossed his arms and stayed close enough to intervene, but far enough away to scope out the crowd.

Mish chatted and laughed as she signed whatever the fans asked her to, except for the one guy who wanted his arm signed for a tattoo.

"I'm sorry." She dropped her shoulders. "Weirds me out to have my signature on someone permanently, you know?"

Poor dude looked dejected. Had to be in his early twenties —still had a bit of baby face to him.

She bumped his arm with her fist. "Besides, it's the whole band, you know? I'm just a part."

"Yeah, but my favorite part." He paused. "What if I got, like, a high heel and a bass guitar?"

Her cheeks ruddied. "As long as you're sure that's what you want. Give it a bit before you decide?"

"Yeah...okay." Puppy-dog eyes. David bit his tongue to keep from laughing.

Couple of people wanted selfies, and Mish obliged. A few more signatures and the fans were all taken care of. But the paparazzi had moved in with their calls of "Mish, Mish, sweetheart!"

Mish rolled her eyes and joined David. "Let's get the fuck out of here."

"That your boyfriend, Mish?" one called out, a smarmy edge to his voice.

"My bodyguard," she called back. "So fuck off." She marched away on those glorious legs of hers, heading toward the nearest subway station.

Well, guess that was out in the open. David caught up, lengthening his own strides to match hers. "I suppose that makes us official."

She glanced his way. "Guess so."

They took the stairs down into the station, swiped their Metro cards and headed to a platform that would take them uptown. Only then did she speak again. "Honestly, I trust Ray. And if Adrian is freaked out, too..." She sighed and pulled her curls off her neck. "Fucking hate when the stations are this humid."

"Summer in the city," he said. "And feel free to use me as interference. That's why I'm here."

Her grin was wicked. "So, you'll save those fuckers from getting their noses punched if they get too close?"

He shrugged and smiled back.

"You're not a man of many words, are you?"

Now, that was an interesting assessment. "I can be, but I usually let the clients set the tone."

He scanned the platform, but everyone was doing that New York thing where you ignored the rest of the world. Except for that one guy by the stairs.

"Also, if I get too chatty, I might miss something." Like that photog trying to get closer. "We've got a straggler from the paps."

Mish closed her eyes briefly. "Every time. Thin bald guy with a DSLR that you could probably kill someone with?"

David met Mish's gaze. Oh yes, she could take care of herself. Aware. Probably had contingency plans. He'd done similar years ago. Keys through the fingers and everything. "Yup."

"He'll get on the train with me—us—and follow me home. Harmless but fucking annoying."

So she'd assessed the threat. A tiny piece of him wanted to scream that the world was unfair to do this to her, but he knew that viscerally. Nothing ever changed.

When the train came, it was as Mish said. Overcompensating DSLR Dude got on with them, found his way to their car, and stayed on.

It was too crowded with the end of the business day to sit, so they stood until Mish tapped David on the shoulder. "My stop."

He'd known that, but kept it to himself. All of the addresses of the band members were public record. Made him itch, but people—even stars—couldn't live in bubbles. And New Yorkers were generally good about leaving them the fuck alone.

Except for people like DSLR Dude, who followed them up to the street. Probably got some good photos of him and Mish walking, too. Well, David had known when he said yes to Ray

Van Zeller that this job would come with lenses trained on him.

"Snap, snap, fucking snap," Mish muttered.

"I could have a conversation with him."

She shook her head. "I've had one. He doesn't care. They pay him to get photos of my lovers, which—" She came to a dead stop on the sidewalk. "You know what really ticks me off about that?"

Her voice was louder now, probably for the benefit of the dude following them. David played along. "What bothers you about it?"

"He's gotten photos of me with my tongue down the throats of people of multiple genders, and they still pull the whole 'is she straight or not' shit on those sites." She turned to stare at the photog. "I'm so so *so* not straight."

Man had the decency to look uncomfortable.

David laughed to cover up the heat in his body at the image of Mish lip-locked with another. "That has to be fucking annoying."

"You have no idea." She continued walking down the sidewalk until they came to an older, high-end apartment building, complete with doorman. "Hey, Lorenzo," she said as they reached the gentleman, who opened the door for them.

"Miss Sullivan." There was a twinkle in his eyes when Mish rolled hers, but her smile said this was a friendly interaction.

"This is David. He's working with the band, so if he stops by, he's fine."

Lorenzo looked David up and down and raised an impeccable black eyebrow. Well, only one thing to do. David stuck out his hand. "David Altet."

After they shook, he dug out his wallet and offered his business card.

"Private security." Lorenzo rubbed a gloved hand over his clean-shaven face. "Watching over Miss Sullivan?"

"Well, the band in general, but yes."

Lorenzo handed his card back. "Best if you let the security desk know."

"Yeah, I will. Thanks, Lorenzo." Mish nodded at the building. "Let's go."

Once inside, David stripped off his sunglasses and tucked them in his shirt.

The movement seemed to catch Mish's eye, and she gave him a smile that was—he didn't know. Friendly. Flirty. Something. David pushed it aside.

They stopped at the security desk. A card, a handshake, and Mish's explanation garnered David another once-over. The woman behind the desk was pleasant and proficient, and kept the card. After she noted his name in a log, he and Mish headed to the elevators.

"Whole thing is key fob controlled. Can't get to my floor if you don't live there." Mish pulled her keys out and jingled them, showing off a small black fob. "And they don't let anyone up unless I give them permission, or I come down to get them."

Not bad security. Load off David's mind, at least until they hit the road. "Pretty good, for an older building."

"Yeah. It's one of the reasons I chose it."

The elevator was also older, but smooth, and when they were deposited on Mish's floor, it closed quietly and slid on its way. There were only three other apartments. Given the size of the building, Mish's had to be downright spacious. And indeed, it was. They entered into a small foyer that led into a sizable living room, complete with terrace. Potted plants swayed gently in the breeze.

A jolt of envy ran through David. He made good money for what he did—but nothing like the amount Mish must have to afford a place like *this*.

He must not have hidden his feelings that well, because Mish twisted her lips. "Yeah, I know. It's huge, especially for one person. And yeah, it cost a lot."

"I didn't..." He caught himself. There was remorse, not mocking in Mish's tone. "You're a star. If you can afford it, you can afford it. Why not?"

"I can afford it because Ray nearly died, and sometimes..." She tossed her keys on the coffee table by the couch. "Sometimes it's a reminder of that. Of everything."

There was more than the troubles with their former band manager and label in that statement.

"From what I've seen of Ray Van Zeller, I don't think he'd be upset that you spent some of your settlement on a nice place to live."

She ran a hand through her curls, teasing out one stubborn copper strand. "No, he loves this place. Practically begged me to buy it, since it was, as he put it, 'so me.'"

David didn't know Mish well enough to assess whether that was correct, but given the length of time Mish and Van Zeller had been bandmates—probably was. Despite its vibrant colors and interesting combination of old and modern furnishings, the place was soothing, and that did describe Mish Sullivan.

She waved at the couch. "Anyway, have a seat. I'm gonna get that glass of something stronger you recommended. Want anything?"

Yeah. An evening off the job with the woman before him, but that wasn't going to happen. He took a seat on the couch. "Just a glass of water, if it's not much trouble."

"None at all." Her smile was bright and warm, like the golden light filtering in through the windows. He hoped that smile would still appear after he showed her exactly why he was in her living room.

The kitchen was a solace for Mish. She needed to catch her breath and get her head screwed on straight.

That fucking photographer. At least David hadn't panicked at her being followed, but she *hated* it. Hated it so much, even if it was the guy's job to get photographs of her.

Mish pressed her palms into the marble of the counter and counted to ten, letting the cool, smooth surface ease the jagged edges of her mind.

This was the side of being in Twisted Wishes that made her want to spend her days in bed sometimes. Mostly, people were good. Fans were great—appreciative, respectful, full of life. She lived for those interactions, the ones that mattered.

She *loathed* being clickbait.

Her hand still ached from the attack and practicing, and now David Altet was in her living room about to tell her about a fucking internet stalker. She didn't need this. The only thing that made it remotely okay was that David seemed to have a good head on his shoulders.

And those shoulders were *damn* nice, along with the rest of him.

She blew out a breath. *Don't even go there.* The trash sites probably already had him listed as her latest fling and the whole "well, maybe she's straight!" shit would start again. Ever since Ray and Zavier had hooked up and then with Dom's love affair with Adrian spread around the internet, everyone was into her business and waiting for her to pick a partner.

She rolled out her shoulders and arms, headed to the cabinet that contained her liquor, and pulled out a glass and a bottle of Elijah Craig bourbon. Maybe the shit that was coming wouldn't throw her that much, but the rest of the day had. A finger of bourbon was enough—being drunk wasn't on her list of plans for the foreseeable future. Too many bad memories there. Her mother's exes. Her absent father. Kevin, their former drummer.

She grabbed another glass and filled it with water from a pitcher in the fridge, then headed back in to hear whatever it was that'd dragged David into her living room rather than a perfectly acceptable bar.

When she entered, David was running his elegant finger over the reproduction of a Byzantine mosaic she'd had set into the center of the coffee table, his dark eyes focused on the path his finger took over the bird's body. His movements were simple, but something about them flipped heat in her stomach and had her body at attention. Maybe the care he took, maybe the intensity. His hands and wrists were thin, almost delicate, despite his height—five-nine wasn't anything to sneeze at, regardless of her earlier comments.

When the wooden floor creaked beneath her feet, he looked up, a smile gracing his lips.

She liked his smile, that touch of bad-boy coupled with honest warmth. Didn't do anything to calm her nerves.

Shit, she needed to get laid. Or at least spend some quality time with her vibrator.

"Like the design?"

He nodded. "It's Byzantine, yes?"

Interesting that he would know that. "Yeah, one that's on display in a museum in Thessaloniki."

"You Greek?"

She shook her head. "Just love the art. Zavier nearly stole the table from me the first time he saw it, though." She eyed David. "You?"

"Part of my family's from Spain, the other part is Eastern European." He leaned back on the couch. "I grew up with a love of icons, mosaics, and incense."

Even though it was expected, she didn't say anything about her heritage. Half of it she didn't know, since *deadbeat* wasn't a nationality. She suspected some Irish because of her hair and her mom's surname, but who knew? Her mom had been beautiful, blonde, and tall. Dutch, she'd said once.

She handed David his water and set her bourbon on a coaster. "So what do you have for me?"

He grabbed one of the other coasters and set his water down. "There's been a disturbing pattern of emails and comments. Not from the same IP or email addresses, but those can be spoofed easy. The content, though, is similar." He played around with his phone, then handed it to her. "Start at the bottom and read up."

She did. At first, she rolled her eyes, because the comments were merely about what the dude liked and disliked about her clothes. Over time, though, the tone changed and a cold chill rose up Mish's spine. They—he—became more demanding. Included photos of her, and not ones she'd seen in the press, either. He deemed her dress wrong. She was too loose and free. When she was finally with him, things would change, he said. He knew the kind of girl she was, knew what she needed. Nothing *overtly* sexual, like the one-offs she used to get from guys wanting her to suck them off or whatever.

Whoever this dude was, he'd homed in on her, and yeah, was following her.

Then came a photo of the lock of hair that had been cut from her head.

"Fuck!" She jerked away. The phone tumbled out of her hand, bounced off the coffee table and clattered to the floor. Shit. Great, just what she needed. Breaking his phone.

She bent to retrieve it, and so did David. Both their heads and hands touched—and that moment, when she jerked her head up and looked into David's eyes, left her breathless. His fingertips on the back of her hand were pleasantly rough.

He was also fucking handsome from this close up, the bastard.

"Sorry," she said. Since she'd gotten to the phone first, she sat up and handed it back to David. Looked like the case had saved it from damage. "It was the fucking hair."

Because those scissors had been sharp, and the phantom sting of her pulled hair and the sheer primal instant of fear before she'd lashed out at her attacker in the heaving crowd flooded right back into her.

"Fucking damn it." She reached for the bourbon, glad now that she'd poured it. Her hands were shaking and goddamn it, she didn't need David to see that.

"I understand. It's hard." There wasn't pity in his voice, only the sadness of understanding.

"You've been attacked?"

His huff was mirthless. "Yeah. Also, I was in the army. Deployed."

Oh shit. Mish let out a long breath. "It's been a couple of weeks." She should've been over it by now, though.

"I know. I should have warned you about those."

Maybe. Maybe not. She took another sip of her drink, letting the alcohol warm her throat. "My therapist says it'll linger. And who knows what'll set the memory off?" She hated that.

He met her gaze and nodded, far too knowingly.

"Please don't tell the boys." It came out unbidden. The guys would flip if they knew she was carrying around that moment, especially Ray, who had enough moments of his own strapped to his back.

"I'll keep your secrets, rock queen." Lovely eyes. Understanding spirit. "But I think they'd understand, and not think less of you."

"It's not that." She leaned back and changed the subject. "I have absolutely no clue who that dude could be."

"No former lovers taking an issue with your life?"

She laughed at that. "No. I don't put up with that controlling shit, and my lovers all knew that from the get-go."

She'd watched her mom put up with men who expected to be obeyed without so much as lifting a finger. All the money, all the love.

Another sip of bourbon eased the memory away. That had been a lifetime ago, and Mish Sullivan didn't even have the same name as the girl who'd witnessed all that.

"It's not anyone I ever dated. Positive."

David seemed to chew on that. "I'll trust your instincts."

"I suspect you've already looked into a few of my exes?"

He laughed, and it was another honest one, as if she'd shocked him. "No, I haven't." He sobered. "I might, unless you object."

She waved the question away. "I don't have an issue with it. *They* might."

"It'll be on the up and up."

She expected nothing less. "It's the thought of someone picking around other people's lives, even if the stuff is public."

A flicker of awareness there, and a hint of sadness. "Yeah, I know. I'll be respectful, Mish. But I do want to cover all the bases."

Not *princess,* or *rock queen,* or *darling*. *Mish.* Hearing it in his bell-like voice made her shiver. She didn't try to hide it this time. Yeah, she liked David, and that was a big fucking problem on the eve of a tour with him guarding her from a creepy-ass stalker.

She downed the rest of her bourbon in one gulp. "Thank you for showing me those. And for saying what you said to the guys, that I should know."

"They care about you."

She snorted. "Don't I know it. And it's mutual. They're my fucking family, all I have." That was the bourbon was talking. "Shit. I should eat." And sleep, and de-stress.

"I should stop taking up your personal time." There was regret in David's voice. At being here or at leaving? Hard to say. But he rose and dusted his hands on his jeans. "Thanks for the hospitality. I concur with Ray...this is a lovely place. Very you, and secure, too."

She climbed to her feet and saw David to the elevator. Felt like she should hug him, would've if he'd been one of the guys. He was new, even if he felt comfortable and fit in as a part of this group. Hugging would mean *touching*. There was danger there, lurking in her body's reaction and in the looks David sometimes gave her.

The whole attraction thing went both ways, but she wasn't about to start shacking up with her bodyguard. She'd watched the damn musical. She knew how *that* ended.

Thankfully, the elevator came and whisked David Altet away, at least for the night.

CHAPTER FOUR

Knowledge was dangerous, Mish realized, and sometimes ignorance *was* bliss. In the days that followed learning about those emails, she found the calm that usually engulfed her on the commutes to and from practice—even with the photog following her—had been shattered. Because *he* could be there. The stalker, and she wouldn't fucking know, despite her general awareness of danger.

She'd yet to spot the fucker. Spent a lot of time looking, too.

At practice, the tension slipped away when they started playing. The music was a haven for them all—always had been. Dom danced, strutted, and played, Ray sang his heart out, and Zavier lost himself in the intricate rhythms he beat out. Hell, Mish found herself singing along on most of the songs, sometimes harmonizing with Ray, other times just singing along like a fan might.

She fucking loved all their songs.

Halfway through "Finding Light," Ray broke off. "Wait, wait..."

They all came to a halt, and Dom and Zavier looked as surprised as Mish. "What's up, kiddo? That sounded great!"

"I know, I know." Ray danced around, hopping from one foot to the other. "I loved it. But I wanna try something different."

Zavier tapped on his kit. "We're all ears."

Ray spun in place, his grin wide and eyes full of energy. He came to a stop when his gaze landed on Mish. "How about you singing on this one? 'Cause I really liked the sound. It looked—it *felt* great!"

Her pulse quickened a bit. "You mean backup vocals?"

Ray shook his head and that smile became toothy. Little shocks of hope fizzed down Mish's limbs. Fuck yes. *Finally.*

"A duet. You and me. We trade off verses or lines or whatever seems to work the best. You guys up for that?"

"God, Ray..." she breathed. "You know I am."

Before she'd joined Twisted Wishes, she used to sing her own sets. Sometimes she lent her voice to Ray's on tour, but it wasn't the same as singing in her own right. She'd never pushed it with Ray, 'cause his voice was so damn unique, like his vision.

But if he were offering her the chance? Hell yes.

Dom nodded, and Zavier's "Of course" put a stamp of approval on the idea.

Ray worked to set up a mic for her—they could've had techs at practice, but they were used to doing this shit alone, so they only used them for recording and live shows. The only other people in the studio were Adrian and David.

"Hey, Adrian?" she called over to him.

"Hmm?" He looked up from whatever book he'd been reading, a half smile on his lips. David had been browsing on his phone, and he too looked up.

"Don't tweet about me singing."

"Oh shit, yeah." Ray fixed a mic to the stand. "Let's keep this to ourselves. I'm sure it's gonna work, and it can be a surprise on tour."

Singing on stage, on tour, in her own right. She caught

Ray's gaze. He was vibrating, or maybe she was. "You sure, kiddo?" She didn't want to steal his thunder, even though she was dying to belt out their songs.

"Yeah. Should have done this sooner. I get a little wrapped up in myself."

Zavier chuckled, and only because Mish was so close could she see the spots of red on Ray's cheeks.

"He's good for you," she murmured to Ray, not for the first time.

The blush grew, and he looked down. "You're all good for me." When he met her gaze again, there was such energy there. "I'm better than I've ever been in my life."

The new songs said that. The music. Everything. She tousled his hair.

He grinned. "Okay. Why don't you start, and we'll do verses first and see how that feels?"

They did just that, with her belting out the first verse of "Finding Light" in her own way, and Ray picking up on the second. They sang the chorus together, her harmonizing with him, and fuck, did it feel good and right and wonderful. She danced through the bridge and they both ended up singing the final verse before bringing the song to a close.

The silence that followed was interrupted by a soft exclamation of "Oh my god" from Adrian. He had the expression of someone who'd been whacked upside the head.

Ray had a shit-eating grin. "Good?"

Adrian nodded. It was David who answered in a voice that rumbled and purred. "That was fucking amazing." His phone lay dark and forgotten in his hands, and there was rapture on his face. He met Mish's gaze and the admiration there—desire, too—sparked lust in her. She was already heated from singing and playing, so she didn't flush any harder.

She slid her gaze from his to the instrument in her hands. God, she loved this band, this song. Everything.

Including the way David looked at her.

"I think maybe we should do it that way in concert," Ray said, snapping her back to the band.

She shook her hair from her face. "Want to try it with alternating lines, too."

"Yeah, okay." He bounced in place, his excitement infectious as always. "And maybe some of the other songs?"

"Kiddo, I'll sing whatever you want me to."

Ray grinned, and Zavier beat out the rhythm, and they launched into "Finding Light" again.

In the end, they went with their first rendition, and played around with her singing on three other songs before they called it quits for the day. Ray was still a bundle of energy, even after everything was packed up for the night. "Damn, that felt good."

Zavier looped an arm around Ray's shoulder and drew him into his body. "Less caffeine for you tomorrow," he said.

Ray stilled when he leaned back against Zavier. "Wasn't the caffeine, you know that."

"Mmm. The music, the songs." Zavier met Mish's eyes. "Seeing something different in the sounds."

Ray's synesthesia. He'd explained more and more about how he *saw* their music over the past year. She didn't have that, but she understood the rightness of a song. There were so many variants of right...and yes, they left her buzzed, too.

"We'll just have to work off that energy later," Zavier murmured.

Dom put his hands over his ears. "La la la, I'm not listening."

Adrian laughed at that. "Babe, come here. We'll go get dinner, then have some dessert." That smile of Adrian's was wicked, and Mish couldn't help a laugh of her own.

The boys were so predictable.

Dom's subtle melt and blush were par for the course, and

he crossed the room to take Adrian's hand. "See you guys later." They slipped out the door together.

Mish dusted her hands and noted that David was still sitting on the far side of the room. He hadn't walked her home since the day he'd shown her the stalker's emails and comments. Sometimes she wanted to ask him to, but most of the time, she was damn glad he hadn't insisted. She might be more paranoid, but this was her fucking home, and damned if she was going to let some slimy bastard ruin that for her.

Still, at the end of every practice, she asked the same question of him. "Anything new?"

Since that day, the answer had been "nope" but given the sad look in David's eyes, that streak must have been over. "There was another email."

Stones in her stomach. She took a breath and another, then walked over and held out her hand. David, with resignation written all over his handsome face, passed his phone over. The email was already queued up.

> *I'm sure you think the way you behave is acceptable, but it's not. A woman should listen to her man. Obey him. You were brought up wrong. When you choose me, you'll see.*

Fucking hell. Those rocks in her stomach tumbled over and over, and every bit of joy she had from practice bled out through her feet. She handed the phone back. "Thanks."

"Mish—" He had that look, the same one the guys got when they wanted to protect her.

She waved any further words away. "I'm fine. I'm gonna get dinner, then go home." She met David's stare. "Alone."

"Are you—" Then he caught himself and shook his head, something like a smile gracing those lips for a moment. "Of course you're sure."

"Damn straight I am." She peered over at Ray and Zavier, staring them down, too. "Same shit, different day. I'll be fine."

Ray seemed at a loss for words, and did that same head-shake thing David had done. "Practice was perfect today, Mish. You're fucking awesome."

A little of the lost warmth came back. "Thanks, hon."

He smiled at that, and Zavier spoke something into his ear. "Yeah, I guess we should go."

They said their goodbyes and headed out the door, leaving her and David in the room.

"Hey," David said, his voice quiet and strangely tentative. "You sounded amazing. Your singing I mean. You always sound fantastic on the bass."

Even more of the warmth—and some of the joy returned. "Thanks. I've sung backup on tour, and I'm always singing, even when I'm not micced up."

A wry grin. "I've noticed."

"David Altet, are you watching me during our practices?" She couldn't help the teasing lilt to her voice.

He stood and rolled his shoulders back. "Technically, I'm watching the whole band."

"Technically?"

His lips quirked, but he didn't reply.

Oh yes, David was into her. But then again, she was into him, more than she wanted to admit. Not that she thought about him or wondered what that beard would feel like on her skin. Or his hands. Or how soft his lips might be.

She glanced away from that smile, heat blazing through her, and sought her bag. "I should really get going."

"Yeah, same." His voice had gravel in it, and he sounded so damn fine. "I'll see you around, princess."

She whipped back to stare at him.

"Rock queen," he amended.

She laughed. "Fuck you, David." No heat in her words.

He blew her a kiss before heading out the door.

Yeah, a week or so in, and he'd already made himself at home with the band. And damn it all to hell, she liked him.

What was going to happen when they were with each other 24/7 on tour?

Holy hell, that was gonna be a nightmare. Or a really good wet dream. She hadn't decided which yet.

Mish was going to have David's head if she realized he was following her, but after that last email, he wanted to make sure no one other than DSLR Dude was trailing Mish, and that meant shadowing her as well.

After her usual ritual of greeting fans, she headed toward the subway. But rather than take the steps down, she continued above ground, in the direction of Midtown.

David huffed in frustration. He didn't mind walking—that would help him spot whether there was anyone following Mish—but damn it, she'd *read* the email. Why wouldn't she head straight home?

The answer hit him sharp and hard, and the echo of it was in his past, too.

She wasn't going home because that's what society told her to do. Run. Be safe. Don't enjoy life. Be afraid.

David's gut twisted. In her place, he'd have done the same thing to prove that he wasn't afraid. Hell, he had been in those shoes and done the same back when he wasn't read as masculine. He understood, and it *hurt* that he understood. Fucking stung that he'd wanted to push Mish to be safer, though that was his job.

At least by trailing her, he could do that part, and she could be herself, even if that meant walking blocks and blocks in the process.

Between dancing at practice and this kind of walking, no wonder she had legs made of sculpted muscle. What *was* a wonder was when DSLR Dude dropped off the hunt after about ten blocks. Guess hiking through the streets wasn't really the photog's thing. There really wasn't that much to capture. Just Mish striding ahead. Pausing at lights. The normal.

There also didn't seem to be, as far as David could tell, anyone else following. He even dropped back a few times to make sure no one was trailing him, but no. The only person trailing Mish was David, and she really would kill him if she found out.

Why she was walking straight toward Times Square, he had no clue. The place was packed full with tourists this time of day, especially now that the weather was warm and summer was around the corner. It wasn't a place for a star to go and get lost. Thankfully, she veered away and headed uptown.

At this rate, they'd end up walking to her apartment, and maybe that had been the plan after all. He almost thought that it was when Mish slowed down in front of a bar, one that wasn't far enough off the tourist trail.

Oh, baby, no. Not that one. Especially not with a gaggle of tourists pointing their phones at Mish.

Of course, Mish went inside.

"Shit." He spoke the word to the sidewalk and pressed up against the wall of a building, pretending to check his phone while people moved past. If he went in, she'd know. On the other hand, pretty sure she might end up causing a scene, especially since the group that had spotted her also went into the place.

Fuck. David tucked away his phone into the front pocket of his jeans and waited another minute before strolling in.

Mish sat at the bar, toying with the edge of her glass, a frown pulling down her glossy red lips. Her shoulders were hunched forward, tension evident. Yup, there were people, both coyly and obviously, watching her. Taking photographs.

The bartender came over and said something, and Mish shook her head.

She'd figured out the issue. Probably pretty fast once she'd taken stock of the place. God, it was hard to watch her sitting there, tense and angry. At the world. Maybe at herself, too.

Seemed like no one had the balls to sit next to her. Good...and bad. Because he was about to blow his cover and probably get reamed for it.

But hey, he had balls to go with his dick. Couple of sets of them, actually.

David slid through the crowd and plopped himself down on the stool to the right of Mish. "Hey, princess, come here often?"

Mish started, then turned, her expression full of exasperation but also a hint of gratitude. "I'm gonna fucking kill you, David."

"Figured you might want to." He eyed her glass of beer. "Should I order one, too?"

She grunted, then nodded. "I hate drinking alone, even when I *want* to drink alone. And I miscalculated this place." She glanced around. "Should have gone over a couple more blocks."

"Yeah, this ain't the kinda bar to be in if you wanted a nice quiet beer and to disappear into the scenery for a while.

"Don't I know it." She twisted her lips. "Lot on my mind."

"I know." He flagged the bartender and ordered a lager off their draft menu. They had a decent list, too. All in all, if it weren't for the tourists, it would have been a fine place to linger.

She took a pull on her own beer, leaving behind a little lipstick on the glass. "So tell me, why the *fuck* are you following me?"

Shit, she *was* pissed. Rightfully so. He toyed with his own beer. "You're probably not going to believe me, but I was making sure you weren't being followed."

Her laugh was sharp and bitter, and David flinched. "Great, so the guy protecting me is stalking me, too." Mish closed her eyes and drank more of her beer.

A sympathetic-looking bartender eyed them both. "You two okay?"

Mish waved him away. "Yeah, he's a friend. Just a fucking annoying one at the moment."

Friend. Okay, *that* was good. "I know, and I knew it would piss you off. The problem with trailing trails is that I *have* to trail you, too."

She contemplated that as David drank, then took another slow pull of her own. "So," she said once she'd set the glass back down, "was I being followed?" A hitch in her voice.

Fear. He hated hearing that. "As far as I could tell—no. Other than DSLR Dude."

She relaxed her shoulders. "Eh, he drops off quickly when he realizes I'm not taking the train—at least now he does."

"Any reason why?"

Her smile was bloodthirsty. "Couple of times early on, I decided to walk around for hours. Even went across the Brooklyn Bridge, and then back. I think the fifteen-mile days nearly wiped him out, so he lets me go when I walk more than a mile, basically. Especially if I'm alone." She rolled her neck out. "I mean, how many photos of my backside do you think the public needs?"

David mocked being in thought, then shrugged. "It *is* a very nice ass, Mish."

She laughed and punched him in the arm. "You're a fucking jerk, you know?" All cheer in her voice.

"I am not!" He smiled back. "And you know it."

Her smile settled into something more private. "Yeah, I do. You're fun. And—thanks. For coming in and facing my wrath."

The way her gaze flicked from his eyes down caught David so off guard. So did the deepening of her smile. "I—

well, I know you can take care of yourself. But it helps to have a friend sometimes?"

"Is that what you are, David?"

Oh fuck. There shouldn't be sparks or chemistry, and he certainly shouldn't be getting hard for Mish. *Again.* "I could be."

She huffed a laugh. "I have to ask, if I were one of the guys, would you've followed them?"

"Yes." The truth rolled off his tongue easily. "If any of them were in the same situation, you bet your ass I'd make sure they were safe. And yeah, I'd make sure no one was following them, too."

"Except it'll never happen to them." She picked up her beer again and drained it. "Doesn't happen to dudes."

"Sometimes it does. Not as often. But obsessive fans can harass any gender, you know?"

"That doesn't make me feel any better." Her smile was too damn sad, as were the creases around her eyes. "The thing is, I'm alone. If anyone were to touch Ray, I'm pretty sure Zavier would break bones. He nearly took out Carl once, but Ray stopped him. And Adrian can be fucking intimidating when he wants to be." She waved at the bartender and handed him a credit card. "Put his beer on mine, too."

David sat up straighter. "I can pay for my own beer."

"Yeah, well, I'm gonna. You have an issue with that?"

Not really. "Next one's on me."

There was that summer-warm smile again. Somehow the lipstick had remained. "Next time, how about we just go out for a beer, rather than you following me?"

Heat rose to his cheeks. "We can do that."

She got her card back and signed the slip. "I bet if it were one of the guys, you wouldn't be putting on the charm so hard."

Putting on the... "Hey, I..." But she had him to rights. He'd not be flirty if he were sitting with any other members of

Twisted Wishes. She punched him in the arm again, and his insides tumbled. "I try not to mix business and pleasure."

Even when every nerve screamed to do so.

"Oh, that's too bad," she purred into his ear, her hot breath caressing the side of his face. One beer couldn't have gotten her that tipsy, so it wasn't the alcohol.

Which meant she knew *exactly* what she was doing. God, he wanted to slip his hands into those curls and kiss her, feel her breath mingling with his. Taste that lipstick. He hadn't been this turned on in ages.

"You're something else, Sullivan." His voice was choppy, and he downed the last of his beer to fix that.

"So they say." She pushed back on the stool as if to stand —but he touched her hand, enough to get her attention, and her long gaze was expectant, her body still tensed to rise.

"You're not alone, Mish."

A tremble in her arm and a whole host of emotions. "I want to be *free*, David. Of the worry. Of the *concern*." She stood then, and turned away.

Free from his concern? Maybe. That was his whole reason for being here, though. He rose and found Mish hadn't gotten far. She stood a step away, a smile that was tired but not faked as the fans he'd seen earlier greeted her.

He waited while Mish chatted with them. A few selfies later, there was fatigue in her arm when she tucked curls behind an ear and nodded at a younger woman recounting a story of how she discovered Twisted Wishes. Sweet tale, and Mish's smile was still genuine, but that earlier tension was back. If she'd gained any relaxation from her beer, it was long gone now.

David shifted to catch Mish's attention, and she glanced his way, long enough for him to raise an eyebrow that he hoped read as *do you need an out?* and not as him pushing her along.

"Oh god," she said. "I hate to run on you, but I've kept

David here waiting." She pulled him closer into the circle. "He's helping the band with the upcoming tour, and we still have things we need to discuss tonight."

He could play along. Wasn't a lie. "Well, but your fans..." He gestured to the group.

"No, no," said the woman who'd been chatting with Mish. "We've taken up enough of your time." They all murmured their agreement, and after another round of "Thank you so much" and "We love you!" Mish headed to the door. David did what he'd done all evening—trailed behind her.

A few patrons eyed Mish as she left, either because they were curious from the cluster of fans or because she was a stunning woman in her own right. None of them seemed to be watching with strong intent or malice. David's skin pricked, though.

He slowed and looked over the last of the patrons, but no one stood out. Either his nerves were shot, or he'd missed something.

He schooled his expression and stepped outside, where Mish waited for him. She'd put her sunglasses on, hiding those expressive eyes. "At this point, you might as well walk me home."

Best plan. If someone was following her, they'd have made him by now. Next time sussing a tail out would be a bust, because they'd be waiting for him. "All right."

They walked in silence for a few blocks.

"I hate this," she said, her voice crackling. "Not you. I like you. I hate *this*." She gestured around them. "Being paranoid. Needing to be walked home. Followed for my own good." She slapped a hand on her thigh. "Stupid fucking patriarchy."

Yup. He certainly knew that set of emotions. "I understand, especially since you can take care of yourself."

"Yet you're here, David. Watching me."

"I am. But, Mish—" He didn't know how to phrase what

he wanted to say, so he just plunged in headfirst. "If you were a guy, I'd still be here. If you took out the stalker but got injured again, where would that leave the band?"

"Fuck." She kicked at a loose stone on the sidewalk, sending it far up ahead of them. "Fucking *fuck*, David."

He didn't say anything.

"I hate that you're right." She gritted out the words. "Because you are."

"Band needs you whole. There's only one of you, like there's only one of each Twisted Wishes member."

"I know." Tight voice. "Stop talking, please." Her voice was all breath.

He shut up. The hurt there, the unbelievable *frustration* reminded David all too well of times he'd been forced into corners he'd hated. And no, none of it was fair. This was why he kept to himself in his personal life. Didn't make too many close attachments. There was only so much he could do to ease another's pain.

When they got close to her apartment, she slowed and pulled him to the side to let others pass. "You know, I do wish this shitty business between us...wasn't. You'd be a hell of a date."

Once again, heat coursed through him. "I can't go on a date with you, but I was serious about the beer. And you did promise me karaoke."

She snorted. "The guys will kill me if I drag them again."

"Then drag me," he said. "As a friend."

"Friend, huh?" Her smile had a touch of the devil in it. "You should ask Zavier about friendships sometime."

He didn't understand what she meant, but how she said it made every part of him take notice of *her*. Every bit of her. "Okay."

That lovely chuckle didn't help at all. "Have a good one, David. See you later." She took two steps backward on those heels of hers, spun with a grace he didn't possess at all, and sauntered past Lorenzo into her apartment building.

He was so fucked. No way this was gonna end professionally.

For the first time in his life, David didn't give a damn about that.

CHAPTER FIVE

Mish tossed her bag onto her berth on the bus, then settled into her normal seat across the aisle from where Ray and Zavier were stretched out like cats in the sun. Adrian and Dom sat at the little cafe table near the kitchen playing some kind of card game while they waited for the crew to finish loading the equipment. Then they'd be on the road, off to their first show of the tour.

There was something about being on the tour bus that made everything fade away to the very first time they'd ever boarded one.

Had been different then, what with Kevin still in the band and Zavier merely a faded piece of Ray and Dom's past. Now Zavier was deeply part of Twisted Wishes, and they had Adrian, too. But that excitement, that flutter of nerves, hopes, and dreams, that was the same. Timeless. Stunning.

They were going on tour and it never fucking got old. Ever. Always a dream made real in the most impossible way.

Now they were headlining, and giving another band the same chance they'd once been given by a larger and more famous group.

She laid her head against the seat and looked up at the ceiling, content to be with this, her family.

"Gin!" Adrian sounded positively gleeful.

Dom's reply was disgruntled. "Fuck! You cheat!"

"I do not!" There was laughter in Adrian's voice.

"You count the cards!" Dom was trying to sound outraged, and pretty much failing.

Laughter from both of them. "It's gin rummy, of course I count the cards. How am I supposed to know what to hold?"

"Your gentleman friend has a point," Zavier said.

Mish peered across the aisle in time to see Ray nudge Zav with his foot. "Fiancé."

"I don't see a ring on his finger."

"Hey," Dom called. "Since when do you care about rings?"

Zavier gave Dom a sly grin. "I don't. I just enjoy teasing you."

Adrian snorted. "He does have a ring, you know. Just isn't on his finger."

"Oh lord," Mish rolled her gaze back up to the ceiling for a moment. "I'm not gonna survive this trip."

Meanwhile, Dom had turned into a little pile of happiness and embarrassment. Zavier was laughing, and Ray had his hands over his face.

Yup, they were definitely back on tour. Felt like heaven. She fucking adored this part.

The bus swayed a tiny bit, and David bounded up the stairs. He paused when he took them all in. "Is this a bad time?"

God, that outfit was pure sin on him. Jeans faded in just the right way to emphasize the power of his legs and thighs, and one of those blue patterned button-downs guys seemed to like. Leather necklace. Wasn't designer anything, but David still looked like a *GQ* model with that dark hair and those darker eyes.

"Nah," she said. "Adrian's oversharing at Dom's expense for Zavier's pleasure." She patted the seat next to her. "Come watch the show."

"It's not for Zav's pleasure." Adrian shuffled the cards. "It's for mine."

"Hey!" Dom was still pretty damn red, but he was laughing. "Don't make me take your phone and reclaim my title as social media maven."

"Please, no," Ray sighed. "Dom, you're my best friend, but you can't tweet for *shit*."

Mish waved a hand. "See what I have to live with?"

"Somehow, I think you love it." David's grin was toothy.

She did. Every single moment. Loved all the guys and the way they all fit together in this group they'd formed. She bumped David's knee with her own. "What's up, Mr. Bodyguard?"

He bumped her back, but glanced around at all of them. "Wanted to check in with you before we got going. I've followed some of your touring online, but I wanted to see how you'd like to handle rest stops and the like."

Ray shrugged. "We usually stop in the middle of the night, and half the time, we're asleep. The other half—well—it's mainly us and truckers, if that. We don't really think about it. Just get our shit and leave. I'm not sure we really need security for that."

David shifted on the couch. He didn't frown, but there was concern there. Zavier caught the look, too, it seemed, because he murmured, "It's never been a problem before."

"Situations change." David gestured with open hands as if to say *what can you do?* "You guys are huge now."

Plus she had a stalker. "I'll stay on the bus."

They all looked guilty. Dom nibbled his thumbnail until Adrian gently took his hand.

God, she hated the restrictions and the necessity. Hated the reason why David was here, even if she enjoyed his presence. "Look, we all know what's going on. Let's not pretend this is about the band when it's about me."

David bumped her knee with his again. "I'm not saying you need to stay on the bus. I just want to know how to handle the stops. You can run them as you always have. Just —be aware of your decisions. The majority of personal security is about awareness and presence of mind."

She spent a few long moments watching him, the open way he looked back, the depth of his brown eyes, and the fucking honesty there.

Dom asked the question she didn't want to. "So, what's your advice?"

David didn't look at Dom when he spoke. "I know that the stops are part of your social media. Ending them would give the stalker what he wants—a change in behavior, specifically Mish's."

"Fuck that," she said.

He nodded, and refocused on the rest of the band. "Keep your stops, but if you don't mind, I'll tag along. And you should be more aware of the people around you in general. There's always the possibility one of you—" he waved at the guys "—might pick up an obsessive fan. Anyone can figure out likely routes for your buses between cities, so it's just good practice."

That last bit—Mish hadn't even thought of that. David was right, though. People knew the tour schedule, knew where they'd be and when. Probably even knew the names of the hotels where they were going to stay.

Everything in her spine tightened and she forced herself to roll her shoulders. "I guess this is the price we pay for fame."

Adrian twisted his face. "It's not been *that* bad."

"Honey, you ain't a women." Though the fans were pretty good to her. Still, she did get more men coming up and making some awful sexual suggestions than Ray or Domino ever did, even when they'd been single.

Then again, with Domino, guys tended to think he was some ultra-dominant top when he was pretty much the exact opposite. Before Ray'd gotten together with Zavier, he'd picked up guys, but they hadn't been the stars they were now. She'd never fished outside the crew for that reason. They knew they didn't own her. Lovers from the outside? Too many wanted control.

David patted her knee. "We'll figure out who this guy is."

Would that be the end of it? The thought of *this* being her professional existence grated hard. She didn't know what to say in return—though she did enjoy the warmth of David's hand through her jeans.

She patted that same hand, now safely back on his thigh, in return. "Thanks."

The driver stepped up onto the bus. "We're going to get moving soon, folks."

"I guess I should head back to the crew bus." David made to rise.

There was that pang of sadness in her that he wasn't around as much. Fucking annoying that the one person she wanted a little more time with was the one person she didn't want to be here because of the damn situation.

David Altet was a fine man. But requiring his presence was hell.

Ray shrugged. "You can ride with us for a while. We should discuss tomorrow anyway."

This time, she bumped him with his shoulder. "Stick around, honey. You'll get to see more of the Dom and Zavier show."

David's grin was infectious and made her body heat with the need to find out what those lips and that beard felt like against her skin. "Darling, I'll never pass up that opportunity.

Zavier, damn his quiet observant ways, chuckled. He didn't say anything. Didn't have to—she was pretty sure they all knew what was going on.

She knew her bandmates' tacit approval when it was there, damn the lot of them.

Best people in the world.

The largest security headache for David so far was the whole VIP encounter process. Great for the fans—an intimate question-and-answer session, and then individual photos with the band. Some of the fans even got to watch the band perform from the side of the stage. Awesome packages. Great experiences. Good revenue for the band.

But what a pain in the ass to coordinate. *Intimate* meant fans got to stand with the band, be right there. All it took was one person to cause an issue.

"We're pretty careful about how the fans interact," Adrian had said when David had sat down with him and Marcella before the tour.

She'd nodded. "We've never had any issues at the encounters. The fans love them, and it's one of the biggest draws next to the signings afterward."

But it was gonna be a fucking nightmare to keep the band and Mish safe. That set David's teeth on edge. Yes, the encounters cost a pretty penny—he'd looked up the prices online—but that wasn't a deterrent to an obsessive fuckwad like the guy who kept sending emails to Mish.

There'd been one before the tour that contained a photo of that bar he and Mish had talked in and a comment that ladies didn't drink beer. That had set every bit of David on edge.

It had unsettled Mish, too. "I guess it's good you followed me home."

Yes, and no. Why hadn't he seen the fucker? It rankled and worried him. Exposure meant less protection, but Twisted Wishes was known for interacting with fans. Guy didn't feel like a fan, though. That soothed and bothered David.

The morning of the first concert, Adrian had texted him from the band's bus, and they'd met outside to go for a run together—Adrian was apparently a gym rat with a fairly extensive training schedule, and runs were part of that. After they'd circled the parking lot enough times to exhaust them both, they'd sat at a picnic table away from the buses, and Adrian had slid his tablet over to David. "This came in this morning."

Another email. Short and to the point.

Only whores wear skirts that short. A girl like you should know better.

These emails were getting more and more personal, as if this guy thought he knew Mish. A boiling, rolling wave of disgust swept through David, and he shoved the tablet back at Adrian.

Adrian flipped the cover over to turn the damn thing off. "Yeah, I know that feeling."

No, he *didn't*. Not the way David did, and undoubtedly not the way Mish did. Fuck, he still remembered some of the shit that had been said to him about the way he'd dressed. Looked. Cut his hair.

David took a deep breath and took in the huge, empty parking lot. "Different IP address again?"

"Of course." Adrian sounded as disgusted. "Easy to open a burner email account. Use a proxy server. Whatever."

They were never going to find the asshole electronically. David doubted the jerk was ready to show his face, even with the ample opportunity this concert provided. If he wasn't a fan, what was the connection?

"Mish is right. This is unfair." He spoke more to himself than Adrian.

Still, Adrian nodded. "It is." With that, he rose from the table and picked up his tablet. "I gotta go schedule some posts and tweets, and prod Dominic out of his pre-coffee stupor. You gonna tell Mish?"

"I'm gonna ask Mish if she wants to know." David wasn't about to throw this at her now, right before the opening concert on their biggest tour.

Adrian smiled, though it was somber. "You're a good man, David."

David watched as Adrian headed into the band bus to wake his lover. Those kinds of compliments, the gendered ones—he'd never quite gotten used to them, even as much as hearing them helped.

He liked Adrian. Enjoyed all of the people that made up Twisted Wishes. He might not play in the band, but it didn't take long to realize Adrian was a big part of it, too.

He should go talk to Mish, but between the run and the sudden burst of anger, he needed a moment to sit in the early morning sun and cool breeze, listen to the birds chatter, and just *exist*. He cherished the tiny moments of peace whenever he could find them—whether in the hustle of New York, in the horror that had been deployment, or right now, in a parking lot at an amphitheater outside of Atlantic City.

A shuffle of gravel drew his attention back over to the tour buses. Mish had stepped out into the morning, and his breath caught in his throat. The sun burnished her hair to shining copper, and she wore a white tank top and denim shorts that rode low on her hips. She had two mugs of coffee, one in each hand.

She really was a goddess. A queen. Awe, respect, and desire all tangled in David, leaving him shifting on the picnic table bench. With arms and legs toned and muscular, she could kick most people's asses. He wanted to do everything in his power to protect her anyway. Was that right or wrong? He didn't know.

She handed him one of the coffees in an official Twisted Wishes mug. Steam curled off the top, and he imagined that might be the way heat curled off his body. Maybe she knew how much she'd affected him, because once he'd taken the mug, she tucked some stray curls behind her ear—a gesture he now recognized as a nervous tic—and there was a hint of color high on her cheeks. Or maybe that was just the way the sun touched her face.

Didn't matter. David looked down into his coffee. "Thanks."

"Adrian said you were out here." She took a seat across the table from him. "Maybe coffee isn't the best thing after a run, but..."

He met her gaze, and her eyes were green in the soft sunlight. "I had a ton of water before and during the run, so this is perfect." He took a sip, and it made the day even brighter. "How the heck do you get good coffee out of a tour bus?"

She laughed. "From Adrian. Zavier used to make the coffee, and it was decent, but one of the things Adrian managed to outdo Zav on was the coffee. I'm not sure if it's the beans he uses or if he's part coffee-whisperer, but..." She gestured to the mugs.

"He fits in with all of you."

"Wasn't a surprise. Any guy Dominic fell for was going be someone we all loved."

"Like a family." He didn't expect the pang of pain that stabbed at his heart. He missed those kinds of connections. Had them in the military for a while. Had them with a few former girlfriends, but over the years of becoming himself, many of those relationships had changed or slipped away. Jobs like this one had him on the road a lot, even with a home in New York. He liked the solitary life, but he still missed what he couldn't have anymore. Not in the long run.

Wasn't his nature.

His silence must have said more than words, because Mish reached across the table and laid her hand on top of his. "Honey, before this crew, I was alone. I know how it goes."

"Thanks." He took another sip of coffee and turned the palm of his free hand to catch hers and give it a squeeze. "Don't mind me being a grumpy old man."

"You're hardly grumpy. Or old." She left her hand in his.

The way his heart thumped in his chest had nothing to do with the coffee or the run. "I'm an old soldier trying to make the world a little better best way I can."

"But aren't we all, in our own ways?" She rubbed her thumb over the palm of his hand. Sparks of awareness shivered down to his dick, but also up to the back of his head. Not all was lust. Been easier if it were.

"Maybe." He moved his fingers against hers. "I do envy your little family. It's clear how much you care about each other."

"It's hard won." Mish ran a finger of her other hand around the edge of her mug. "We lost Kevin along the way. He's in a better space and doing things he loves, but still." Her shoulders dropped. "We nearly lost Ray permanently. Puts things in perspective."

Yeah, that would.

"We do tend to pick up strays." She smiled before drinking more coffee.

"Am I a stray?" Was he considered part of this group after a little more than two weeks? God, these people were unreal.

"You're a man who cares, David."

Despite the coffee, his throat felt tight. "You have to care to protect, if you're doing it properly." But not too much. Not get involved emotionally. He'd already blown way past that point, sitting here holding Mish's hand. Given the jumble of emotions, this might as well be high school, and him sitting with Tricia at lunch, secretly holding hands under the table.

Except their hands were out in the open, and no one

would beat him up later. Reluctantly, he slipped his fingers from Mish's.

"I do care about the band, about you." Especially about Mish. "I don't want to hide things from you. You've already had that happen with your bandmates trying to protect you." He waved at the bus. "But I gotta know *when* you want me to tell you things. Right before the show doesn't seem the best time."

She wrapped both hands around her mug and made a face. "Tomorrow. Whatever it is, tell me tomorrow. I can't have that shit in my head tonight." She sounded apologetic. "That might seem selfish..."

"Fuck no, Mish, it isn't selfish! You need to be on your game, especially for the first show."

"Thank you." Her smile was *everything*.

He couldn't keep from grinning back. "With all those stellar practices, you're going to do great, rock queen."

She rose and navigated to his side of the table, mug in hand, and bent down to kiss him on the cheek. "Keep that up, honey, and I'm gonna expect you to worship at my feet."

Oh fuck, that more than the chaste peck made him squirm. This woman? Hell yeah, he'd worship her. David craned his neck to meet her grin with one of his own. "You saying you don't deserve worship?"

She laughed. "I'll see you around, David."

Man, everything about that woman left him in a daze, from her kiss to the way she moved as she headed back to the tour bus.

Yeah, that whole professional line was crossed long ago. Still, he had a job to do.

He took his coffee and headed back to his crew bus to catch a quick shower and get ready for the rest of the day. The roadies and the engineers didn't quite know what to make of him, though he had joined in on their poker game last night.

The bus was empty except for one of the younger crew

members, Faith, zipping up her duffel. God, they *all* seemed young to him. He guessed the rest of the crew was at work unloading and setting up equipment.

She eyed his mug. "You getting coffee from the band?"

He shrugged. "Mish brought me a cup."

She pulled her long, dark braids into a ponytail. "Oh, just like *that,* huh?" There was a hint of teasing in her voice.

A touch of heat rose to his face. "It's not what you think."

"Mmmhmm." She leaned up against the berths near his. "I've been on these tours before, and let me tell you, Mish is a hell of a woman."

"Believe me, I've figured that out."

"She also knows exactly what she wants. She doesn't bring coffee out to just anyone."

Oh. *Fuck.* He blew out a breath and made a calculated decision. "Do you know why I'm here?"

Faith straightened up. "Ray said you were security."

He nodded. "There's been some pretty creepy messages coming in."

He saw when Faith connected the dots. "Oh fucking hell," she murmured. "That asshole from the pop-up show wasn't the only one?"

He shook his head. "I'm watching after her." His turn to lean against the berths. "But she sure as shit can take care of herself, too."

"That's a damn needle you'll be threading." She crossed her arms. "We'll keep our eyes open, you know. Most of us did the last tour with them, and there ain't a better band in the business."

"Appreciate it." He hefted his shower bag and grabbed a pair of jeans. "I should go get my ass clean." He headed back toward the shower.

"Hey, David," Faith called.

He turned back. "Yeah?"

"Doesn't mean Mish doesn't know what she wants." She grinned at him. "I hear she's a hell of a fun time."

He coughed a laugh. "I guess I'll see, huh?"

When he got to the bathroom, he locked the door, then rested his head against it. He *hadn't* been imagining Mish flirting with him. Well, *shit.* Now he had to figure out what the fuck he was going to do about *that.*

Nothing. Do nothing. David stripped off his clothes and hopped into the tiny shower. Easy enough to get clean with minimal use of water. He'd done that before, on tours of duty. All the while, his mind slid around Mish and he ignored the heat in his dick.

Yes, he wanted her. No, he shouldn't. Even beyond the sexual attraction, he liked Mish. Wanted to know more about her. Maybe knowing more would help him figure out who the fuck was stalking her. Not a fan. Too personal.

More and more, he suspected someone from her past.

CHAPTER SIX

A couple of hours later, and the quiet of David's morning had vanished. Orchestrated chaos rolled around the venue. There were techs and roadies and equipment everywhere. Their staff, the opening band Two Times Strong's people, and folks from the venue moved around, on stage, in front of, and behind it. It took all of David's concentration to remain vigilant for any weirdness.

Especially since *weird* was the normal state of existence for most of these people. Security for the venue lurked everywhere, but fuck if David trusted them to keep Twisted Wishes safe. Two Times Strong had staff that acted as bouncers, which was good, since a couple of the venue people looked decidedly uncomfortable with the whole queer vibe that permeated both bands and their crews. Lots of the bands' staff bucked gender norms and were obviously and openly not at all straight.

The amphitheater was perfect for big summer tours, but behind the stage was a labyrinth of buildings, rooms, and trucks. Everything had to be orchestrated so fucking carefully. Of course, being the height of summer meant that even though it was before noon, the weather was already hot and sticky.

At least there was enough water to go around to keep them all hydrated. In fact, David needed to do something about all the water he'd been drinking. He took in the stage again, but everything looked fine. Twisted Wishes themselves weren't out yet—they had an interview with a local radio station, some meetings with the press, and some business Marcella needed to discuss with them before sound check. They were watched over. Perfect time to head toward the restrooms.

Once there, he found one of the roadies from Two Times Strong's crew lingering outside the building, looking uncomfortable in a way David knew all too well. The signage was very gendered, there was no family restroom, and one of the venue security guards was eyeing the poor kid.

David walked up to him. "Hey, don't worry about that dude. I'll head in with you."

Kid started and turned, looking at David's badge. His had *Eric* on it. "Shit. Um. Okay."

He clapped Eric on the back and they made their way to the men's room.

"Must have had a giant sign over my head, huh?" Eric's neck was red, and David twinged sympathetically.

"Eh, been there, done that, mastered the stand-and-pee."

Now *that* made Eric's head whip around. "No fucking way."

"Way," he said, like it was still the '80s. They went in and did their business in peace.

Most of the venue staff were polite and respectful to him and to the other various members of crews, though. Yeah, maybe some of the "regular joes" thought they were strange, but this was a fucking concert venue. They'd likely seen it all.

His main concern was safeguarding Mish. With all the entrances and exits, he wasn't sure they could keep Mish's stalker out of the restricted areas if he wanted to waltz in. Anyone could be charmed, and it only took one lax member to look the other way while someone snuck in where they shouldn't be. Never mind that they couldn't keep the guy out of the venue if he bought a damn lawn ticket.

In theory, it shouldn't be that big an issue, but in practice, Mish had been attacked in a crowd, so the shithead knew he could get to her.

He'd already caught one would-be fence jumper trying to climb in, and pointed him out to venue security. Groupies were also hanging at the back gate as the crews unloaded. David watched them for a while, but the crew and the venue security kept them in check. It was all normal concert stuff, but also shit that could hurt the band.

He headed back down toward the stage where the crews had finished unloading the equipment for both bands. There'd be two sets of sound checks and then they'd get the stage prepped for the evening's concert. Two sets of everything existed. There were two crews with a careful plan for the placement of equipment so that Two Times Strong's setup could be removed and loaded while the Twisted Wishes crew set the stage after the opening act.

The band had discussed what would happen on tour, but seeing all the chaos in person before the start of rehearsals gave David a taste for the intensity that would be this assignment, even without guarding Mish.

God, that conversation this morning. Holding her hand. What Faith had noticed. They were definitely heading in the direction of hooking up, and god, that was such a bad idea.

This damn band. He liked them all too much, and yeah, he wanted Mish. Probably would let her take this where she wanted it to go. Entirely the wrong thing to do, but he couldn't help it.

Well, no. He could. He was an adult, but one that was tired of being alone, even if that was his natural state of being.

If Mish wanted him, he wasn't about to say no to her, regrets or not. He was enough of a professional he could keep from being distracted, couldn't he?

How much he was lying to himself, he didn't know. Twisted Wishes hadn't even played a concert yet, and David already had a hard time not sinking into the music.

Didn't help that Mish had worn jeans, fucking *killer* boots, and a bright green T-shirt that clung to her in all the right ways to sound check. She'd danced and played and even sung a little into the mic—ostensibly to check the levels—though Mish would sing with Ray, not behind him, tonight.

Luckily, when they were on stage, David could relax. Only so many entrances and they were all covered.

All he had left before the concert was the meet-and-greet, where the band would hang out with a couple dozen fans who practically vibrated with excitement. They'd set them up in a bar area away from the stage. Good location. They could control the flow of traffic. Check for wristbands. The VIP experience folks who worked for the band were efficient and friendly. Among the fans, there was a good mix of ages, races, and genders—a lot of rainbow everything given that it was the start of Pride month. Helped him relax a little.

The guy stalking Mish? *Had* to be straight and white. The sheer amount of hubris told David that. He was probably in his late forties or early fifties, given his speech and text patterns, at least according to David's forensic linguistics buddy, Salha. He'd sent some samples to her for a profile.

No one seemed nervous in a way that wasn't also coupled with excitement. No malice or slippery feelings among the VIP guests. The hair on the back of his neck didn't stand up. Everything felt good.

A stirring in the crowd made David rotate to watch Adrian climb the short flight of stairs into the bar, cell phone out and his Twisted Wishes all-access badge bouncing against his crew T-shirt. The tee stretched tight over his chest, making him look more bouncer and less social media expert.

He also had quite a few fans swooning, despite not *technically* being part of the band. But everyone knew Adrian Doran belonged to Domino—that had been all over the internet last year. Though, after watching the practices, David had a feeling the whole "belonging" thing swung in the opposite direction. Dom melted when Adrian was around.

Would be interesting to see how *that* played out in concert.

Turned out, Dom in public wasn't the soft-spoken, demure man David had encountered during practices. Domino Grinder was—quite literally—something else. Loud and brash, though he wore the same smile. His glances at Adrian were steady, steely, and sinful. It was as if Dom had turned the extrovert dial up to eleven. Adrian merely smiled back at his lover and filmed the rest of the band entering.

David's breath caught in his throat. Mish was wearing the same jeans, shirt, and boots combo as before, but now sported a loopy silver necklace with some kind of glass bauble, and a silver-and-turquoise ring on her right hand. They shone in the sunlight as she, Ray, and Zavier followed Domino into the shade of the covered bar area.

She flashed him a smile that was brighter and warmer than the sun as the band filed to the chairs that had been set behind a folding table. Each had a mic, but it was Ray that started them all off.

"Hey there! How ya doing?" There was more than a little Jersey boy in Ray's voice, which was fitting for the venue—they couldn't be too far from where most of the band grew up.

The fans were nervous and quiet.

"Oh, come on now," Domino said as he swept his gaze over the crowd. "You can do better than that!"

This time, there was laughter and some clapping. Ray smiled, and laid down the ground rules for questions and answers, and they were off, talking and interacting with the fans. There was an ease to all the band members as they joked and answered questions, and the laughter came more freely from the fans, their smiles wider.

None of the questions were inappropriate. Some were interesting, including one that asked each for a favorite memory of touring.

That was a question David couldn't answer. All he had were these moments right now, and though they were brilliant, he had a feeling they'd be eclipsed. Probably as soon as Twisted Wishes took the stage.

Someone asked Mish about her childhood, and she laughed. "Oh, there's not much there to tell." There was a tightness to her smile. "Dirt poor. Moved around a lot." She took another question.

David turned that answer over in his head. He'd run simple background checks on all of Twisted Wishes, and that mostly jived with what he'd learned of Mish. There wasn't anything about her before she'd begun her career as an entertainer at dive bars and clubs in the years prior to when she'd met Ray Van Zeller. In the area where she'd grown up—the Poconos—class disparity could be large. With the types of jobs Mish had held, no way she was a child of one of the Manhattanites who owned a big weekend house in rural Pennsylvania.

No known enemies. None of them had any, notwithstanding their former manager, who knew better than to come anywhere near Twisted Wishes, given the no-contact part of his plea deal. That fucker's focus had been on Ray, not Mish.

The meet-and-greet went on, with a question thrown to Adrian about whether he'd join the band. "No, I have no musical talent at all. I'm lucky I can hum a tune."

Then they set up for individual photos with the band. That set David's teeth on edge, but in the end, nothing happened.

The line moved fast, everyone had fun, and no one tried to cop a feel. The members of Twisted Wishes all left with smiles on their faces and the fans looked more than a little starstruck.

David followed Adrian out. "That went well," he said.

"Yeah, it usually does." Adrian glanced at his phone, then pocketed it. "Really wasn't worried, to be honest, even with the emails."

That was interesting. "Any particular reason why?"

Adrian slowed as they made their way back behind the stage. "Because the rest of the band was there. And the fans. This guy interacts with her—or tries to—on an individual level. All the other people would have been competition."

Adrian was smart, for sure. The theory was a decent one. "Could be. I'll keep that in mind."

"So, I'm on your team now?" Adrian sounded amused.

"Aren't we all on the same team?" David caught Adrian's gaze. "You're the front line. You see what comes in. Your opinion counts, too. And yeah, you're on my team."

Somehow, Adrian managed to look both pleased and worried at the same time. "I don't like it, though. Seeing that shit."

David sighed. *Yeah, same.* "Still, your insight gives me something to think about." A second set of eyes and a good mind were never a problem.

Right before they made their way to the backstage area, Adrian put a hand on David's shoulder and pulled him to a stop. "Glad I can help. And use me if you need muscle. I'm not a brawler, but I know what I look like."

He chuckled at that. "Especially in a tight T-shirt?"

Lo and behold, the smile that touched Adrian's lips was slightly embarrassed. "Don't tell Dominic, but I enjoy being his boy toy."

"I bet he knows." David slapped Adrian on the back. "Come on, I want to know what the game plan is for tonight."

Usually before the first concert of a tour, Mish found herself so full of excitement, she physically itched to get out on stage, as if her bass and the audience had her roped in and were pulling her out to play. She belonged there with Ray and Domino and Zavier, with the music and the beat and the screams of the fans.

Tonight was different, though. Ray'd run her through vocal exercises—they'd been doing that since they'd decided to sing together. Now they'd finally do that, in front of a very unsuspecting audience. Yeah, she itched to get out there, but deep in the pit of her stomach lay something she hadn't experienced in a while.

Nervousness. Stage fright.

She stared back at her reflection in the dressing room and finished putting on her makeup. Maybe it was bolder tonight. Dom wasn't the only one who crafted a persona for the stage—they all did, just not to the same extent that he had created Domino.

That shy girl who'd sat by her mother's side in the hospital wasn't the one in the mirror. Hadn't been in a very long time. But a hint of who she'd been was in her eyes now, and Mish didn't know *why*.

"You okay?"

Mish started at David's voice, even though he'd spoken softly. He stood next to her station, his sunglasses hooked on his T-shirt again, this time a Twisted Wishes one in red. The color suited him.

"Honey, I've been doing this for years." Not exactly an answer to his question, but she had a feeling if she lied, he'd know.

"True." A smile touched his lips. "But you're getting to do something you've wanted for a long time tonight."

It shouldn't have been an issue. "I've sung before." Her mom had always said she had the voice of an angel.

There it was again, that flutter in her stomach. *Shit.* Mish sorted through her lipsticks and ignored the emotions. And David. "Dom, honey, Blood Blue or Violet Massacre?"

Dom, at his own station, craned his neck around and rolled his eyes. "With that skirt? Please. Blood Blue." He waved a hand.

She could have gone either way, but Dom had an eye for color and makeup. Hell, half the time he gave her tips. She put on the blue and half watched David from the corner of her eye. He was looking at her skirt, which was leather and electric blue.

The violet would have popped against her sleeveless top, which was short and purple. When she ran out on stage with the band, she'd wear a short white jacket over it, but that wouldn't last long. Her boots were white to contrast against the black net stockings that had rhinestones scattered here and there.

The rest of her makeup pulled the starkness of both those colors up to her face and mixed it with the others. Once she finished with her lips, she realized that Dom had been absolutely correct—the blue was the only choice. The violet would have been too much, and none of the other colors in her arsenal would have worked as well.

She didn't know if she was still replying to David, or speaking to herself. "I've sung before." This time her nerves were rock steady when she met David's gaze.

His stare raked over her. "Damn, you are something." He shook his head. "I shouldn't say that, I know."

"Darling, I appreciate a man who appreciates me. These boys see me all the time, and they ain't interested anyway."

"I appreciate you," Marcella said from across the room, humor in her voice.

"Yeah, but you have a no-dating-the-band policy." She winked at Marcella.

The other woman laughed. "You bet I do. Bands are *trouble*. So *much* trouble." Her smile fell to something friendly. "Besides, pretty sure I'm not your type."

Mish was pretty sure of that, too. Not that Marcella wasn't into women—Mish was almost certain she was, but she never got the vibe that Marcella was all that attracted to *her* in particular. Still, Mish enjoyed teasing Marcella anyway.

She fucking enjoyed teasing *all* of them.

Her eyes strayed back to David. This one, too, with his dark eyes and hair and intense stare. "I'll be fine," she said, finally answering his original question.

Seriousness had settled onto David. "I have no doubt. I know we've joked about it, but you really are rock royalty, Mish."

She spied Ray smiling in the reflection of his mirror.

Okay. She liked David. "You're a charmer."

"I don't know about that." His expression was sly. "I'm too unvarnished not to tell the truth."

"Unvarnished." She laughed. "You know, I'd kiss you on that cute cheek of yours, but then you'd be stuck with a big old blue lip print, and everyone would know where you got it."

He offered his cheek anyway, and she patted it. "Maybe later, honey."

"Can't wait, darling," he drawled.

"Hey," Ray said, breaking into the conversation. "You guys keep that up, and there's gonna be rumors."

Marcella rolled her eyes. "There are always rumors about the band, Ray."

"Yeah, but they're usually about Adrian and me," said Dom—and this was more Dominic than Domino. "Though I don't wish a boy toy rumor on you, Mish."

She waved away Dom's words.

For his part, David's smile never wavered. "I'm gonna go check the stage out."

Ray got this look, then shook it off. Mish knew the source, they all did, except David. He'd seen Ray, too, though. "What's up, boss?"

"Sometimes I like to watch the opening band perform from the side of the stage, but we shouldn't tonight."

"Not on opening night, no," Zavier echoed. They were both wearing black leather—Ray a vest and Zavier those tight pants of his. "We'd make them even more nervous."

David rocked his head ever so slightly, a gesture Mish had learned to interpret as him having an opinion or suggestion. She wasn't disappointed. "You could go watch toward the end. Wouldn't throw them off, and would show support."

"Someone give that man a job," Marcella muttered. "He's smart."

A burst of heat swept through Mish, coupled with something that felt like possessiveness. "He has a job."

David held up he hands. "I do. And I'm going to go do it. I'll scope out a spot good for viewing."

"As out of sight of the audience as you can get it," Ray said.

David waved a hand above his shoulder on the way out of the room. When the door clicked shut, Mish let out a breath. "He fits in too well."

"He fits in just fine," Zavier said. He was wearing lipstick —violet to her blue—and his lips were curved into a knowing smile. "You know it.

Yeah, she did. She decided that wasn't a problem.

After putting a few finishing touches on her makeup and waiting for the rest of the band to get their act together, they made their way to the back of the stage. Two Times Strong was ripping through one of their better-known songs, taking it to a higher level.

Their lead singer, Lane, was genderfluid and had one of

those voices that was like honey and light itself. It wasn't any wonder Ray enjoyed listening to the band, given the tones and timber of the words when they danced with the music. Two Times Strong's style was a little different from Twisted Wishes—lighter and more airy—but having them open made so much sense. Another band not afraid to be who they were. Another singer who defined the sound.

Except tonight, on the stage, Mish would be lending her voice to Ray's vision. More than lending. She took a pull of water from a bottle one of the crew had handed her earlier.

The rest of Twisted Wishes was focused on Two Times Strong, so none of them saw her press her palm to her chest and whisper a little prayer up to any force that might be listening.

Fingers brushed her elbow, and she turned. There was David, by her side. He gestured for her to lean down, probably wanting to speak into her ear, so she did.

"I've heard you. I've seen you. I believe in you. You're gonna slay them tonight, Mish." His voice was like a caress.

His voice saying her name, right into her ear, sent a shiver down her back and woke a heat in her core that chased away all her fear. In the dim light behind the stage, his eyes were so dark—yet so warm, shining and reflecting the color of the stage beyond.

God, the need to kiss him burned through her. Her expression must have given that away, because his smile deepened into something more private. He touched the tip of her nose with his finger. "Still owe me a beer, darling."

Just then, Two Times Strong finished their song, and the audience roared, jerking Mish and David back from their too-close, too-private conversation. Two Times Strong's crew flew out onto the stage as Lane said goodnight.

Moments later, Two Times Strong was backstage, and Ray was shaking Lane's hand and patting them on the back. "Fucking awesome set. You guys are fantastic."

Their band was high on the music and the crowd. Seeing Twisted Wishes seemed only to push them up higher. It was a whirlwind of conversations and thank-yous and praise, then the other band was bouncing off like they'd won the jackpot of feelings and emotions.

Which they had. A grin stretched Mish's mouth until it hurt. She remembered that rush and high. Hell, she still got that every fucking concert.

And this one? She'd *sing* at this one.

They headed back to the greenroom while the crews pulled Two Times Strong's equipment off the stage and into the waiting truck, and set up for Twisted Wishes. Tension filled the air—the anticipatory kind. The whole area was filled with it.

When Marcella gave them a nod, they whirled through the dressing room one last time to check themselves, then they were back in the wings. This time, the butterflies in her stomach were large and happy, and Mish couldn't stop smiling.

Ray caught her look in the dim light. "Can you believe our life?"

She would have answered, but the house lights flicked off and the audience went wild. Screams and cheers and stomping.

Sometimes she *did* believe their life. This was one of those times, the noise from the crowd a physical hum in her bones. Ray bounced on his toes in that way he always did before he ran out on stage, and Mish's heart leapt. Then they were off, Ray in the lead, onto the stage and the screams fell over them like waves crashing on a beach.

"Yo, Jersey!" Ray shouted into the mic, his own New Jersey accent thick. "How you doing?"

Hard to believe those screams could get louder. They always did, especially near where Ray, Dom, and Zavier had grown up.

Ray tossed a look over his shoulder at Zavier—and with the beat clicking off on those sticks—they spun headlong into their first song. It was fucking glorious. The sound, the rhythm, Ray's voice rising and Dom's guitar following. Mish's bass anchored them as they flew into the chaos and emotion they were so known for.

One song led into another, and she danced across the stage, flirting shamelessly with the fans in the pit, then with both Domino and Ray. Everything was music and the throbbing beats she understood better than her own pulse.

They paused after the next song to more shouts and thunderous applause. She downed half a bottle of water that had been placed for her on the raised platform that held Zavier's kit. Fireworks went off in her chest. Third song, "Finding Light." This was it.

Zavier quirked an eyebrow and gave her a questioning look.

"I'm fucking ready." No idea if Zav heard her over the audience or Ray's ramping them up, but she bet he could read her lips well enough, since he grinned back.

She swung around and found Ray waiting, mic in hand, teeth blinding in the spotlight. They were playing this part cool—not letting the crowd know anything was different. So they'd decided to start "Finding Light" like they always did, with Domino's guitar sliding over notes and Mish adding a rhythm. Then Zavier joined his beats to her bass and they settled into a kind of duel until Ray layered his voice on top for the first verse.

Mish danced over to Ray, then shimmied backward to the mic that had been set up for when she'd lend her voice to backup vocals. She sang the refrain with Ray, which wasn't that unusual, but when it came time for Ray to sing the next verse, he danced away, and Mish's voice rose above Domino's guitar.

For a moment time seemed to drop away. Everything

happened—nothing stopped—but that instant when the words poured out of her throat and rang into the screaming, shifting throng before her, when the realization hit that she and not Ray was singing, when the energy and sound slammed back into her—that carved itself into her memory and soul.

Ray bounded next to her for the chorus, throwing his arm over her shoulder and staying there while she played her solo. Then they were both dancing away when Domino took over. Ray sang again, then she did, and this time she saw the outstretched hands and the open mouths—some singing, some screaming, some in ecstasy as her voice soared, carrying words and love into the night.

When it was all done, the stage shook from the reaction of the crowd. Mish waved.

Ray chuckled, and though that was amplified, it still bore all the love he had for her. For them all. "Honey, you do have your own mic."

It was an unguarded line, one that was pure Ray and would have been at home on the bus or in the studio. She slid up to hers. "Well, how 'bout that? I do!"

Laughter and shouts from the fans.

His grin was joy. He turned to the audience. "You like Mish singing?"

God, the noise. Part of her wanted to cry from happiness. She leaned in. "Thanks, everyone." She plucked out a cord on her bass. "Been wanting to do that for a long time."

She saw, then felt Domino bump up next to her. "I think you should sing with Ray more often." The venue went wild again. Dom rarely spoke during concerts—and there was more than a little of the wry, sneaky Dominic in the quirk of Domino's blood-red lips.

She hip-checked him, and he laughed and spun away. "Maybe I will," she said.

From Ray's beaming, she was sure she would. She swung

her gaze out over the people in the pit and their smiles, and met the smoldering gaze of David Altet, who stood between the pit and the stage, looking up at her. He had on one of his soft smiles, and everything about him, from his stance to his crossed arms, spoke of pride and fulfillment.

Of course he'd be out there in the crowd, watching over her. He nodded once, his smile curving up, before he mouthed two words she read easily on his lips.

Rock queen.

Heat rose to her cheeks and a smile followed, and she backed away from the stage's edge to grab a few swigs of water before they started their next song.

The rest of the concert flew by, and when they were done, they bounded off the stage, much as Two Times Strong had. Performing never, ever got old. Not when they were here, and now, and living their dreams.

CHAPTER SEVEN

Mish was still buzzing a high from the show. The way the audience had responded to her singing—wasn't anything better in the world than those screams and the joy in those faces. Even now, as she sat and signed and talked to the fans, they were glowing and complimentary.

The woman who came up next had bright-red nail polish and lipstick—close to the color of Mish's guitar—and she wore a pendant with the band's logo on it. Bright eyes, brighter smile. Probably college-age.

"Oh my god, you were amazing. I mean, I've heard you backing up, but like, tonight was so amazing." She pushed a poster toward Mish. "Oh god, I'm babbling. I'm sorry. I'm sorry." She was blushing furiously.

"Hey, it's okay. And thanks. Been wanting to sing for you all for ages." She pulled the poster over. One of the few that featured Mish in the center. "You want me to make it out to you?"

"Yeah," she breathed. "I love you. I mean—your music." Her blush grew.

Mish couldn't help her smile. She got it. She'd also had

crushes on so many of her musical idols. "Gotta know your name if you want it on the poster." She winked.

"Oh. Claire. It's Claire." Then spelled it out.

Mish wrote *To Claire, with love, Mish* and slid the poster back over. The woman gushed, and the staff, bless them, directed her away.

Mish held up her hand to the next fan. "Give me a sec." Singing tonight had stressed her voice more than normal, and she needed to soothe her throat a little.

The fan was polite enough while she took a swig from her water bottle. Her right hand ached, probably leftover from her injury, so she took her ring off—a simple turquoise and silver band she'd bought back as a teen—and flexed her fingers before setting it down on the table. Then she gestured him over.

He had an actual vinyl album—they hadn't printed many of them, but some of the fans loved old-school, even if they were a little young to remember playing records on turntables. She got his name, and was in the middle of signing the album cover when a scuffle spilled out in the line behind him.

A guy—of course it was a guy—broke through the line and lunged at her table. She reared back as David yelled something and leapt after the dude. But rather than touch her, he grabbed her ring and took off past the other shocked band members and the venue security.

Fuck *no*. She'd had that ring since high school. Her mom had loved it, had given her the money to buy it back when they'd had so little and spending any got Momma in trouble with her shit-ass boyfriend at the time.

She was halfway over the table when Ray caught her arm. "Mish! You can't!"

She sure as hell could. Hadn't cost much, but it meant everything to her. "Get off me."

He didn't let go. "Mish," he ground out again, "David and Adrian went after him. We need you here."

Fuck. *Fuck.* So much of her wanted to bite Ray's head off, but his last words hit her in the heart and the head. She let him pull her into her seat.

Her gut tumbled and her hands shook. That fucking stalker. This was part of that, she was sure. He'd take her, piece by piece, whoever the hell he was.

Bile rose in her throat even as fury made every muscle in her ache. "Ray."

"I know. I *know*. But the fans need you," he said close to her ear.

Yes, she heard them, the crowd murmuring and whispering. The tone had gone from excited to frightened and worried. All because some shithead had it out for her. Mish swallowed her anger and hoped to god her hands stopped shaking soon.

When she met Ray's gaze, all of his emotions were written onto his face, as they so often were. "And I'm selfish. I can't handle seeing you hurt again."

She had to laugh at that. She knew that feeling all too well. "You don't play fair, kiddo." She *was* hurt, though, but not in a way any of them could see.

"I don't play at all. Not in this." He patted her arm and finally let go. "Did the ring mean something?"

She shook her head. "It wasn't worth much."

"That's not what I asked." Ray's stare held her. "And you know it."

Fuck, sometimes she hated how much he'd grown and matured. But a brush with death did that, she suspected. "Yeah. It meant a lot to me. My mom gave me the cash to buy it."

Ray sat back, his lips drawing into a tight line. She'd talked a little with the band about her past, enough that they knew how her mom had died and how hard that had hit her back then.

"We'll get it back," he said.

Except they wouldn't. She knew that already. Just—knew. Hurt like fucking hell. Couldn't let anyone see that, so she nodded, settled back into her chair, and looked up at the fan in front of her. His eyes were wide and he'd gone pale.

She pulled the album cover back over. Thank fuck the pen hadn't smeared. She'd gotten his name—Dayton—written, but that was all. "Hey, Dayton, you okay?"

He took a breath. "Yeah." He glanced at the other band members. "I—Sorry. I'm sorry. I should have grabbed him or something."

"Oh, honey." She finished signing her name on the cover. "Wasn't you. Don't ever blame yourself for the actions of assholes." She handed the record back to him. "Don't let 'em ruin this night for you, either."

Ray bumped his leg against hers under the table, and she resisted rolling her eyes. Dayton moved on, and the line flowed along again.

The next fan was a young Black teen with her mom in tow. The girl was twelve, maybe thirteen. So hard to tell at that age. She had tears in her eyes, though, and was clutching a T-shirt to her.

Mish bit her lip. Yeah, Ray was right—the fans needed her cool, calm, and okay. "Hey, hey. I'm fine."

The girl had a death grip on the shirt, her knuckles ashen. "You sure?"

"Absolutely. What's your name?" Mish held out her hand, and with a little prompting from her mom, the teen handed the T-shirt over, along with a silver paint pen.

"Alysa," she said. "This is my mom."

"Liberty," the woman said. "I'm a fan, too, but this is Lysa's first concert."

Mish signed the T-shirt. "Did you have fun?"

"Oh my god. It was the best thing ever." Alysa's dark eyes were wide and held wonder and joy. Her gaze drifted to the hand where Mish's ring had been. "I'm so sorry, though."

Mish waved the concern away and handed the T-shirt back. "Some people are just jerks. Don't worry about it."

Kid looked at her mom, and Liberty nodded. "If you want to."

Alysa took a breath, then pulled a silver ring off her finger and handed it to Mish. It had a sun design stamped into the band. "I don't know if it'll fit, but I want you to have it."

"Oh god, I can't!" The words came out so fast, Mish couldn't stop them.

Alysa's eyes filled up with those tears again. "Please?"

Reluctantly, and with moisture in her own eyes, Mish held out her hand and Alysa dropped the ring into her palm. "Thank you. I'll treasure it." Like she'd treasured the ring from her mom.

The smile both Alysa and Liberty gave her almost made the tears spill, but Mish didn't cry at concerts. Tried not to cry at all, if she could manage it.

The pair moved on to Ray, and Mish found another fan in front of her. Another set of worried eyes. Her heart twisted, and she did her best to smile and laugh and set the fans at ease.

"Get out of the way!" David shouted as he ran through the packs of people heading to the parking lot, swerving around those that didn't move. They were gonna lose the fucker if he got to the entrance. Too many cars, too much land to cover.

He'd outstripped the venue security when they'd all taken off after the man who'd stolen Mish's ring, but Adrian ran next to him, his focus as intent on the fleeing guy's back. "Too fast," he said between breaths.

Yeah, the fucker was running pretty damn quickly. Probably fear and adrenaline keeping him moving. The knowledge that bad things would happen if he got caught. David had chased his share of thieves in his time in security. Knew how this went.

Hopefully the guys behind them had called ahead to the gate security.

God fucking damn it. He should have noticed that guy lingering, not being as happy and bouncy as the other fans. Impatient to get to the front. Should have caught him before he'd lunged out of line. David fucking should have been closer to the signing table, but with all the helpers and security there, he'd figured it would be fine.

He'd been wrong, and put Mish in danger.

He really fucking wanted this asshole.

For once, something went their way, and the crowds thickened near the gate as security temporarily slowed people leaving—enough that the dude who'd stolen Mish's ring came to a stop, then frantically looked around for somewhere else to run.

"Cut left," David shouted to Adrian.

Adrian did, no questions asked. Good. Because if David read the guy correctly, he was going to break—left. Adrian saw and gave an elated shout, which was perfect, since it made their quarry spin right back around and head straight for David, the short, unassuming guy.

David grabbed the man's arm, pulled him around and laid him flat on the ground. "You have something that doesn't belong to you, asshole." He pressed a knee into the guy's back, as Adrian and some of the venue security guys came up.

"Let me go. I didn't do anything!"

Guy was maybe in his early thirties. Wiry build. Light brown hair. White as a sheet, despite the exertion and the sweat on his skin.

"Dude, we watched you snatch Mish's ring," Adrian said. "Where is it?"

"It's just a fucking ring. Not like she needs it, with the cash she has."

Anger spun through David and he pressed down harder. "Doesn't matter. You're giving it back."

The guy grunted and panted. "I can't breathe, you fuck!"

He wasn't pressing that hard, but there were more than a few boots of the venue security that shuffled forward at that, so David took his knee off the guy's back. "You can breathe. And you better start talking."

"We should wait for the cops," one of the security guys said. More murmurs in agreement.

Yeah, he should have expected that. The venue had to deal with insurance and all that. Technically, so did he. David let go of the guy completely. "All we want is Mish's property."

"I don't have it." The guy sat up to kneeling and shook out his hands. "Gave it to some other dude."

Fuck. This had been coordinated.

The venue security guards looked confused.

"To who?" Adrian asked. Standing there, uphill from the ring snatcher, he looked like the broad, intimidatingly big guy he was.

The thief shook his head. "Called himself Stan, but that can't be a real name, can it?" Dude spread his hands out. "Said he collected souvenirs from stars. Shit they leave around. Paid me to stand in the line and snatch something of that chick's. Anything she left unguarded."

"You're not even a fan." Adrian raked his hand through his hair and looked at the venue security people. "You ever hear of anything like that before?"

One of them, a woman, shrugged. "People try to steal shit from the bands, sure. But they're usually super-collectors or overenthusiastic fans." She rubbed her chin and looked at the thief. "Not some random guy."

"Tell me about this Stan." David folded his hands over his

chest. But it was too late, because from the entrance strolled in two uniformed police officers.

Dude saw them and shook his head. "I didn't do a damn thing. I don't have anything. You can't keep me."

He was, as it turned out, right about that. Once the cops took over, the thief clammed up. Even though plenty of people saw the ring being snatched and could point at the dude as the perpetrator, the actual cost of the ring was minimal. Maybe thirty bucks, if that. Petty theft, *if* Mish wanted to press charges. The guy got a ride to the station from the cops for the night.

No more about Stan, the man who'd bought the guy's services. And no ring to return to Mish.

Fucking *shit*.

And now that the cops were here, that meant a mountain of paperwork. Going over the event only drove home how David had screwed up, how much he should have seen and didn't. The man's nervousness, the way he didn't fit into the scene. Everything.

This was the first concert and he'd been too damn wrapped up with the client, too willing to be her friend and fall into this group of wonderfully supportive queer people. He longed for community, and they'd sucked him right in where he didn't—shouldn't belong.

That was bad for business. They weren't his *friends*, they were his *job*, and the sooner he got that through his head, the better for all of them.

The tale of the ring snatching must have been passed down the line or over social media, because by the time the signing was over, Mish's insides were scrambled, her mind a mess, her eyes way the fuck too wet—and she had a pile of beautiful rings of all sizes, shapes, and materials from so many fans, she couldn't keep count.

One of the crew collected them up. "We'll take care of these."

It was Zavier who touched her shoulder and helped her out of her chair—she hated how much her legs shook. "I need a fucking drink," she said.

"I think we all do. Let's get on the bus and I'll get you a glass of wine," Zavier said. He fell in step next to her.

"Fucking want something stronger." Because she would not break down, not at the loss, not at the incredible generosity of their fans. Even though it hurt and hurt and hurt and all she wanted to do was rage and scream and let the tears fall.

"I'll find something stronger," Zavier said.

The trip to the bus was a blur, but true to Zavier's word, he brought her something other than wine. Into her hand, he placed a white Twisted Wishes coffee mug with at least an inch and a half of amber liquid that smelled gloriously like the lack of regret with a hint of oblivion.

She blinked down at it. "It's the color of Ray's eyes."

Zavier huffed a laugh and did something so uncharacteristic that it froze Mish into place: he kissed her on the forehead. When she met his gaze, his smile was full of depth and affection. "We care for you, too, Mish."

Fucking Zav was gonna make her cry, that asshole. She took a sip of the booze—bourbon, it turned out—and let the warmth slide down her throat. Zavier fell onto the couch across from her, next to Ray.

Tears still pricked at Mish's eyes, but they were contained. "Adrian back yet?"

Dom answered. "No. There was some paperwork to do with the police." He stood close to the bus entrance, clutching his phone, still in most of his makeup and leather, though he had thrown a clean geeky T-shirt on.

She had no idea what that meant—not in terms of catching the guy or finding her ring. "It's gone, isn't it?"

Dom turned his phone over in his hand. "They caught the guy, but he didn't have the ring anymore. Said he give it to another dude."

Her stalker. So he *was* here. Mish shuddered and took another swig from the mug.

Ray's question was soft. "What can we do to help?"

God bless that boy. He always tried to protect them. Lead them. Take the brunt of whatever the world threw at them. Ray Van Zeller was their soul and their heart, and tried to be their shield. His bourbon-colored eyes were intent and open, staring back at her.

Her shoulder finally unlocked, the booze doing what it did best—making her not hurt for a little while. "Kiddo, you're already doing it." The tears she despised suddenly were *there* and she shook her head, pinching the bridge of her nose. "Shit."

Ray moved in an instant, taking the mug from her and handing it off before he pulled her into his arms.

That was the end of every effort to not let the pain, hurt, and rage bubble to the surface. 'Cause Ray Van Zeller held her tight and said nothing as she buried her face into his shoulder and let the tears and the sobs go.

She hated crying, but if she had to do it anywhere—here with her family was the safest place. And maybe, just maybe, she could let them take care of her tonight.

Once David and Adrian had finally finished with the police, the venue was calm and quiet, with only the cleaning staff and security left in the public areas. On the walk back to the tour buses, David raked both hands through his hair, recalling the evening and every wrong move he'd made, every thought and action that had led to failure.

Beside him Adrian let out a long breath. "Don't do that to yourself."

David glanced over to find Adrian regarding him. "Do what?"

That got him an eye-roll. "Beat yourself up because you didn't see that fucker coming," Adrian said. "No one did."

"I'm not *no one*. I'm trained. I'm usually careful, and yes, I should have picked him out as a threat before he got close to Mish." Sharp, angry words.

Adrian grunted. "The fans are always agitated in the signing line. He could have been perfectly fine. It's not your fault."

David came to an abrupt halt and Adrian followed suit, staring back at him.

"It *is* my fault," David said, wrapping each word in disgust. "I fucking *failed* at my job."

In reality, Ray should fire him. Or he should resign. But that would leave Mish even more exposed, and fuck it all, he wouldn't do that to her.

Adrian closed the distance between them to less than shouting length. "David—"

"Adrian." David's jaw tightened, but he worked hard to keep from grinding out each syllable. "I'm the professional here. I know when I fail."

Rather than be defensive, Adrian sighed. "Look, I get that it feels that way—"

"It is that way," David snapped.

Adrian held up his hands. "But I know the band. I *know* them. No one is going to blame you for not spotting that guy."

God, these people. "You don't get it. In this, I don't care what you—what the band thinks. I know the mistakes I made." Got too close, too fast, which led to distraction. That would change. It had to.

Adrian looked like he was fishing around for words. "I can't stop you from taking the blame. I get that you think you should have caught that guy. That's not the important bit."

"Not doing my job isn't the important bit? Jesus Christ." David stomped away. The sooner he got back on the crew bus, the sooner he could get his head on straight.

Adrian and his fucking long legs caught up with him. "The important bit is not treating Mish any differently now."

David slowed and his heart flipped around. He *had* to treat Mish differently. That was *exactly* what he had to do. Why didn't Adrian see that?

Adrian's chuckle was a bitter thing. "Yes, I know it's easier to push her—push us away. I understand the reasons behind it."

"I have to do it to protect the band." Protect himself, too.

"Yeah, well, here's the thing." Adrian's voice took on the sharpness that David's had. "Nothing matters more than the band. Not you, not me, despite my relationship with Dominic. The whole name of the game is to keep the band playing every night with the intensity and love that they need. It's what they want and what the fans deserve."

"Fuck," David said under his breath. He saw the way Adrian's argument was going, saw it clear as day.

"You cut Mish off now, she'll blame herself for the whole thing, even more than she already has been." Adrian waved at the path in front of them. "I love every single one of them, but they're all primed to shoulder blame and misfortune onto their backs, even Zavier, and he's level-headed."

"*That* guy's got a sore spot?"

"You wanna see Zavier flip his shit? Hurt Ray. You wanna hurt Ray? Hurt *anyone else* in the band." Adrian let out a breath. "Just...don't back away. Not like I know you want to."

"I got distracted." By Mish. By the band, the excitement of

the concert, and the love the fans poured out onto Twisted Wishes. He wanted to be a part of that.

"You can't see everyone in a crowd," Adrian countered. "I mean, I was standing right by that guy and I didn't see him, either."

"It's not *your job.*" But it was David's. He looked up at the bus and stopped. "I don't know if I should go in or not."

Adrian clapped him on the shoulder. "Yeah, I'm kinda wondering that myself, and I'm *on* that bus." He gave David's shoulder a squeeze. "Let me see what's going on."

The litany of curses wound its way through David's brain. He needed to step away at the same time the band needed him to remain exactly where he was. Adrian was right—Mish would blame herself if he gave her the cold shoulder.

His shoes crunched on the gravel as he turned to gaze back at the venue. The concert had been astounding, Mish's singing transcendent. A wild crowd, singing and dancing to every one of Twisted Wishes's songs—and open with who they were, too. Rainbow flags in the audience. A multitude of queer people in the crews.

He didn't want to turn his back on that, or freeze out the people who'd made that dream come to life for so many of the fans—a dream he'd have loved to have back when he'd been younger.

He rubbed his forehead, anger finally abating. Yeah, this wasn't going to be an easy job. Was rapidly starting to feel like more than a job, too.

Behind him the thud and crunch of gravel sounded as someone exited the bus. David turned to see Ray Van Zeller heading his direction, exhaustion draped over him like a cloak.

David swallowed. "How's Mish?"

"Shattered. Though if you asked her, she'd say she's fine." Ray scrubbed a hand over his face. "I'd be tempted to believe her, if she hadn't spent a half hour crying in my arms."

David couldn't help the wince or the deep, deep stab of guilt. "Sorry. This is my fault."

"Adrian said you'd say that." Ray waved the words away. "It's bullshit."

"I—" But the shrewd look he gave David stopped the words in his throat.

"The only people responsible for the theft of Mish's ring are the guy who took it and the stalker."

So Adrian had told them that much. "The thief said that the guy's name was Stan, but I doubt that's a real name, especially considering the fan meaning." He paused. "I should have noticed the thief, though."

Another hand wave from Ray, but no words.

"And I didn't get her ring back." He regretted that so much. "Police are gonna want to know if she wants to press charges against the dude who stole it."

"She won't want to." Despite the large parking lot lights that illuminated the area, Ray's eyes were weirdly shadowed and unreadable. "That's not the part that broke her down, you know, losing the ring." He kicked a piece of gravel and sent it flying toward the grass at the edge of the lot. "The ring was important to her, don't get me wrong. But what tore her heart out was the fans giving her *their* rings. Like—she's got dozens now. Maybe even a hundred." He tipped his head up, and now David saw the sadness there. "We don't deserve the fans we have," he whispered.

"Now, that's bullshit," David said.

Ray huffed. "Stalemate."

Maybe. But not really. "We should talk about all of this tomorrow, when we're not so tired."

Ray gripped David by both arms and gave him a little shake. "Don't you dare think of leaving us now. You're too important."

"But not good enough to protect you."

An odd smile lifted Ray's lips for a moment before it

vanished. "There's all kinds of protection." He let him go, then nodded. "We'll talk tomorrow."

David could only answer one way. "Okay. Tomorrow."

"Night, David. Try to get some sleep."

He doubted he would, but it was a nice sentiment. "Thanks, Ray. You, too." He turned away and headed to the crew bus, the shifting of the gravel under his feet an echo of Ray's steps back toward the band's bus. Where Mish was.

He shook his head and climbed onto the bus. The soft murmurs of the crew halted when he boarded, and they all looked at him.

"Hey," he said, and slipped past the folks who hadn't yet crawled into their berths, intent on his own.

"David." It was Faith, and she held out a mug. "Take this."

He did, and peered down into it—but it was the scent that gave the whiskey away. "God." He breathed in the fumes, then swallowed a huge mouthful, both wincing at the burn and loving every painful second as the heat slid down his throat and the alcohol into his bloodstream. "Thank you."

"No problem. You did good tonight."

Why did everyone keep thinking that?

"I did shitty tonight." His next swallow wasn't quite so large. He leaned against the wall close to his berth.

"You chased down and caught that dude."

"I should have never let him near Mish."

Faith shrugged. "He had a wristband. Not like you could have stopped him."

David blinked at the booze in his mug and then at Faith. "He had a wristband?"

She nodded, confusion in her eyes. "Yeah, you know. For the signing event. You had to buy them in advance, kinda like the VIP encounter—but a lot cheaper."

Despite the alcohol seeping into his system, David's brain processed that information. He knew the dude's name. "Is it like with the VIP—the person who orders needs to pick up the wristband?"

"Yeah. Name on the ID needs to match."

Maybe they could figure out who bought him the ticket. Follow the money.

David drank down the rest of the whiskey and handed the mug back to Faith. "Thank you. I needed that. And not just the booze."

She gave him a lopsided grin. "Go to bed, hotshot. That lead will be there in the morning."

Despite not thinking he'd be able to sleep, as soon as David's head hit the pillow, the warmth of the booze and the rhythmic swaying of the bus on the highway dropped him straight into darkness and oblivion.

CHAPTER EIGHT

Crusty morning eyes were the *worst*. Mish spent a couple of minutes lying in her berth blinking and rubbing the gunk out of her eyes so she wouldn't look like she'd spent a good portion of the night crying into her pillow. Fucking tears. Once they started, they were so hard to turn off. Damn Ray for being so understanding and giving her the affection she needed.

She loved the man, inside and out—a brother from another mother, as the saying went.

It was early, but the others were moving around the bus, given the murmurs, the clink of ceramic, and the wonderful smell of Adrian's coffee. When she was sure she only looked like death *half* warmed over and not completely, she crawled out of her berth and stumbled to the bathroom. Emotional hangovers were worse than alcoholic ones. She didn't get drunk that often, but when she did, she could blame the nausea and headache on being foolish.

This wasn't foolishness, but her life. Emotions she couldn't bottle up and some dude doing what they so often did—made her life hell because they thought she was public property. Or worse, their property.

When she returned to the front of the bus, Adrian handed her a steaming hot mug of black coffee, and she could have kissed him for that. Whatever magic he wove with those beans of his, he'd taken their tour bus coffee from fine to transcendent. "Thanks."

His smile was sleepy. "No problem." He claimed Dom's seat, since Dom hadn't emerged from his berth.

Zavier and Ray were in their usual spots—opposite ends of the same bench, legs twined with each other. They had similar expressions, but it was Ray who asked the inevitable question. "How do you feel?"

Mish pursed her lips and stared into the depths of her coffee. Shaken. Unbalanced. It wasn't a good place to be, especially since they had a concert tonight. She didn't want to tell them that, but they'd vowed to be honest with each other.

She took a sip of coffee and sat next to Adrian. "Fragile. It's—" She shook her head, trying to sweep the dust bunnies from her mind. "I think once we get to the next place and I can get on stage, I'll be better." Too much time to think on the bus.

Ray grunted. "Yeah, I hear you. Performing's the best. It's all that exists when you're doing it."

It was. Ray interacted with music in a way Mish didn't, but they all sank into their songs when they played. In those moments, only the music, the stage, and the fans existed. She needed that more than anything right now. "When do we get there?"

"Couple hours," Zavier said. He flipped the cover of his tablet closed. "Though I believe we'll be hitting a rest stop soon."

Over by the berths, Dom finally rolled out, blinking into the light of the day. "Please tell me there's coffee."

"Babe, it's me. Of course there's coffee." Adrian rose to pour a cup.

"I fucking love you," Dom said. Adrian handed over the

mug and stole a kiss, which led to Dom leaning against his fiancé.

They were adorable together, which both warmed and broke Mish's heart. Hard not to be happy for Dom and Adrian—or for Ray and Zav, for that matter. But it was a reminder that though this was her family, she was alone in that regard. Sure, Ray was a shoulder and a brother, and the others were as supportive, but there were different connections she missed. Physical ones. Emotional ones, like the way Dom relaxed as Adrian steered him to his usual spot on the couch.

Dom sat and bumped her shoulder. "Hey. You feeling better?"

"Yeah," she said, because it was true. "Your man makes a mean cup of coffee."

His grin was still edged with sleep, and he drank deeply before turning those eyes back onto Adrian. "Second best part of the morning." The heat in that look probably could have fried an egg.

Adrian laughed and booped Dom's nose with his finger. "Shush, you."

Zavier rolled his eyes, but was smiling. "Ray doesn't want to know."

"Damn straight," Ray said. "Some things can stay private." He took a sip. "I'm gonna need to talk with David when we stop. Didn't last night because we were all too tired."

"I thought you did talk to him." Mish had watched Ray bound off the bus when she'd gotten up to get ready to sleep.

He looked up at the roof of the bus for a moment, obviously thinking of how to word what he wanted to say. Finally, he met her gaze. "I did, but that was to make sure he wasn't going to quit on us, or shoulder all the blame."

Shock zinged through Mish and she sat up straight. "Why the fuck would he blame himself?"

"'Cause he didn't see that asshole coming," Adrian said. "Thinks he should have."

She shook her head. "Men."

Zavier chuckled. "More like 'protectors.' Pretty sure you'd have done the same thing, had your roles been reversed."

She grunted. Zavier had a point. "Touché."

Ray scrunched up his face. "Marcella's also gonna ask you if you want to press charges against the guy who stole your ring."

"Ugh. No." The thought of having to deal with that incident for much longer made her skin crawl. "I love that ring, but it's not worth the press on my ass or dealing with lawyers."

"Yeah, she figured. But she's gotta ask," Ray said.

Mish grabbed her phone and texted Marcella, then grabbed some fresh clothes. "Gonna go catch a shower."

Didn't take her long to get washed and dressed. The guys all got themselves together, too, and soon they slowed down onto an exit ramp. Mish nudged Ray with her foot. "I want to talk to David, too."

"Figured you might." Ray's grin made sense. She hadn't exactly been subtle about her interest in David. His smile slipped away. "I'll let him know."

Only then did it occur to Mish that maybe David wouldn't want to talk to her. She was the job, after all. *Shit.* "Did he really try to quit?"

Ray shook his head. "I think he knows he's in this for the long run. But he was angry and upset. It gutted him, not being able to return your ring, even though he caught the shit who took it."

Because David took his job seriously. She knew what would come next: the professional face. No more *rock queen* or *darling* designed to make her laugh. "Well, it gutted me, so at least we have that in common."

"You have a lot of things in common," Ray said.

She wanted to ask him what he meant, but the bus swung into a rest stop with a lurch, and Ray was out the door as soon as the bus was parked. She and the rest of the band were slower, but Mish spotted David almost immediately. Ray was already talking to him. Even so, she met David's stare and tried to smile. Probably failed, since he looked down before saying something to Ray.

"Come on." Zavier stood next to her, hands in his pockets. "Let's go check out the breakfast options. I bet there are hideous donuts to go with Adrian's brilliant coffee."

A laugh bubbled up in her from underneath the weight of the preceding evening. "Okay. But we're only buying them if they're obnoxious colors, 'cause normal donuts aren't worthy of Instagram."

In the end, they found neon blue and green frosted donuts and bought a half dozen before boarding the bus. David joined them on the bus too, and he and Ray headed to the back lounge, where things were a little more private.

Dom raised an eyebrow. "He's not keeping us out of the loop, is he?"

"No." Zavier sat when the bus started moving and eyed the donut box Adrian was holding. "He's doing that leader thing he does."

"Want a donut, Zav?" Adrian's grin was wicked.

Zavier rose and stood over Adrian and the donuts. "I still believe food should not be this color."

"Except you're the one who bought them." Adrian got out his camera. "And I know you desperately want that neon green donut, so you better pose biting it."

Zavier flipped open the box and claimed one of the donuts. "Fine." His voice was rich with laughter. Photos were snapped, of the donuts, of Dom and Zavier chowing down. They were pretty good in the end, despite the scary color of the frosting. They even left two—for Ray and David.

Of course, Adrian's photos were artful and cute and

featured them and Twisted Wishes mugs of Adrian's coffee. Mish approved the one of her laughing, donut in hand. She wanted *that* one posted.

"People are worried about me. Our fans." The image made her look happy and carefree—more so than she felt. But she could get there again. The weight of hurt, fear, and loss was lifting.

From the chatter on the internet and on the band's site, lots of folks were upset on her behalf.

"Yeah, the fans are," Adrian said. "They adore you. It's not all bad out there, though."

"I know. One rotten apple shouldn't reflect on the bunch." An apple with minions, though.

Zavier settled back into his seat. "The press about the show has been phenomenal. The critics very much enjoyed your duet with Ray."

"It was fucking fantastic," Dom said.

"Really was." Adrian flipped open his tablet. "Let me show you the fans' reactions."

She scooted closer to him, and he flipped through Twitter, Snapchat, and Instagram. Each one warmed her heart. The OMGs and the wows and the comments on how good her voice sounded. People wanted more. They thought she and Ray were awesome.

The stabbing edge of pain from the night before was gone, and she gave Adrian's arm a squeeze. "Thanks, hon."

"Anything for family," he said, his voice gentle. "I see the good, too, and there's a lot more of that."

She believed him. But somehow, the bad always weighed more than the good. "Glad you joined us." She punched him in the arm with no force.

"Me, too," Dom said.

Zavier's grin was legendary, but he didn't say anything.

Just then, Ray came up from the back of the bus, and paused by Adrian and the donut box. "I think I've waylaid

David's fears and self-incrimination, and he threw some ideas around about tonight's concert which we wanna run by all of you." He picked up the last green donut. "But he'd like to talk to Mish in private, if that's okay?"

Her stomach tumbled from nervousness, but she wasn't sure if it was from thrill or apprehension. "Yeah. I'll head back." She poured another cup of coffee for her, one for David, and grabbed the box with the remaining donut. "I'll even bear gifts."

Ray planted a kiss on her cheek. "Go get him."

There was more to Ray's statement than she really wanted to admit.

Despite the rocking of the bus, David paced the floor of the small lounge, his heart in his throat. The engine covered most of the noise from the front of the bus, but murmurs of speech still filtered to him, and Mish's voice chattered across his nerves. Was she mad? Upset? How would this go? He needed to apologize, even though Ray had been vehement that David needed to do no such thing.

The flutter of the curtain between the sections heralded the arrival of Mish, who was carrying a box in one hand and two mugs of coffee in the other. He closed the distance between them and retrieved one of the mugs. "This for me?"

"Some of Adrian's magic bean juice."

Hearing her voice, so normal, so right, was perfect. "His coffee *is* magic."

Her smile was magic, too. She held out the box. "And here's the last of the scary, scary donuts."

Inside was one of the hideously colored confections the band had bought at the truck stop. "Thank you, I think." He took the box, then gestured at the couch. "Sit and talk?"

Her smile dimmed, and he swallowed his own apprehension. "Yeah, sure," she said.

He placed the box between them, though the last thing he wanted was a barrier right now. Maybe this would go better if they kept some distance. "Ray's told me four times that I need to stop beating myself up about last night."

"Only four?" Her smile was faint. "He's slipping."

"Well, four so far." David sipped his coffee and let his eyes flutter shut for a moment as the brew hit the back of his throat, warm and perfect. "Fucking hell. If I were into men, I'd marry Adrian just to have this coffee every morning." He met Mish's shocked silence and shrugged. "Though I don't think I'm his type."

"You're straight?" Her voice pitched up and she wrapped her hands around her mug. "I mean, I don't want to assume, but..."

"I prefer women, yeah. I don't like the label *straight*, because it's so often used in opposition to queer." He took another sip of his coffee and steeled himself for what was next. "And I'm queer as fuck."

"You're..." Mish didn't seem upset, just confused.

That was pretty normal, a drawback to passing as cis. He preferred it to shock and horror, though. Not passing had grated on him, but sometimes passing did, too. Fucking assumptions. But he did need to have this conversation—regardless of his interest in Mish.

He pointed at the donut. "I'm gonna eat that. 'Cause the rest of you did, and didn't die from the horrendous food coloring. But blue isn't my favorite color. Neither is pink. Too wrapped up in gender."

"I get that. Blue is for boys, pink girls, like color has a gender." Mish rolled her eyes, then took a sip of coffee. "What are you trying to tell me? I'm...missing it, aren't I?"

"Missing what I'm trying to tell you? Maybe. But I'm not being clear." He inspected the donut, then picked it up.

"Part of it is that my mother used to make me wear these pink dresses with scratchy eyelet lace edging right up until the moment in time I told her I was a boy and tired of that shit." He took a bite of the donut. "She didn't believe me 'cause it was the '80s and people didn't understand being trans that well, but at least she didn't force me into another dress."

Mish's eyes widened a faction, then she got a faraway look, as if running things through her mind. Finally, she took a swig of her coffee. "Yeah, okay. That makes sense."

Nothing else. No waver in her voice. If anything, she'd relaxed more. Then again, her chosen family was pretty damn queer.

What *really* surprised him was the taste of the donut. "This thing isn't half-bad!" Even the frosting was good.

"I know. We were all expecting nightmares and they're actually decent. I guess that's what we get for snarking on rest stop donuts."

"Don't judge a book and all that?" Not that she'd judged him.

Mish grinned. "So, is Ray gonna have to tell you a fifth time not to beat yourself up?"

David took a breath to settle himself. He hadn't intended to come out to Mish, at least not like that, but the conversation he'd had with Ray had made him realize that if he didn't pull back, he had to be completely open with Mish. He knew why, too—that sparkle in her eyes, the way he felt when she touched him, smiled at him, and teased him.

"Maybe," he said. "I *am* sorry about last night, and I keep going over it in my head. I *did* run after the dude, which left you alone. In retrospect, that wasn't smart, especially after what we learned." Each time he thought about the night objectively, the more he picked his actions apart. Ray was right—he needed to stop beating himself up.

She waved his words away. "Eh, I've already punched out

one guy. Wasn't like I was alone—the band was there, and the venue staff."

"True. And yeah, you can throw a mean punch, but Ray would have my hide if you couldn't play for six weeks." There was that heat deep inside him again. "Even though your singing is fucking out of this world."

That's what shocked her. Not that he was trans, not that he'd failed to return her ring. Those words of praise. A blush rose to her cheeks and she looked into her coffee mug. "I know I'm decent, but I'm not sure about *out of this world.*"

"Stunning," he said. "Beautiful." Just like her. Rock royalty. "You weren't out in the audience. People were screaming their heads off."

"Stop." She put up a hand. "Please. Adrian already showed me how the fans reacted."

"You're a goddamned rock queen." He couldn't help the gravel in his voice. "People should worship you."

The look she gave him wasn't anger or annoyance, but there was too much tension in it to be friendly. She set the empty mug down on the floor of the bus. Moved the donut box behind her, then reached up, her hand hovering close to his cheek. "May I?"

"Fuck yes." His throat was dry and every nerve in his body was primed.

She cupped his face with her palm. With her other hand, she drew her fingers along the edge of his beard. "You want to worship me, David?"

God, he was hard, leaning into her touch. So much for not getting involved. "Can't help it, princess."

She chuckled. "Still not a princess, darling." She stroked his jawline, sending sparks down his arms and legs.

He settled his hands on her hips. "You okay with this?"

"You touching me? More than." Her breath ghosted over his lips.

"You gonna forgive me for screwing up?" He whispered

the words. Wanted absolution from this beautiful woman who held him in her hands.

"No. Because you didn't screw up. You did what you thought correct in the moment and it *was* the right thing, David."

"But—"

Her lips finally met his, and he groaned against their softness, against the bitter taste of coffee and sweetness of the donut. When she deepened the kiss and drew him closer, their legs touched and he tightened the grip on her waist.

Her fingers drifted into his hair, nails scraping against his scalp, bringing a hint of what more might come if they went beyond this one meeting.

He broke the kiss and whispered against her lips, "This is such a bad idea." He wanted to keep going, drown in her, in this mistake.

Her chuckle was heaven. "What's a bad idea? The whole 'me getting close to you because I trust you and don't know how to tell you you're okay' bit?"

He kissed her neck. The gasp she made only increased the heat in his veins and his desire to slip off this couch and kneel on the floor of the bus. "Gonna make it harder for me to keep you safe."

She pulled back, and her hazel eyes had taken on the greenish hue he so loved. "I don't know about that." She straddled him until there wasn't a gap between their bodies and her rocking hips pressed his packer against his dick. God, he couldn't help the moan, or matching her movements. Her lips took his again, kissing and nipping until he couldn't breathe through his need for her.

She spoke between kisses. "Closer you get, the closer I am to you."

He wanted to rake his hands through those copper curls. Strip everything off. Unwrap his entire being. He barely even knew Mish. "Fucking hell, you terrify me, baby."

"Ditto, David." She mouthed his chin. "At least we're in the same place."

Was that good or bad? One of them ought to have their head on straight. Right now, he was so keyed up by her body against his and the way her hips rolled. "Jesus, Mish. You're gonna make me come. What will the band think?"

The vibrations of her laugh only made him want her more. "Zav will roll his eyes and ask what took us so long. Ray won't care, and Dom will stick his fingers in his ears and not wanna hear about it at all." She stilled herself. "Though you're right that I shouldn't take you apart in the back of the bus with them on board."

He pressed his forehead against hers and worked to catch his breath. "So you're gonna make me ache instead?"

There was a bit of the devil in her chuckle. "Don't think it'll be the first time." She stole a kiss. "And I get off on my lovers wanting me that badly."

He shuddered. *Lover*. Okay, so they were going there. "You're right about it not being the first time." He took a kiss back. "And yeah, I wanna worship you, Mish."

"Good." She kept straddling him. "I'm gonna love that. A guy like you on his knees for me."

He rolled his head against the back of the couch. "I'm so fucked."

"Not yet." Oh, the humor in her voice. "Just you wait."

He twined his fingers into her hair then, and pulled her into a long, deep kiss. When he broke it, he spoke. "We should talk about work."

She groaned, but it wasn't with pleasure. "Yeah, you're right. I—just wanted to set you at ease." She slipped off his lap, and he missed her warmth and weight immediately. "Want me to get more coffee?"

He nodded. "Yeah." That would give him a chance to get his dick and brain back under control. "Please. And maybe Adrian, too?"

"Okay. But first..." She kissed him again, and fuck, he loved every second of her mouth on his. When Mish relented, she scooped up the two coffee mugs, winked at him, and vanished past the privacy curtain.

David stared up at the ceiling of the bus. That hadn't gone like he'd planned. He should've been worried—instead, relief washed through him, along with anticipation and delight.

He was *fucked*. Completely.

Of course Zavier raised an eyebrow at Mish when she returned to the front of the bus. Ray's husband always seemed to be able to spot connections and relationships in an instant. She gave him a cocky-ass smile, and took the last of the coffee. "Should I shut the pot off, or are you gonna make more?"

Adrian looked up from the book he'd been reading. "Eh, we're close to the venue. Turn it off. I'll give it a cleaning."

Dom was sprawled out next to Adrian, his nose in a book of his own. "Venue coffee sucks." He didn't even look up.

Adrian poked him in the side. "Yes, but I don't want you to get complacent and replace me with some other coffee brewer."

Dom started and looked up. "Never in a million years. You're fucking stuck with me now."

The smile on Adrian's face was radiant and so personal, Mish looked away. "Could we borrow your boy toy for a bit, Dom? David wants to talk to him about work."

"He's not my boy toy." Embarrassment in Dom's words.

"Quite the other way around," Zavier murmured. Then looked even more smug when Ray thwapped his thigh.

"God," she said. "Can you guys stop for even a minute?"

"Pot, meet kettle," Ray said.

Heat to her face. She didn't think she looked different, but that make-out session with David had every bit of her body tingling, so maybe there was a neon sign the same color as donut frosting above her head blinking *Got some. Gonna get more.* "Adrian? Can we borrow you?"

He set his book down on Dom's chest and stood. "Of course. Even though you took the last of the coffee."

Dom shifted on the couch. "Hey! Am I furniture now?"

"Now?" Adrian absently ran a hand through Dom's hair.

Ray huffed. "Okay, I'm gonna agree with Mish here."

Talk about smug smiles. Both Adrian and Zavier wore similar ones. Ray rolled his eyes. "Go work." He made shooing gestures at the back of the bus.

Adrian grabbed his tablet, and they went. He still had a grin when they entered the back lounge, and yup. David's color rose like he'd been caught with his hand in the cookie jar.

Mind you, she did want his hands in her—"Fuck you all, you have me doing it now."

Adrian laughed. David looked bewildered. She handed David a mug. "They're a bundle of innuendo up there, that's all."

"Exactly how is that different from any other day of the week?" David seemed to relax. "Because you all are primed for it."

"I'll give you that," Adrian said.

Yeah, she had to admit that they did get into the thick of it damn often. "Yeah, all right. I don't help, either."

Adrian snorted. "You *encourage* it, sweetheart." He took a seat on the couch. "But we're here to work, right?"

"Well, I'm not into ménages." David seemed less embarrassed, though the blush remained on his neck. He sat as well.

It was Adrian's turn to look a little uncomfortable. Maybe David was *his* type, though Adrian and Dom were completely committed to each other. Monogamous, too.

"What did you want to talk to us about?" Mish wanted to

crawl into David's lap again, partly because throwing Adrian off was such a treat. She sat next to David instead. Not a ménage, but David *was* between them.

"When I got on the crew bus last night, I talked a little bit with Faith. I think she works with the VIP crew?"

Adrian looked sharper and he was the one to answer. "Yeah, she organizes the extras. Been with the band longer than I have, first as a roadie." There was an edge to his voice. Yeah, he was protective of the band, too.

Before Mish could intervene, David held up his hand. "She's good people, I know. Told me something that got me thinking of how we might find this stalker asshole."

Cold spiked through Mish. Fuck that goddamned dude. "How?"

"Faith said that the guy had a wristband, so I couldn't have kept him out of the line."

Adrian got a look like he'd been poked in the back of the head. "Oh fuck. The credit card. Of course."

A second later, she got it, too. "If that fucker paid for that guy to be there, we can figure out who he is." They knew the name of the guy who'd taken her ring, so in theory, they could work backward.

"The only thing I'm not sure about," David said, "is privacy rights. I mean, I know you guys have the info, but I'm not a cop."

Adrian mulled that over. "Yeah. We might have to bounce this off someone legal."

More ice in Mish's spine. She rubbed her hands over her face. Going to the police would mean public records. Sure, the attack earlier and the ring theft were known, but they'd kept the whole stalker thing out of the press. Easy enough to do. Everyone expected Mish to have some overenthusiastic male fans, since she was a woman.

"If it's the last resort, let's go to the cops."

David patted her thigh. "I want to keep as much of this as

I can out of the public eye. Pretty sure this guy *wants* to be known. Feels like he needs there to be a connection."

Adrian scratched his stubbled chin. "What if there is one?"

They both looked at him.

"I mean," he said, "the guy seems familiar with Mish. At least to my reading."

Jesus. She was *sure* it wasn't an ex. "Maybe I need to look at everything."

Oh man, did David look unhappy with that statement.

"Really?" She stood and looked down at him. "You're the one who said they shouldn't keep things from me."

David caught her hand, and Adrian raised an eyebrow at that, but fuck him. She focused on those dark eyes of David's.

"I don't intend to keep things from you. But you have a concert tonight."

As if to punctuate his statement, the bus slowed and shifted and she nearly lost her balance. Rather than topple over, she sank down next to David. "I didn't mean right this instant," she muttered.

Adrian looked at the privacy curtain, his brow furrowed. "Let me see how much info I can get without involving lawyers."

"Legally, please." David hadn't let go of her hand. She squeezed his.

Adrian's smile was all teeth. "What do you take me for, some black hat hacker?"

"Oh," David said, "I suspect your hat's a little on the gray side."

That smile didn't fade from Adrian's face. "We should get ready for the show. How about once we get to the hotel in New Hampshire, we all have a meeting? With the rest of the band, too?"

Shit, yeah. "We shouldn't leave them out of this." Mish reluctantly slipped her hand from David's. "Especially since I yelled at Ray about that."

The bus came to a stop with a jerk. Outside the darkly tinted window was a view of another vast parking lot surrounded by trees—another summer amphitheater. Back in her youth, she'd dreamed of having enough money to buy lawn seats to those blockbuster concerts. That girl would never have imagined performing on stage at one.

David stood. "That good with you? Adrian sees what he can find, then we lay it all out on the table?"

Mish tore her attention from the window. "Yeah. It's a good plan." She paused, then added, "I still don't think it's anyone I know, but I'll consider that, too."

"Don't let it throw you off your game." Real concern in David's voice. And a twitch in Adrian's smile before the latter left for the front of the bus.

She closed the distance between them and took David's chin in her palm. "There's something else I want in New Hampshire."

"Yeah?" His eyes were wide, and the thrum of his pulse was visible in his sleek neck. "Tell me, baby."

"You inside me." She drank his moan in with her lips, and relished the way his hard body fit against hers. A beautiful man. Tough and headstrong. So, so pliant in her arms. She relented, too aware of the voices in the front of the now much quieter bus.

"Any way you want me," David said, his voice low but clear.

"Exactly." She took another drink of him, then untwined their bodies. "I gotta go work."

"Me, too." The way he looked at her in that instant didn't help the wobble in her knees. "Got the best seat in the house. Go knock 'em dead, Mish."

She would. Then later give David the show of his life. Maybe a bad idea, like he'd said earlier. But the best things in her life only happened when she'd taken the initiative and grabbed that one chance.

Mish blew him a kiss and sauntered up to join the rest of the band. They were waiting for her at the front of the bus. Ray wore a smirk, and she punched him in the arm. "Shut up."

He mocked being affronted. "I didn't say a word!"

"Didn't have to." There was joy in her heart, especially when David worked his way forward, a soft smile on his handsome face.

They'd kill the show tonight, then head to New Hampshire, where she'd set a certain personal security guard on fire. *That* thought was much more pleasant than dwelling on her creepy-ass stalker.

CHAPTER NINE

The crowd for this concert was thicker than their first one. David hadn't expected that. He stood by the soundboards before Two Times Strong took the stage, and surveyed the venue. The Twisted Wishes meet-and-greet had gone off reasonably well, with both the fans and the band having a huge amount of fun, despite one overenthusiastic fan rushing the band as they made their way to the pavilion where the fans waited.

David grabbed the guy around the waist and hauled him back before he got anywhere near the band. "Hey, hey. Nope. We're not gonna do that."

The crew was smart enough to notice the scuffle and delayed the band from entering.

The kid—he couldn't be more than twenty—squirmed in David's arms as he shoved him back. "Sorry, I just—I want to tell them how much I love them."

David moved him another couple of feet into the pavilion. "Plenty of time for that, kid. But if you rush 'em like that you're not gonna see them at all."

That deflated the kid. "I—Okay."

David sat him in the back row, and clamped a hand on his

shoulder until Twisted Wishes entered and took their seats at the table up front.

Once the band started talking, the kid was wrapped up in listening. Good. David didn't think this guy was an actual problem, and he didn't have any of the vibe of Mish's stalker. Sometimes fans just got ahead of their brains. The band acted like nothing had happened at all.

Ray was on-point as the leader, and Dom his outlandish self. Mish was loud and brash and sexy, while Zavier played the cool, quiet type, throwing out occasional quips.

David did have a harder time looking away from Mish this meet-and-greet. Maybe because he knew the way her mouth felt along his neck and the heat of her body against his.

Or because she'd changed into an outfit that was both low-key and hot as sin. White flowing pants that were slit up to her knees, along with a top from the same material that showed glimpses of her abdomen and arms. Her jewelry—as well as her nails—was blood-red. How she'd painted them in the scant hours since they'd gotten off the bus, he didn't know. That kind of thing had always seemed like magic to him.

He'd kept an eye on the fans, especially the kid, even as he'd admired Mish and enjoyed the banter of the band. They answered questions and picked on one another the way siblings—and lovers, in the case of Ray and Zavier—did.

When it was all over and the fans had been escorted out to their seats, Ray clapped him on the shoulder. "Thank you for spotting that."

"That's what I'm here for."

It was. And a little proof to himself that he could do this job, despite his attachment to the band. To Mish. Still might not be smart, but it was workable.

Now Twisted Wishes was changing for their set, being looked after by Adrian, the crew, and venue security. Access to this venue's backstage area was tightly controlled, so David took his time scoping out the crowds while the techs prepared the stage for Two Times Strong, who'd be out in short order.

The pit by the stage was packed with fans decked out in Twisted Wishes T-shirts and tanks, waiting for the main attraction. He'd walked along the barrier between the stage and the pit, and nodded to the security stationed there. They eyed his badge and let him go past.

The main seated area was filling in. There'd be lots of empty spots during the opening act, but he also spotted pockets of fans here to see Two Times Strong. The lawn, however, was a mass of blankets, people, alcohol, and probably some weed. It really wasn't a summer concert without *that* scent drifting through the air, no matter how much the venue security inspected the bags at the gates.

He should be on edge. Instead, excitement built in him to see this show, what Mish would wear on stage, what songs they'd play tonight. Twisted Wishes never played the exact same concert twice. Sets were similar, but the band liked to mix it up and give each city a unique experience—and that had really worked this past concert. According to Adrian, the internet had exploded since Ray and Mish's duet.

David wanted to watch that again. Wanted to see her safely through this night, and then on to New Hampshire, where he'd let her do whatever the hell she wanted with him. Some of that was lust, but he'd clicked with her the moment she'd snarked at him. He knew something of Mish behind the rock star...wanted to find out more, too. Share pieces of his life and experiences with her.

He was the last person who should be hooking up with Mish, becoming part of this strange Twisted Wishes family. This was not the way the job was supposed to go. His logical brain told him he needed to step back and tell Mish they couldn't get together. But another part remembered the earnest expression in Ray's face, in his eyes, when he'd told David not to back away.

Not backing away wasn't the same as running headlong into fire, though.

David rolled his head to release the tension in his neck, and resumed his walk through the covered pavilion. He should join the band backstage. They might want to watch Two Times Strong perform from the side of the stage again. Ray said Five Asylum had done similar for them, and they wouldn't have gotten where they were without that support.

But if Twisted Wishes were visible, the fans would react.

David dodged between people entering the pavilion, and headed toward the entrance that led behind the stage. Close to the gate, someone tapped his arm. "Excuse me?"

He halted to find a woman inspecting him from head to toe. "Yes?"

"Aren't you that guy who's been with Mish?"

With Mish? Jesus, he needed to ask Adrian about *that*. Yes, he'd been seen frequently with her in New York, but there hadn't been much muttering in the press, especially since they'd established that he worked for Twisted Wishes.

"I'm security for Twisted Wishes." He was a little gruff, but he and Mish hadn't hooked up yet, and they hadn't talked about how public they were going to be if they did. When they did.

The woman got one of those smiles that made him apprehensive. "So you're *not* with Mish?"

He wished like hell he'd been wearing his sunglasses, because he wanted a shield to hide behind. This wasn't a normal fan question. "I'm sorry...who am I talking to?"

"Oh, my apologies, I'm Vicky Heydel, from the HitsDaily website. Rumor has it that you're Mish Sullivan's latest fling, and I'm trying to confirm that."

Now he really wanted his sunglasses, because his first instinct was to roll his eyes. "I'm sorry, I'm not available for interviews, and I have a job to do. If you'll excuse me." He turned and walked away.

Thankfully, the reporter didn't follow to press for information, and he'd been around enough important people in his career that his response was fine. Still, he made it a point to track down Marcella. Easy enough to do, since she was chatting with Adrian in the hall outside the dressing rooms. But when they broke off their conversation to look at him, they both had long faces. His stomach dropped an inch or two. "What happened?"

Without a word, Adrian handed over his tablet, and there was yet another email from yet another address. This one had an attached photo of Mish's ring.

> *My dear, I'm surprised you even have such inexpensive trinkets now. After all, you are the serpent who shed her skin for fame and fortune. But such a thing does belong on your finger. I'll be sure to slip it on again once you're mine.*

David handed the tablet back to Adrian. Talk about crawling skin. He practically heard a slick, ugly voice while reading those words. He'd run into this type of guy before. Far worse was when he ran into them *now* because they no longer filtered themselves around David.

The world was different on this side of his transition, but no less scary.

"You haven't showed this to Mish, have you?"

Adrian shook his head. "I know better. That's also why I'm out here. I need to burn off my anger before I head back, or Dominic will read me like a book."

Marcella waved in the direction of the stage. "I take it all is fine out with the public?"

"Yes. This venue's tighter with the security and has less access points." David paused. "As far as the crowd, the fans are even more excited than the last show."

Finally, a smile appeared on Marcella's lips. "Get used to that. You're going to see it at each stop. I don't know how the band manages it, but they only get more energetic and wilder as the tour goes on, and the fans are the same way."

He chuckled at that, then sobered. "I also ran into some reporter from HitsDaily. She asked me point blank if I was Mish's latest fling."

"Are you?" Marcella's voice was entirely neutral.

He could have denied it, but that wouldn't have been truthful. Plus Adrian had a look that meant David wouldn't get away with hedging his bets.

"I don't know yet," he murmured. "I'm letting Mish decide that."

Her lips twitched upward. "And what did you tell the reporter?"

"That I was security for the band, wasn't available for interviews, and that I had a job to do, before I excused myself and walked away."

That grin grew wider. "Good man."

He didn't know if she meant how he'd handled the reporter or his earlier statement.

"You didn't happen to get the reporter's name?" Adrian tapped away on his tablet. "Because there really hasn't been scuttlebutt about you and Mish, other than that stuff early on. But that doesn't mean sites aren't going to sniff around to try to find out more. They always do." He flipped his tablet closed. "They're still trying to figure out if Dominic and I are really together, since there's been no announcement about a wedding."

David rattled off the reporter's name. "How do you guys put up with that shit, anyway?"

Adrian made a face. "By ignoring it. It bothers Dominic something fierce, but I've gotten used to it."

Marcella cleared her throat. "We try to keep the band's personal lives as private as possible."

"Not like I'm going to kiss and tell," David said. "I like my life private as well." Especially since being in public more might mean being outed to more people than he wanted as the paparazzi traced back his past. He didn't particularly care about being known as trans—it was the fucking stupid questions about being trans that he hated with the passion of a million suns exploding at once.

Marcella nodded. "One of the reasons Ray preferred you for this job above the other candidates."

Just then, the door to the dressing room opened, and Ray poked his blond head out. "Everything okay?"

"Fine," Marcella said, her business face on. "Just getting updates from David and Adrian."

Ray rolled his eyes, as if he knew what they'd been discussing. "Okay, we'll talk about it tomorrow." He slipped out into the hall and closed the door to the dressing room before leaning on it. "Tell me how it is out there." His eyes met David's. "The atmosphere."

"Thick with excitement. Pit's full. Lawn is filling up. Seats are a little empty, but I gather those sometimes are for the opening act."

Ray twisted his face and looked just shy of sticking out his tongue. "They're missing out. Two Times Strong is great. Speaking of which..."

Oh, that imploring expression. "Yes, there's a spot you guys can watch."

"Fucking awesome. I'll let the others know." He stole back into the dressing room.

Soon after, the rest of the band made their way out into the hall, and David damn well lost his mind when Mish walked through the door. From white and flowing to a short black leather dress and hot-pink fishnets, makeup, and jewelry. Quite a contrast, but equally as sexy and scorching hot.

His desire must have been obvious, because her smirk was

out of this world, and she fucking winked at him. "Like what you see?"

Marcella chuckled low. Thank god Adrian was focused on Domino.

David fell in step next to Mish. "Of course I do. You're stunning in everything you wear."

"Mmmhmm. I've seen you look at me before and I saw you look at me now, and there is a difference, David." Her eyes danced. They were hazel in the light of the hallway, and framed in black and pink.

"There *is* something about leather," he said. The thought of peeling Mish out of a dress like that before going down on her flickered through his mind and he nearly tripped over his own feet.

She kept her laugh soft, since they'd made it backstage. David touched her shoulder. "Need to show Ray where to go." He worked his way past and her hand skimmed his ass.

Oh yeah, they really were gonna do this.

He ignored the uptick to his heartbeat and found Ray at the front of the pack, a step ahead of Zavier. David tapped him and spoke close to his ear. "Over this way."

They wove through until they reached the side of the stage. From this vantage, they'd be able to watch the show but be hidden from all but the performers and techs. In fact, Two Times Strong was also in the wings, waiting for the signal to go on stage.

Ray worked his way up to the front. "Hey," he said. "Knock 'em dead."

Lane laughed. "If we kill them, who's going to watch your show?"

There was that stunning grin that Ray Van Zeller was known for. "Eh, we'll just bring 'em back to life when you're done with 'em."

Just then, the house lights turned off, the crowd cheered, and Two Times Strong ran out onto the stage.

Once more, a hand landed on David's ass, then slid up to his waist, and he was entirely unsurprised to find Mish next to him, towering even taller in her heels. She murmured into his ear as Two Times Strong struck up their first song, her breath hardening his dick. "This okay?"

He leaned into her embrace. "Baby, more than."

"Good." Her lips grazed his ear, and it was all he could do to not gasp or moan. Not that anyone would have heard it over the music from the stage. Through the buzzing in his brain, the thump of the bass, and the beat of the drums pounding through his body, it occurred to him that being *this* blatant with Mish might not be the smartest idea, especially with a nosy reporter running around out there.

But at least David knew exactly where Mish was. And right now? No one was getting any closer to her than him.

Mish's heart pounded. Two Times Strong's set had been stellar and pumped up the crowd so much that when the house lights went down for Twisted Wishes, the screams and shouts of the audience had been mind-numbingly loud, even through her ear protection. They'd burst out onto the stage and those calls and yells got louder, like the roar of a storm, and they were all for them.

When Ray leapt across the stage, Zavier burst into the beat of their opening song. Mish and Domino crashed into sound and then Ray's voice was there, and they were off, blowing their fans out of their shoes.

Mid-concert, Mish's head spun with so much passion, she didn't know how she was still on her feet. Especially given the heels she'd strapped on. But hell, she'd played these kinds of concerts before, the ones where the fans were screaming and dancing, and each note played was a love letter to them.

Ray was already shirtless. She danced through the end of "Haze," then met with Ray away from the mics.

He had the devil's grin. "You ready to sing?" Over his shoulder, the audience pulsed like a giant heart.

"Kiddo, you know it!" Singing at the previous show had been a dream come true. Doing it again would be unreal. "Let's go."

Ray bounced on his toes, then sauntered to his mic. "Hey, Syracuse, you all having a good time?"

The roar of the crowd was intense.

"So are we!" Ray pumped his fist into the air. When the crowd quieted down a tad, he continued, "You probably heard we're doing something a little different with 'Finding Light,' right?"

More screams, which sent pinpricks up Mish's arms.

They could probably see Ray's grin from the lawn without the projection on the screens, it was so wide and brilliant. "Wanna hear Mish sing with me?"

Louder screams. Holy shit, David had been right—this crowd was primed.

"Okay." Ray stripped the mic from the stand and did his bounce-bounce-jump move toward the very edge of the stage. "Here we go!"

They launched into "Finding Light," and Mish danced and played through the opening bars, then shimmied up to the mic and belted out the first verse. As soon as she sang the first words, the fans in the pit went wild. Beyond that, she could only make out a throbbing mass of humanity and hear the roar over Dom's guitar and Zavier's drums, and her own deep bass.

Last show, Ray had sung the first verse, but they figured switching it up would keep the fans on their toes. Ray joined in for the chorus, and she crossed the stage to play with Domino for the next verse. From the pit, fans reached for them and the look in their eyes was ecstatic. She'd never been sure the band deserved that, but they worked to live up to every expectation.

By the end of the song, she was flying on adrenaline, the crowd, and the rush of the music. This was the best fucking job in the world. During the cheers while they all took drinks of water, Mish spotted David near the entrance to the pit, his arms crossed, which only showed off his muscular arms. His smile was stunning. Maybe it was the lights, but his eyes seemed to drink her in. She shivered.

Usually after these concerts, she was a heady combination of exhausted, wired, and horny. David was more than a chance to curl her toes and burn off excess energy, though. He was—god. She didn't know. Fearless. Funny. He cared about her, but *listened*, too, which was so damn rare.

She nodded his way, which he'd see, but the fans would take as an acknowledgement of them—which it was as well.

David nodded back. He'd called her a goddess, but at the moment, he was a magnificent god watching over her. Over them all.

Ray took the mic again, much to the delight of the fans, and they launched into another song. On and on it went, until they'd reached the end of their set.

Two stellar, heart-pounding encores later, and they were heading back to the dressing rooms. All Mish wanted to do was find David, a wall, and some privacy, because that had been an amazing show.

But she and the rest of the band had to clean themselves up enough for the signing event, then make it through talking to a hundred buzzed fans. Then she and David would pile back into their very separate buses and head to New Hampshire.

However, she fully intended to have him in her hotel bed before she fell asleep tonight. Or tomorrow. Whenever the fuck they made it to the hotel. That boy was going to be *hers*.

Thank god nothing unusual happened in the signing line.

She was careful not to lay anything on the table, and their crew had told the fans that the band couldn't take any gifts. She got smiles, wide eyes, and stories that left her breathless and misty-eyed, but no more jewelry.

When the last person passed through, she leaned back in her seat and closed her eyes. "That was fucking awesome." How was it that everything kept getting better? Then again, they'd been through some pretty rough shit to get to this point, so maybe this was payback for that.

"It really was." Ray sounded happy and exhausted, much like her.

Zavier cupped the back of Ray's neck with his hand and had this look of supreme satisfaction as he stared out past the table, probably at nothing at all.

Domino—well, Dom now—had his head on Adrian's shoulder. The latter had taken a seat next to his lover once the final fans had left. Adrian's lips were moving, but whatever he was saying to Dom didn't travel to her ears. Zavier must have overheard, though, because he chuckled.

Dom, without even looking, lobbed his empty water bottle toward Zavier, who caught it out of the air. Probably something kinky, then. Those boys tried so hard to stay on the downlow and failed miserably every time—mostly because Zavier really had no shame at all.

God, she loved them.

Into her field of vision walked David, and yes, she still wanted to push him up against the nearest wall and taste those lips again, savor the heat of his hands on her body. See if he *really* wanted to worship her like he claimed.

"Hey, honey," she said. "We done here?"

He laughed. "Darling, you've conquered all and taken the spoils. Time to head north!"

She leaned back in her chair, tipping it onto two legs. "I haven't conquered you yet."

"Get a room," Ray murmured. "God, you're nearly as bad as me."

This time, Zavier's laugh echoed around the nearly empty pavilion. "I'll show you bad," he said in a voice that had them *all* blushing.

Fifteen minutes later, they were on the bus, rolling out, and Mish couldn't sit still. It was one thing to talk about hooking up, another to actually *do* it. Was she out of her mind for flirting so damn hard with a man working for the band? Sure, she'd fooled around with the crew before. A fling with Dane, then something a little more with Sasha. That could have turned serious, if Sasha had wanted more than a summer tour fling with a hot rocker before heading off to grad school.

But that had ended with their last concert that year. Had hurt a little, but Mish hadn't blamed Sasha at all. Had to be on the same page with your partner to make something stick.

David wasn't a member of the crew, not like that. He worked *directly* with her and the band. Given that she tended to gravitate more toward femme regardless of gender, she couldn't exactly tell why he pinged her so hard. That was exciting and a little scary, which...was also exciting.

Fucking brains. Never could figure out her own.

Yes, David was handsome. Compact. Hard. Bearded. The kind of masc she *did* tend to like, when her attraction turned that way.

"Fuck," she muttered before getting out of her seat and heading to the back. At least there, she could pace a little. And maybe—*maybe*—the boys would leave her alone.

No such luck. Ray waited a good ten minutes before joining her, though. As the band's leader and her best friend, he had every right to be worried. Relief trickled through her. Maybe she needed to talk to someone. She'd been Ray's sounding board often enough, even after he'd married Zavier.

She met Ray's gaze, and his smile turned wry. "Oh, come on," he said. "You expected me."

"Course I did. You're predictable, kiddo." He was the glue that held them all together. Family.

He sank down onto one of the couches. "Don't tell the press."

"Wouldn't dream of it." She gave up the pacing, because it wasn't helping at all, and took a seat next to him.

He angled his body. "Wanna talk about it?"

Yes. No. She dropped her head into her hands. "What if I said I didn't?"

He huffed a laugh. "Consent, as Zavier likes to say, is important. If you really don't want a shoulder, I'll head back up." He tapped her knee with his finger. "But somehow, I think you want me to stay."

There was a hell of a lot of maturity in Ray. Not that he'd been immature before—he'd just been a bundle of worry that had thrown his bright mind off track. But in the past two years, he'd come into his own.

"I really like David."

"Well, duh." Ray bumped her knee. "Sounds like you want to do a little more than stare into his eyes, too."

Oh god. Ray was teasing her. Weird to be on this side of that. "Yeah, well. I'm pretty darn tactile."

He laughed outright at that. "You and the rest of us. I get that, I really *really* do."

They were all touchy people, and not ashamed of sex at all—not even Dom, for all his blushing. They'd had their various flings at one point or another, before Ray and Zavier, and then Dom and Adrian, had hooked up.

"But am I into him because you guys are..." She waved a hand.

"Fucking in domesticated bliss, or something close to it?" Ray leaned back and looked smug.

"Yeah, *something* like that." She shrugged. "Being serious

for a moment, sometimes I do feel weird being the only one not paired up. Maybe I'm jumping on David *because* of that."

Ray's smile vanished. "Okay, that worry is valid. And maybe that's a catalyst, but I'm not sure it matters in this case. I mean, I've pretty much wanted to jump Zav's bones since high school. Turns out there was something beyond lust there."

"Quite a bit more, in the case of you and Zav." She'd heard them. Seen the toys. Been to their house. Yes, Zavier was aromantic, but that man wanted Ray like the ocean wants the shore. There was an inexpressible pull between them.

Ray's sly smile was back. "You'll know if there's more there than a need to bone, but there's nothing wrong with blowing off steam with him, if that's what you both want. I mean, dude *is* hot and smart. He keeps up with your mouth, too."

"Your eyes straying, Ray?" She had to get in a *little* teasing.

He held up the hand with his wedding ring. "I'm Zav's. Happily. Entirely. I'm a little too monogamous and he's a little too possessive. But we both appreciate the appearances of others, you know. You, though, can go *touch*."

"If he wants that." God, she hoped he did. There was flirting and then there was actual fucking.

Ray's expression leveled off. "Honey, when that man looks at you, there might as well be a sign saying 'lay me out and fuck me' above his head."

That made her cheeks heat. "It's not that obvious, is it?" Good god, the press would be all over David, and she was damn sure he didn't want that.

"Well, to *us* it's obvious. Plus, not like you two have been subtle with the flirting." He scrunched up his face. "But maybe not to others? You guys are pretty pro in public."

She tried to be. David did, too.

Mish leaned back against the leather of the couch. "So basically, jump his bones?"

Ray patted her on the knee. "Yeah. He's a good guy. You like each other. And..." He trailed off.

Mish leveled her gaze at him. "And *what,* kiddo?"

He matched her stare, his golden eyes steady and true. "He fits in. With you. With us. Like Adrian did."

Oh. That was the thing that made her insides tighten in both joy and fear. Ray saw that, too. Maybe Zavier and Dom did as well. "I—Okay."

"I've rendered you speechless," Ray murmured. "That's a first."

She punched him in the arm and he laughed, then rose. "I'm gonna head back up. You always tell me not to think too hard. Works both ways." He vanished through the privacy curtain.

Mish watched it sway in the chaos of Ray's passing, then settle into a rhythmic pattern similar to the motion of the bus. Yeah, Ray'd grown up a *lot* recently, and she did feel better. Calmer.

She still wanted to fall into bed with David Altet. Maybe more than that, too. Time would tell. But whatever happened, Ray and the band had her back.

CHAPTER TEN

No one on the crew bus had racked out in their berths to sleep, which was fine by David. Joking around and laughing with everyone covered his agitation and need to be at the hotel in New Hampshire right fucking *now*. God. Here he was, at forty-three, acting like a horny teenager. Even when he'd started on T and went through all that had entailed, including having a teenaged libido again, he hadn't been *this* needy.

Then again, it wasn't entirely about sex. He'd gladly lie in Mish's arms or sit near her and talk for hours. Whatever she wanted. Unusual for him, but also freeing. He'd been the pursuer in every single one of his relationships back to high school. Whether butch, masc, or male, he'd been expected to fill a role.

Mish didn't want a role. She wanted *him*. And the reverse was true. He'd caught glimpses of the woman behind the bass guitar, and wanted to see and hear more from her.

On his knees? Sure. Inside her? Yes, *please*.

The rumble and vibration of the road didn't help at all, and he nearly groaned in frustration. They had several hours before they'd arrive. The next day would be free from activities—a time for the band to rest and the crew to relax. The following day, they'd pile back on the bus and head to the nearby venue.

Hours and *hours* to get to know Mish in whatever way she wanted. Also hours and hours he should be *working*. There was information they needed to share with Mish and the rest of the band. They had to figure out how to stop this clown. Nothing had happened at *this* concert, but David had expected a lull in activity—that was normal. A way for the harasser to gaslight the victim with *See, I'm gone, you're safe* before striking again.

How could David claim to be working to protect Mish while getting too damn close to be able to do his job properly? He needed distance to be objective and observant. To not be fucking *distracted*.

He knew better, knew what happened when someone looked away from their objective. People *died*.

The creeping taste of sand edged up his throat. He hadn't screwed up on deployment, thank god, but he'd seen that outcome too many times and had the mental scars to prove it.

Marcella lifted an eyebrow, then swung across the aisle to sit next to him. David forestalled any questions by asking one of his own. "So why is it you ride on the crew bus and not with the band?"

Shock overtook Marcella, then she laughed. "I could ask you the same, you know. Would make more sense for security to be riding with them."

David looked away, focusing on the floor of the bus. Yeah, that did make more sense, and they had the berth space, too. "They're such a tight-knit group."

"That's exactly why I'm here and not there." She folded her hands into her lap. Well-kept nails with green sparkling nail polish at the ends of slender fingers. They went well with her dark hair and golden complexion. She'd changed out of her skirt and suit into jeans and a blouse, but looked a hell of a lot more put together than he did. "Back when I took this job, I knew I would have to be a stellar manager, fight for the band *and* to prove I could do my job. I also had to step so carefully. This band was put through hell by that asshole before me. Ray nearly *died*. Part of what I needed to do was to give them the space they needed to heal and grow after that. To become the family they were already forming for each other."

"But Ray trusts you." He saw that in Ray's smile and the way he spoke to Marcella.

"*Now* he trusts me," she said. "That wasn't always the case. I had to earn his trust."

Something in the way she'd said that set him on edge. "You think I don't have to earn his trust and respect?"

"Of course you do. And you *have*, David." She cocked her head and studied him. "You're also being very careful about your friendship with Mish."

This time, he looked out at the highway as they sped along. "I'm not being careful. I should be, but I'm not."

"Some bonds are important to build."

That made him snap back and study her. "You're saying I should build *bonds* with Mish?"

"I'm staying that Twisted Wishes has its own rhyme and reason. Their dynamic is different from any other band I've worked with. They build friendships. Relationships. Passion that isn't just in their fans. Ask anyone who's ever worked for them. Being closer to Mish isn't going to hinder you on the job. If anything, it'll only help."

"You can't know that." But he did know what happened getting too close. He'd seen it happen with others in similar situations. He'd fucking lost people.

He pushed the thought from his mind. He didn't need those memories, either.

She pursed her lips in that *maybe, maybe not* way. "I *have* been working with Twisted Wishes a little longer than you."

True. He raked a hand through his hair. Everything about *this* job, about Twisted Wishes, threw him for a loop. "What about the press?"

She laughed outright at that. "Oh, leave them to me. That's why I'm here, after all." She turned thoughtful. "Don't have any scandals in your closet, do you?"

He shook his head. Everything that happened overseas had been the price of war. The only item in his closet was his birth name. "But I do have stuff I want to keep private, you know?"

"Don't we all. Such is business. Like I said, leave the press to me. Also, no one here will think one way or another if you fall in with Mish. Or if you don't. Or if you two just—" She waved a hand. "Everyone loves her, and you're a good guy."

"She's gotten close to the crew before?"

A wry smile. "So did Ray, I hear, before Zavier joined the band. It happens."

But did it happen to him? Should it? David grunted. "You know, bouncing at events and corporate security was easier than this."

"Well, yeah. Rock's got its own rules. But it's got to be more fun than a room full of suits."

"Oh yeah." Couldn't help the smile. "This is the most fun I've had. But also the most frustrating." He held up his hand. "And I'm not talking about Mish. I mean her stalker."

That sobered Marcella. "I know we're going to cover that in detail tomorrow, but I wish you could find the guy."

"Me, too. Would make life easier." And his mind less conflicted.

She blew out a breath. "I'm curious about your theories, but I also don't want to work myself up, so let's table that until tomorrow as planned. And if you do decide to hook up with Mish, I'll keep you and her out of the press until such a time you both want to *be* in the press. Deal?" She stuck out her hand.

He clasped it. A warm and firm handshake. "Deal."

She let go, then shimmed up toward the front of the bus. "Hey, are there any more of those beers left?"

David folded his arms across his chest. He could use a drink, in some respects. But he wanted to be completely sober when they arrived at the hotel.

He knew exactly what he was going to do. Mish had invited him...he was going.

David closed his eyes and listened to the road, hoping yet again he wasn't making a huge mistake.

Mish stayed in back for a little longer after Ray had left, but the laughter from the front of the bus drew her out of her funk and sent her back up. Turned out Dom was trying to balance a spoon on the tip of his nose and failing miserably, since Adrian kept poking all of his ticklish places. The end result was a happy Dom wrapped in Adrian's arms.

They were so predictable. But it brought her joy to see Dom so free and easy with his life—no longer conflicted between the stage persona he loved and inhabited on tour, and the much more reserved dorky version of himself he'd hidden from everyone *but* the band.

Adrian had helped Dom bridge that gap, and that had allowed Dom to settle deeper into Domino whenever they were on stage.

On one of the other couches, Zavier was his usual bad-boy self, all sprawled out and stunning. Except she knew better. He gestured Mish over to join him, pulling up his legs to make space. Ray sat across the aisle, scribbling in his Moleskine.

"He's caught the song bug again," Zavier said.

"Shush," came Ray's replay. "Busy."

Mish chuckled and sat, and like a cat, Zavier shifted his legs over her lap. "Feeling better?"

She thought about that. "Maybe. A little, yeah."

"You want my advice?" Zavier's blue eyes were bright and it was pretty obvious he was in one of his way-the-hell-too-overstimulated moods.

"I know your advice, honey. You're gonna tell me I should fuck him."

Zavier grinned. "Maybe tie him down first."

The spoon Dom had been playing with hit the floor. "Zav!"

He looked over at Dom. "What?"

But Adrian was speaking into Dom's ear, so whatever he'd been going to say was lost in a gulp of air. Dom muttered, "That's not fair."

Adrian embraced Dom from behind. "Totally is, babe."

She shook her head. Tying David down did have an appeal, but she had no idea if David's bedroom play even ventured into kink. Not everyone's did, even if all her bandmates were kinky as hell, and *loud*.

Thank god for earplugs. Even in the expensive hotels they stayed in, the walls didn't keep all the noise out.

Zavier shifted his legs to gain her attention, and the humor had fled into profound seriousness. "You enjoy his presence. You're both interested in each other. You should totally fuck him."

Ray shut his book. "That's Zav's solution for all relationships."

"It is *not*." Zavier wiggled his toes in his socks. "My solution is friendship, then trust, then fucking." He ticked each off on his fingers. "*Then* commitment, if you both want that. But start with friendship and trust. There's nothing more important."

She patted Zavier's legs. "Honey, you're a good soul, you know that?"

"Don't give him an ego," Ray said, and there was laughter in his words.

"Give?" Zavier looked affronted. "I already *have* an ego." He crossed his arms behind his head.

"Mmm." The look Ray gave Zavier was like watching sunshine. Bright and warm. "You do."

These men were all perfect for each other. Even when they snarked and argued.

"You want your husband back, Ray?" Mish patted Zavier again.

"Nah. Keep him for a while. He's good company."

"So says our fearless leader," Zavier quipped.

"You're all good company." Mish leaned back and closed her eyes. Friendship and trust. Then fucking. That was a reasonable plan. Zavier tended to see through all the bullshit.

"You like David," she murmured, knowing Zavier would hear and answer.

"Yes, I do," he said. "More importantly, you do. And you aren't a fool, Mish Sullivan."

She huffed, then lapsed into silence, enjoying the warmth of Zavier's legs and the murmur of conversation that ebbed and flowed around her.

They pulled into the hotel fairly late, but this one was used to hosting stars, from rock to sports. Everything went smoothly in terms of getting their rooms and unloading their personal items. Marcella was there, talking quietly to the night manager, David by her side. He glanced up at Mish and held her gaze for a long moment before that dropped away and he addressed both managers, all business again.

God, he was stunning. She watched his proud back as he followed the hotel manager and Marcella into the lobby.

Zavier bumped her from behind. "Come on, princess. Let's go to our rooms."

She snorted. "I'm not your fucking princess either, Zavier."

"Mmm. So very true. But the sooner you're tucked in, the sooner your handsome prince can come a-knocking." He had his devilish grin on, but the giddy nature of his voice belied how tired he must be.

Ray grabbed his arm and tugged. "Hey, *your* handsome prince wants to go to bed. Shall we?"

Zavier turned that sly smile onto his husband. "Yes, by all means, let's *go to bed.*" The way he said it made Ray blush. Perhaps Zavier wasn't *that* tired after all.

She shook her head and followed Ray and Zavier through the sliding glass doors.

CHAPTER ELEVEN

The hotel was secure, thank god. David's nerves settled down to something near normal. After talking to Marcella on the bus, he'd spent the rest of the time worrying that if, *if*, he chose to go off with Mish, he'd be leaving the rest of the band unprotected, even though he'd be sleeping, too.

Didn't matter where he slept, in reality, but a part of his brain was already thinking about setting up shifts to sit in the hall and working on that with the hotel security.

However, Twisted Wishes wasn't the first well-known group to come through this location. They were hardly the most famous. There was an entire floor of the hotel that was locked out to the rest of the guests. And honestly, at the cost *per night* for these rooms, he doubted any of this hotel's guests would be crass enough to venture up to catch a peek at Twisted Wishes, not when they could pay for a fan encounter or just call up Marcella if they were well-known enough. There'd been a few famous folks who'd done that in the past.

They shouldn't have any issues. The night manager seemed a competent, thoughtful, no-nonsense woman. She'd answered all of his and Marcella's questions, and everything had gone smoothly.

So yes, his nerves were settled. Right up until the moment fucking Ray Van Zeller winked at him, as if he knew what the hell was going down. Or might go down. The band was tight-knit indeed. They *were* like a family, and they'd tacitly invited David into that little world. He didn't know if he could belong or wanted to. He'd been on his own for so long.

Whatever was between him and Mish, they needed to sort some of that out tonight, before tomorrow brought a host of emails and speculation about the stalker none of them wanted to think about.

Before he'd headed to the crew bus with a stack of keycards, Mish had caught his hand with hers, pulled him close, and whispered, "Please come to me tonight."

It had happened so fast. If anyone had blinked, they would have missed the slide of their bodies, and that second of intimate connection. The *please* had destroyed him, as had the lust in her breathless whisper.

Now, after stowing his gear in the room assigned to him, he stood at the door of Mish's room. David took a deep breath and knocked on the door.

A few heartbeats later, the door opened, and Mish stood there dressed in a T-shirt that didn't cover her bright pink lace panties. Fucking hell, *that* was a look. All that leg. The curve of her body. The V the lace traced from her hip straight to her mound.

He didn't even have time to croak out a hello before she beckoned him in with a crooked finger and a wicked smile, like something out of a *very* hot porno, and yeah, his body and mind responded the same way. Dry mouth, hard cock.

He stepped inside her room, the door swung closed, and he was pressed up against the unyielding wall. Mish's lips devoured his in a bruising hot kiss. He kissed her back, and he let his bag fall to the floor so he could grab her ass and pull her closer.

She moaned into his mouth, or maybe he moaned into

hers. Couldn't tell. God, he wanted more of her grinding against him.

They were doing this. No shame, no worries—only a sense that this moment was right and wonderful.

She broke the kiss. "I was worried you wouldn't come."

He couldn't help the deep chuckle. "I don't think you're going to have to worry about that." He slid his hands up her sides, grazing his thumbs against her breasts—no bra under the T-shirt.

She shivered at his touch, and her laugh was light. "Oh, fuck you."

"Isn't that the poi—"

She swallowed the rest of his word with a kiss that had him on his toes, heat burning through every part of him. Her hands roved down his body and slipped under his shirt, and it was his turn to shudder at the touch of her skin on his. The small of his back had always been sensitive, and Mish's nails trailing over the flesh there had him pressing up into her arms and gasping.

When she came up from their kiss, her lips were plump, her eyes dancing, and her smile wicked. "Well, yes. But I figure we should talk first."

He leaned his head back against the wall. "I like *this* idea of conversation, though." He was burning and breathless and there was fire in his veins. He skimmed his hands down until the lace of her underwear grazed his palms. "Have to admit this isn't the most *comfortable* position for a conversation like this."

Once more, she laughed, then opened space between them. "True, and we'll get to the more comfortable part soon enough, I promise." She took his hand. "Come on."

He scooped up his bag and went where she led, into the sitting room of the huge two-room hotel suite. His own room, bathroom and all, would fit inside the first, with space to spare. "Well, shit. I guess it's good to be the rock queen."

She snorted and pulled him over to the couch. "Yeah, at least when it comes to hotel rooms." She eyed the duffel he set down on the table. "What's in the bag, honey?"

"Toothbrush, deodorant, condoms, dicks. That kind of thing." This had the feeling of the bumbling first times he'd had with women after he'd transitioned. "Might be presumptuous to bring toys, but better to be prepared than to be running back to my room for a bigger cock." Especially given his room was one floor down and a long corridor away.

She clapped a hand over her mouth to smother her giggles. "Okay, yeah, that would kill the mood." She took a long inhale. "Though I am curious what you mean by *bigger*."

Bet she was. Her gaze shifted from the bag to him, and oh god, the way she inspected every inch of him.

"I also want to see what's under all this." She tugged at the sleeve of his tee. "You've got quite the body."

So did she. Legs that went on for days. Arms strong and toned from playing bass and, he suspected, from working out, too. Sensuous curves at her hips and breasts he wanted to cup and kiss and—

"You're staring," Mish murmured. "That's not usually what happens when I tell a guy they're hot."

"Well, you're beautiful. I got distracted." He reached for the hem of his T-shirt and pulled it off, letting it fall to the floor at their feet. "Better?"

Mish's breath hitched before she answered. "Yeah. *Much*."

He'd thought Mish's roving eyes had been full of heat before—but that had been a slight warm breeze compared to the way her gaze licked over him now. "Is there anywhere I shouldn't touch? Anything off-limits?"

He considered the question. Lovers in the past had paid too much attention to parts of him and not enough to others, but in general, he loved his body. "Not in particular. There's a scar on the back of my thigh I'd rather not be touched, 'cause the nerves are fucked up, but other than that..." He shrugged. "You?"

Her expression shifted as if he'd startled her. "No one's ever asked me that before."

Oh. Huh. "It's a good question." He slotted his fingers between hers. "Every person has likes and dislikes. Areas they'd rather their lover not dwell on."

"I used to hate my feet. They're...huge. But I had this boyfriend who adored them and..." She gave a shrug.

"You saw them in a new light?" He glanced at her feet. They were bigger than his, but given the four inches she had on him in height, that made sense.

"Yeah. It's weird. I still don't understand *why* he liked them so much. It's not my thing, you know? But that helped me not be so critical." A blush ruddied her neck. "I also learned that with the right partner, there's not much I don't like."

"Oh, ditto." So much ditto. With the right person, everything was exquisite.

David gave their entwined hands a tug and Mish slid a hand up his arm and pulled him forward for a kiss. The taste of her uncurled lust in his belly. If he was gonna be half-naked, so was she.

But before he could grip the bottom of her shirt, Mish's palm skimmed over his abs and she drew back enough to whisper, "Penetration?"

Fuck, just the thought made him even harder. Two images that flashed through his mind. Him in her. Her in him. "You or me, darling?"

She nibbled up his neck and stroked a hand over one of his pecs. Her touch had him sucking in air. "I really want you to fuck me, David. Nice and hard." Hot breath in his ear. "I also want to suck your dick so badly."

Her words turned the fire within him to an almost unbearable inferno. Talk was fine, but now he wanted more. "I like the sound of both." And with that, he caught the hem of Mish's shirt and yanked up.

She laughed and let him pull the thing off, baring her fine abs and even finer breasts. "Jesus, you *are* a goddess."

"Queen," she said, tugging him to her. "Come here."

He went. Skin against skin. Lips, mouths, hands roaming everywhere, exploring. He teased one of her nipples into his mouth and she arched into him on a breathless moan. After he'd done the same with the other, she lifted his mouth off her breast and occupied it with her lips and tongue instead. That was fine. Every piece of her was so damn *fine* it hurt to contemplate for too long.

When Mish cupped his package, he pressed against her palm. "Damn, baby."

She chuckled against his lips. "Hard for me," she said, and traced him through his shorts, the pressure softer and indistinct.

"It's a packer." She probably knew, but he'd wanted to say it anyway. "But yeah. I am." He was, too. *Painfully* hard underneath, and neither her ministrations nor his own thrusts helped that situation any.

Well, they *did* help—but this wasn't his favorite way of getting off. Far from it.

"Should I stop?" She moved her hand to his thigh. "Or keep going?"

He met her gaze. "Well, you did mention something about wanting to suck my dick."

"Yeah, I did, didn't I?" Her hands were back on his shorts, this time to unbutton and unzip him. They made quick work of getting him naked, all while Mish looked at him like she wanted to eat him alive. Maybe she *did,* given that goddamned fiery stare. "If you were in my business, you'd be a fucking rock god with a body like that."

"Security god sounds ridiculous." He kept in shape for the job, but also partly out of habit—it had kept the dysphoria at bay for so long. Maybe that was *his* body issue, but the outcome was that he could take out people taller and thicker than him, and in his line of work, that was good.

That Mish loved the results? Even *better*.

He cupped her face and ran his thumb over her lips. "You got a bed in this place, baby? 'Cause I think we'd be more comfortable without a coffee table *right there*." Especially not one with a glass top.

She rose in one fluid motion, and David found himself eye level with the one piece of clothing Mish still wore. He grabbed her hips and planted a kiss on her mound, delighting in the gasp she made. She smelled of lust and salt, and he couldn't wait to get his mouth on her.

"Bed, David. Now." She tugged at his hair. "Or we're gonna end up on this coffee table after all."

"Not gonna say no to you and bed." And banging on a glass table wasn't his idea of fun. He paused long enough to grab his duffel, then followed her out of the living room into *another* huge room. This one had a king-sized bed, more couches, and a huge TV. Plus a freaking wet bar in the corner. "Fuck me, this place have a swimming pool?"

"Hot tub in the bathroom." She swung him into her arms, pulling him close so the lace of her panties slid across his dick.

He murmured, "You're killing me, Mish."

"Then drop the bag and get on the bed, David, so I can kill you even more." Her voice was low and commanding, and she didn't need to tell him twice.

They broke apart, and he set the bag by the foot of the bed, then crawled into the middle of the huge plush white space, flipped over and laid his head on the pillows. He didn't have time to make any of the snarky comments on the tip of his tongue, because Mish was right there above him, her long, warm body weighing his down, and that damn lace rasped against him again. It was torture, both her slow kiss and the way she moved her body over his.

He brushed his fingers through her hair, then down over her back to her ass, and ground up against her.

Given her huff of laughter, his actions amused her. "So I *do* turn you on."

He kissed her shoulder. "Fuck, woman. You turn me inside out." He thought about simply flipping their places and going down on her, because he really did want a taste. "I *like* this." Her on top, making the first moves. Seemed right.

He could *relax* this way. Enjoy himself. No expectations, just two people enjoying each other.

She levered up and hovered above him. Not a shiver or shake in those toned arms—god, she was strong. "So, you don't want to possess me?" There was surprise in her voice, maybe even delight.

"I want to *protect* you." That came out without thought. Hell, he wanted to keep all of Twisted Wishes safe. The band, the crew. Everyone. Mish, though... She was a kindred spirit. He didn't understand all of the how and why of it, but she *understood* him in ways a lot of people didn't, and that was rare, indeed.

Mish didn't move, complex emotions playing over her face.

He ran his hands up the taut muscles of her arms. "No, it's not the job, baby. It's who I am. I want to protect the people I care about." Beneath his fingers, he felt the tiniest tremble in those arms. "Possessing someone, the way I think you mean, is the opposite of caring about them."

Mish's face softened, and she lowered herself until her lips met his and her whole body pressed him down into the mattress.

This kiss, this embrace, wasn't full of lust—it was slow and sensual and had the taste of promise and entanglement and affection. A different heat flared in David, one that tightened his throat and spiked a little fear into his mind. He knew what was happening, that spinning helpless feeling of falling and falling.

And who wouldn't fall for Mish?

She worked her mouth down over David's jaw, mouthing at his beard, then under his chin and down to suck on his collarbone. He arched off the bed.

She laughed. "Sensitive?"

Before he could answer, she nibbled the spot again, sending lightning into his veins and he bucked up against her.

"A little." Came out raspy and breathless.

He stroked his fingers down her body again, finding the edge of her breasts and gliding a finger over the soft, warm skin there.

She let out a cry and twisted. Delicious. So he did it again. This time Mish grabbed his hands and pushed them up over his head. "Be a good boy, David."

"I *am* being a good boy." He smiled up at her. "I did say I wanted to worship you, after all."

She kissed the tip of his nose. "Worship, not *distract*. Hands on the headboard, David."

He did as told, and she slid back down his body, kissing and nipping. Down his chest, stopping to kiss a nipple. It had been a fifty-fifty chance, but she'd found the more sensitive of the two, and he twisted on the sheets as she lavished attention on it and his pec. The wood of the headboard bit into his palm. "Fuck, baby. Please!"

"Getting there," she murmured against his chest.

He could *feel* the devil in her smile against his skin. God, he wasn't going to survive this night. He'd barely had a chance to touch her. Not that he minded—but his brain and body were about to shatter into a million pieces.

Letting go once in a while was a good thing. He'd done it so rarely, he'd forgotten what it was like to be out of control of the situation and out of his mind with anticipation and desire. The wanting and needing and pleading. The way every piece of his skin, every nerve ached for Mish's touch and how utterly turned on he could get from kisses and licks and fingers dancing over flesh. He tightened his grip on the headboard as Mish slid her mouth over his abs, to the juncture of his leg. She kissed each thigh, and blew a warm breath over his dick.

"Mish!" he hissed. Torture. Pure torture. It took all his will not to let go of the headboard and guide her mouth where he needed it to be.

"Want something, darling?"

"Your fucking mouth around my fucking—"

She sucked him down so suddenly, and everything became fire and light and breathless pleasure. He moaned against the tension coiling in his belly, back arching off the mattress. God, of course her mouth would be as talented at *this* as it was at everything else. She eased off a little, swirling her tongue around his girth while humming into him. The vibrations sounded all the way up his bones to his fingertips digging into the wood of the headboard.

She teased and sucked and tongued him and yeah, that would get him off. Light danced in his vision. One of her hands was on his stomach, the other on his thigh, holding his leg. His breath came in harsh grunts, and oh god, he was so damn close he could taste the pleasure on his tongue, his body winding up and up, grunts becoming gasps as he sought air and the courage to say the words that were really fucking hard to say. Because he hadn't been clear when she'd asked before.

He wanted more than just her mouth. "Mish!" That came out as a moan. He tried again. "I need you inside me."

She hummed again, an agreeable sound that had his toes curling, then her fingers were sliding into his hole, stretching him, fucking him, and it was too damn much and exactly right. He didn't care that his hands weren't on wood anymore, but curled into Mish's hair as he thrust and pleaded. His vision turned hot and white and every nerve fired at once as he came on her mouth and hand.

She let him down slowly, kissing his inner thigh. "Damn, boy. That was some ride."

He smoothed his fingers through her hair. "Not over yet." He gulped down air and stared at the ceiling, his heart slowing. God, he felt good. Liquid. Content. First time in...he didn't know how long. "Just need to put my brain back in my head." He tugged gently on her hair. "Come up here, please?"

She slid up him, and that was glorious and right, their legs entwined, the scent of sex hanging in the air. He kissed her, tasting himself, and deepened the kiss until she was the one squirming. When they came up for air, she brushed a lock of hair off his forehead. "I take it you approve."

"Baby, I haven't come like that in a while. Fuck yes, I approve."

Mish smoothed a hand on his chest, and her smile was somehow sly and shy at the same time. "Glad I could help."

"More than." He closed his eyes. "You have no idea."

She kissed him, then nuzzled against his chin. "I have *some* idea, David." Humor there. That shifted to something more content. "God, I love your beard."

"Some women find it annoying." There'd been several who had told him that. But he loved how it looked on him, loved how he looked when he stared back in the mirror. A reminder in the morning of who he was. He wasn't changing that for anyone. Too hard won.

Her fingers teased over his chin and up the side of his face to his ear. "Well, it takes all kinds, as my momma said. Their loss. And my gain."

He shifted, surging up to kiss her and hold her beautiful face in his hands. "My gain, too." Didn't take long or all that much effort to roll until they'd switched places, David above and Mish underneath him. She laughed and arched her neck back and god, all he wanted to do was kiss her everywhere.

Well...not *all* he wanted to do. But it was a good start.

She had a dusting of freckles on her shoulders, and he pressed his lips to those on the way to her collarbone. Cupping her breasts and toying with her hard nipples had her squirming and gasping.

"Yeah, that's good." Each word was breathless.

He licked the tip of one nipple. "Nice to know." Her laugh turned into a low moan when he closed his mouth over her breast. She tasted of salt and heat, the scent of whatever she'd used in the shower still lingering, despite all that they'd done so far.

Now it was her turn to curse and tangle fingers into his hair. "Fuck, David. It's too much." He backed off and met her wild gaze. "I mean, it's good. Really fucking good. But also too good."

"Slower, then?" He kissed the valley between her breasts.

"Actually, *lower*." Her smile was lazy. "If you please."

Oh, that he could do. "Maybe you should grip the headboard."

"Nah. I like your hair. And besides, my bed, my rules."

He laughed against her belly button. "Fair." Then he licked circles around it, savoring how the muscles underneath trembled, how Mish's breath hitched.

"Lower," she murmured again.

"Getting there, baby." He drew his hand over her thigh and up between, slipping his finger along her slit, even as he worked his mouth down her body so slowly.

"Fucking tease!" Her fingers tightened in his hair and she urged him down farther. To take her in his mouth. To slip inside.

"Turnabout, sweetheart." He kissed her mound, then slid his tongue over her clit.

She bucked against him, her cry low and so sexy. God, he

could get used to that. Used to this. Her banter, her taste. He slipped a finger inside her while licking slow circles around her nub.

The grip of his head tightened almost painfully. "Like you *mean* it, David." Mish practically growled the words. Commanding. Compelling.

"As you wish, my queen." Then he gave her exactly what she'd asked for, and that was perfect, too. Her cries, the tug on his head, the way her thighs trapped him there. He sucked her clit and fucked her with two fingers, curling and stretching until she was practically levitating off the bed and shouting his name loud enough that the whole damn floor probably knew who'd made her come.

He slowed a little, easing her down, but not stopping completely until she pulled him up. "How big a dick you got in that bag of yours?"

He met her passionate, desperate kiss with one of his own. "Why don't I show you, and you can pick?" he said against her lips.

Her exhale was a moan. "I can do that."

God, the most exciting, fucking wonderful thing about this night was Mish being turned on by *him*. By his body. By his bag of dicks. The *normalcy* of it.

There'd been little awkwardness—and what had been had come from him. "You're fucking magical, baby." He claimed another kiss.

She smiled against his mouth, then laid a hand on his chest and pushed. "Dicks."

He laughed at that and crawled to the foot of the bed to retrieve his harness and cocks from his duffel. He handed the bag that held the dicks to Mish. Three dildos, all pretty much the same length, but of varying thicknesses. Different colors, though.

He enjoyed that he could have a purple dick. Or neon

blue. Why not? They were an extension of him—might as well have some personality.

The one Mish had pulled out of the bag was the thickest. She turned it over in her hands, her eyes a little wide. "It's...tie-dyed."

Not exactly the response he'd expected, and he laughed. "It is, yeah. I liked the colors."

"It's also huge," she murmured. "God, David. I can't even imagine."

He couldn't help his grin or the gravel in his voice. "You don't have to imagine, you know."

She shivered, and handed that one to him. "Yeah, all right."

He tucked away the others and pulled out a condom and some lube. No questions from Mish. She'd probably been around toys before, which didn't surprise him, though he did wonder if she had her own collection of strap-ons.

"Can I watch you put it on? I know some people don't like that, but..."

The way she sat, how her eyes were wide and shaded toward green, the flush of her body. "It turns you on to watch," he murmured.

"Fuck yeah, it does. It's... I don't know how to describe it." Her gaze traced over his body. "More intimate than being naked."

That wasn't far from the truth. "I don't mind." Other lovers had minded watching him, even back before he'd transitioned, so he'd usually step into the bathroom to avoid the awkwardness.

But Mish cut through all that. He let her watch as he strapped his dick on, and god, it did turn her on. Enough that she was fingering herself, which only made him want her more. "Fuck, baby. We should have done this ages ago."

She laughed, breathless and full of joy. "Yeah, probably. Except we haven't known each other that long."

Three weeks. That's all. Seemed short and far too long.

He closed the distance between them and devoured that mouth of hers. She answered back hungrily until he had to break the contact to catch a breath. Before he could say anything, she lowered her head and took the tip of his cock between her lips.

The sight of her mouth spread wide and the pressure against him had him raking his fingers through her hair. Might was well be his dick—hell, it *was* his dick. Every bob, every pull sent fire pouring into him.

Mish hummed, a content sound. Same one she'd made sucking him off before. Beautiful, with her copper curls between his hands and falling around her face and her lips stretched around the festive colors of his cock.

But after a few more times swallowing him, Mish pulled off. Her breath came in huffs and her pupils were huge with desire. "I need you inside me. David. Hard. Fast."

He paused just long enough to slip the condom and some lube over his dick, then crawled over her. "I can do that."

He was glad for the lube, 'cause she was *tight*. And moaning, and demanding that he just fuck her already.

"Yes, ma'am." Was more breath than anything else.

Mish slapped his ass. Hard enough that he hissed at the pain and the afterglow of pleasure. "Don't you *ma'am* me, David fucking Altet."

He laughed and claimed her mouth. Didn't take long before he was sliding his thick length in and out of her, which had her nipping at his lips, her eyes closed and every inch of her meeting his strokes. "Yeah, like that. God."

"Rock queen is a size queen," he murmured. He pistoned in and out of her, enjoying her cries and the shivers that ran through her body.

Mish grabbed his hair with both hands and dragged him down into another bruising kiss. When she let him go, her eyes were fire and her smile devilish. "Shut up and fuck me."

He did. His hands on her hips, thrusting as fast and as hard as he could. Nails scraped against his skin, and Mish threw back her head, each breath a groan of pleasure that only served to turn David on even more.

God, he was going to come. So was Mish, if the tremors in her body and the changing pitch of her cries were any indication. He shifted his angle, licked his thumb, and found her clit.

Mish's eyes flew open and lighted on his. "Oh fuck."

Then she broke apart beneath him, coming hard and fast and so damn loud. Yeah, he was gonna get some stares tomorrow from her bandmates.

David didn't fucking care, because he was there, too, his own groans as loud, his vision a haze, and his body one long, trembling mess.

He pulled out, then sank down next to her, his breath sharp and heavy. Legs still tangled with Mish's. Fuck, that had been something else. Blinding, wall-banging sex. With Mish Sullivan.

David stared up at the ceiling. *Holy shit.*

Fingers traced over his jaw, through his beard. "Hey." Mish's voice was soft. "You okay?"

He started at that and propped himself up on his elbows to get a better look at her face. "Isn't that my line?"

She snorted. "Not if I get there first."

He let himself fall back onto the mattress. "Yeah. I'm fine. Better than fine. Just...you blow me away."

She caressed his cheek again. "Ditto, David. Ditto."

Warmth spread through him, even as his mind whirled. He'd take that, too.

"Stay the night?" She pressed a finger into the cleft of his chin.

"Baby, yeah. If you want." He wasn't really sure he could walk that far anyway, and the idea of spooning up with Mish sent little sparks of pleasure through his arms and legs. How long had it been since he'd held someone during the night? Been held?

"I want," she said.

They both rose to clean up. Condom ditched. Dick cleaned and put back in its bag. David brushed his teeth, leaning heavily against the counter. His reflection looked very much like a man who'd just had some of the *best* sex in his life. But also a guy who was about to fall over from exhaustion. It was late, and after a concert.

"Glad there's not much going on tomorrow," he said when he exited the bathroom.

"Mmm." Mish had slipped under the sheet on the bed. "We do that on purpose. Give ourselves some time to fuck off."

"Or fuck?" He bent down to retrieve one more item out of his duffel bag: Marly.

"Or fuck." Her reply was a soft echo of his, and she eyed Marly curiously. "You have a bear?"

He did. An old, somewhat worn teddy bear. The one thing he had left from his childhood. His dog tags were looped around Marly's neck. "He's...a talisman, I suppose. A touchstone. Was in the desert with me. And also high school."

She shifted under the covers. "Which was worse?"

He laughed, but considered the question anyway. There was also some truth there. "The desert, but not by much." He set Marly down on the nightstand, then crawled into the huge bed.

Mish drew him into her arms, into her warmth, and her smile tumbled all the emotions he'd shoved off into the back of his brain. Hope. Fear. Longing.

"I'm glad you brought him," she said.

"Why?"

"'Cause it means you trust me. And it means you wanted to stay. Planned to. Weren't just gonna fuck and run." There was a bitterness there.

"Oh, baby, no. If you'd wanted me to go, I'd have gone, but I want this. Not—"

Not a one-time thing.

She laid a palm on his cheek. "Things are gonna get interesting, David."

"You don't say..."

She smirked, then rolled over enough to turn off the lights. In the darkness, they curled into each other's arms, and David fell asleep with the scent of Mish's hair close by and the warmth of her body pressed to his.

It was heaven.

CHAPTER TWELVE

Morning came slowly to Mish. The whir of the hotel's air conditioner, the smell of the sheets, the warmth of David next to her and the pleasant ache of her body, both from the concert and the intense, fantastic sex she'd had with him.

God, even thinking about that sent a shiver of goose bumps over her arms. David was all that she liked in a partner—giving, snarky, passionate, and willing to let her lead. His body was tantalizing and perfect.

She ignored the voice in the back of her head that wondered if this was wise, if they could remain professional now that they'd fucked. None of her bandmates cared—they'd rather she be happy with David.

But she'd been happy with Sasha and Dane on tour before, and neither of them had stuck around. Granted, she hadn't said that they should, nor really wanted them to—they'd had their own lives and dreams. David, though...

She moved slowly, to not disturb his sleep, and looked over the bare expanse of his back, marked with scrapes and scratches from her nails, to gaze at the teddy bear that sat on the far nightstand. Marly had been obviously well loved, but also well cared for. Mish focused on the dog tags looped around his neck. There were times and moments David would likely never speak of, that he'd shared with this bear, this touchstone.

She'd never dated a man ten years older than her, and maybe that was the strangeness of it all, the way everything felt deeper and—more. Or maybe it was because everyone else in her band-family was, for all intents and purposes, married. Couldn't tell.

Her aversion to older masc lovers wasn't fair, but too many of her mom's boyfriends had taken an interest in her during the bad days when they'd scraped by and moved around and her mom—

Mish ended that line of thought. She missed her mom something fierce and with a pain that would never go away. She hoped that if there was an afterlife, her mom was pleased with how her daughter's life had turned out, with her chosen name and with the family she'd found.

Her gaze drifted to Marly again. There were things she'd never tell anyone else, too. Parts she'd never share. Dollars to donuts that David would understand *that*.

When she shifted, he stirred, propping himself up on his forearms. "What time is it?"

She had no idea, mostly because it didn't matter. Or shouldn't. Except they had plans to meet with the band today. "Don't know."

"Be right back." David slipped out of bed. God, that body. There were more marks, too. On his shoulders and ass. She hadn't realized how rough-and-tumble they'd been last night.

He headed into the other room, and returned with his jeans and cell phone, frowning at the latter.

That wasn't the look of a relaxed lover. "What's wrong?"

"Nothing. Just some emails from Adrian."

Fuck. "They up already?"

He laughed, and the tension washed out of his body. "Well, it's after eleven, but given these came in five minutes ago? I doubt they've been up that long." He tossed his jeans onto a nearby chair and set the phone down next to Marly. "Gonna take a piss."

She rolled her eyes. "Didn't need the announcement."

Another chuckle. "Didn't want it to seem like I don't wanna crawl back in bed with you."

She waved him toward the bathroom. "Go, and go. I'll order some coffee from room service."

He got a look she knew—at one point, every member of Twisted Wishes had gotten it when one of them had suggested doing something abnormally expensive. "There's a maker—" David pointed at the wet bar.

Yeah, there was. It was even one of those pod types, and stocked with better than average coffee. She scrunched up her nose. "After practically living with Adrian for this long, that coffee doesn't cut it. Neither does the room service stuff, but it's better, and there's more of it."

He shifted back and forth. "The delivery fee alone's gotta be more than the coffee."

It was, practically. "David. I'm a fucking rock queen."

He shook his head as if to clear it. "Okay. Coffee would be good." With that, he turned and headed into the bathroom.

She flopped back down onto the bed and groaned, regretting her last words. She loved being Mish Sullivan, loved her life, but she'd had a suspicion she'd opened up a gulf between her and David she desperately wanted not to exist.

She *was* a rock queen, though. No denying that. That hadn't been her only existence, however. Twisted Wishes had fought their way up, and before that, she'd clawed her way to playing at bars and clubs. Before that...she'd been a teenaged daughter of a disadvantaged single mother with cancer.

That ache and nausea that came when she dwelled on her past too much crept into her gut and helped propel her out of bed. Yeah, coffee. And yeah, from room service, partly as a fuck-you to her past. If David couldn't handle her present, then he wasn't the right person for her.

She could explain her past to him—but she'd buried parts of herself with her mother, and those she didn't want to unearth. She called down to room service and ordered the damn pot of coffee.

After she hung up, she sank onto the bed, this time on David's side, and picked up Marly. The fake fur was soft under her fingers, especially the inner ear portion. The dog tags bore David's name.

David's *name*.

She was running her fingers over the text when he came out of the bathroom. She didn't look up, just started talking. "I know it seems like a waste of money—the coffee—but it's also a small pleasure. Past me would be horrified, too. But past me hasn't gone through what I did."

When she finally looked up, David nodded. He stepped lightly through the room, grabbed his briefs from his jeans, and put them on. Then he sat next to her on the bed, gesturing for the bear in her hands. She handed Marly over.

"We all have pasts." David touched the tags on the bear.

She nodded at the bear. "Your name is on those tags."

"Yeah. I had another set made after I transitioned. If my name weren't on those tags, I couldn't live with them now." He stroked her cheek. "The past can stay where it is, Mish. Unless you want to share."

She didn't. She did. The past was a part of her, the foundation. The heart. She snorted, mostly to herself, but David raised an eyebrow.

"I was thinking about Dom and Adrian and when they met. Dom was so anxious about telling Adrian who he was, and I didn't understand his fear. I really should've."

"Different situations are different."

"Thanks, Captain Obvious." She knocked her shoulder against his, garnering a chuckle.

"Pre-caffeinated me isn't pretty," he said.

Morning David was stunning. All mussed hair and sleepy eyes and that lovely, nearly naked body. "I wouldn't say that." Mish kissed him on the cheek and rose from the bed. "My turn." She headed to the bathroom.

When she returned, David was murmuring thanks to someone at the door to the suite. Hopefully that was their coffee.

Indeed, David stepped to the door to the bedroom, holding a tray with a stainless steel pot, ceramic mugs, and all the fixings. "Where do you want this, Ms. Queen?"

Delight shivered down her spine. She loved his mouth and his voice and those words. "In here."

They ended up at a little table by the window, each in their own chair. She'd found her panties and her tee and put those back on. Neither of them spoke as they took the first sips of coffee. David grunted appreciatively.

The coffee was good. Not Adrian-good, but enough that she knew where David was coming from. After a few more sips of her own, she asked a question that had been flitting through her mind all morning. "Did you enjoy last night?"

David nearly choked on his coffee. After a short coughing fit, he pinned her with disbelief. "Fucking hell, Mish. Did you really just ask that?"

Heat to her face. "Okay, foolish question. But was everything okay?"

He set his mug down. "Baby, last night was perfect. Couldn't have asked for better." He tilted his head. "You okay with everything we did?"

Her turn to give him the skeptical look. "Yeah. Of course."

"Then where's this—" he gestured between the two of them "—coming from?"

That was a decent question, and the coffee unlocked a little more of her brain. "I don't know what you like in bed. I mean, other than the obvious." Fucking her. Going down on her. Her going down on him.

"Well, that's part of this." Once again, he gestured between them. "Right? We'll discover all that." He gave her that quizzical look again. "You want something, just ask. I'm not gonna be offended."

"So not a one-time thing?"

His smile was full and warm. "I'm game for more, if you want that. I *would* like to find out what more you like in bed."

Everything, including fucking him, if he was willing. The intense desire came as suddenly as a possessive streak, and both blazed through her hard, leaving her breathless. Hadn't felt like that for anyone in forever.

She sipped her coffee. "Oh," she said. "Good."

Whatever David was going to say was cut off by the ringing of Mish's cell phone. They both jolted, and she scrambled out of her chair to find the damn thing because it was Ray's ringtone. She didn't ignore that one.

"Hey," she said, once she'd found and answered the phone. "What's up?"

"Really hate bothering you two," Ray said, and she heard the delight in his voice. "But we kinda want to figure out our day, so when can you meet?"

Right. The stalker. The band. The tour. All of the things they needed to get back to. "Soon, I think. We're caffeinating."

"Is that what kids are calling it these days?" Ray's New Jersey accent was a little thicker than normal as he spoke. Had she been near him, she'd have playfully shoved him and given him the finger.

"I'm still older than you, kiddo," she said. "So get the fuck off my lawn."

He laughed. "So, ready in...an hour? Half hour?"

She lowered the phone. David had his inquisitive look on. "How soon can you be ready to do that meeting thing?"

He looked away for a moment, his lips twisting in

thought. "Getting dressed is easy. It's getting my brain in gear and looking over those emails again that'll take a bit."

"Hour?"

"I think we all want to get this out of the way. Half hour. I can shower in my room and get my shit together."

She relayed the info to Ray. "Mmm," he said. "Let's make it forty-five minutes, to give everyone time. And come to my room."

"Sounds to me like someone else isn't quite ready for a meeting yet," she teased.

Ray's chuckle was soft and devilish. "Something like that."

"Okay, kiddo. See you in a few."

By the time she'd hung up and relayed the time and meeting place, David had completely dressed and packed away his dicks and his toiletries. All that was left was Marly. She picked up the bear and hugged it, pressing her face into the top of its plush head.

"I don't suppose I can get a hug like that, too?" David's voice was gravelly.

Heat raked through Mish, and something else—the need for more beyond their sexual chemistry. To know the man this bear belonged to, to build up that friendship. To let herself explore this new relationship.

What had Zavier said? Friendship, trust, and fucking? They were on their way.

She pulled David into a hug. Rather than the top of his head, she kissed and nuzzled his hairline, breathing in a scent that was all David. Raw and spicy and human.

"I wanna spend more time with you." She whispered the words against his hair.

"Same, sweetheart. Same." He pulled back a little. "I still owe you a beer, don't I?"

"You do," she purred. "Maybe after this meeting we can lounge by the pool?"

He went up on his toes and pecked the tip of her nose. "Deal." He stepped away. "I should go and get ready." He'd fallen back into his business voice.

Mish tightened her fingers around Marly. "Don't forget your best friend." She held the bear out for him.

His smile was so quirky and fond when he looked at Marly, Mish's legs nearly buckled from the sheer cuteness. And the utter unabashed, pure moment of David. "Why don't you hold on to him for the day? I have a feeling I'll be back later."

God, she hoped so. "All right."

That same fond, unguarded expression fell on her. For such dark eyes, David's practically glittered when he smiled. "See you in a bit, Mish."

He sauntered out of the room, then the suite door opened and clicked shut. Mish pressed her face against the bear again. "I really like your dad, Marly. I trust him. I want him as a friend. Think you can help?"

Marly, as all plush bears tended to be, was silent. Mish felt connected to David anyway, as if an invisible thread had been wrapped around her and tied off to him. David would keep her safe.

And for the first time in her life, Mish didn't resent that.

David found it strange not having Marly in his room when he returned there to shower and dress. But a jolt of excitement ran through him at the thought that Marly was with Mish. Maybe she was holding him. Maybe he was back on her bedside. Didn't matter that the bear was an inanimate object —he was a piece of David's heart, one that still clung to the wonder that hadn't been scrubbed out of his childhood by bigotry and war.

Marly would watch over Mish and keep her safe when David couldn't. Because that's what bears did.

A foolish thought, most of his mind said. He gave that part a giant mental middle finger.

As he'd predicted, he was out of the shower and dressed in about fifteen minutes. He took some time to more thoroughly clean the cock they'd used because he hated putting those away without doing so. Once that was complete, he turned his attention to his laptop. He'd been reading most of Adrian's forwards on his phone, but if he was going to share this stuff, a bigger screen was better.

He took some time getting reacquainted with the material. It was grueling, especially now that he and Mish had hooked up. All of it felt personal, and that twisted guilt into his chest. The *last* thing Mish wanted or needed was a man being possessive with her or making *her* pain about him.

Wasn't right. Wasn't needed. And was why he'd wanted to review the stalker's communications—so he could rid himself of these toxic reactions.

He'd been hired to protect the band, to watch over her. Nothing more. That he cared for her didn't mean he got to own her pain or problems. She'd kick his ass for doing that, and rightly so.

By the time he reached Ray and Zavier's suite, he was centered. Focused on business.

The rest of the band, plus Adrian and Marcella, were spread out in the living room part of the suite. It only took one look at Mish to throw David off-kilter. The visceral memory of her flooded back into him. The way they'd fucked, his own taste in her mouth, the feel of her skin against his lips, their moans in the air.

Her smile was slow and sexy as if she saw right through him—and maybe she did.

Luckily, Ray stepped into his line of sight. "Going old school?" He gestured at David's laptop.

That was all he needed to recover, to drag his sorry mental ass back to being a goddamned professional. "Figured a bigger screen would be better, you know?"

"A man after my own heart," Adrian said. He sat on the couch with Dom, both wearing what David recognized as their casual clothes. For Adrian, that was jeans and an old, worn T-shirt. For Dom, it meant jeans and a button-down that pretty much covered all his ink. He leaned against Adrian.

Damn, David wanted Mish in his arms like that.

He shook the thought away. "Where's the best place to put this?"

"Coffee table." That came from Zavier, who was lounging against the door to the bedroom. "But we'll need to rearrange the furniture, or some of us will have to sit on the floor."

Marcella shrugged. "I'm limber enough."

David eyed the huge TV. "Damn shame I didn't think to bring an HDMI cable."

"I have one." Adrian made to rise.

"Guys!" The strangled quality of Mish's voice stopped them all in their tracks. "I don't want my stalker's emails on a huge fucking monitor. I just want to—read them. Not go over them in detail."

David breathed out. "Okay. Yeah. That was..." The only consolation was that everyone in the room sans Mish also looked sheepish. "Why don't I...give this to you?" He held out the laptop to Mish.

She took it and placed it on the coffee table. "You and Adrian have seen these, yes?"

David nodded, his mind still churning in embarrassment.

"Okay. That leaves Dom, Ray, Zavier, and Marcella."

"I've seen most of them," Marcella said. "I can catch up on the rest later." She wandered over to a table that contained a fruit basket, bottled water, and a carafe, poured herself some coffee, and took a seat there.

Dom moved to sit on Mish's one side. Ray took the other, and Zavier came around to the back of the couch.

"This okay?" Zavier's voice was a concerned murmur over Mish's shoulder. Not feigned, either. David doubted he feigned anything with the band. There was an open honesty about the man despite the sharp control that lay there.

"Yeah." A quiet reply from Mish.

The four of them settled in, and David resisted the urge to pace. He took a seat in one of the very white chairs. Adrian glanced his way, expression mirroring David's own inner turmoil.

Mish had seen many of the emails, but not all.

"Fuck," murmured Dom at one point. "Is that your..."

"Yeah. My hair."

Silence fell again, except for their breathing. David wanted to drop his head into his hands. Close his eyes against Mish's hardening expression and the revulsion in both Zavier's and Dom's eyes.

"And my ring," Mish said.

Ray was focused but shuttered. Tiny twinges snuck through in the flicker of his eye, a twitch in his cheek, or the way he scowled, but David couldn't put a finger on the emotion. Wasn't anger. Or maybe it was far deeper than that.

After a while, Ray sat back and met David's gaze, his own grave. "Now I'm even more glad I convinced you to stay."

A mix of shame and pride and worry punched into David. His gaze flicked to Mish's, but she wasn't looking at him.

No, her focus was on Ray, and she was pale and a tightness had gathered in her whole body. "And why's that?"

Ray shook out his neck. "Not because you can't take care of yourself, Mish. I met you in a bar that scared the pants off gay old me, and you had the whole place by its ear. Literally and figuratively."

That put color back into her cheeks. "Gay *young* you. You were, what, twenty? And scrawny."

He glanced at his hands and smiled—a quick flash of teeth —before that fell away. "David can have your back in ways none of us—" he gestured to the band, Adrian, and Marcella "—can."

Finally Mish's gaze met David's, and hers was warm and steady. The heat that curled into David's chest wasn't lust. It was...he didn't know. Complicated—that's what it was.

The words were out of his mouth before he even thought about saying them. "If you'll have me."

The crinkles at her eyes weren't from tension now. No, there was a happiness there David didn't understand. "Yeah. I will."

Zavier grunted, and that man's expression was one of supreme satisfaction.

Dom was the only one not focused on them. His focus was glued to the screen and he chewed on one of his nails. "This fucker." His voice was jagged and sharp. He sat back, not looking at anything, but working his jaw.

"Babe," Adrian said. "It'll be all right."

Dom closed his eyes. Mish patted his knee. "Sweetheart..."

He exhaled. "I know. I have no right to be angry."

"Yeah, you do," Mish said, echoing David's own thoughts. "We're family."

At that, Dom opened his eyes and wrapped Mish in a hug.

The pang David felt was an intense longing he'd never experienced before. That need to have what these people had. He could hardly breathe for the way that desire tangled into his soul.

Family. His hadn't been *that* bad, just...distant. Especially after his successive coming-outs. He barely talked to his sister anymore. He exchanged emails with his parents a couple of times a year. Most of the folks he'd known in the army had fallen away.

He was used to being alone. *Liked* being alone, or so he told himself.

He shook the feelings away. "This guy isn't a fan of the group, I'm sure of it now."

"Why?" Mish asked.

"The way he talks in those emails. It's focused on you and your look. Not on the music, or your playing. Or how you interact with the guys or fans."

Dom sat back on the couch. "Huh." That seemed to be the voice of everyone's thoughts.

Zavier straightened. "Then how does he know Mish?"

That was the thing. "Don't know." David paused. "It's just a theory."

Mish stirred. "Like I said before, I don't think it's a previous friend or lover. They weren't...like that. Even the ones who were jerks."

"What about from high school or—" Adrian waved a hand "—someone who knew you before you were famous?"

"I don't think so. I didn't look like this in high school." She gestured at herself. "We moved around a lot. Plus, after my mom passed, I changed my name."

David's world tipped sideways a little. "You changed your name," he repeated. His former name slid across his consciousness and away. "First and last?" He'd only changed one.

She nodded. "Mom's last name was Sullivan. She never married the sorry sack of shit that sired me. I didn't want his name anymore."

In the silence that followed, no one asked her what her name had been and David rejoiced. Her family—the people in this room—understood the power of names.

It was Marcella who broke the silence. "Here I thought Mish was short for Michelle."

Mish grinned. "Nope." Her smile fell away. "Honestly, I can't think of anyone from my past." She dug out her phone. "I keep a photo of my mom and me on here. Hang on." She scrolled a bit, then handed her phone to Ray.

He blinked a few times. Zavier leaned over. "Oh. Yeah. I see what you mean," he said.

Mish shoved him. "Hey!"

His smile belied any hurt. "I'm not saying you were ugly. You're just not you now."

Ray handed her phone back, and she passed it to Dom next. He cocked his head, then passed it to Adrian. After that, it went to Marcella, and she brought it to David.

He didn't have to look up to know Mish was watching him. He felt her stare from across the coffee table. More than just her, he bet, but Mish's was the only one that mattered.

He studied the photo on the screen. He both saw and didn't see her in the two women in the picture. One woman—had to be her mom—had blond hair with the same curls that Mish bore. Her eyes were darker, though, and her face rounder. Mish was young, maybe sixteen or seventeen, on that cusp between youth and adult. A redhead like now, but cut so short the curls were gone. Green eyes that were shy and set into a face that hadn't developed the long lines of Mish's. Her clothing was conservative and she was lanky, not the muscular musician she was as an adult. Only if you knew she was the same person could you pick out the similarities.

With an entirely different name, how many people would know that this girl and Mish Sullivan were the same?

He nodded. "You grew up a lot." He rose, leaned over the table, and handed her phone back. Her fingers brushed his gently. Almost a caress.

Then she was leaning against the couch again. "That's one way of putting it."

"Okay, so it's unlikely to be someone from the past." David lowered himself into his chair. "Still doesn't feel like a fan gone bad, but I suppose there's no other avenue."

Mish rocked her head back and forth. "Or it's some MRA-type dude who saw my photo and thinks I'd make the perfect wife."

"Maybe." David didn't think so. There was something to this he couldn't put his finger on. Gut instincts were so fucking vague.

"Question is..." Marcella rose and joined the rest of the group. "What can we do about it? What are we going to do about it?"

That was the issue at hand. The answer was simple, but unsatisfying. "Nothing," David said. "Block email addresses. Keep logs. Keep an eye on Mish. But that's pretty much all we can do."

Adrian shifted in his chair. "I looked into the credit card connection."

Ray shot him a look. "Legally?"

"Yes, of course." Adrian sounded a little miffed. "Card was that dude's own, not the mysterious Stan's. If the thief got cash from that guy, I can't find out...legally."

Ray relaxed a fraction. "Sorry for the assumption."

"No illegal hacking, Mr. Doran," Marcella said.

"None planned, Ms. Crane." He grinned. "I really do know better."

She snorted. "I'll believe that when I see it."

"Stan? Who the fuck is Stan?" Mish looked between David and Adrian.

"Name the thief gave. Doubt it's his real name." David struggled with keeping calm. "I wish I had caught that little shit sooner, before he'd handed it off." Guilt gnawed at him, especially since he'd missed the handoff. The stalker had been at the concert, too.

Mish skewed up her face. "Well, Stan rings no bells. I bet you're right." She closed David's laptop. "So you recommend business as usual."

He hated that, but there wasn't any other choice. No way to draw the fucker out. "You were right all those weeks ago. Changing your habits just lets this guy think he has control."

She nodded. "But now we all know."

Dom fidgeted, picking at invisible lint on his pants. "You gonna be okay?"

"Yeah, hon. I'll be fine. I have all of you and I've got David there."

Zavier rubbed his chin, but said nothing. Which, David had learned over the past weeks, meant the man had something to say, but was unwilling to say it. So he called his bluff. "Zavier?"

Caught off guard, Zavier started and locked eyes with David, and there was that open expression again. "I was just wondering...at what point we go to the police? Where's that line?"

No one in the room said anything in response. Mish stared at the closed laptop, then looked over at David. The pain in those eyes ate right through him.

"That has to be Mish's call."

"I'll let you know," she whispered. "I'm not a fool, Zav."

"I know you're not." He laid his hand on her shoulder, and she reached up to hold it. "But sometimes we wait too long to confront things. And it's burned us before."

It was Ray who swallowed and looked up at Zavier, at his husband.

Mish didn't look away from David. She did let go of Zavier's hand. "It's going to be fine."

"But he's right," Ray said.

"Zavier's always right," Dom said.

At this, the man rolled his eyes. "I am not, and you fucking know it."

Mish looked up at him. "Wait, can we quote you on that?" That broke the odd tension in the room.

Zavier waved the comment away. "Are we done? Because I'd like to try out that nice pool I saw."

David nodded. "Yeah. We're on the same page. Pass anything weird along to me." He stood and stepped closer to

Marcella. "Would you let the crew and all know to be on the lookout for anything strange?"

She sipped her coffee, then spoke. "Already on my to-do list."

Man, it was nice having everyone with him rather than second-guessing him. Then again, this team actually cared about each other.

"That's it, then," he said to no one in particular.

"Good." Mish climbed to her feet, grabbed the laptop, and handed it to him. "You got swim trunks in your luggage?"

He did. A last-minute addition, since he generally didn't go swimming. But he thought lounging in a hot tub while on the tour would be needed after sleeping on a bus and working odd hours. "Yeah."

"Oh good," she purred. "'Cause we're all going swimming."

Marcella was backing away. "I've got calls I need to make."

"All means all." That came from Ray. "You always say we should relax on our rest days." His grin was sly.

Marcella looked up at the ceiling. "Fine. Because you'll bug me if I say no."

"If you honestly don't want to swim with us," Zavier said, "we won't make you."

"I know. You guys are good about boundaries. I'll meet you there in ten or fifteen."

Ray nodded. "David?"

The twinkle in Mish's eyes told him he wasn't going to get out of the group swim unless he had an objection—and he didn't.

"I'll be there with bells on." He paused. "Figuratively."

Zavier's lips twitched, and David knew that expression as well. He didn't even come *close* to asking if he had bells. Because if *anyone* in this group did, it was Zavier Demos.

CHAPTER THIRTEEN

By the time Mish made it poolside, Ray was splashing around in the water, his inked arms shining in the sunlight. Zavier was standing near the edge, sunglasses on, shirt off, exposing his own set of tattoos. None of the other members of their extended group were there.

Zav had that smile he only got around Ray. A deep friendship, one that would abide the years, he had once told her in a guarded moment. That's why he'd married Ray.

That expression deepened to something far more devilish when Ray splashed water at him. She couldn't hear what Zavier said or what Ray did in response, but the way Ray tossed his head, even while treading water, was pure sass.

Zavier dropped his glasses on a nearby lounger, then plunged into the pool. Ray yelped and tried to swim away. No such luck. They ended up in a tangle of limbs and pushing and laughing, until they'd both dunked each other under the water.

Those two. She wasn't sure who'd rescued whom in that pair.

Mish strolled to the shaded bar and ordered a tonic and lime. No alcohol yet. She wanted to take a dip, plus the conversation earlier had her unsettled and aching in her heart.

All those emails and comments. The photos. Her hair. Her ring in someone else's hands. She shivered, opened a tab on her room, and took the drink to the edge of the bar where she could sit in the shade, yet still watch the antics of her bandmates.

Dom and Adrian were the next to appear, and lord, did the eyes of the pool crowd follow them. They were a sight. Dom, wiry and muscular from dancing around with his guitar, sans his stage makeup but with all his ink on display. Adrian stood several inches taller, broad in the shoulders and chest. He stripped off the T-shirt he'd been wearing.

"Lord," a woman at the table next to Mish's said. "Will you look at that?"

Mish chuckled and the other woman smiled.

"I mean, there's quite the view at the moment." She waved her hand to encompass Mish's other band members. "But the arms on that one..."

They *were* something, Mish had to admit. Especially when Adrian scooped up Dom to mock protests, and dropped him into the pool.

"Aaaaaaand taken." The woman sighed and sipped her white wine. "Of course."

If the woman had been a fan of the band, she'd have known that already. "Very taken, yeah."

"Lucky them."

That was true. Both couples were lucky.

The next person to arrive was Marcella, in a colorful one-piece suit of reds and oranges covered in a white sheer flowing wrap. She headed for the bar and then, with a glass of rosé in her hand, joined Mish. "Your man keeping you waiting?"

The woman at the other table raised an eyebrow, but Mish ignored her. "I'm not sure he's *my* man."

"Bullshit." Marcella sat down next to her, then sighed in contentment. "I so needed this."

"What, the pool or the wine?"

"Both." There was a flash of a grin, then it settled to weariness. "They look happy." Marcella nodded at the pool. Adrian had jumped in at some point, and all four men were acting more like rowdy teens.

"They need that, too. Helps Adrian to feel like part of the whole."

Marcella sipped her wine. "Mish, doll. Sometimes I think you're the glue that holds this whole damn band together."

Mish couldn't say anything, because her throat was suddenly too dry. She picked up the tonic and let the cold fizzy liquid ease some of that out. Truth was, they held her together. The band. The music. Adrian and Marcella.

David. That thought rose unbidden, and her heart flipped. David, who'd been both gentle and fierce in bed. Who'd let her lead, and also had her back. David loved her *voice*. He'd left Marly with her—because he'd be coming back.

"I care about 'em. And you." She blew Marcella a kiss.

And got a grin in return. "I know." Marcella nodded at the bar. "And there's your dude."

Heat rose to her cheeks. She was certain the woman at the other table was checking out David's very fine ass in the swim trunks that clung to his hips. No shirt. She shivered a little. His arms weren't Adrian's, but they were built and perfect and she knew the strength in them.

Her dude.

When David turned, bottle of beer in hand, his sunglasses hid his eyes, but his smile was as warm and bright as the summer sky above. He picked his way around tables. "I guess I'm late to the party." He took a seat next her, one that was—thankfully—away from the woman at the other table.

"I see your bandmates have already tried the pool." He took a sip from the bottle, then set it down on the table.

"Mmm. You missed Adrian tossing Dom in."

"Poor dude." David laughed. "He didn't stand a chance, did he?"

Marcella was the one to wave away the words and answer. "Eh, Dom loves being manhandled by that man."

Mish nearly choked on her tonic water. What she said was true and not a great secret, but she'd never heard Marcella comment like *that* before about any of them.

David was laughing, but silently.

"Oh, come on." Marcella gestured at the couple still bobbing around in the pool.

"It's not that..." Mish stopped, put her glass down, turned to Marcella, then gave her a gentle punch in the arm. "You're comfortable around us now, huh?"

Marcella leaned her head back. "No idea what you mean, Mish Sullivan."

This time, David's chuckle was audible.

"Don't you start." Mish leveled a look at him. "Or I'll throw you in the pool, too."

He crossed his arms. "I'd like to see you try."

Oh, it was *so* on. She sprang on him, and luck was with her, because he must not have anticipated her moving *that* fast. She got him over her shoulder in a fireman's carry before he croaked out a curse.

They weren't that far from the pool. Only took a couple of steps to cross the distance.

"Mish." David sounded both exasperated and amused. "Don't do something you'll regret!"

The boys were cheering from the pool, egging her on.

"Don't think I'm gonna regret this." She pitched him forward into the pool, but he caught her arms as he fell, his grin wicked, and there was no way she could pull back from his weight taking them both into the cold water of the swimming pool.

Her laugh and his mixed during that fall until there was

only the crash of water, then silence when she dropped below the blue surface until she burst forth into the air.

Before they'd hit, David had let go. She had no issues coming up for air. Neither did he—though he'd lost his sunglasses somewhere in the pool. His teeth flashed in the sunlight, dark eyes crinkled with joy and laughter.

Her heart tried to leap from her chest from the sight and the sound.

There was a splash behind her and a streak of red-orange, then Marcella's dark head broke the surface. They were all here and *hers*. Her family, her shield against the world and all the fears in her heart. Her strength to move forward, to perform and play and sing the words and music Ray crafted.

She didn't even care if there were photographs. She floated over to David and pulled him into an embrace, one he slid into easily, as if their bodies already knew each other.

They did. He laid a hand on her shoulder and his smile was brilliant. "No regrets?"

"None," she said. They treaded water together, lazily rotating in the process. "Thank you."

A flash of confusion. "For what?"

"For being here." This wasn't his job. This was friendship. And trust. She flicked her gaze over David's shoulder and found Zavier hanging on to the pool's edge, chatting with Marcella and Ray.

David turned and followed her focus. "You once told me I should ask Zavier about friendship."

"I did. You should."

His expression was thoughtful, but after a moment, it turned devilish. "Later, I think." Then he dunked her under the water.

Well, she deserved that. When she surfaced again, she splashed him, which turned into an all-out water fight between them all, until they were laughing too hard.

Ray held up his hands. "I'm turning into a prune. I gotta get out."

They all did then, but not before David dove to the bottom of the pool to collect his sunglasses. After drying out a little and collecting their things, the whole lot of them ended up back by the table Mish had claimed before. The woman from earlier had gone, but new guests had arrived, and everyone seemed to eye their group.

She glanced at David and yeah, he'd already scoped out the other guests. "I'm guessing there will be pictures up of all of that by tomorrow."

Adrian snorted. "A photo of Mish launching you into the pool was posted about a minute and a half after you two hit the water."

She'd figured that would happen. "Let me guess, 'Boy Toy Toss'?"

"Oh, nothing so clever." Adrian made no move to grab his phone. She'd left hers up in her room. David frowned.

She poked him. "You're not upset, are you?"

His expression lightened. "God, no. Just contemplating 'Boy Toy' at my age." A falter in his expression gave away that there was more. She cocked her head. "I wonder how well that's going to go over."

She didn't have to ask with who. Her fucking damn stalker.

He caught her hand in his and gave it a squeeze. "This afternoon was some of the most fun I've had in years. It's..." He glanced around at the rest of their group. "I'm usually alone. Not part of the group."

"Welcome to Twisted Wishes," Zavier murmured. He was a table away, but of course David heard. They all had.

"We're kind of a strange land," Ray said. He ran a hand through his wet locks. "And tumultuous, but we're fun."

David's fingers tightened around Mish's and she wasn't

sure if the thrumming was her pulse or his. His dark eyes were steady when they met Ray's. "Thanks for inviting me."

And that was the moment, Mish realized, when David finally accepted *them*.

Dinner that evening was apparently what Ray liked to call "busting out of jail." David learned that this particular tradition had started during their fateful tour as Five Asylum's opening act. That had been the tour where Ray'd nearly died.

After he'd returned from the hospital, they'd desperately needed to get out of the hotel where they'd been holed up for days—so the band had walked out, no holds barred, to have dinner at a swank restaurant.

That night had turned into a reoccurring event where all of Twisted Wishes dressed up and headed out on the town, as if they owned the world.

They weren't even the biggest act in the States, and the band knew that, but Marcella chimed in that they'd gained a lot of respect from that defiant act years ago now, and it was as much of a treat for any fans they met as it was for the band.

This time, Adrian, Marcella, and David were coming with them.

David was taken aback. "You mean, you just...show up at a place?" He'd sputtered that, much to his chagrin, when they'd told him about their plans at the poolside bar.

"Yes, exactly." Zavier's smile was wicked, and David realized he was being teased. Zav seemed to get a kick out of doing that to his friends, which was both heartwarming and fucking *annoying*.

"I don't suppose I could talk you all out of it?" David asked.

"Nope." That from Ray. "Not a chance in the world."

So they were heading back to their rooms to shower off

the chlorine and put on their Twisted Wishes best, which for David was going to be...trying. "I have no fucking clue what to wear," he muttered. "God, you people."

He'd hadn't thought much beyond "security guard for a rock band" when he'd packed. So denim. Black T-shirts. The usual. He had one button-down, but that was at the bottom of his laundry bag.

Mish slid a hand up his spine that set every nerve of his on fire. "Need my help?"

He started at her touch and tamped the sudden shock of desire down. "Yeah, maybe." If anyone could pull together an outfit for him out of his sorry wardrobe, it was Mish. Though it might prove too much for even her.

Dom chuckled from the rear of the elevator. "Careful, or she'll have you in smoky eyes and lipstick."

David laughed at that. Might be interesting to see what he looked like in makeup now. But no. "Not really my thing."

"That's fine." Mish stroked his back again. "I'm sure we can find something."

When the elevator reached his floor, he and Marcella exited for their rooms. A half hour later, David was surprised to find Mish at his door. For some reason, he'd figured she'd take longer than that to shower and dress, but no. She strode in on red boots that made his mouth water, and a black-and-white dress that clung to every one of her curves. Her hair was down, and she carried a clutch purse in one hand and what looked like a mini tackle box in the other.

His gaze lingered on the box. "What's that?"

"Makeup." He met her gaze, a trickle of fear slipping through his mind. She stuck out her tongue at him. "For me, not you, doofus."

Heat to his cheeks. It only dawned on him *now* that she wasn't wearing any makeup. "Oh."

She chuckled and bumped past him. "Come on, hot stuff. I've seen you naked, now show me your clothes."

He did, and a mere two minutes later, she was rolling her eyes. "Really? I saw you in a button-down the first day! That whole outfit would be perfect for tonight."

David cringed. "It's in my dirty laundry bag. I don't have any other button-downs."

"Damn it, David!" But she was laughing.

He held up his hands. "I'm security! You guys said there wouldn't be any fancy dress parties." He lowered his hands and sank to the bed. "Jeans and tees. That's what you have to work with."

She looked him up and down, and that was all the more sexy in that dress with those boots and from that height. "Oh no, it isn't." She whipped out her phone. "As I recall, you and Dom are the same height. And your basic body build isn't *that* different."

Fucking hell. He tried to argue. "I'm broader in the shoulders. And I'm not gonna look good *at all* in Domino Grinder's gear."

"But you'll look stunning in Dominic Bradley's." Those warm eyes pinned him to where he sat. "Do you trust me?"

"Yeah. Yeah, I do." Of course he did. She'd thrown him into a pool. They'd lain in bed together. Fucked.

"Good." She dropped her focus to her phone and started tapping away on it. A moment later, she bounced on her toes. "I'll be right back." Then she was gone.

David sat down on the bed and sorted through his emotions. This was—fucking amazing. He was going to dinner with Twisted Wishes, not as a security guard, but as a friend. Part of their inner group. And, most likely, he was going to do it in some of Dom's clothes.

Mish returned with an entire garment bag. "I grabbed a few options." And by few, she meant several button-down shirts, some ties, a few vests...and suspenders.

David boggled at the choices. "He travels with all this?"

He fingered the shirts, all good quality and colors that would work with David's skin tone.

"Honey, Dom is a clotheshorse. The only one worse is Zavier, but don't tell him I said that. He keeps his shoe collection on the downlow."

In the end, through much laughter and several outfits, David wound up in a pair of his own black jeans, a brick-red button-down paired with a dark blue tie. The suspenders didn't work with the jeans, and the vests made him look like a waiter, so they did without those, though he liked the suspender look. Maybe when they got back to New York, he'd look into expanding his wardrobe.

Mish had him dig out the leather necklace he'd been wearing that first day. He'd put it away while on duty—the less shit for people to grab at if he got into a scuffle, the better.

Coupled with the boots he'd been wearing earlier, his reflection in the mirror could be called *stylish*. He looked like *himself*. Air caught in his throat, emotions welling up so suddenly. These moments, the simple ones when he saw the man he'd always wanted to see staring back at him—they always left him breathless.

He turned away from the mirror and worked to settle himself. He was *here* and himself, through all that had happened in his life. It was a fucking miracle sometimes.

"David?"

"I'm fine," he said, though his voice was husky. "I look good."

She bumped his hip with hers. "You always look good."

He grunted, and a smile tugged at his lips. "Thanks."

Mish did her makeup, and a few minutes after that, they were walking through the lobby. Damn, they *all* looked fine. Mish had chosen well. Might not have been planned, but there was something of a theme of black, white, red, and blue going on among them. They certainly turned heads. David offered Mish his arm and she took it, her grin a flash of white that was as bright as a camera's.

There were plenty of those, too. "They're gonna write about us," he said.

"Oh, honey, they already have. It's been *hours* since the pool."

He laughed at that.

They piled into a limo—a stretch one—and when David settled in, Marcella tapped his foot with hers. "We're going conspicuous."

And yeah, they were. The restaurant they rolled up to wasn't the most expensive in town, but it was pricy. They swung past the bar and were seated toward the back of the establishment without any waiting.

"How the heck did you manage this?" he asked Marcella.

"I didn't. This was Adrian's doing."

Adrian shrugged. "Despite Zavier's teasing, this *was* planned. I enjoy fine dining, so I took the liberty of researching places and made a reservation once the tour was finalized."

Adrian was a food nerd? Who'd have thought? "So not just breezing in."

"Oh, we've done that." Mish took his hand and laced her fingers between his. "But after a few food misses, as Adrian likes to call them, he took over planning."

Domino was almost too quiet during this whole exchange. He noticed David watching. "Adrian knows what he's doing when it comes to restaurants."

"And this place has *pie,*" Adrian said.

For a moment, the rock star was gone. "Oh," Dom said. "Damn."

David glanced away. Adrian's return smile was too personal, too private.

"Yeah," Mish murmured. "They can be a bit much."

"I'll say." Marcella poked his shoulder. "Don't you two start in like that, please."

They didn't, though they did hold hands while ordering, until food and drinks appeared at the table. Most of the group split two bottles of wine, but neither he nor Ray had any of that. Ray didn't drink much and, though he wasn't on duty, David wanted to remain sharp, just in case.

There was much eating, talking, and laughing. Random stories were told, some of the early band days. Zavier told one about traveling with the symphony he'd played with years ago.

When the conversation wove around to David, he held up a hand. "I was in the army. Those stories aren't funny, or good dinner conversation."

But eventually, they pried a work one out of him. "So, I was working as a bouncer for this club that did concerts—little ones. Small acts, not like you guys now."

Ray nodded. "I remember those kinds of clubs."

"Well, this was supposed to be an easy night. Not thrash. Not metal. Not rap. Folk music, they said."

"Oh no." Zavier hid his smile behind a sip of wine. "Famous last words."

"Right? Turns out it was an Irish folk band with a rock edge."

Adrian choked on his drink. "Oh, you poor thing," he sputtered.

Dominic nudged him. "Some of those bands are really good."

"Babe, I *know*." He set his wine down. "Bet it wasn't the band that was an issue."

"Exactly right." David took a sip of water. "The crowd was *chaos* incarnate. Masses of bodies. People singing and dancing, then getting mad when they crashed into others. Worse than a mosh pit, 'cause when you mosh, you expect to be hit, you know?" He shook his head. "Hardest concert I ever bounced, I swear. We had to call an ambulance when someone accidentally elbowed a woman in the head and knocked her out. Adrian's right. The band was very nice. Treated all of us well and the concert was a good one."

"So we must be a cake walk," Mish said. Her fingers brushed his thigh.

Except for the stalker and the guy who'd stolen Mish's ring, sure. David didn't say that. "Well, less bruises in the line of duty, for sure."

Mish leaned in and whispered into his ear, low so no one else heard. "And when you're not on duty?"

Oh yeah, he had some bruises from the other night. He smiled back at her, their faces close enough to kiss. "Marcella told us to behave."

The table turned into a round of laughter at that, and lo and behold, there was a touch of pink in Mish's cheeks, but both her voice and her eyes sparkled.

Dessert was an *experience*. That turned into one big round of sharing everything the restaurant had on the menu. David noticed that despite the plate in front of him, everything Domino tasted came off Adrian's fork. Another intimate glimpse that made him focus on other things.

He looked up from his own plate, now covered in chocolate sauce, to find Zavier watching him. A smile graced the drummer's lips. He nodded, and that was all.

He didn't understand that look—but the moment seemed important, an approval of sorts. He set it aside for later. Right now, he'd focus on the food and the fun, and the beautiful woman sliding her hand over his thigh.

The ride back to the hotel was sedate. Mish enjoyed that as much as when they were rambunctious and loud. Given that they were full and happy and all of them but Ray and David were a little buzzed from the wine, it wasn't too surprising. It was a comfortable, warm stillness.

Mish had David's hand in hers, their arms twined together like lovers, his body warm and solid against her. Into the soft noise of the road, he spoke low, close to her ear. "That was nice."

It had been. No stress at all. There'd been a few fans waiting for the band when they'd come out, but those interactions were a joy, not a burden. They'd even asked David, respectfully, for a few selfies. One young man had shyly said he'd been so happy to see David shirtless in the pool photos and videos. He'd just started on T, he'd said.

David had pulled the kid aside to talk a little. That hadn't gone unnoticed either, and they'd all given David and the kid time and space.

Mish snuggled against David in the limo. "That's why we go out. Sometimes we need nice."

Of course, Zavier was watching them, with his hooded eyes and half smile, like the pleased little string-puller he thought he was. He had nothing to do with her and David. Zavier hadn't really had anything to do with Dom and Adrian either, but Mish saw pride when she caught him watching those two. The arrogance of that man was annoying, welcome, and not malicious at all.

"Good food with good friends." Zavier leaned back against his seat. "One of the best things."

"One of," Ray murmured.

Zavier patted Ray's thigh, his smile deepening, but said nothing.

Ah, those two. Partners who complemented each other so well—the very best of friends.

The limo pulled in at the hotel. Another small group of fans waited for them, so they signed a few more items, then strode—far less quickly than before—through the lobby to the elevator. David's hand was at the small of her back the entire way.

Once the doors of the car closed, David sought out Dom. "I'll get your shirt and tie back to you tomorrow, if that's okay."

Dom waved his hand. "Eh, whenever. Heck, keep them. They look better on you than me anyway."

They did, though David had one of his perplexed scowls on, as if he couldn't believe what he was hearing.

Adrian cocked his head. "Maybe. Though I do like the brick red on you."

"Biased," Dom said. "And I have other shirts that color."

Adrian made a little humming noise in the back of his throat, and looked way the hell too pleased.

When the doors opened onto David and Marcella's floor, Mish stepped off with them. "Gotta get my makeup."

Totally an excuse. What she wanted was David. His lips and hands on hers. His mouth open in ecstasy, and that deep, sexy moan of his.

Plus, she really didn't want to hear Adrian and Dom tonight. They were so damn loud when Adrian got *that* look.

"Uh huh." Ray didn't sound convinced. But then, he knew her too well. "Have fun."

She laughed as the doors slid closed.

Marcella rolled her eyes at them. "Do remember we have a radio interview pretty damn early in the morning. I don't want to be banging on your door because you two spent the night..." She waved her hand. "But Ray's right, you guys *should* have fun."

With that, Marcella marched down the hall to her room.

"It's like they think we're gonna have sex or something." David's eyes met Mish's and heat curled inside her, every inch of her longing for those strong hands and that *very* talented tongue.

"Well..." Mish kept her voice low and quiet, since the rest

of the crew had rooms on this floor. "There's probably a reason for that."

She took hold of his tie, just under the knot, and pulled him forward until their mouths met in the kiss she'd denied herself all evening. This one was all lust and desire, her need coupled with his. David's hands drew down the length of Mish's back to her ass and pulled them close.

She groaned and broke the kiss. "Okay. Your room. Now."

That was an order she didn't need to repeat. They scrambled to his room, and once inside, with the door safely shut and the bolt thrown, Mish grabbed David by his shirt and pressed him up against the nearest wall. She swallowed his muffled *oomf* in a hard kiss that had him melting. His hands found her ass again.

God, she loved the feel of him against her, the tautness of his muscles, the firmness of his thigh between her legs, the strength he surrendered to her.

Mish worked the knot of his tie. All these lovely clothes needed to be off both of them, and soon. She wanted her skin against his. That beard tickling down her torso. She nibbled up to his ear, loving the texture of his beard under her lips.

"Been wanting you all night." She finally got the damn tie free and tugged at the collar of his shirt.

"Careful, darling, or you'll rip Dom's shirt." When he kissed her throat, her fingers fumbled on the buttons.

She pressed him harder into the wall. "Pretty sure the shirt's yours now." She got the top button undone, even as he worked at the zipper of her dress. Then it was a race to see who could get the other naked the quickest.

Except David stopped moving when he'd stripped the dress from her, which she'd expected. *She* knew what was underneath. White lace bra and panties, with matching garters to hold up her stockings. Plus she was still in her red boots and jewelry.

David seemed to drink her in. "God, whatever the hell you want to do to me tonight, I'm all yours."

He certainly was. "I should have borrowed some rope from Adrian or Zavier. Tying you down would have been fun."

His neck reddened. "I'm fine with that. But I just learned more about your bandmates than I should know."

She pulled him off the wall. "There are very few secrets on the road—at least in the band." She paused and added, "You'll figure that out fast, after a couple of days on the bus with us."

She saw him register what she said, and the meaning behind her words—she wanted him on *their* bus. "And tonight?"

"I think we can work something out as soon as you lose the rest of your clothes."

He did that quickly and efficiently. Damn, she loved the sprinkling of hair on his chest, the darker line that trailed down his belly.

David chuckled. "You know, that's a look I'm not used to getting."

She flicked her gaze up to his very dark, smoldering one. "Then your lovers were fools."

She stalked toward him until she had him backed up against the bed. The heat of his body seared through lace and sent fire racing to her core. The things she wanted to do to this man. Maybe she *would* borrow some rope at some point, but right now?

She caught his face between her hands and devoured that mouth again, relishing the groan. David slid his hands up her arms, then over her back, but made no move to undo her bra. Just—held her tight to him as she kissed and rocked their bodies together.

God, she wanted his mouth on her clit and his fingers

buried in her. She also wanted to suck him off and hear the strangled cries he made when he came. There was time enough for both, even if they did have to get up damn early for that interview.

She drew her hands down to his chest, then pushed him backward onto the bed. "Why don't you pretend I've tied you down to your bed and am about to make your every filthy wish come true?"

David's black eyes widened a fraction, and his breath hitched. "Anything you want." His voice was slurred with lust. He scrabbled backward to stretch his arms out and grip the headboard.

She grinned down at the length of his body. "Call me *princess*."

The croak that came out of him and the accompanying shudder was worth everything. She climbed onto the bed, boots and all, up over David and hovered above him on her hands and knees, their lips almost touching.

"Princess," he whispered, and that one word was the most glorious music in her ears. She kissed him, taking her time to tease a guttural groan out of him as he squirmed and thrust on the bed. The muscles in his arms flexed, but he kept his hands up, kept holding on to the headboard, as she'd told him to.

A powerful and heady moment. No question David was physically stronger, even though she had him on height, but tonight he was hers in all the ways that mattered. She turned that thought over in her head as she worked her mouth down his jaw and neck and over his chest.

She stroked his sides and he twitched, his breath coming in gasps. "Oh fuck!"

But he kept his hands above his head. Left them there, even when she closed her mouth around his dick, when he arched off the bed and begged her to keep going every time she backed off. God, she was wet. Throbbing, and aching for him to touch her, be inside her. But she fucking loved David like this, too—so strung out, so near the brink of orgasm that his voice was full of moans and grunts. His arms had turned to cords of muscles as he fought to hold on to the headboard, fought to *obey* her. Such a little thing. Such a *powerful* thing.

"Please, baby." David was nothing but air and lust, his body trembling underneath her. "Please!"

"I love you like this." Before he could say anything more, she took him in her mouth fully, sucking and licking, then slid two fingers into him and pumped until he was thrashing and shouting unintelligible words to the ceiling of the hotel room.

She slowed but kept going until he keened in his throat. "Fuck, baby, you gotta stop. I can't..." David's breath caught and his whole body shook in orgasm, and she let him down slowly until they were both panting ragged breaths.

"Unfair," he whispered. He was still clutching the headboard, though his arms were slack.

"Totally fair." Mish kissed his thigh. "Figured I could get you off more than once."

He grunted. "First person in a while, to be honest."

Mish crawled up his body, and they kissed, gently this time. "Lucky me."

"Lucky *me*." He closed his eyes. "God, you are a fucking queen."

She tapped his nose. "Princess."

That smile was so damn bright. "Princess. Queen. Baby. Doesn't matter. You're royal and beautiful, and I..." He stopped there, his eyes widening. Staring up.

She pressed a finger to his lips. "It's okay. Keep that for now." Because it was too soon, and so close on the heels of pleasure. Her own heart flipped and ached when it came to David, but she didn't know whether she wanted to pin a name on those emotions yet. There was something there, beyond a fling. Different from her other sexual friendships.

Trust. Comfort. She laid her head on David's chest. "You can let go of the headboard, you know."

His laughter was more vibration than sound. "I was curious to see when you'd finally let me go." He wrapped his arms around her. "I liked that, by the way. Wouldn't mind being tied up."

"Mmm. Good to know." Maybe she'd ask Zavier about rope or something. That man was far too wicked not to have a stash of toys on the trip, and he'd probably get a thrill out of her asking. Zav so loved to be up in everyone's business. Mostly because the damn fool cared about all of them.

"Mish?" There was laughter in David's voice. "Are you still wearing your *boots*?"

"Yep."

"In *bed*?"

"Yep."

"Oh my god." He rolled them both over until he was looming over her. "My turn." The smile matched the humor.

"Oh? And what are you going to do?" She stretched like a cat beneath him, but he was the one who purred.

"Why, I'm going to strip those boots off. And that bra and those panties." His voice grew deeper. "And then I'm going to wreck you as hard as you wrecked me."

"That... Yes. *That*." More than anything else, she wanted to shout this man's name when she came. "Then I want you to fuck me."

"With pleasure." He stole a kiss, then set about doing exactly as he'd intended.

Pleasure it was, too. Raw and uninhibited, and she screamed his name more than once. When they finally wore each other out, it was later than she wanted to think about. They both dragged themselves out of bed to clean up, then fell right back into it.

As she was drifting off, a thought had her wide awake and struggling to sit up. "I left Marly in my room."

David grunted in dismay. "He's just a bear." He didn't sound any more convinced of that than she did.

"You're going to think I'm silly, but I don't know if I can sleep, knowing he's all alone up there."

"Don't think you're silly at all. He's my bear and I haven't been without him in years." David spoke the words against her back.

"I'll go."

He caught her around the waist. "Baby, no. You only have your dress. Give me your keycard. I'll throw on shorts and a tee and be back down before you know it." He paused. "I don't think I could sleep without him, either."

They crawled out of bed. Mish extracted her card from her clutch and handed it to David, who somehow managed to look sexy in a pair of black gym shorts and an olive-green tee. He nudged her toward the bed. "Relax."

He slipped out the door of the room. Maybe they were both childish in this, but a talisman was a talisman. She crawled back in bed, her body aching in pleasant ways and her mind buzzing with the memories of David's arching back, when he came, and the taste of him. How he teased and kissed every inch of her skin. How full she'd been when he'd fucked her.

If they hadn't pushed each other to the brink of pleasure a few times, she might even have been turned on, but exhaustion made another round impossible. The sleepy high was nice, though.

True to his word, David was back quickly, Marly tucked in his arm. He handed the bear to Mish, undressed, and crawled into bed, once more wrapping his arms around her. Usually she was the bigger spoon, but she *liked* this.

"Hey, is it okay if I hold Marly?"

"Course." David's voice was slurred but happy, and his breath warm against the back of her neck. "I do sometimes, when I need to."

She didn't ask why. The dog tags on the bear were explanation enough.

Mish pressed back into David and snugged Marly under her chin.

CHAPTER FOURTEEN

Way the heck too early the next morning—and after a round of coffee that wasn't as good as Adrian's—the seven of them piled into a luxury mini bus, the kind David usually saw used as party buses. Thing was *huge*. "This is less obtrusive than a stretch limo?"

Marcella gave him a *look*. "It's easier to maneuver and park, and yes—less obtrusive. Plenty of vans and small buses out there, especially in the mornings. Ride shares. Trips to the airport."

"Not like we're going to have the party lights and be dancing around one of those poles," Ray quipped.

Zavier got a wicked grin. "I think I'd enjoy you pole-dancing."

That earned him a snort from Ray. "Oh, I'm sure you would."

Mish grabbed a pole and rotated around it. "I worked as a stripper early on, you know."

Something tumbled in David, even as the others chuckled. Mish must have seen his expression, because she raised an eyebrow. "This you have a problem with?"

Even though her tone had been gentle, it itched across his

mind, and he was brought right back to his initial shock of emotion.

David took a seat on the couches that lined the bus. "No, not at all. I'm sure you were spectacular." He hadn't known this little fact about her, even after running a background check on her. "Was this before or after you changed your name?" There was a certain *possessiveness* to Mish's stalker, in the way that asshole thought he owned her.

Mish froze, then sank onto the couch across from him. "Before, right after I turned eighteen. With the cancer treatments, Mom was having a hard time working, and it seemed the quickest legal way to make some money. I couldn't risk getting jailed for turning tricks or escorting. Though I did think about that."

Marcella rubbed her neck. "That's a lot to handle at eighteen."

Zavier looked thoughtful. "I've done sex work. There is that risk, for sure. You're right—a barely legal woman attracts more attention from the cops."

"This bus ride is turning into a confessional," Adrian said.

Ray shook his head. "I don't think anyone here feels guilty, Adrian."

"Granted," Marcella said. "But let's keep this part of your collective pasts out of the limelight, yes? I have no issues, but the scandal sites would have a field day."

There were general agreements about that. Throughout the conversation, Mish's gaze never left David's. "You think this guy knows me from that? I only stripped for about six months, until our finances settled out and I was getting gigs singing in bars and could switch paths."

"I don't know." It was an honest reply. "I still get the sense that this is personal. That he knows you from somewhere that isn't Twisted Wishes. And while your high school photo isn't anything like your image now, I bet your look while stripping was closer to Mish Sullivan, the rock star."

She frowned in thought. "Yeah, I carried some of that over to the musical stage. It was empowering."

"I want to ring that fucker's neck." The words were low and harsh, and it took David a moment to realize that Dom had spoken them. He was Domino now, all leather-clad and spike hair, with makeup that was on point and so unlike the man Dom was in his off time.

The depth of anger was out of character, though.

"Sweetheart," Mish murmured.

Dom's eyes were pools of fury. "I'm not kidding. If I knew who this guy was, I'd hunt him down and strangle him myself. No one fucking deserves what you're going through. Even the goddamned press is more respectful than this fucking fucker."

Given Dom's loathing of the public spotlight and the press, that was saying a lot. While all of Twisted Wishes was salty with the language, he'd never heard Dom string together *that* many curses in a row.

"Babe." Adrian's voice was soft. "Please don't kill anyone. You might look good in orange, but that's going a bit far for fashion." He rubbed circles on Dom's back.

Dom bristled, but softened. "I just want Mish to be safe."

"I love you all, but I don't need your protection."

"Yeah, you do," Marcella chimed in. "And don't you give me any lip, Ms. Sullivan. I'm immune to your charms."

"You are so not," she purred. "After all, I did manage to get you into a bikini that one trip."

Marcella opened, then closed her mouth. "Okay, I'm not *entirely* immune," she amended. "But the statement stands. You need protection. Ray needs it. And Dom." She eyed Zavier. "You—even you need someone watching your back from time to time."

"We all need friends and family," Zavier said.

"The Zavier Demos motto." Mish leaned against the couch. "Thank you for caring. It's not like I don't appreciate it, but shouldn't we be worried about this damn radio interview?"

David thought she had a point, but Ray snorted. "We can do radio interviews in our sleep."

"You *have* done them in your sleep," Marcella muttered, and David couldn't help laughing.

"Hey now." Mish met him with a smile. "No taking sides."

"No sides when it's the truth, darling."

"He's got you there, Mish." Ray swung his legs over Zavier's lap and lay down on the couch.

Zavier locked an arm around Ray's legs. "If you roll off this thing when we go around a curve and knock your head, you only have yourself to blame."

Ray grinned.

The antics continued until they pulled into the station parking lot. There were a few fans there—how did they know? David cast Marcella a glance.

"Oh, the station's been hyping this for weeks. But it's early enough in the morning, and on a weekday, figured it shouldn't be an issue."

It was just after six—their interview was for seven. It was a wonder the band had energy this time of morning. Then again, the day off had done them all wonders.

After signing a few items, the band made their way into the studio, Marcella leading. David strode next to Adrian. "You ever feel like a groupie?"

That got him a laugh. "Never. I didn't know who Dominic was when I met him, so it wasn't like I was pining over the band. Just Dominic Bradley. Who turned out to be in the band." Adrian held his gaze. "You?"

"No, but sometimes I do feel like I'm an extra."

Adrian clapped him on the back. "Dude, you're not. And you're doing a more important job than I am at the moment."

Wasn't so sure about that, but David let it go. They'd

warmed to him at the pool, pulled him in, had kept him in their family. His relationship—or whatever it was—with Mish left him unsettled from a professional standpoint. Didn't help, though, that he was the last one through the door as they marched in.

That station security was tight, including metal detectors. He raised his eyebrow at the guard on duty. "This necessary?"

In return, the guard gave him an impassive stare. "We had an incident with a shock jock get out of hand at one point."

Fucking hell. That was just great. Volatile listeners *and* employees. Well, at least he wouldn't have to worry about anyone sneaking into the station.

After meeting with the morning show personalities, the producer, and the station manager to go over the ground rules, David, Adrian, and Marcella were ushered into a small room with a clear view across the hall from the studio where the band was setting up with the radio hosts. Mics. Earphones. They were given all the expected things, and donned them like they'd done this a million times.

They probably had. This wasn't their first tour—just their biggest and in support of their latest album.

Mish's gaze snagged on his and she blew him a kiss. He gave a small wave back, heat rising up his neck. Adrian clapped him on the back again and Marcella grinned.

"What?" he said to both of them.

"Nothing." Marcella's humor belied that.

"You guys are adorable." That from Adrian. David elbowed him gently in the ribs before he could even think about it. Adrian laughed outright. "See? Family."

Marcella made an agreeable noise.

He would have said more, but there was a flurry of activity in the studio, and a check of the clock showed it close to the top of the hour. Interview time.

There was a goofy intro to the morning show, then the

hosts acted upbeat and irreverent before they introduced Twisted Wishes. The band all gave a round of hellos, and from the smiles, everything was going the way it should. Songs were played. Commercials. The hosts asked several questions about the new album.

One host, Morning Coffee Clark, turned to Zavier. "This is your first album as a member of Twisted Wishes. How'd it go? Were you prepared? How'd it feel?"

That led to a very amused laugh from the drummer. "It was a phenomenal experience, of course it was."

There was a general murmur of agreement from the rest of the band.

"As for being prepared, touring before recording helped, my relationship with Ray notwithstanding." He paused. "And it felt *good*. Kevin Schmidt was a great drummer, extremely competent, but our styles are different, so it was nice to get into the studio and make my own mark on the sound."

"Beyond the one you made touring," Ray said.

"Well, yes." Zavier's smile was sharp and personal and aimed at Ray.

Questions about the album continued, then they turned to Domino's reveal of his non-persona side.

"So what was that like?" asked the other host—Amy in the AM, if David recalled her moniker correctly. She had a mellow voice that was smooth, with a hint of sultry. "Letting the fans see behind the mask?"

Domino—in his makeup—never lost that sharp edge to his smile. "It's not a mask." His voice was not nearly as smooth as the hosts'. There was a gravel in it David hadn't heard before. "It's part of who I am, as much as my more private life is." The bark of Domino's laugh was normal, though. "After all, it's not like I could dress like this at a desk job. I get to wear what I want, when I want. Leather, glitter, and all."

Beside him, Adrian was nodding, probably unconsciously. "You tell 'em, babe."

There was a little more banter about glitter getting everywhere and whether the band shared makeup—they did—before they moved on to Mish.

Clark chimed in. "Mish, these past couple of concerts, you've been singing with Ray! How'd that come about?"

Mish's laugh was deep and David sat up straighter to cover the growing heat in his body.

"I began my career singing and playing in bars. That's how Ray found me. But many of our earlier songs weren't in my range—"

"Or were me musically yelling into the mic," Ray chimed in.

Mish nodded, though no one listening on air could see that. "Exactly, so they weren't right for my voice. But 'Finding Light' is one I sing along with all the time when we practice—"

"And I'm not a fool," Ray said.

"Honey, sometimes you are."

There was laughter from all the band and the hosts.

"Fine, I'll grant you that," Ray said.

Mish looked through the hall and met David's gaze, the giant black headphones stark against her copper curls. "Sometimes we try new things. This one worked."

This one worked. Yeah, they worked. David worked with the band. Still, a voice said that getting in this deep would make Mish vulnerable.

"Ray, are you going to write a song for Mish?" Amy asked.

The whole band shifted in their seats. "Been toying with the idea." Ray's voice had a slyness to it.

Mish's smile was just as sneaky. "We'll see."

"I can see we're not going to get more about that!" Clark had one of those performer smiles, the ones that lifted your voice but were too exaggerated to be real. "Let's play 'Dare to Be' from your album, and when we come back, we'll take a few calls from listeners."

The hosts rattled off the phone number to call, then music started.

"So far, so good," Marcella said.

Adrian slumped back in his chair. "I hate when they ask Dominic about masks."

"Hits close to the bone?" The unveiling of Domino Grinder had been in all the entertainment magazines before they'd moved on to other scandals and news, and Adrian had been tangled up in all of that—as Domino Grinder's secret boyfriend. Dom's romantic rescue of Adrian from in front of their practice studio had spun across the internet—and changed Adrian's life. For the better, it seemed to David.

"No—well, yes." Adrian shoved a hand through his hair. "We all wear masks. I wore suits to work every day. They put me in a different headspace, but I wasn't another person." He waved at the studio. "Dominic is still Dominic."

David grunted. "They're all themselves. We get to see more of that behind the scenes. And you see even more with Dom."

Adrian's lips quirked. "Could say the same about you and Mish."

Marcella clicked her tongue. "Let's keep that under our hats, shall we?" There was no one else in the room, but that was a damn good reminder that though the photo of Mish tossing him into the pool was out there, they hadn't discussed how they were going to handle the press. Was David going to be known as more than the band's guard? Would they play those photos off as general band horseplay?

Both he and Adrian settled down into silence as the Twisted Wishes song wound down and they went to commercials.

"This is the tricky part," Marcella murmured. "Let's hope we get a good batch of callers."

"Don't they screen them?" David glanced at the studio, then to Marcella.

"Of course. But once the caller is live—all bets are off."

Well, shit. Guess that made sense from the little time he'd spent listening to morning radio shows. They sat and waited until the commercials were over and the show started again. The hosts led in and they got ready to take their first caller.

Every member of the band was tense now, more focused—which meant that these calls had been issues before.

"What happened in the past?" He didn't look away from Mish or how high her shoulders were and how taut her mouth.

But Marcella was right there with him in thought. "Personal stuff. Asking about sex. Or Ray and Zavier's marriage—prying questions."

Right. That would bug the shit out of everyone.

The first question, though, was a gushing fan who wanted to know how they decided what songs to play on tour.

David had seen that—it was a group decision. Led by Ray, yes, but with a ton of input and ideas tossed around until they were all happy with the results. They had a base list of songs and swapped ones in and out, mixing up the sets. Kinda drove the techs working the concert up a tree, but they were used to it by now.

The next caller asked about Ray's process for writing songs and how that worked with the rest of the band. That took a while to discuss—and it was fascinating.

"I don't talk about this much, 'cause people don't always understand, but I have synesthesia," Ray said. Then he went into how he saw songs. Sometimes the music came first, sometimes the words. Once he had a sketch, he'd play it for the rest of the band and they'd go from there, each adding their own unique takes.

"We only have time for one more call," Amy said. "Hi there, you're on the air with Twisted Wishes!"

There was a pause, then a masculine voice spoke out from the speakers. "Yes, my question is for Mish."

The tone of that voice, the way Mish's name had been spoken, had David on his feet. Every nerve alight. Fucking *hell.*

"David." A whisper from Adrian.

Mish glanced at him before speaking into the mic. "Go ahead."

"You were wearing those slutty tights again, at the last concert, and I want to know why. I told you—" The line cut off abruptly.

Both Ray and Zavier were standing. Marcella had somehow materialized on the other side of the hall by the studio door in mere seconds, probably because she had more training in management than either he or Adrian did.

David was rooted to the ground, mouth dry, heart pounding, every instinct to lash out at the threat that wasn't there. Not physically, at least. His hand flew to his chest, but his tags weren't there. They were on Marly and he was safely tucked into Mish's belongings, ready for their next leg on the bus.

In the studio, Mish sat still, pale but for red high on her cheeks. She wet her lips and leaned into the mic. "I wore them because I wanted to. Because they make me feel good. Because no one dictates what I wear." Her voice was low and smooth, but carried the force of her passion. "Clothes are a personal choice. Wear what you want." She leaned back.

Both Amy and Clark had the same wide-eyed and shocked expression, but Amy spoke in that upbeat voice of hers that only belied a little of the chaos in her expression. "I think we can all agree to that! Why don't we treat you to another song off Twisted Wishes's latest album? This is 'Born in Fire.'"

Music started to play, and both hosts slumped over. Marcella was in the studio in a flash, talking quickly, but nothing came out the speaker except the song.

Mish sat still, her eyes closed, in the studio as everyone moved and gestured around her. David fought the urge to go to her side. There were already too many people in that small space.

Domino sat next to her, still and silent. His focus seemed to be on his hands.

"Shit," Adrian murmured.

David thought of Dom's comment on the bus. "Don't worry about Dom. I'm going to ring that fucker's neck first."

Silence stretched before Adrian spoke again. "You know, you'd look hideous in orange, David."

Maybe. He rubbed his chin. "I don't like death. I've seen too much of it. But this fucker..."

Mish opened her eyes and flicked them up to meet his. Her shoulders dropped. She rose, seemingly oblivious to the people around her, and strode out of the studio. That unrooted David. He met her in the hallway.

Everything in his chest was painful and full of danger. All the words in his mind. He uttered only one. "Mish."

She gave a single shake of her head. "I need air."

He pushed his own anger and fear away. "Let's see if there's somewhere private you can go." Because the front parking lot would still hold fans, all of whom had just heard that creeper speak.

They worked their way to the reception desk, and David spoke to both the guard and the receptionist while Mish stood back. When he returned, she held her body so rigidly and her lips were set in a line so sharp he could have used them to slice stone. "There's a loading dock in the back of building. There's only one way back there from the outside, and there's security, so there shouldn't be any fans."

"Good." That was all she said.

He led her in the direction the guard had told him. Down a corridor, around a corner, and through a nondescript door out onto the dock. The area smelled of cool concrete and oil, but beyond the rolled up dock doors shone sunlight. He headed down another short set of stairs and out into the day.

The guard had been right—there was little back here but a few cars, a high chain-link fence and a driveway that turned around to the front of the building. Mish had stopped in the shade of the dock, and he gestured to her. "There's no one here. It's safe."

She slid out into the light, her arms wrapped around herself as if it were late autumn and not June.

"Nowhere is safe." Her eyes glistened and she shook, maybe in rage, maybe in pain. Quite possibly both.

David knew that cacophony of emotions when he'd wanted to scream and hit and cry until unfairness bled away. Never really left him.

"Right here and right now, you're safe." He kept his voice soft, but firm. "There's no one else. Just us."

It was almost a laugh, her huff of breath, but there was too much sorrow in it. Mish loosened her arms, then craned her face up at the sky.

There were tears in her eyes, though they didn't fall and made no tracks down her cheeks. "I'd scream, but I have to sing tonight."

If there was one thing in the world that meant everything to Mish, it was being there for the fans. Mind, body, and tonight, voice.

"I guess punching something is out, too." David shoved his hands into his pockets.

This time she did laugh. "Unless you have a hidden talent as a bass guitarist and can replace me tonight." She flexed her fingers. "Otherwise, I need these in one piece."

"I never learned to play an instrument, beyond those plastic recorder things in elementary school."

"Ah, the flutophone." Mish's sharp expression was gone. "I had one. My mom couldn't stand it. I think that's why she got me a guitar."

This was a better avenue than talking about the stalker. "How'd you learn bass, anyway? You said you moved around a lot."

A nod. "We did. But I loved music. Wouldn't stop playing that damn flutophone, so Mom found a half-decent acoustic guitar and some books at a thrift store and gave them to me. The music teacher at the elementary school at the time indulged me. She taught me basic fingering and we were learning to read music. So I just...studied those books. Played as much as I could." She paused. "I was heartbroken when the guitar got smashed in a move."

"Shit." He almost tasted the shock and agony of a young girl discovering her beloved instrument broken.

"I cried for hours. One of two times in my life I've done that."

He didn't have to ask the other—he had a very good idea what that moment had been.

Mish rolled her head around her shoulders. "Couple months later, my mom dated this guy who played bass. I kinda wish he'd stuck around because he was nice—nicer than the rest of them. But he was chasing fame." She stopped. "I get that now. Didn't then, though. I was ten."

"I remember ten." He'd been so torn, wanting the jeans, shirts, and shoes all the guys had. Wanting to be accepted as one of them. Instead, he was "cute" for emulating the boys and shoved back into the dresses he hated.

Mish had a smile now, thin, but there. "When I saw Danny the bassist's guitar, I asked if I could play it. He thought I was joking, but when I started to get chords and notes out of it, he realized I wasn't—and spent time teaching me." Another huff. "Sometimes I wonder what happened to him. I mean, he was something like twenty-five, so he'd be around fifty now. Not too old. Maybe still out there, playing." She paused. "Before he left, he got a new bass, so he gave me his old one."

There were tears in Mish's eyes again. David's throat was tight. "That was kind of him."

Those eyes—green now in the summer light—trained on him. "It changed my life."

He let the silence settle between them. After a while, Mish kicked at a stone. "I miss my mom so much. It's been years, but the pain never leaves."

He could only nod. "My parents are alive, but we—drifted apart." Joining the army. His transition. All those internal scars that never seemed to go away.

Mish raised her face to the sky and drew in a breath. "She called me her little smish. That's why. That's..." More tears traced down her face. "I took a name that was all her. Because she was everything to me."

Her pain was so raw, so intense, David couldn't move. Didn't have the right to interrupt. To speak.

She took another breath. "Can I ask you why you chose David?"

"Because he defeated Goliath." So had he, in his own way.

Maybe Mish understood that, because she met his gaze. "It's you."

It was. And Mish Sullivan was her. Every inch.

Mish kicked another stone across the lot. "I think you're right. This shithead is from my past, somewhere. There's something about his voice that's familiar, but I can't place it." She pursed her lips. "Why couldn't someone like Danny drift back into my world instead of this creep?"

So, his instincts had been right. David took no pleasure at all in that. Instead, he focused on Mish's happy memories. "I don't know, baby," he murmured. "Maybe when this is done we can try to find Danny? I bet he'd be thrilled to see how far you've come."

"Yeah, I'd like that." There was brightness in her words again. An ease in the way she moved. "David?"

"Yeah?"

Mish opened her arms. "Thank you."

Of course he went. For this woman, he'd always step into her arms.

He expected the hug. What he hadn't anticipated was her kissing him. Wasn't the passion of the night before, but her mouth still threatened to take David to his knees. There was affection in that kiss. A homecoming. And a need so deep and profound answered in him that it shook him to his marrow.

This wasn't a job anymore. Hadn't been for some time. This was—if he let it be—a road to the future. One he could walk along with others. With Mish. A path he'd never ventured down before with any thought that it might actually work. He wasn't built for company. He'd been a loner all his life.

But this woman—with her fingers in his hair, with softness, pain, and hope in her lips—with this person, there was a glimmer that the path might be different. Be shared. Be true.

David was frightened and angry for Mish, yes. But in that moment, he was also terrified for himself. Because hope opened doors, but it also shattered lives.

Silence. That had been Mish's life since Marcella had found David and her in the back lot of the radio station. In fact, they pulled the van around to the loading dock and they'd all boarded there.

The drive to the hotel, where the bus waited to take them to the concert venue, was quiet but for the road noises and the occasional shifting of bodies on seats, shoes on the floor.

Mish's fingers were twined with David's. That touch kept her grounded and present even as she replayed the stalker's words in her head, listening to the memory of that voice. Examining the timber.

The words hurt—the whole damn thing cut her—especially that voice. Something stirred in her mind, but she couldn't grasp it, couldn't match the sounds to anything she knew.

Each one of her bandmates was caught in a silence of their own. Ray looked sad. Not hopeless—probably because he knew something could be done. Something had been done. Still, he sat with his eyes downcast. Zavier had his hand resting lightly on Ray's thigh, as if to remind Ray that he was there.

Dom's eyes were closed, arms crossed, and Adrian was thumbing and typing on his phone, as was Marcella. Probably dealing with the inevitable social media—and every other media—storm.

All she'd ever wanted to do was play. Play songs and sing and be heard. Lose herself in the music, both in her heart and in the hearts of others. Ray had plucked her out of a bar and offered her a path to that dream, one that he shared with such fierce passion, she'd believed in him even that first night.

Her mom would be so proud. Had been so supportive of her music, even if the shrillness of the flutophone all those years ago had been like nails on a chalkboard. Even when Mish had taken up stripping to support them, her mom hadn't berated her.

And deep inside her came that wailing that always did when she thought about her mom too long. Because death was unfair and awful and *final*.

She tightened her grip on David's hand and got a squeeze in response. He turned in the seat—that much she saw out of the corner of her eye, but she kept her gaze focused in front of her.

Momma would have liked David, thought he was a good, decent man, so unlike the ones she'd dated. *Beggars can't be choosers,* she'd said once, when Mish had asked why she dated so many awful guys. *Don't ever be a beggar, my beautiful child.*

To this day, Mish didn't understand what she meant. Her mother had been a bright star in the galaxy of her life. Not a beggar at all.

Mish closed her eyes. This wasn't good, this train of thought. They had a concert to play tonight. So she took a deep breath, then another and another, and listened to the rumble of the van and the stillness of her bandmates and worked to clear her mind of thoughts of her mother, of that awful voice she'd heard over the phone, and of her pain and sorrow.

David's hand was warm in hers, and she drew strength from that. She was here. Her dreams were *here* and manifest. So many would look to her tonight to give them a taste of that hope.

When they reached the hotel, the tour bus was already there, which was good. There were also fans, which normally lightened her heart, but her heart felt like a stone of iron falling and falling down into something dark and shadowy.

"I don't know if I can," she whispered as the van pulled up.

Ray answered in a quiet, soothing voice. "You don't have to. We can sign. You and David can head to the bus."

Another squeeze from David, which felt less like agreement with Ray and more like support for her—for what she wanted to do. Mish looked up at the ceiling, hating that this...fucking asshole...was getting to her. Had gotten to her.

No matter what she did, his comments, his actions, and that damn call changed how she behaved by making her think about how she should act. How each motion would be perceived, how that damn man would respond.

"Fuck." She whispered that, too. "No. I'll go. Can't be any worse than after the ring."

David finally spoke. "Would you like me there? With you?"

"With me with me, or just with me?" The question tumbled out, though she hadn't meant to ask it.

He cocked his head. "Either. However you need me, Mish."

She needed him. Right now, she needed him by her side. She didn't know what the future held—didn't want to think beyond the concert and the stage and the freedom that was playing and singing. After tonight, maybe she would. "Come with me. Stand with me. Be with me."

"Okay." That was all he said, though his eyes, the curve of his lips, and the warmth of his hand said so much more.

They filed out from the bus.

In the end, signing for the fans lifted her spirits. They were all kind and bright-eyed. Hopeful and excited. They couldn't wait to hear her sing. See the band play live. They were astounded to be able to talk and hug and take photos with Twisted Wishes.

She was here and now. Because that's what was important. *Hold on to those moments tight,* her mom had said so many years ago. *Never forget them.*

I miss you, Momma.

David was here, his hand occasionally touching her. His soft smile lifted his cheeks, even if she couldn't see his eyes behind his sunglasses.

There were pictures taken of them like that—David close. Closer than a guard would be. The pool toss, the night out. All of those would be catalogued, too, along with that horrible phone call. Such was her life in the spotlight.

But Mish's life was also what was before her now—a young woman's bright smile. Another from a college-age fan wearing a pronoun necklace that read *they*. The laughter from a group waiting to see the band. All of this was her life, too.

When they finished signing, she waved to them. "Thank

you. You have no idea how much this means to us. To me." Then she boarded the tour bus.

David followed. The whole band was there. Ray had sorrow in his eyes when she met his.

"Aw, kiddo," she said, and pulled him into a hug. "I'll be okay."

"I know," came his muffled reply from her shoulder. "But I also know it hurts."

She gave them all hugs, after that. Kissed Dom on his forehead and Zavier on the cheek. Marcella even opened her arms, though she was the least touchy-feely of them all.

Then she drew David into her arms and let him take her weight and rock her. "Baby." His voice was full of the grit he got when emotions were in play. "You're gonna knock 'em dead tonight."

Right words. Right time. Tears welled, and though she hated them, she let a few fall, then pulled back to wipe her eyes. "Yeah. I want to."

The bus shuddered to life, rolling forward, and they all found seats. "I want us to walk out there and play like it's the first concert and the last concert. The only one we get."

Ray nodded and Zavier was rubbing his chin, eyes bright. Dom—Domino—had his grin on. "All right. Let's do that," he said.

Ray dug out his Moleskine. "Let's get to work."

Mish took David's hand in hers, and they all leaned in to make this the best Twisted Wishes concert ever.

CHAPTER FIFTEEN

David prowled around the concert venue, passing each entrance, each pathway that led anywhere, and inspected them all. He had time—a couple of hours. Sure, there'd be the VIP event, but he'd already checked out *that* area thoroughly.

He'd also inspected backstage and grilled the head of venue security. Marcella had been there, and between the two of them, they'd imparted how tight security needed to be tonight.

And it was, too. Thank god. Venue security had shooed away the groupies. There'd been a few people who'd tried to sneak in, but they'd all been caught quickly. He should have been able to relax.

He couldn't. Not after watching Mish run through her emotions that morning, not after the fans and then the way the band came together. They would shake this venue down tonight. Give their fans one to remember. All of them were pumped and raring to go.

It was an infinitely better use for their energy than anger. That emotion had run through them all. It still flowed through David, which in turn made him both sloppy and sharp. Stomping around the venue was also about clearing his mind, letting go of the worry and fear for Mish. He doubted the stalker would strike again today—he'd want to see Mish's response first—but they couldn't let down their guard.

David wanted this concert to be a success. While he could be strength and support for Mish, right now Twisted Wishes needed each other. Even Adrian was letting the band hole up in their greenroom.

So *of course* David ran into that reporter again. No idea how she'd gotten early access to the venue, but it didn't matter, since she was wearing the paper wristband that marked her as someone allowed in before the official gate opening time.

Fuck.

He veered away, but she caught up with him easily. "Mr. Altet!"

He kept the sigh inside, slowed and turned. "Ms.... It is Ms., yes?"

That question brought her up short. "Well, yes. What else would it be?" She paused. "I suppose Mrs."

He shrugged, glad to have the upper hand. "Could be Mx. if you're non-binary. Or Mr."

Her mouth hung open for a moment. "That's true." Her gaze turned inward for a moment. "Thank you for asking, but it is Ms."

"All right. Then what can I do for you, Ms. Heydel?

The whole exchange about honorifics seemed to have taken the wind from her sails. She studied him. "Still security for Twisted Wishes? After those photos of you and Mish?"

"Still security, yes." He paused. "Why wouldn't I be?" Maybe the key to throwing reporters off was asking his own questions.

"I mean, you and Mish seem to be much closer."

He gave another shrug. "I'm not going to comment, you know that."

"Fine," she said. "Then tell me this, does Mish Sullivan have a stalker? Was that why you were hired?"

Oh, the effort to keep his face schooled and his hands still. At least he had his sunglasses on this time. "I'm not commenting on that, either."

Marcella wanted to put out some kind of statement. Mish had vetoed that. They still hadn't come to a consensus on how to handle the situation from a PR perspective, and probably wouldn't until after this concert. There'd be time on the drive to Boston, but not before.

"I don't think you have to," Heydel said. "It's obvious you're here for her, and not the rest of the band. I'm just wondering how professional it is for a security guard to be sleeping with his charge."

David tensed, then cursed inwardly. This time he didn't hide his exasperation. "I really don't have time for this nonsense, Ms. Heydel. I hope you enjoy the show." He turned on his heels and strode down the pavilion, toward the stage where the techs for Two Times Strong were setting up for their sound check.

He could at least inspect the pit and the space between it and the stage. He ignored the fact that Heydel was entirely correct—it wasn't professional to be sleeping with Mish. Getting close—being her boyfriend.

By the time he'd surveyed the pit, Heydel was nowhere to be found. "Shit," he muttered, and headed backstage to find Marcella.

He found her with Adrian in a room adjacent the one the band had retreated into. When he relayed the conversation he'd had with Heydel, Marcella patted his arm. "We'll work out a statement. Don't let her get to you."

"Also," Adrian said, "general consensus is that you're smoking hot and the only bad thing about you dating Mish is that it means you're off the market."

Embarrassment wove through David. "Smoking hot?"

"Mmmhmm." Adrian flipped through his phone, then held it out to him. On it was a photo of him from their evening outing.

He looked like a movie star. Or rock star. "This is—Well, shit."

"Yeah, I know," Adrian said. "I'm not used to it, to be honest." His shoulders dropped. "I mean, I'm a nerd at heart, but everyone treats me like some kind of heartthrob."

"You guys need to fucking look at yourselves in the mirror sometime." Marcella went back to scrolling through her own phone.

David bit back his reply, because it sounded suspiciously like something Adrian might dissemble—which proved both their points. So he shifted gears. "Band doing all right?"

"Oh yeah." Adrian tucked his phone away. "They're a bunch of little matches next to a can of kerosene, just waiting to burst into flame."

David laughed from the absurdity and accuracy of that image. "Well, I suppose that's good."

"As long as they don't burn anything down for real, or burn themselves out," Marcella said.

"I don't think they could ever burn themselves out." Adrian looked rueful. "They've a ton of energy and I have a feeling they're only starting to use it."

Good. Something fantastic needed to come from this damn mess.

For the concert, Mish chose to wear her neon-pink fishnets again, and her short black leather skirt with a fuchsia corset and a jacket that matched the skirt. She also pulled out heels that made her two inches taller. She applied makeup that curled her toes and made her feel fantastic about herself, and added silver jewelry to remind her of the stars and her mom.

Fuck that damn man. She would dress sexy and sharp and use every ounce of that on stage. If Ray could prance around topless in leather pants that left nothing to the imagination, then she could wear her damn tights. No one got on their cases for their stage clothing choices—or lack of clothing.

Besides, she felt *good* in her outfits. That was the *point* of clothing—an expression of who you were and a way to confront the world with power and love. That's who she'd always been on stage, both for herself and the fans.

Two Times Strong kicked ass during their performance, getting the crowd on its feet and dancing. The vibe was already incredible, but when Twisted Wishes ran out on stage, the audience erupted into sound and movement. They'd shaken up their entire concert set, this time starting off with "Your Only Shot"—a loud, hard-pumping anthem about the ecstasy of being your own person. They were all near the front of the stage, even Zavier on a set of standing drums he somehow managed to play while bouncing around nearly as much as Ray.

Mish flew across the stage, dancing, wheeling, and playing, pausing at a mic to lend her voice to Ray's during the chorus. From that song, they slid straight into "Dreams unto You," a fan favorite that had everyone screaming.

Outstretched hands waved at Mish as she stalked up to the edge. She glimpsed smiles, even tears from some of the folks in the front row.

It was fucking heaven, and they were only two songs in.

By the time they made it to "Finding Light," Mish had stripped off her jacket and was flush with joy and excitement, soaking up the energy of the crowed, then throwing it right back at them.

She grinned at Ray, then unslung the bass from her shoulder.

Oh, the confusion in the crowd, the absolute sense of anticipation, as if they were all holding their breaths.

Ray always claimed he couldn't play their instruments, which wasn't true. He'd taught himself over time. He wasn't quite as good at their parts as they were or as versed. But he could play pretty darn well if he needed to.

And tonight, he'd need to, at least for this one. They'd decided during the bus ride that Ray and Mish would switch places.

When she handed off her bass to Ray, she leveled a look at him. "You take good care of her, kiddo."

Ray laughed. "If I don't, have Zav beat me later."

There wasn't any time for a snappy comeback. The audience reaction overwhelmed them, even through their ear protection.

In theory, he should've had his own bass, but part of the exchange was theatrics. Thankfully, he could play hers comfortably without adjusting the strap, making the switch easy. The techs had just about had a heart attack when they'd popped the idea on them. But they were rolling with it.

Mish strode up to Ray's mic stand, claimed the microphone, and spoke. "Hey, Boston. How you all doing out there?"

God, she felt the response vibrate through her. "We figured since I've been singing on this tour, it's only fair to give Ray a shot at bass. You think he's up for it?"

More shouts. Ray bounced on his toes and gave a shrug. But his fingers picked out a few chords expertly—and the bass was still in tune.

Good. "Yeah, I think he is, too. So here we go."

Zavier led into the song, and they were off. When the bass line came in, Mish's head spun, even as her hands twitched—one on the mic and the other at her side—with the need to play. The notes weren't hers. They didn't sound like hers, which she'd expected but hadn't been prepared for. She glanced over at Ray, and while he was moving with the beat, he was focused inward, his fingers flying like hers usually did.

A moment later, she was belting out lyrics, this time entirely by herself. Even when the chorus came around, Ray stayed off the mic. His grin was tremendous, though, and she sang a few words to him before leaping down the stage to serenade the left side of the pit, then back up. She waved out at everyone she couldn't see through the stage lighting.

Domino took over with his guitar solo, playing near Ray, and god, that was amazing to see. Those two best friends, grinning like only the music existed and they were back in high school. Then Zavier's drumming picked up and rolled over them all. Ray closed his eyes in ecstasy while Domino yelled and ran up onto Zav's kit, hovered there for a moment before leaping off to the right side of the stage.

Mish put the mic up again and sang her soul out. When they finally struck the last chords of the song, the applause and screams went straight to her heart. Everything felt light and magical and her eyes misted.

She looked out over the crowd. "Thank you all! Do you think Ray did a good job?"

Of course, they approved. He'd played well. Maybe with less flourish than she did, but Ray was a fucking genius, so everything he touched turned to gold.

Ray strode up to her mic, the one she used to sing backup vocals, and winked at her. "Totally not as good as you play," he said. "But I think you're gonna give me a run for my money singing." He turned to the audience. "What do you think? Should we write a song together?"

The fans reacted as if Ray had asked each and every one of them to marry him. The response was furious, and she felt the stage vibrating.

"Well, okay then!" His smile was a million dollars.

"I can't fucking wait." She said it to Ray more than the crowd, but it didn't matter. They were all there. Zavier laughed and Dom pirouetted, which was pretty impressive for someone in the boots he wore. Mish set the mic back in its stand, then claimed her bass from Ray.

"You were incredible." Unvarnished, open truth in his face. "Seriously. You could head your own band."

"I don't want to be anywhere but here with you guys." She set the strap of her bass back on her shoulder. "You know that!"

Ray grinned. "We're fucking lucky to have you." He waved at the bass. "You make that sing as gloriously as you do." With that, he turned and snagged a water bottle from the side of Zavier's kit, then bounced up to his mic. She grabbed a bottle, too, and downed half of it before setting it by her mic stand. She checked her chords, caught Domino's eye, and they made sure they were still tuned. Then, with the tapping of Zav's sticks, they were into another song.

Mish danced across the stage, playing with the band she loved more than anything else. This was her home.

By the end of the show, she was soaked with sweat and absolutely flying high. They'd done exactly what they'd set out to do. During the bows at the end, she tossed her guitar pick to a young woman in the front row, who burst into tears when she caught it.

There were tears in Mish's eyes, too, and for once, she wasn't that bothered by them.

CHAPTER SIXTEEN

After the show, in the chaos of cleaning up and changing for fan signing, David found himself grabbed by a sweaty, beaming Mish. She pulled him to her and claimed a kiss that nearly had him on his knees. "Ride with us tonight," she murmured. "Please. I need you there."

He hadn't been planning to. He'd traveled from the hotel to the venue with the band, but despite what she'd said when they'd been in bed together, he wasn't sure that was the right move, especially after his run-in with the reporter. But with Mish kissing him like that, and her breathless plea, he would be on that bus. "Sure."

She stole another kiss, then sprinted off to change. He found Marcella and let her know about the travel plans. Oh, the twitch of her lips when she tried not to smile. "I figured that would happen."

David could only rub his forehead. "Should I? I mean, there's a world of trouble lurking there."

Marcella sighed in an exaggerated way. "David. Go get your damn bag from the crew bus and put it on the band bus. Mish and the guys are safe and sound, but they need to clean up enough not to kill their fans with body odor."

He nearly choked on his laugh, then he went. Most of the crew was breaking down the sets and loading the truck, but a couple of folks were hauling instruments to the buses. "Hey, I'm heading that way, too. Need an extra set of hands?"

Travis nodded and handed him two guitar cases. "Those are Domino's. Don't drop them, and follow me."

He did as instructed, and Travis stowed them in the crew bus. "They don't ride with their instruments?"

"Nah. Domino's got an acoustic on the band bus. That's what they use when they're writing new songs. I hear Mish tends to sing the bass part, and Zavier can drum on any damn thing and make it sound sweet." He shook his head, then eyed David. "You hooking up with Mish?"

The parking lot was bright enough David had no doubt Travis saw him blanch. "Yeah. She asked me to ride with them to Philly."

Travis smiled and held up his fist for a bump. "Good. She needs someone to make her happy." He paused. "And to look after her." He waved a hand at the band bus. "She takes care of the whole damn band, you know? Those guys are like her brothers, and she'll stand against the world for 'em."

"It's all pretty mutual." David stared at the band bus.

"Still. Good that she wants you there."

He considered that. "Does that happen a lot?"

Travis cackled. "God, no. Mish fooled around with people, don't get me wrong. But you're the first she's ever asked to ride with her and the band." He sobered. "I've seen her watching you, my man. There's no mistaking *that* look."

"What look?"

He shrugged. "The same look she gets every time she's on a stage."

Oh shit. "I better get my bag."

Travis nodded solemnly, then headed back toward the venue.

David bounded up the stairs of the bus, greeted the driver,

threw together his bag, and headed to the other bus. That driver regarded him. "Joining us?"

"Yeah, looks like."

She grunted as if that had been expected. Which seemed like it had, for everyone but him.

When he got back to the venue, it was time for the signing. That was a whirlwind. David stood near Mish and kept a sharp eye on the fans, but nothing bad happened—only good. Fans sharing their stories. Beaming. Some crying. All the joy in the world.

The band was in that giddy stage of tired by the time they boarded the buses. David sank down onto a couch. They were all wiped out from the Boston show. Band, crew, Adrian. Even Marcella had the glassy-eyed look they all shared. Too much adrenaline, plus the stress of the morning, coupled with the absolute joy that had been that show.

"I need a fucking beer," he murmured, mostly to himself.

Domino—Dom—rooted around in the fridge and pulled out several beers. "Mish, you doing beer or wine tonight?"

"I could really use a shot of whiskey. But a beer will do." She leaned against David, her hand on his thigh.

Adrian rose from his seat, reached into his berth and pulled out a hip flask. "Why not both?"

"Adrian, you brilliant man, you." Mish held out both hands, and he tossed the flask. "Got a shot glass?"

"Nah. I figure if one of you gets sick, we're all getting it anyway."

"Shut your mouth, Adrian Doran," Dom said. "No one is getting sick."

Ray laughed. "I wouldn't worry. No one's ever gotten sick on our tours!"

"Shut it, Ray," Dom said. "You know that's not true."

"Eh." He waved Dom's words away. "Nothing more than a small cold."

God, these people. "Are they always like this?"

Zavier took one of the offered beers. "After a show like this? Yup."

Cold glass touched David's arm. "Endorphins," Dom said. "An hour after we're on the road, we'll all be crashed out and snoring."

"Except me, because I don't fucking snore," Mish said.

"No, you don't." Zavier took a pull on his beer. "That is, in fact, Ray's job for all of us."

"Hey!" Ray looked indignant, and David couldn't help laughing.

Mish downed a gulp of Adrian's whiskey, then chased it with a swallow of beer. "Damn, I needed that." She snuggled in closer to David. "Need this, too," she said.

If the others heard, they were polite enough to pretend they hadn't. Which, David guessed, was bus etiquette. He put his arm around her. Given that Ray was pretty much draped over Zavier, he suspected that was fine.

Zavier gave David a little grin and stroked Ray's hair.

True to Dom's words, once the bus was moving and they'd consumed their drinks and babbled for about a half hour, everyone slinked off to their racks. David had thrown his bag on one of the empty berths, figuring that's where he'd end up. After they'd all gotten changed, Mish pulled him into the lounge in the back and closed the curtain.

"If the curtain's drawn in the middle of the night, chances are there's something going down." She paused. "Or someone."

"Don't think I have the energy, darling."

"I know I don't." She did cup his face and kiss him. "I'm glad you're here, though. It's—better. As long as it's okay with you."

He took her hands from his face and held them in his own. Because he had to be honest with her. "Mish, what's going on between us is wonderful. Amazing. No idea where it's going, but I want to see."

"But?" She had a wry look.

"I'm still here to do a job. To keep you safe. To keep the band safe. I'd be lying if I told you I wasn't worried that getting this close, feeling what I do, is gonna get in the way of me staying sharp and keeping you—all of you—out of danger."

"But?" Her look had softened.

"I'll be where you need me to be. I can't help what I feel." Sometimes he saw years and years when he looked into her eyes. "You want me here. I'm here for you, princess."

Her next kiss had passion and longing and everything David was afraid to name. He knew what the tumble and lurch in his chest meant. Understood exactly why his soul soared every time Mish touched him.

He was falling in love with his rock queen.

They left the lounge and moved to their respective racks. Not enough room to share one comfortably, though they both eyed Mish's with the same thought. In the end, David put Marly in her hands. "I think he enjoys you better, anyway."

She'd laughed and kissed David once more before slipping into her berth.

Once he'd settled in his own rack, he didn't think he'd fall to sleep given how he was turning the day over and over in his mind, but the sound of the road cut through his mind, slipping him out of his thoughts. That's all it took for slumber to find him.

So weird to be in a venue *this* early for a concert. It wasn't even noon yet. Mish had already sucked down several cups of Adrian's coffee in the greenroom and was on another now. Somehow, Adrian had managed to insist that he provide the beans and make the joe, rather than relying on the catering service the venue used. Guess being a big-name band helped smooth over that.

Twisted Wishes had never been obnoxious in their needs, so insisting on their own coffee was probably way low on the Band Diva list.

After the tumult of the day in Boston and the show that'd blown all of them away, they'd played another stellar show in Philadelphia. Now they were between Baltimore and DC for a stop at a music festival, as one of the headlining big-name bands.

Five Asylum was there, too, and that was also strange—to be meeting up with them as equals this time, not as their opening act. On social media, Adrian was all over the two bands meeting again. He'd been strategizing with the woman who was his counterpart, along with Marcella and a man she recognized as Five Asylum's band manager.

Gregor Daye, Five Asylum's lead singer, pulled Ray aside for a private chat, and both men returned with smiles, though Gregor's was more subdued. He also took a cup of Adrian's coffee—then lobbied to hire Adrian for himself. "What the hell you put into this? And how much do I have to pay you to leave these louts?" It was all said with humor and amusement.

Adrian grinned. "The ingredients are top secret."

"And he's mine," Domino said. "Or I'm his, or whatever."

"And Dominic is priceless," Adrian said.

"Oh god." Gregor mock grimaced. "Aren't you two stinking cute?"

Mish, though, had kept away from most of the action. Everything felt off. Nothing had happened at the concert in Philly, and both David and Adrian swore up and down that no new messages had come in. Marcella backed them up on that.

"I'd tell you," David had said. "You know that."

She did. Adrian might demur, but David wouldn't lie.

Every day they got closer, their relationship firmer, and Mish fell more for the man. If she were honest with herself, she liked that he was there, at her back, watching out for her. Sure, Twisted watched out for each other, but no one had her back like David did.

It should've made her relax. But that horrible sensation she'd had during the radio show hadn't let up. Somewhere out there was a man obsessed with her. She'd heard his voice and still couldn't place it. Many voices sounded familiar, but this one had made her stomach tumble and her anxiety soar. She shivered in the heat of the day.

Gregor must have noticed, because he sauntered over. "Hey, lady. How're you doing?"

She wasn't in the mood to lie, even if Gregor had helped them find a kick-ass lawyer during their scare with Ray. "I've been a lot fucking better, to be honest."

"I heard scuttlebutt about an abusive caller. The shitty assholes will get to you every time."

She couldn't help a small smile. "Yeah, well." She gestured at herself. "Hence the mood."

"Fucking world. You play harder and better than pretty much all the men out here, and you get crap for it." He grunted. "And here I am telling you what you already know."

His words unlocked something in her chest and lifted her spirits. "That acknowledgment is nice. Thanks, Gregor." Mish held out her hand, and he clasped it and pulled her into one of those backslap hugs she'd seen him give other band members.

At least some folks treated her like an equal and not a piece of meat or a porcelain doll.

"You take care, Mish. And don't let the jackasses get you down, as my grandpap used to say."

She laughed. "He give you any advice on how to handle them?"

"Oh yeah, but I don't recommend what he said to

anyone." He shook his head. "Pappy's advice consisted of a shotgun, the backwoods, and the fear of god."

She couldn't help her bark of laughter. "Yeah, not my style." Even though a part of her wanted to strangle the unknown dude.

Gregor gave her shoulder a squeeze. "We gotta get ready, but we're gonna watch you play, for old times' sake."

"Thanks," she said. "I hope we still live up to the hype."

"Of course you guys do."

He and Five Asylum filtered out, and Twisted Wishes got down to business. There was no fan encounter at this event—no time between their warmups, sound checks, dressing, the show, and all the other acts. Plus the general chaos of the festival crowd was intense enough without all the extra bits.

Juggling all the sets and bands and sound checks was hard on the techs and venue staff, yet somehow the crews made it work. Twisted Wishes went on for their sound checks at about the time they'd been told to be ready, got off when asked, and managed to be dressed to play their abbreviated set when they were supposed to. The concert even started reasonably on time.

The vibe of the afternoon crowd went a long way to settling Mish's nerves. The throb of the audience, the vibrations of their instruments magnified by the huge speakers. The music played down in her bones. Zavier's drumming, Domino's screaming guitar, and Ray's voice were inside her, part of her movements and her own soul.

Wasn't anything better than being on stage. Not a fucking thing in the world. She danced and played with Domino, sang with Ray, and flirted with Zavier, and her heart soared. Unfettered, she was giddy with excitement and pleasure.

Music relaxed her more than sex did, though it was a close contest—both were intense. But when it came to playing in front of fans in tears because Twisted Wishes was *there,* right in front of them—that was something she never wanted to get used to. *That* was love.

They gave the fans joy and pain and anger and hope, all tossed out on a messy but perfect string of notes and beats, twined around Ray's words and his voice, and then it was all thrown back at them, through screams and singing and the sparkling of tears and sweat and smiles on a sea of faces. Love returned in outstretched hands and shouts of their names.

What could be better than that?

In the moment when they'd finished playing "Lightning" and before they launched into "White Hot Midnight," Mish spied David in his black T-shirt and jeans, a smile on his face and his gaze fixed on her as if she were the only one that mattered in the universe.

That look wasn't part of his job at all. Mish's chest ached even as her heart screamed upward like the opening notes of Domino's guitar. She closed her eyes and let her fingers and her bass answer what she'd seen in David's eyes.

The hope and fear there. The love neither of them wanted to admit they felt.

Mish looked over to Ray, then spun close to the mic to lend her voice to his. This was the way she knew to express how she felt. Note by note, song by song. She hoped David understood, that he got it.

Mish always performed her best for the fans. They were Twisted Wishes's lifeblood. But today, she played for David. For their unknown future and their simmering present.

Ray must have noticed, because he gave her such a *look* when they finished, but there was no time to probe. Zavier led them directly into the next song.

Mish threw her heart and soul into that one, too, and the next, until the end, when the crowd screamed and she tossed her pick and blew Adrian a kiss before disappearing back behind the stage with the band.

Mish was a live wire who desperately wanted privacy, David, and a good fuck. She made do with water to quench her thirst.

As the adrenaline and joy wore off, the tightness in her body and mind returned, that unsafe feeling, and that voice—that damn voice over that damned phone line.

"Fuck," she said under her breath. Thankfully, no one heard.

She went about changing and cleaning herself up enough to head back to the bus. Ray perched on a rotating stool and spun himself around. "We should go out tonight. There's that club we can get into now, and I hear it's karaoke night."

Adrian held up his hands. "Not it this time!"

Mish said nothing. Usually she loved going out, wanted to tonight. But her mood was tanking fast. 'Cause she'd have to figure out what to wear, and what if that got her another call at another radio station or another email or...

This time, the *fuck* came out louder.

"Mish?" Ray stood and crossed the room.

She held up a hand. "Sorry, kiddo. I'm—thinking too much."

"We can nix the idea. Not gonna leave you out of anything." He gave her shoulder a squeeze.

There it was, the other issue. Her problems trickling out to the others. "No, the club sounds great. I want to go. I—god. I'm a mess."

"You're not." He glanced at Zavier, and something seemed to pass between them. Those two were so often in sync. Ray focused on Mish again. "Not any more than the rest of us."

Yeah, they'd all had their moments, but she hated spinning out of control. Then again, Ray'd been at that point not so long ago. "Let's go. I can do this."

Ray nodded, and over his shoulder, Zavier slipped out the door. "You change your mind, let us know? We've got your back."

"I know you do, sweetheart."

They all did. All the important people in her life. Still, Mish felt like she was letting everyone down by not being able to shove this shithead situation into the back of her mind and enjoy their rise to fame and the love of their fans.

And David. Then again, she wouldn't have known David if not for the shithead.

Mish rubbed her forehead and got back to cleaning herself up. She'd go. Find an outfit that wasn't...so fucking controversial, or maybe throw every caution to the wind. She could do this. Even if she hated the thought of stepping out into public right now.

CHAPTER SEVENTEEN

David was surprised when Zavier tracked him down after the show. He'd stayed to watch Two Times Strong, and also to recover from the dizzying effect of watching Mish with Twisted Wishes. He'd okayed it with Ray and Marcella—security was so tight even he, with a freaking crew badge and all-access pass and the right damn colored bracelet, had a hard time getting backstage.

He downed half a bottle of water he'd claimed from security and upbraided himself for becoming so distracted during the show. He had to stop watching her on stage, because doing so wasn't going to let him see any threat to her should one appear. He was consumed by Mish and the band when they performed, like everyone else in the audience.

But sometime after Twisted Wishes left and before Two Times Strong came on stage, Zavier slipped out from backstage and wandered up the aisle toward David like he wasn't a fucking big-name rock star.

Fans stopped in their tracks. Venue security did a double take.

David met him halfway down the aisle. "What the hell are you doing?" His voice pitched up a notch, which should have annoyed him, but didn't because fucking Zavier Demos was walking around in public at a music festival and he was going to start a riot.

"I came to talk to you." Zavier's eyes were hidden by sunglasses, but his smile was full of that devilish charm he was known for.

"You can't just—" David gestured with his hands. "You'll start a scene."

"Nah." He clapped David on the shoulder. "I've got security with me." Now there was laughter in his voice.

David dropped the volume of his own. "Oh, fuck you." Didn't put any heat into it.

"Not your type, I think. Besides, turns out with Ray I'm hopelessly monogamous, which is a strange thing, indeed."

That was a train of thought David decided not to follow. He led Zavier up to the soundboard—there were techs there, but also added guards who would keep fans away. They moved away from the techs so no one could overhear, especially with the music that was playing from the pavilion speakers.

"So why are you risking life and limb and your husband's ire to come talk to me?"

"I enjoy causing a little shock and awe once in a while," Zavier murmured. "And Ray asked me to find you."

David's heart dropped to the ground. "Did something happen to Mish?"

Zavier held up both hands and his expression fell open. "No! Nothing!" He ran a hand through his hair. "I should've thought about how that might sound, rather than playing Mr. Obnoxiously Cool."

David laughed, part in humor, mostly in relief. "Well, you play the part very well." He dusted his hands on his thighs. "So what do you need from me?"

That earned him a rueful smile. "We—the band—were

thinking about going out tonight. To a club. Blow off a little steam."

God, a club could be a nightmare. "What kind of club are we talking? Logistics-wise...that could be an issue."

"I'm not—we're not asking for you to be security. It's a well-known place." He rattled off a name, and yeah, it was. "And they're known for their security and we certainly wouldn't be the first names to drop in."

David rubbed his chin. "Or even the most famous."

Zavier shrugged in acknowledgement. "Truth."

"So if not security, what do you need from me?"

In a rare moment, Zavier looked sheepish. He even slipped off his sunglasses before answering. "To talk Mish into going."

A thousand thoughts bumped off each other in David's mind. He grasped at the most important one. "Zavier, if Mish doesn't want to go, I'm not going to coerce her."

Once more Zavier held up his hands. "It's not like that. She's..." He let out a frustrated sigh. "Mish is fine on stage. Playing. On the bus, because you've been there. But Ray and Dom are worried, and so am I."

"So you want to make her go to a club." David knew his voice was flat, and his temper was showing. These three should know better.

For his part, Zavier looked damn uncomfortable. "I'm not explaining this well."

"Which is unusual for you." Zavier knew what he wanted, and said what he meant. "So try again?"

He met David's gaze, and his blue eyes had more than a hint of concern in them. "I'm worried about her. Deeply. That makes me less precise." He seemed to chew on some words before continuing. "Mish *wants* to go to the club. We decided as a band, like we do with everything. But she's worried about the publicity, her mood, the next show, what to wear. *Everything*." He spread out his hands. "The very idea is stressing her out, and the whole point of going is to *relax*. When Ray offered to nix the idea, she insisted we should all go. But...it's also obvious she's not happy about it."

Okay, so he had an idea of what Zavier and Ray were asking of him. "You want me to help Mish unwind at the club. Give her a reason to go."

Zavier considered this. "Yes, something like that." He dropped his voice. "She's scared, and I haven't seen her this scared since—" His face tightened and flickered with anger and sorrow. "Since Ray nearly died. Ray never saw that fear, so he's more worried than Dom and me. We want to help her, but leaning on us is uncomfortable for her sometimes."

"Other times, it's exactly what she needs." Because David had seen that, too. When she wanted a hug or needed a laugh. Family.

Zavier glanced down, then nodded. Agreement without using words. A strange form of reluctance, and David wondered how many people ever saw this side of Zavier outside of the band.

"Not this time. Right now, she needs *you*." Zavier paused, and that sly smile came back. "Plus, there's karaoke, and I hear you owe her a beer."

David almost broke into laughter, but he kept it to a huff of breath. "Okay, payback might pique her interest. Especially if I promise to sing for her. I can do what you're asking." He gestured to the stage. "Shall we head back?"

Zavier looked around. "I wonder if they'd let us watch Two Times Strong from here. In the wings is fine, but it's been a damn long time since I've been out in the crowd at a concert."

Well, there was only one way to find out. David asked the sound guys and the guards and no one seemed to care, as long as the fans didn't bother Zavier or cause a scene. Since they hadn't yet, they likely wouldn't. Zavier texted Ray, and stayed and watched. He didn't sing along to the songs, but he nodded and bobbed with the beats. David sang, and that got him a smile from Zavier.

When Two Times Strong's set was over, Zavier leaned over. "Mish does need to hear you sing."

Heat to his cheeks, and a flip in his stomach. "I can't sing like she or Ray does."

Zavier's smile was a flash of teeth. "I'll let them judge that." He nodded toward the stage. "*Now* we should get back."

They did. Didn't take long for Zavier to get cleaned up and changed before a limo arrived, this time an SUV for the six of them, since Marcella begged off. "I need to take a stab at some press releases I've been putting off."

Mish crinkled her nose, but she was focused on the topic Zavier let slip earlier. "I can't believe Zav heard you sing before I did," she said.

"I'm not sure it was really singing. More like belting out lyrics at Two Times Strong." David shifted in the seat, his leather jacket creaking in ways that sent shivers down his spine. Always loved that sound, but good leather was pricy. This jacket he'd borrowed from Domino.

"Still." Her fingers were in his and she smelled of vanilla. She wore a green dress that was short and sparkled when she moved. Silver and emerald jewelry and a set of patterned black stockings rounded out the look. Her heels were killer. He didn't need to ask if she'd dance in those, given what footwear she wore on stage and how she could move around while playing.

His outfit was pretty tame for club-wear. His own jeans again, tight in a way he liked, a brilliant blue tank top, and the jacket, with all its studs and chains, like something he'd only dreamed of wearing during his punk days.

"You like Two Times Strong?" That from Ray.

David tore his attention from Mish's legs and met Ray's gaze. "Yeah, they're really good. I didn't know them before they were your opening act—well, I'd heard 'Like A Little Light' but didn't know it was them. I looked them up when you said who you were touring with."

"You like us or them better?" Domino had a smile that was just shy of a smirk, until Adrian poked him and he twisted in his seat. "Hey!"

"That's not a nice question." Adrian's voice was mild. He was in dress slacks, but wore a dark red T-shirt that clung to his frame. He also sported a leather cuff similar to the one Domino wore.

It wasn't a *bad* question. David understood where Dom was coming from. "Your style is different. You're more punk, they're more electronic pop. But you're also similar. Energetic, loud, and queer. I can see why people are fans of both bands. You guys are phenomenal and the more mature band, hands down. I'm not saying that for the paycheck, either. I'm out there hearing you play, same as the crowds, and I know what I'm hearing. There's a level of skill in Twisted Wishes that's several notches above Two Times Strong." He glanced out the window, then focused on Domino. "But they're gonna go places in a year or two, mark my words."

Zavier had one of his thoughtful looks on. "Yes, they will."

The conversation shifted to what Ray thought of Two Times Strong and how Twisted Wishes was helping them up the ladder, as much as they could.

"They're good kids," Mish said. "They'll be fine."

"And they've seen us navigate the pitfalls," Zavier added.

"Or not navigate them." Ray shook his head. "Lane's got balls. They'll be more fine than I was."

A few minutes later, they pulled up to the club and stepped out into a flurry of exclamations and flashes of cell phones and more professional cameras. Mish took David's hand.

"You know," he murmured. "People are going to think we're together."

"Good," she said.

They strode into the club with more ease than David expected, but then he should have seen that coming. He was with Twisted Wishes. Some of his bewilderment must have slipped through because Adrian huffed a laugh. "You'll get used to it."

Maybe. Maybe not. He'd been with corporate movers and shakers and they could unlock doors. The way Twisted Wishes moved through the world was completely different, though. Plus he had no idea what would happen when the tour ended and his contract ended, too. Business was why, ultimately, he was here, except everything professional had been thrown out the window by the woman holding his hand.

He shoved those thoughts aside when they entered the club proper. The atmosphere was loud, thumping, and both dark and bright. Mish's laugh was worth hearing, though. "Okay," she said. "You win. I'm glad I came."

Ray had the biggest fucking grin on his face. He wore a mesh shirt that both hid and exposed his tattoos, and leather pants that were probably going to have to be peeled off him at the end of the night. Zavier snaked an arm around Ray and pulled him close. That man wore all black, from his pants to the tight tank top that showed off his drummer's arms. The look in Zavier's eyes was one David had glimpsed a few times on the bus—unguarded and intense—as if he were trying to figure out how he could possess all of Ray at once. Then it shifted and he smiled. "Care to dance?"

Ray's expression was one of bliss and happiness. "Of course." Then they were gone, out into a sea of people, with Adrian and Domino following a few moments later.

Mish tugged David to her. "Dance or sing?"

"Can't we do both?" He'd give about anything to see Mish

move on the dance floor and be right *there* rather than down in the pit or up in one of the aisles when she shimmied her way across the stage. "Besides, I'm gonna need a drink before I sing for freaking Twisted Wishes."

She laughed at that, and did the unthinkable—stole a kiss from him right there and then. The artificial sound of cell phone cameras whirred nearby.

Half of him was ecstatic, the other half deeply worried.

"Let's go check on the other guys." Mish tugged him in the same direction the other couples had gone.

Couples. They were a couple. No taking that kiss back. "Marcella's gonna have our heads," he said.

Oh, her smile. "I'm sure she had a statement all written up." Mish hugged him and he wrapped an arm around her waist. In for a penny, as the saying went.

The dance floor was a colorful mass of writhing bodies, moving in time with the music. They spotted Zavier and Ray —how could you miss them moving against each other the way they were? The look on Zavier's face was one of sublime satisfaction. Ray had his eyes closed.

"There's no doubt that they're together, is there?" David spoke the words close to Mish's ear.

She shook her head, a wide smile lighting up her face. Then she pointed over at Adrian and Domino, and holy shit, Adrian could dance. And keep up with Domino as they careered around the floor in movements that looked like ballroom crossed with thrash.

"I think you're gonna find me a piss-poor dancer after that."

"You're gonna be fine. I've seen you move." Mish's voice was sultry and hot in his ear. Before he could think otherwise, he pulled her out onto the floor. They fell in together, turning, twisting, Mish twirling in a move he recognized, and he caught her hand. They flowed together, stepping in time with each other and the thudding pulse.

"You sly shit! You ballroom dance." Her eyes sparkled in the ever-changing lights.

His answer was to swing her around in the tiny space they'd carved out on the floor. "Might as well give the cameras something to love."

"I'll give you something to love..." It came off as a challenge. The music changed and picked up the pace—and so did she.

He let her lead because his heart and soul ached. She'd given him someone he could love if he let himself. If the circumstances were a little different.

If he wanted to take that leap of faith.

God, dancing with Mish was like heaven and hell all rolled into one. She moved like magic and his body responded to her, the beat that thrummed through his bones, and the need that sang in his veins. He didn't know how long they were out—long enough that they swapped who was leading several times—before Domino broke between them. "Ray wants to catch his breath, get a drink, then hear David sing."

"Well—" Mish spun Domino around. "Who are we to keep Ray Van Zeller waiting?"

Dom led them to the bar where some of the club patrons were belting out a rendition of "Love Shack." Wasn't bad as far as karaoke went. Adrian, Ray, and Zavier had already acquired drinks. Both he and Mish opted for beer.

"I'd do shots," Mish said. "But we need to be on the bus later."

Ray closed his eyes and leaned against Zavier. "Don't remind me."

Whatever Zavier whispered into Ray's ear earned him a groan. "You're fucking evil, Zav."

"It's why you married me," Zavier said.

"I thought we got married for tax purposes."

Zavier laughed, a rare, uninhibited bubbly sound.

"There's a story there," David said.

Mish huffed. "Oh yeah. But part of that is true, even if they're gonna grow old together and end up bitching about the weather while sitting in rocking chairs on some porch somewhere in sixty years."

Ray still had his eyes closed but was smiling. "That'll be fun."

"It's not much of a story, really." Zavier tucked his hand into Ray's pocket. "I'm aromantic, that's all. But yeah, Mish is close. Ray and I will probably argue about using the peanut butter knife in the jelly jar more than the weather."

"I hate dirtying a second knife." Ray's smile hadn't faded.

"And I hate picking peanut butter out of my jelly."

Ray opened his eyes and met Zavier's gaze. "I *know*." He grinned from ear to ear.

Zavier's lips twitched up. "Oh. I *see*."

David absorbed the information and the banter. "So do I." Everything he'd observed fell into place with Zavier's statement. Queer band, indeed.

"You gonna sing me a song?" Mish's breath warmed David's ear.

Yeah, he was. In front of the rest of Twisted Wishes. Someone else was waiting their turn, which gave David time to compose himself and pick a song. He'd already half a mind as to what to sing, figured they'd never have it, and was both pleased and a little shocked when he found it in their database.

Yeah, maybe it was somewhat on the nose, but what the heck. After a rendition of "Carry on Wayward Son" by the person in front of him, David took the stage. Of course Twisted Wishes whistled and clapped, which intrigued the crowd, and there were the cell phones being held up.

Well, in for a pound, too.

When the opening notes of Erasure's "Chains of Love" started, David jumped right in, singing loud and strong. He also ignored anything out beyond the end of the stage, because fuck if he was going to stare out at that crowd, those cameras, or Twisted Wishes. He'd stumble over notes and probably off the stage, too.

Now he understood why Dom had a rock persona. It was one thing to sing while tipsy with friends at the local queer bar, another to sing at *this* club in front of strangers, a famous rock band, and the woman he was falling for.

When he got toward the end of the song, he did look out over the crowd and found Mish. Joy suffused her face, though she wasn't grinning. Her expression was profound and full of love.

He was so fucking glad the song ended, because he wasn't going to get another note out of his throat after seeing Mish like that. He walked off the stage to clapping and cheering, and worked his way through a crowd of smiles and photos. Mish held out her hand and he gave his to her.

Mish pulled him into her arms. "That was fantastic," she said into his ear. "Zav was right about your voice."

"Still ain't like yours, rock queen." He pulled back from the embrace. "I think I need the rest of my beer."

She chuckled but let go, and David downed the rest of his brew in a few swallows. Someone else was up on the stage now and that singer drew attention away from their corner of the bar. Thank god.

"Mish's right." Ray's tone was serious and professional. "You've got pipes and excellent control. You *could* sing."

David considered that. His voice had changed a lot—vocal cords thickening—but he'd kept singing. Even joining a queer choir early on. Plus Ray wasn't the type to lie, especially not about music. "Maybe. I don't have the passion you guys have. Singing's fun, you know, but I wouldn't want to do it for a living."

Ray laughed, then coughed. He took a swig of his drink. "Fucking dry air."

"Does take passion to do what we do." Mish nursed her beer. "Lots of downs to go with all those ups."

"I'm not cut out for that. Or for the spotlight." David spotted another cell phone pointed their direction. "Though I'm getting used to that."

"The spotlight is a blessing and a curse," Domino said. "Everyone has their way of dealing." He was sober for a moment, then grinned. "Mine's being me." He grabbed Adrian's hand. "Dance with me? I want to show you off some more."

Adrian laughed. "Dancing's fine, baby. But who's showing who off?" He let Domino take his hand and pull him away from the bar.

David watched them go. "I don't know if I can do that." The words slipped out before he thought about what they meant.

"Date a rock star?" Mish's words were soft.

"No." Except that sounded wrong, too. His heart leapt into his throat. "Adrian makes it look easy." He met her gaze. "I'm here *with* you, but this is new to me." Wasn't what he should be doing, not as a professional. But damn, his heart and soul wanted this. "I'm just saying, I need to figure it out."

She seemed to take those words in and turn them over in her head. "I get that. I don't want to be a burden."

Those words weren't just for him. Out of the corner of his eye, he saw Ray shift. "You're not." David took her hands. "You most certainly are not." Through their entwined fingers, Mish trembled, the tension evident. "Wanna go show up those guys on the dance floor? We do make a pretty good pair."

Mish's grip softened. "Yeah, we do." She paused. "I'm glad you're here."

By the bar, Ray shifted again, leaning into Zavier and whispering something.

"Me, too," David said.

Mish led them back to the dance floor, and they ended up spinning and sliding and dancing circles around the other couples. By the time the night was over, David's legs ached and his face hurt from smiling.

When the band flopped back into the limo, Mish pulled him close. "Thank you. I needed to get out for a while. Not think."

"It was my pleasure," David murmured.

Mish kicked Ray in the shin—not hard—but enough to make him start. "Hey!"

"Don't think I don't know you planned this, kiddo. You and your coconspirators."

"Me?" Ray grinned. "No idea what you could mean."

The whole limo dissolved into laughter that turned into murmurs of conversation until they returned to the tour buses.

When they climbed out, Marcella was waiting for them, looking both smug and annoyed. "I see you all had fun." She waved her phone.

Adrian shrugged. "Photos and video happen when we go out."

Oh god. Video. David wiped a hand down his face and over his beard. "My singing's out there, isn't it?"

"Yeah, it is. Nice voice." She paused. "You and Mish playing tonsil hockey is *also* out there." Marcella's expression hinted at concern. "You guys making this official? Or should we *no-comment* it?"

He met Mish's gaze, and the same hesitancy and need lay in her, too. David cleared his throat. "It's probably too late to put the cat back into the bag."

"I should probably make a pussy joke here, but I'm gonna refrain." Mish managed her most innocent smile.

Marcella rolled her eyes. "*Thank* you."

Ray looked like he might choke for laughing so hard. It ended in a coughing fit.

"Yeah," Mish said, her tone serious. "Why don't we say we're dating?"

Something flipped in David's chest. Warmth. Joy. Fear. He swallowed. "That's fine with me."

Marcella nodded, as did Adrian. "Got it covered," he said. She strode to the crew bus while the rest of them boarded the band bus.

Dom headed to the bathroom to strip off his makeup while the rest of the band changed into more comfortable clothes. Not much privacy, but then none of them were getting naked. David followed their lead and pulled on sweatpants and a T-shirt.

A soft touch on his back alerted him to Mish's closeness. "You fine with us?" In the quiet of the bus, the others had to have heard. But they were minding their business.

"Yeah." He was. Mostly. "You're a hell of a woman. I'm honored." He paused. "Dating's gonna make the job interesting, I can't lie about that. But I'll have your back, and the band's, too."

"Good." She dropped a brief kiss on his lips. "Don't think I don't know what you did for me tonight."

"Your bandmates love you, too, you know." The words came out before he even considered the meaning. *Shit.* Because it was still too soon for his heart to be so involved.

She leaned in and kissed him on the forehead. "I know." That seemed to be an answer for both what he'd said and what he insinuated. "Come have some water. Wind down with us. Pretty sure we're all gonna crash soon."

They ended up spread out among the couches and the table by the coffeepot and sink, chatting about nothing in particular until yawns and bleary eyes overtook David. He rose, gave Mish a quick kiss, then excused himself to finish his nightly routine and crawl into his berth.

The rumble of the road threatened to pull him down into sleep almost as soon as he hit the mattress, but a thought kept him awake and peering up at the dark, close roof above his head. He was dating Mish Sullivan. Openly.

There was the media to contend with, but in the grand scheme of things, they were harmless.

Mish's stalker wasn't going to take kindly to her change in relationship status. That drove fear deep into David's heart. This wasn't a job anymore. The whole thing was so far from a job that he felt unmoored for the first time in years.

He flattened his hand over his chest where his tags would've been, if they weren't on Marly, and that brought a kind of comfort—soon those would be with Mish in the little cubicle she'd sleep in.

A little piece of David, close to her heart.

CHAPTER EIGHTEEN

The delicious aroma of Adrian's magical coffee roused Mish from her sleep, though the rumble of the bus and the soft feel of Marly pressed against her neck enticed her to stay curled up in her pod until she identified the voices murmuring softly at the front of the bus. Adrian, of course, but also Zavier, and the voice she'd come to love so much: David.

She couldn't make out the words, but the usual thrum of snark and laughter were missing, and that set her on edge. So much for relaxing.

She checked the time on her phone, gave Marly a boop on the nose, then crawled out of her berth. "Please tell me there's a mug of Adrian's coffee with my name on it."

"I didn't see any mugs with your name on them, but get me a Sharpie and I can fix that." David rose from his seat and headed for the coffeepot.

"Now there's a thought," Zavier said. "Individualized mugs. Maybe Ray'd stop stealing mine."

"Never in a million years." Adrian clicked off his phone. "Besides, you like it when he steals your things."

Zav's smile was all devil. "Yes, I do."

David handed her a mug of deep, rich coffee and she

inhaled. "God, I feel like I'm in one of those old coffee ads." She sank onto one of the couches. "Best part of waking up."

"I'm honored to jog a jingle memory." Adrian grinned.

The banter died immediately, like the guys didn't know what to say. Something big hung over all their heads. *Fuck.*

Mish sipped her coffee and peered at the men around her. "Okay, so what happened?"

David looked all kinds of unhappy, and even the normally unflappable Zavier squirmed. Adrian turned his phone on, tapped at the screen, then handed it over.

She set the mug aside and took the phone. An email. She skimmed the contents and cringed. Yup. Her stalker. More orders she didn't read as she scrolled. At the bottom was a photo of her and David, from after he'd finished singing, when they'd kissed. She handed the phone back to Adrian and wished she could unsee the email.

Her next swallow of coffee was larger. "Well, we expected photos to be out on social media. I'm not surprised he emailed." Revolted, but not shocked. "I didn't read the message, though. Guessing it's the usual?"

David nodded. "I am not nearly man enough for you as well."

"Oh, for fuck's sake," she muttered, and downed another gulp of coffee.

"Thing is, he doesn't know I'm trans, so that was normal masculine bullshit. Comments would have been worse if he knew." David refillled his mug, then sat next to her. "You okay?"

"Like I said, I figured this would happen. I have no regrets." Mish patted David's thigh. "Except that we're on a bus and I couldn't take you to my room last night." She cupped a hand around his neck and pulled him into a lingering kiss.

When they came up for air, David chuckled. Adrian was

smiling, and Zav's grin was more smug than usual. She mock glared at him. "What?"

"Nothing." Zavier drank his coffee. "Just wondering if you took my advice."

Oh *god*, that man.

"Advice?" Of course David asked.

"Zav said to become friends first. I think we managed that."

"Friends before love?"

"Friends before anything serious," Zavier said. "You'll have to ask someone else about love."

"You really did get married for tax purposes?"

That made Zavier laugh, and pretty loudly, too. "Well, and wanting Ray and his friendship for the rest of my life, yes."

David, nodded. "I understand that."

A moan rose from Dom's bunk. "Jesus, some of us need our beauty sleep."

Adrian sauntered over to the berth and opened the curtain a sliver. "Eh, you're cute as you are. There's coffee if you want to get up."

"Fine," Dom said.

This was what she needed. Her lover. Her band. The banter of family. Mish shoved that email away. They had a show tonight—that was the important thing. The tour and her family.

"Speaking of beauty rest, where is our fearless leader?" Everyone was up but Ray.

Zavier twisted his mouth. It didn't hide his worried expression. "When I prodded him this morning, he groaned and buried his head under the pillow. I hope he's just tired from our night of fun."

God. Mish prayed that was the case as well. But Ray had taunted the gods of touring earlier. She matched Zavier's expression.

"What?" David's question was spoken softly.

She wrapped an arm around his shoulder. "I'm sure Zavier wore him out dancing, that's all." She would not *think* of Ray being sick. Would not.

Zavier's mouth quirked, as if he wanted to say more but thought the better of it.

She jostled David. "You're not upset that your singing is out there on the internet, are you? Or...us?"

David bobbed his head side to side. "Not upset. It's strange to hear my voice, though. Last time I heard a recording of my singing, I had a different range." He sipped his coffee. "And I'm not upset at being seen kissing you."

She laughed, despite the rock in her stomach. Someone *else* was upset at David kissing her, but she wouldn't let that fucker spoil all she'd worked for. Nor what she wanted. David was a gift that had emerged out of this mess—and she'd take that.

Another round of coffee for all of them led to a discussion of the perfect karaoke songs, until a raspy cough from the bunks sent a shiver of fear down Mish's spine.

Oh no. No, *no*. Ray was not sick. He couldn't be sick.

When Ray emerged from his bunk, he looked groggier than he should've. Zavier was on his feet in an instant, but Ray waved him away. "Just need coffee." His voice was only thin air and the expression that crossed his face after was one of pure dismay. "Oh shit."

Oh shit, indeed. Mish leaned against David, and he looked worried, too.

Zavier felt Ray's forehead. "You're warm."

Fuck.

They still had a concert that night. They could cancel, but no one wanted that, least of all Ray. Mish rose and poured Ray a cup of coffee. Both Adrian and Dom had tight, horrified expressions.

Ray pushed Zavier back a few inches. "I just got up." That came out of him in a whisper. "I'm fine."

Zavier snatched the coffee from Mish's hand. "You're not fine. And you're going back to bed."

Ray's mouth set into a firm line. He glared at Zavier, then pried the coffee from him and took a sip, then another. "Look," he said, and his voice sounded stronger, "in this, you don't get to be the master. It's still the band, and I'm still the leader."

Every muscle in Zavier's body tightened and he huffed before stomping off to the back of the bus.

Ray shut his eyes. "I adore him," he murmured. "I do. I do."

Dom shifted on the couch. "You'll kill your voice if you sing tonight."

Ray met Dom's stare and nodded, but shrugged. Likely trying not to talk too much. Rest the voice.

"What are you gonna do, right?" Mish spoke the words that were likely on Ray's tongue.

A wan smile, but he tapped his head.

"You've got an idea?" Mish patted the seat next to David. "You wanna sit down and drink your coffee? I can talk to Zavier."

She couldn't describe the complicated expression the passed over Ray's face, but he sat. Then tapped her arm and nodded at the back of the bus.

She gave David's shoulder a squeeze. "Watch over him, huh?"

David nodded and Ray rolled his eyes before sipping more coffee.

Mish steeled herself and headed to the back. Wasn't surprised to find Zavier pacing the small length of the lounge, but it wasn't anger emanating from him, it was *worry*.

"Zavier," she said.

He didn't look up. "He's sick. He needs to rest."

"He's *Ray* and we're on tour. You think a cold is going to stop him, honey?"

Zavier halted and met Mish's gaze.

Oh yeah, this man was one giant bundle of angst. She beckoned him forward, and he gave a kind of frustrated grunt before stepping into her arms. "He's gonna be fine, sweetheart. It's a cold. He'll dose up on lemon tea, pantomime things for a couple of hours, scribble in that journal of his, and we'll do some longer solos. It's happened before. He says he doesn't get sick, but that boy has a short memory."

"He hasn't been sick while I've been here." His voice was muffled against her shoulder.

"I'm sure he's gotten a cold."

"Sure. At home. Where I can take care of him." Zavier pulled back. "It's foolish, but I—don't do well when he's ill."

No shit. "It's not foolish, not after what we went through, what *you* went through."

That elicited a painful smile. "He's right to be mad at me. I can't protect him from everything."

"If you could keep people from getting a cold, we could make a lot more money bottling you up and selling you on the open market."

That got her an actual laugh.

She patted his shoulder. "And yeah, he's right to be annoyed, but he says he has a plan. Wanna go see what your husband's got up his sleeve?"

"All right. Just—I worry so much about him, you know?"

"You two are the most important people in each other's lives, Zav. Of *course* you worry. Ray knows that. But he's right about being the leader. And we do have a concert tonight. He needs your support."

Zavier scrubbed a hand over his face. "Fuck. Okay."

When they returned to the front of the bus, Ray was typing away on Adrian's tablet. David rose, and Zavier took his seat next to Ray. "Apologies," he said.

A smile tugged at Ray's lips, and he stopped typing. He

took Zavier's hand in his own and pressed his lips to Zavier's knuckles. That seemed to unlock the tension in Zav.

Mish's own tension ebbed, even more so when David wrapped an arm around her waist. "They're adorable together," he said close to her head.

"Heard that," Zavier muttered.

Ray blew out a breath and thrust Adrian's tablet into Zavier's hands.

Zavier read what Ray'd typed. "Well, that'll work."

"What?" The word out of Mish's lips was echoed by Dom. Zavier handed her the tablet first.

She read Ray's missive. Then a second time. Her heart and head both warred with a reaction, though her stomach had settled for gymnastics.

"You want me to sing? Like...all the songs?" Her voice pitched strangely, which she hated. David gave her a squeeze. Supportive. Warm. She was so thankful that he was here with them. The fear inside her, the little voice from her past and that big fucking annoying one from the present whispered that girls—women—like her couldn't do what Ray asked. One song was one thing. An entire show?

"Technically, Ray suggested most of them," Zavier said.

That wasn't better. She leaned on David. "Most, then."

"Um, guys?" Dom held out his hand.

"Sorry." Mish handed the tablet over. "Little shocked here."

Didn't take Dom long to read. "Yeah, I can see why. But Ray's right. This is gonna work."

Beneath the initial shock bubbled something else: excitement. Pride. Confidence that shattered and hushed the words in the back of her head. Ray *was* right. The fans would love it.

She could do what Ray asked—fill in as lead singer.

They hashed out the rest of the plan. Ray'd rest his voice—dose up on lemon tea and honey—and he'd sing a few of the songs. The rest would be Mish's. They worked up a set list with songs her range could handle well—and ones for Ray that wouldn't shred his voice.

Luckily, they had a small break between this show and the next. Hopefully that would give Ray enough time to recover.

When they finished, Ray sat back against the couch, obviously relieved.

Goddamn, singing tonight would be fun. Yeah, she could do this. *They* could do this. "This is gonna work."

Dom cracked a brilliant smile. "Damn straight!"

"Ain't nothing straight about this band, honey."

David nearly snorted his coffee at that. "Oh my god. True, but warn a guy before you say something like that." He dabbed a hand at his beard, then got up to grab a paper towel.

Mish eyed Adrian. "Not a word on the 'net, though."

He laid his hand over his heart. "I know better than to let something this big out of the bag!"

One of Ray's shit-eating grins split his face.

The moment reached up and grabbed Mish so hard her breath caught. For one night, she'd be the voice of Twisted Wishes. She stood and set her mug in the sink. "David? Can I talk to you for a moment in the back?"

Smart man that he was, he rose and placed his mug in the sink as well. "Whatever you need."

She needed him, in so many ways it wasn't funny. But that would have to wait until they weren't sharing a bus with her bandmates. Sure, the others fooled around quietly and she'd been known to rub one out in silence, but if she was going to jump David's bones, she wanted loud, wall-banging sex.

She wasn't above bringing *him* to his knees, though.

Thankfully, the others kept their mouths shut while she and David made their way to the lounge. She pulled the privacy curtain closed and turned to find David watching her. Mish gestured at the couch, and he took a seat. She chose to stand straddling his legs, and leaned over him, her hands to either side of his head. "I really *really* want to fuck you right now."

His lips parted before he swallowed and spoke. "You can, if you'd like."

"Thing is, I'm noisy and I like making you scream." She leaned down a little. "I don't want to share those with the others up there."

His breath hitched. "Oh." His gaze never left hers, his eyes nearly black in the dim light of the lounge.

His strength would never stop heating her blood, the assuredness that allowed him to surrender to her desires. "How quiet can you be, David?"

A cocky smile. "As quiet as you want me, darling."

Maybe they could play. Her body hummed like a transformer, and she didn't want that to end, the power there. Creativity. Exhilaration and control. "I want to see you come," she murmured. "I want you to jack off right here, right now. I want to see how much you need me."

That earned her a long exhale. "Baby, I can do that. Question is, can you be quiet watching me?" He worked open the tie on his sweatpants, staring up at her.

God, it was glorious to watch, too. The way he shifted on the couch to give himself more access, how he slipped his packer out and set it aside with care. The flicker of his eyelids when he started to stroke. His head lolled back against the seat.

She leaned in and kissed his chin and jaw, his wiry beard rough against her lips. David's breathing shifted, but that was all the noise he made. Mish climbed onto the couch, still straddling David as he worked his cock. Their lips brushed, and she moaned from the taste of coffee and desperation, and combed her hands into his hair.

His lips beneath hers slid into a smile, so she bit the lower one gently, then drew back. "I never said I'd be quiet. Only that you should be."

The response was a silent laugh that morphed into a soundless moan when she tightened her fingers in his locks. David's breathing stuttered. Gorgeous. Perfect.

"Yeah, that's what I want to see," she whispered. "You falling apart for me."

His eyes met hers again, wide and lovely, face flushed, lips plump and inviting. She took them into a hard kiss that had her moaning, even as he rocked beneath her. His need for air between bites and tongue thrusts, how his body shook—she knew he was close.

Mish slid her mouth down David's neck, nipping at the flesh there. "Come for me."

He did, and that was beautiful, too. The way his hips rose off the couch, his closed eyes, open mouth. David's whole body shook from the pleasure she'd asked him to find. A single perfect moment, one he'd given to her because she'd asked.

This was power. And satisfaction. "Thank you."

David flicked open his eyes and smiled. "Pleasure was all mine." Soft, soft words.

"Not all." She might not have come, but deep within her lay a calm that he'd given her with his actions.

"Good." He lolled his head. "I should put myself together."

"Mmm. Yeah." Mish stole a kiss, then took her time with another—and that one got her a moan from him. When she pulled back, she grinned.

"So I wasn't a hundred percent quiet, but your lips are killer."

She laughed and climbed off the couch. "So are yours." He was sexy and perfect especially tousled like he was, post orgasm. "Do you want more coffee?"

"Yeah." He closed his eyes. "After that, I need it." When he looked up again, he was grinning. "Mish?"

"Yeah?" God, every nerve in her body sparked like that smile.

"I'm still up for you fucking me until I scream."

That turned her insides into a fucking volcano. "Oh good. We even have a hotel room tonight."

His laugh was glorious. She blew him a kiss, then sauntered up to the front of the bus to get more coffee. The guys looked amused, even Ray, despite his cold.

Mish didn't care. Tonight, she'd sing for all of them, and for David.

Tension laced through the air as David prowled through the venue. This time, they were playing in a concert hall—not the outdoor amphitheaters they'd been playing. Seats. Balconies. Even little boxes on the side. The building was easier to secure, and that led to a more intimate atmosphere. The stage seemed smaller, though it wasn't by much.

The band couldn't hide the fact that Ray was sick, not with his voice on rest and everyone but him answering questions during the VIP event. Especially not after his coughing fit that had him looking miserable and put Zavier on edge. David had thought the drummer might split open the water bottle he clutched in his hand.

Mish was their saving grace. Calm, cool, and beautiful, and so open and inviting with the fans. She took point during the VIP encounter, joking with the group, asking her own questions. Ribbing silent Ray and tense Zavier until they relaxed.

Domino followed Mish's lead, so the reviews of the encounter out on the 'net were positive, Adrian said. But everyone knew something was up with Ray. That was even evident in the conversations David overheard as he made his rounds. Fans nervous that Ray'd hurt his voice or wouldn't sound good.

Or that there'd be a last-minute cancellation. Everyone was primed for something to happen tonight.

Part of the reason David was out in the venue was to get a sense of the vibe. Plus the band had sequestered themselves in their dressing rooms and even Adrian had been shooed away. To keep his own nerves from fraying, David focused on work.

The audience here felt closer to the stage as well. They weren't. The perception came from the closeness of the seating and the lack of a lawn. Didn't help that he was well known now. Fans watched him and snapped photos. Someone had even asked for his autograph, and he'd had to beg off. He didn't sign things. He was just security.

Only he wasn't anymore. He was *dating* Mish Sullivan. The proof of it was in all those photos on the internet. There was also that recording of him singing to Mish, out there for all to see. Including that reporter, Vicky Heydel, who spotted him at *exactly* the same time he saw her.

Oh, fucking *great*. He couldn't retreat, because there weren't as many aisles to stomp down. Besides, Marcella had cautioned him to be nice. And truthful. While there still was no *official* comment on his and Mish's relationship, they couldn't demur anymore, so David stood his ground.

"Ms. Heydel," he said when she strode up to him.

"Mr. Altet." Her smile was triumphant. "Do you care to make a statement now?"

Couldn't help the painful chuckle. "Not really, no."

And yes, her lips twitched a little, hitching into satisfaction. "But you are dating Mish Sullivan, are you not?"

There it was, the question he couldn't avoid. He could play coy, or he could get this over with. "Yes. I am. We are." He gave a shrug. "Probably obvious from the other night."

Heydel smirked. "It's been obvious for a while. But I'd like to know why."

"Why what?" He racked his brain to come up with a reason for this line of questioning.

"You've stated you're security. Rumor has it that Mish Sullivan has been receiving some interesting comments online —certainly have been some of those on the photos of you two." Her expression was shrewd and expectant.

Shit. *Shit.* He had an inkling where this was going. "I can't comment on social media postings."

"Can't or won't?"

"Both." He shook his head. "I'm sorry, Ms. Heydel. I do have a job to do." He made to disengage, but she blocked his path.

"Mr. Altet, does Mish Sullivan have a stalker, and are you play-acting a relationship to flush him out?"

David froze. "Play-acting?" He hated how his voice rose on the last syllable, even more when Heydel's eyes glinted with that *got you* look. "We're not play-acting."

"So, a real relationship, then? Not trying to draw out a stalker?"

Damn it, damn it. "Could you not write about that?" The words were out before he had the sense not to say them.

Much to his surprise, Heydel hesitated. "Shit, there is one?"

"No comment." But the cat was out of the bag, David knew. "Just...please don't run with that? For Mish?"

She blew out a breath and nodded. "I'll table that topic for now." There was a pause. "But what about your relationship with Mish?"

"I *really* have no comment on that." He did his best to slip past her without touching her.

"Thing is," she said to his back, "Mish doesn't keep any of her lovers long. What happens to you after the tour, Mr. Altet?"

He kept walking, throat tight and body tighter. That conversation had gotten completely out of hand, and he'd fucked up. Not that he'd said anything in particular, but too much could be inferred from his comments.

God, he was a fool. This was why you didn't mix business and pleasure. And then there was the thorn Heydel had shoved into his side at the end.

What *was* going to happen when this tour was over? Touring was living in another reality, one where everything could happen—and had. But at some point, they would end up back in the real world, where he was a bodyguard and Mish was a huge rock star.

Their lives meshed now, but in the world outside touring, outside of the job? If this relationship with Mish continued, he couldn't keep his job with Twisted Wishes.

David scrubbed a hand down his face. First things first: find Marcella and let her know what had happened. The rest he'd deal with later. Because this show? This show was Mish's, and if nothing else, he'd be here and work his hardest for her, no matter what the future held.

Thankfully, Marcella didn't seem too concerned about Vicky Heydel. "She's gonna dig and dig, David. The evidence is out there, as is the speculation. There's nothing Heydel's reporting that's new."

At least there was that.

"Something else eating you?" Marcella clicked her phone off and gave him all her attention.

Shit. He schooled his face. "Nothing in particular." A lie, but he covered it. "The fans know there's something up."

She gave him a long look. "Yeah. Adrian said the chatter about Ray's gone up a ton. Fans were hit hard by his previous illness, so collectively, they worry about him almost as much as Zavier does."

Illness. That was a gentle way of putting Ray's near-death experience. "I don't blame them. Or Zavier, for that matter."

Another nod, then silence, until Marcella cleared her throat. "I know deflection when I see it. I've been in PR too long. I'm going to let it go—but you know we're here for you. This whole 'taking care of each other' includes you, too."

"I'm not—" But Marcella had gotten him dead to rights. "Okay. I'll keep that in mind."

That earned him a smile. "Doesn't have to be me. Any of the guys would be there for you."

He gave her a little salute and headed down the hall. Two Times Strong would be on stage soon, so he should make one more round, and check in with their crew again. As David walked away, he realized that Marcella had meant "guys" as in the other men in their circle, which meant she'd guessed the source of his disquiet. Then again, that was probably obvious.

After he'd checked in with Two Times Strong's crew, he made his way toward the house seats, and ran into Adrian in the hall.

"I'm sure it's fine," Adrian said, in lieu of a greeting.

He stopped. "What's fine?"

"Whatever it is you're off to check on now." Adrian tucked his phone into his pocket.

"Doing final rounds." David didn't have much time left.

"You've done rounds three times already." Adrian crossed his arms and leaned against the wall. "I've counted."

God, these people were so damn frustrating sometimes. But even as he glowered at Adrian, part of him took warmth in the man noticing.

"Look, we all have ways of dealing with the stress. Yours is marching around like a man with a mission," Adrian said. "One of mine's cooking, which is really hard to do on the road, let me tell you."

"Hence the coffee?"

A laugh, then Adrian sobered. "I also know you marching around isn't all about tonight."

"God, not you, too."

Adrian pushed off the wall. "Oh really?"

"Marcella. She..." David gave up and slapped a hand against his thigh. "You all are too perceptive." He searched for words, but didn't find the right ones. "I'm mulling my future, that's all." The one person he should discuss that with was the one he couldn't. He wouldn't distract Mish tonight—or any night—on the tour.

Whatever happened between them would happen, and they'd figure out shit after they returned to New York.

Heydel was right. Mish never settled on one lover for very long. While his heart ached with the thought of walking away, that was on the table. Had been from day one. Day one, when he'd known he shouldn't have gotten involved.

David met Adrian's thoughtful expression. "I'll be fine. These jobs are always weird when they get personal."

Something in Adrian's expression shifted. "I see."

David's muscles tightened. "I should go and..." He waved in the direction of the stage and the audience.

"All right," Adrian said. "But David...it's not a job for us."

There was the line he had to decide whether to cross. "I know. Like I said. Thinking ahead."

He turned away, because he didn't want to see how Adrian's expression changed. How much all of these folks felt. They were family, one he could be a part of—maybe was. He didn't know anymore.

He was dating Mish Sullivan, and that seemed to shake up everything in his head. Worse when he thought about his paycheck and the contract he'd signed.

Once out in the theater again, he pushed the turmoil aside. The focus had to be the job. Regardless of his feelings, he had to keep her and the band safe. If he couldn't do what he'd been hired to do, then he might as well not be here at all.

CHAPTER NINETEEN

Mish had expected her stomach to be in knots at the thought of taking the lead on singing. But the rhythm of getting ready for the show, the banter with Dom and Zavier, knowing David, Adrian, and Marcella were out there, had eased the anxiety from her mind.

As expected, Ray's voice was still a fucking mess, even though he'd been downing tea and not saying a word. He'd manage a few songs, but no more than three. They rearranged the set list, practiced with Ray singing and some songs with her singing, but only on ones she'd already sung, to keep that she'd be singing the majority of the night a secret. The meet-and-greet went well. And now? Now they were in the wings, waiting for the house lights to go down so they could burst out onto the stage.

She could do this. She *would* do this. Ray clutched a bass guitar—another one of hers. He'd play some of her parts, too. He nodded at her, his smile wide and pleased.

Yeah, they'd be fine. Maybe the show'd be messy on the edges, but they'd roll with it.

The lights dimmed, the audience screamed—and they moved. A moment later, Zavier clicked his sticks to set the beat and they exploded into sound as the light bathed them in brightness and color.

While the crowd had been loud before, they were tumultuous now. Mish danced across the stage to the opening bridge of "River of Pain," then spun up to the mic and belted out the words that had been Ray's, but that they all had felt at one point or another. Ray picked up her bass line as she slid her guitar out of the way, planted her feet, and sang her heart out.

Oh god, what she got back. Like before, the screams, the outstretched hands she could spy from the first couple of rows before the stage lights robbed her of vision. The singing coming *from* the audience was magnified by the wooden walls of the theater, and it shook through her like they were standing inside a giant guitar.

When another musical interlude broke through, she swung her bass around, and she and Ray played together until the lyrics came around again. She sang and sang.

By the end of the song, the din from beyond the stage was wild.

"Hey, Charlotte, how y'all doing?" She raised her hand to block out the stage lights enough to see some more of the theater. "Having a good time?"

Of course, they screamed back at her.

"Good." She slung her bass off and a tech took it from her hand. "So we're mixing it up tonight. You might have heard that Ray's a little under the weather."

Ray put on his best pouting face, and it was a good one. Got him a bunch of laughs, including from Zavier.

"He's not quite up to singing the whole night for you. So if you don't mind, I'm gonna sing a lot more."

Shouts and cheers.

"Ray'll sing, too, don't you worry."

More clapping and thunder from the audience.

"Right! So here we go!"

Zavier started them off again, and they launched into another song. Mish sang and danced her way through two more before a tech handed her bass back and Ray took over with "Dare to Be," which only he could do justice. His voice held out well enough, though he ended up heading behind the drum kit afterward for a coughing fit and to down some tea the crew had waiting for him. She mouthed over *You okay?* And he threw her a thumbs-up.

As planned, she sang two more before Ray belted out another one—and then they threw in an instrumental before closing with Mish singing "Time Runs Out."

While they lurked in the wings and the fans stomped and clapped and demanded an encore, Zavier pulled Ray into a hug. "Can you manage one more?"

Ray snorted and nodded against Zavier's shoulder.

"He ain't gonna be talking tomorrow, though," Dom said.

Yeah. Knowing Zavier, Ray'd probably end up ensconced in bed for the entire day. "You guys ready for this?" She nodded at the stage.

They all straightened and, following Ray, ran back out.

Ray took the mic and gave it his all, his voice damn strong for being a wreck. The audience ate it up when he let them sing the chorus for him. They killed the first song of the encore.

The second one? That was a little surprise. She turned and nodded to Zavier, and he started up a beat different from most of the Twisted Wishes songs—and Dom led them straight into a cover of Erasure's "Chains of Love"—the same song David had sung for her.

She grabbed the mic and sought David out where he usually stood for the last song—and found him gape-mouthed and staring back. She blew him a kiss, then launched into singing the words he'd sung to her.

The fans? They danced and sang and shouted as she

finished, screaming and clapping even when the band took their bows, left the stage, and the house lights came up.

Backstage, Ray collapsed against the nearest wall and croaked out, "Fucking hell, we did it." He pointed at Mish and gave two thumbs-up.

They *had* done it. Every bit of Mish glowed, every part vibrating with energy. Thank god they had hotel rooms tonight. She needed about twenty hours of sleep, right after she fucked David into oblivion.

Zavier drew Ray into his arms, his expression a combination of relief, worry, and protectiveness. "Up for the signing?"

Ray nodded, and opened up a little space between them. "I'm not gonna die."

"I hate when you say that." Zavier loosened his hold. His tone was mild.

Mish understood. They all did. "Kiddo, you keep that voice of yours resting, and let your man take care of you."

Ray rolled his eyes, but smiled.

"Speaking of your man..." Domino bumped Mish. "Yours is looking fine tonight."

Her man. Warmth bubbled up in Mish as David walked down the hall. He *did* look fine. Black jeans and a dark purple Twisted Wishes shirt. Wasn't the clothes, though. He had this look that could melt paint from the wall. Passion and fire, all contained in those dark eyes and the way he sauntered toward them.

He met her gaze and his lips quirked up, but when he spoke, it was to all of them. "You folks gonna get ready?"

Right. The signing.

"Yeah," Zavier said. "Give us ten." The guys headed toward the dressing room, but Mish lingered, never taking her eyes off David.

"That was some final song," David said. He slid a hand around her waist. "Was that for me?"

She pulled him against her body. "Well, and a couple thousand fans. But mostly for you."

He laughed and she shut that up by stealing a kiss that quickly became a demand for more as she gave in to his heat, the press of his body, and the thrum of her own pulse.

She fucking needed this man in bed.

He broke the kiss and spoke against her lips. "You gotta go do the rock star thing, darling."

"Yeah, I do. But when I'm done, I'm gonna do you. Just you wait."

"Baby." It came out as a groan. He stepped away. "Gonna hold you to that." So much depth to his voice.

Not an issue at all. She always delivered on her promises.

Thank goodness for the fans. Their energy and enthusiasm kept Mish focused on them and not David standing a few feet away. Though she'd practically burned for him as she'd changed, as soon as the band had sat down behind the tables, that took a backseat to all the fans and their joy and stories.

However, once they were at the hotel, every ounce of that desire came rushing back. The need to touch and kiss David. To strip him down and make him beg and scream.

Mish paced over the carpet of her hotel suite. David was with Marcella, making sure the rest of the band and the crew were settled and secure. There was too much time spent waiting and too much emptiness in this sterile, bland room.

Marly sat on the nightstand, but *David* wasn't here. Mish stopped moving and closed her eyes. He had a job—one that took care of them all. She had to be patient.

Still, it seemed like forever until she heard a gentle rapping at her door. A glance through the peephole verified that it was the man she wanted. Mish yanked the door open, pulled David inside, and had him up against the wall before the door clicked shut.

His muffled grunt turned into a groan. He gripped her hips and pulled her closer, even as she used all her weight to keep him right where she wanted him. "Fuck, baby," he murmured between kisses.

"That's the plan." She threw the dead bolt on the door, then hauled him off the wall and into her arms. God, she loved how he let her do that. David was all muscle, but he let her manhandle him, draw him across the suite in a tangle of limbs, punishing kisses, and discarded clothing, until he was half-naked and she pushed him down onto her bed.

His grin was astounding. And goddamn, he was beautiful. Toned chest. Those thick legs. "Man, I wish I'd thought to pack my strap-on. Kicking myself now."

He laughed. "Always pack the dicks. That's the one rule I've never been disappointed to follow." He stretched those arms of his up and tucked his hands behind his head. "More seriously, I have no issues with you using *mine* on me, though not my harness."

Fair enough. She crawled over David and teased his lips with hers. "This is gonna be fun."

She peeled the rest of his clothing off, then slowly stripped off her own as well while David watched, propped up on his elbows. His gaze flicked all over her. "You're something else, Mish. You could have anyone you wanted."

She'd had a lot of the people she'd wanted over the years. Not all, but that was fine, too. "Right here, right now, I want you." His compact form, his muscles. The way the hair trailed from his chest down to his sex. Those fucking powerful thighs.

His smile was golden. "If you're serious about wanting one of my dicks—" He pointed his chin over to a duffel against the wall. "I asked the hotel to bring that bag to your room."

She's noticed earlier. "How thoughtful."

All tooth and sexy posing. "Figured you wouldn't mind."

Especially not now. "May I?"

He nodded, and that was all the encouragement she needed. Like before, the array of dicks was impressive, and this time, there were more. Some were realistic. Others were not. One was smooth, a thickness she liked, and bright orange.

"Safety orange?" She brandished the dildo.

He threw back his head in laughter. "It's not one that requires a warning."

No, there were thicker ones. But this one? She liked this one. She grabbed a bottle of lube and a condom and sat on the edge of the bed. "You sure you're okay with this?"

"If I wasn't, I'd tell you. I like my body—all of it." He paused, and his voice dropped in tone. "And I've been fantasizing about you filling me. So, you gonna use that on me or not?"

Game on. She grabbed his shoulders and met him halfway in a blistering kiss that left them both breathless. Finally he used his strength, hauling her to him, and they tangled into each other. Flesh against flesh, his thigh between her legs. She rode that hard muscle, thrusting against it, then pushed him against the mattress before straddling him around the waist. God, the heat of his body. She smoothed her hands up his chest, over his pecs and nipples, then down those impressive arms.

He rocked his hips, seeking friction of his own. Those lovely hands of his coasted over her belly and up to cup her breasts. He teased her nipples. "Come here."

"Demanding now?" She lowered herself, then moaned as he took one of her nipples into his hot mouth.

He might not be all that sensitive there, but she sure was. Took all her concentration not to pull out of his mouth or collapse down on him, and the moans that fell from her lips sounded wanton and needy, even to her.

This man would undo her before she even had a chance to fuck him. Especially when he rolled so they changed their positions. He switched breasts, licking and sucking the other nub until she thought her nerves might fry from the shocks and sparks flying over them.

Time to turn the tables. Wasn't hard to reach between his legs and find his dick. When her fingers teased him, David lost all his control. "Oh fuck."

"Again, that's the idea." Mish rolled him back over, then slid down his body, biting and licking as she went.

David's warm hands caressed her head. "God, yeah. Suck me."

She did, taking his dick into her mouth and relishing his harsh curse and how his hips lifted off the mattress, how he spread his legs to give her access. He tasted of salt and smelled of musk and she couldn't get enough.

Her own body flared in response to his moans and bitten-off curses. Fingers laced into her hair. "Baby, god..."

His front hole was warm and tight and wet against her fingers, and the gasp he made was worth every second she lavished on him. God, she'd needed this. Needed to break him apart. Finger him. Suck him off and hear him moan. Better than anything in the world.

Mish pulled back and gazed up at David, his face flushed under his beard, his chest heaving. His fingers brushed her cheek. "God, you're beautiful," he murmured.

Only one thing left to do, really. She grabbed the dildo, quickly rolled a condom down on it, and added some lube. He was wet, but tight enough the extra slick would help.

She entered him slowly, her gaze not leaving his until he threw back his head. "Fuck, fuck, oh god..." His hips drove the dick in deeper.

That was a sight. Him hard and spread open by her. She

eased the cock out, then drove it in again, finding a rhythm that made the sounds pouring from David loud and plaintive. Then she took his dick back in her mouth.

David writhed under her as she held him down, his dick in her mouth. She pistoned the slick orange cock in and out of his front hole, her own body humming as his pleasure reverberated through her. She might get off like this, making David come, fucking him relentlessly. His breath came in gasps and groans, and she tasted him on her tongue and felt the sharp sting of his hands tangled into her hair.

He came long and hard beneath her, crying out wordlessly as his body jerked and trembled. She didn't let up, though, fucking him straight through one orgasm and into another that left him pleading with her to stop.

Mish had never been so turned on in her life.

Once she'd slid the cock out of him, he pulled her up so that they were lip to lip. "Fucking hell, woman."

"You liked that?" He was still trembling. Or maybe that was her.

His answer was a kiss that scorched her down to her toes. His hands cupped her ass as she rode the hard muscles of his leg, trying to seek relief for her overstimulated body and not finding enough.

When she groaned in frustration, David rolled them both over until he was on top, leering down at her. "Don't think I'm too tired to take care of you."

Their mouths met and devoured each other in equal measure, and his fingers found her clit between her slick folds.

Didn't take long before she couldn't see through the light and the pleasure ripping through her, sending her up and up until she shattered on his hand. She pulled away from his mouth and gasped for air. She'd been so keyed up fucking him, it wasn't surprising she'd come so fast.

He let her down slowly, but didn't stop entirely. "Want more?" He mouthed her chin. "Can give you more."

Except she was wrung out, and even the gentle movements of his hand were almost too much. "Not—now." She let out a breath as he slid his hand up to her hip. "God, you're too damn good."

He grunted. "Hardly did a damn thing."

"Oh, but you did. You let me have you. I fucking love that." She nuzzled his neck.

He pulled her close, their limbs shifting until their bodies slotted neatly against each other, as if they'd been made for this. Utter joy spun through Mish like light breaking through the clouds, and that was almost as intense as her orgasm had been. "Can we stay this way forever?"

His soft laugh was more of a hum and movement than sound. "I wish we could." A hint of sadness there.

Life moved on. After a time, they both heeded the call of their bodies, cleaned themselves up, and finished getting ready for bed.

Tomorrow would be a lazy morning before boarding the bus again. After that, another hectic run of concerts. A life she loved and wanted. But stopping like this, holding David like this—she wanted that, too. He was the one bright, shining delight in this whole business with the stalker, and she hoped that would never dim.

CHAPTER TWENTY

David relished the quiet early mornings in the bus before Adrian woke and made his coffee that had them all crawling out of their berths.

After Charlotte, they'd played in Atlanta, with Mish singing half of the songs. Ray's voice was well and truly on the mend. Tonight, they'd play in Nashville, and Ray was itching to get back into his top form, even as they juggled around sets to let Mish sing, too. You gave it your all in Music City.

Though staying at hotels had been a nice break, there was a simplicity to the hum of the road, the darkness of the sleeping berth, and the utter silence of humans asleep around David.

Reminded him, in some odd way, of barracks. He had often woken up early then, and lain in the dark contemplating all that he didn't dare think about during the day. Back then, it had been his gender, his sexuality, his role in the world, and how he'd been running and running and running from the truth.

Now it was about the tangled mess that was his job, this band that felt like family, and how fucking much he was falling for Mish Sullivan. On top of all of that, there was the stalker. Every blip in the news, every photo of David and Mish together—even the ones when he was in the background—those threatened to infuriate that asshole. Make him act out.

He hadn't. Even the emails and comments were gone. Oh, he was still out there, both David and Adrian were sure of that, but they hadn't heard from him. Not a comment about Mish's singing. Eventually the asshole would come out of the woodwork. But when and how? They were getting pretty close to the end of this leg of the tour.

That niggled another worry in the back of David's brain. Eventually, this tour would be over. The job he'd been hired for would be done. What then? Was he another Mish Sullivan fling? He didn't think so, but there were no guarantees. They had gotten close so fast—fallen in lust. That didn't mean love. Or the kind of commitment Ray and Zavier had for each other.

Hadn't minded the thought of a fling when they'd started this. But now his heart ached to be with her. He loved being on the bus with the band, too, and the friendships he'd formed. The deeper he got with Mish, the more reason he had to step back from the very job that put him here to begin with.

When this leg of the tour was over, he really ought to tell Ray and Marcella to find another guard for Mish. Help them find someone. In reality, the whole band could use a security detail, not something cobbled together out of him, Adrian, and the crew.

That left the most looming question: when he left this job and took another, how the hell was he going to date Mish Sullivan? Could he even?

Yeah, maybe boy toy fling was the best way to look at himself. Thinking through the logistics of Mish touring and him off on some other job made his brain and heart hurt. There wasn't a way they could be together after the tour.

He reached up to touch the ceiling of his berth, to run his hand over the surface, the texture under his fingers cool and soothing. Life went on. It had after the army. After he'd come out, then come out again. He'd left family behind. Friends. Fellow soldiers. Ultimately, he was a loner and functioned best when he could move through society on his own terms.

Once he heard Adrian drop out of his bunk to brew coffee, David folded up his thoughts and tucked them away. He had to be here and now. What might happen later couldn't impact what he was here to do. His fling with Mish couldn't impact that, either.

When he heard someone else besides Adrian in the main area of the bus, he crawled out of his berth and started his day as part of the Twisted Wishes inner circle.

Went pretty quickly after coffee. They pulled into the venue—another amphitheater—midmorning, then the day was full of sound checks, banter, walking the setup and talking to the site's security. Mish caught him about halfway through the day for some very heavy kissing in a quiet corner backstage.

Just like that, all his resolve to keep his feelings contained burned up in his veins. He ran his hands up her sides and teased her breasts through her shirt.

"God," she whispered, "I want you to make me come. Hard. Fast."

"Not here." Might be quiet, but it was still far too exposed for his liking.

"Right here." Mish nipped at his beard.

"Reckless." But he was already hiking up her skirt. He fucking needed to get a grip, but his heart was pounding too damn hard. "Someone might see."

"So?" He felt Mish's smile against his neck. "Come on, baby. You've got talented hands and a talented mouth."

He shouldn't do what she asked, but he also couldn't help himself. Everything about her was heady and hot. He took her mouth in his, and pressed her against the wall. He found the edge of her silky underwear and pushed the fabric aside. When he slid his fingers into her folds, she moaned into him. God, she was slick and hot and ready.

What he wouldn't give for more time and a far more comfortable place? He was hard and as needy. Pushing a finger into her got him a groan and a hissed "Yes, please." He circled her hard clit, and she gasped, riding his hand. He alternated between fucking her shallowly and lavishing attention onto her clit, until she was crushing him in her arms. "Oh fuck, oh shit."

God the power in undoing a woman like Mish. Only took a few more strokes and she was coming hard, burying her head against his shoulder, her breath warming his neck. They hung there for a moment, his fingers in her folds as she came down, her arms around him. His own breath was harsh against her hair.

"Fucking hell, baby." He pulled his fingers away, all too aware that they both smelled like sex.

A chuckle. "You better believe it." Mish smoothed down her skirt.

Despite all his years of experience, nothing had prepared him for what to do after a moment like this. Wiping his fingers on his shirt seemed...gauche. So he did what came to him next—sucked them into his mouth and licked the taste of Mish from them.

Her eyes widened. "Fucking hell yourself." She smiled, ruddy-cheeked and breathless. "I think I love you."

The words shot through David faster than any bullet he'd ever taken. He couldn't even respond—didn't know what to say. Elation and terror. The sense that his world had shifted.

In the next instant, Ray's voice punctuated the air from down the hall. "Yo, Mish! We gotta do sound check! Where the hell are you?"

Mish—oblivious to David's turmoil—rolled her eyes.

"Duty calls." She stole another kiss, then slipped away, heading in the direction of Ray's voice.

Duty calls. David licked his lips, tasting Mish on them. Holy fucking hell. He should be out there, too. Watching over the band. Looking for Mish's stalker. Instead, he was leaning against a wall, with absolutely no sense of himself anymore.

This wasn't good. Nothing about this was right.

He peeled himself away from the spot and headed for the men's room, aching from too many emotions and memories. He washed his hands and tried to rein himself in. The cool flow from the sink over his hands helped. So did a later chug of water as he headed out to watch the sound check.

Mish was in love with him. His own feelings echoed hers. That should have been a happy thing, the start of something grand. But he wasn't cut out to be more than a rock star's fling. Didn't *want* to be more than that, really. He had his own life, his own sense of self.

At the same time, he wanted to give Mish everything in the world. She deserved that, someone who could sacrifice themself for love. Be willing to let go of everything for this one shot at happiness.

He wasn't that person. He was fundamentally flawed in that regard. He—had to live for himself.

That inner turmoil, that war raging over this tangled mess he'd helped create was probably why he failed Mish again.

The concert was their best yet. Ray's voice was back, the fans loved when he and Mish sang together, and every song they played was top notch. No problems with the fans, aside from some drunk shoving in the pit that was handled quickly by the venue.

Then the signing happened.

There was a dude eyeing Mish while he stood in line. David resisted the urge to roll his eyes because it was obvious he was checking Mish out, even as he went to the other band members. Kid needed to knock it the fuck off.

Heat and rage rose in David—and he mentally kicked himself in the ass for it. He was *not* getting jealous of a fan, was he? God. Yeah, he fucking was, and that was an issue and a half *right there*.

Still, he took a step closer to Mish's table. Just in case. But not too close as to be the damn overprotective boyfriend.

Of course the guy asked for a selfie with Mish. Of *course*. Not intervening took all of David's professional demeanor. Didn't stop him from gritting his teeth when they both leaned over the table and the guy wrapped his arm around Mish before snapping the photo.

Then the dude snagged the necklace around Mish's neck and yanked.

Happened in the blink of an eye. One second the photo, the next Mish shouted and clutched at her neck as the guy took off.

David froze. He should have seen it. Should have stopped the dude. David had been right there. Horror and anguish at his sheer *incompetence* rolled through him. This was his job, and he'd failed completely. Breath halted in his lungs. Time stood still.

Holy fucking *hell*.

He burst into movement after the guy and the venue staff, who'd been more quick-witted than him.

Thank god the chain had broken easily—must have been thin. Thank *fuck* Mish hadn't been hurt. Ray was going to have his head. Hell, the whole band would probably be gunning for him.

By the time David caught up to the staff, the guy was gone, vanishing into the crowds that were milling around and heading to the exits.

Fuck. Oh fucking *hell*. Just like last time—only worse, because he'd noticed the guy. Seen him. Just been too damn caught up in his *relationship* with Mish to do anything useful. Now the dude was gone along with another one of Mish's belongings, straight into the hands of her stalker. Who was probably here.

David resisted the urge to punch the nearest inanimate object and scream. All his muscles tensed, and his throat was raw with rage—at the dude, at the stalker, and at his damn self.

One of the venue staff ambled over. "Did you get a good look at him?"

"Yeah, but it's not going to help." This thief had been pretty nondescript. White. Mid-twenties. Medium build. Brown hair. Brown eyes. Black concert T-shirt and jeans. Matched half the men at the concert. They'd never find him.

The venue guy eyed David. "You were right there, weren't you?"

David bit down on his tongue to keep from snapping back, then ground out, "Yep. Guy was fast."

And David had been slow. Motionless, in fact. He saw the contempt in the other man's eyes. He deserved that—and more.

With the thief gone, there was nothing to do but head back.

By the time he returned to the signing area, Domino was consoling Mish. Some great boyfriend David was. Hadn't even fucking *been there* for Mish. Not as a bodyguard, either. Waste of space. This was exactly the kind of shit that had killed people in the desert. Inattention. Lack of focus. At least Mish was fine, physically. A small abrasion marred her neck, a nick from where the chain had bit in before it had broken. Barely any blood.

"Fucking hell," she murmured, then sat back in her seat.

The band, of course, insisted on finishing the signing, against the better judgment of Marcella, the site, and David.

There were statements to give the police. Reports. Each time he told his part, the recriminations in the eyes of the officers became more and more apparent. Yeah, great bodyguard he turned out to be.

When it was all over, he sought out Marcella and Ray. They were by the band bus, with Adrian. Ray must have known what was coming, because he raised both hands. "David, don't."

"You have to find someone better, Ray. For Mish, for all of you guys. I fucked up. Shouldn't have taken this job."

"The only way you could keep this sort of thing from happening," Marcella said, "would be to convince the band not to have public interactions."

"That's exactly what I should have done," David ground out. He'd gotten too close to all of them. Hadn't been strict enough.

"Yeah, well, that was never gonna work." Ray folded his arms.

God, they were all so infuriating. "I saw that guy. He was eyeing Mish. I should have stopped him from getting anywhere near her."

Ray released his arms. "Lot of fans eye us up. We're—whether we like it or not—part of people's fantasies."

"Yeah, so what? I failed at keeping her safe, for the second time."

No one said anything. Adrian shifted and had the gall to look hurt, which made no sense at all.

"What?" David snapped at him.

Adrian didn't flinch. "Mish is *fine,*" he said. "People ask and take selfies with the band all the time. Maybe we should stop, sure, but that's not on you. It's not a failure on your part."

"It is." David tightened his hands into fists. "Look, you all have been kind to me. And yes, I'm well aware that Mish likes me. But you need someone better for this. Someone who will tell you the truth and not be won over by all of your damn charms."

Ray stepped forward. "So that's it? You think you fucked up, so you leave us—leave Mish in the lurch?"

Marcella shook her head. "This is not the appropriate time to talk about this. We're all rattled and tired and none of us has a clear head."

David hadn't had a clear head since he'd walked into that studio and met Mish Sullivan in person. Felt like he finally had one again. "Break's coming up in July. I'll stay on until then, and help you find another person—or a team."

Marcella sighed and Ray rubbed his forehead. "Yeah, we're not doing this now, David. Go get some sleep." He nodded to the bus.

David stared at it. No way in hell he was spending the night on the band bus. "I'll get my things and head to the crew bus."

All of them had the good sense not to argue with him about that. He climbed on board the bus and gathered his belongings.

Marly was sitting in Mish's berth. David fingered the dog tags—they weren't the ones he'd worn so many years ago. Those were in a box in his closet with a couple of other mementos. Still, these ones had been with him for years. And Marly had always been there. He patted the bear on the head. "You take good care of her, since I can't."

Then he hoisted his bag and walked off the bus.

Sometimes you had to do what hurt the most to make everything better. He'd been hired to do a job—that he'd failed to do. Regardless of what Mish or Ray or Adrian or anyone a part of Twisted Wishes felt—he had to go. For the band, for Mish, and for his own sanity.

The police were kind in taking Mish's statement, but she'd had it with the whole situation. After the ring fiasco, all of the jewelry she'd worn had been decorative, not sentimental. She didn't give a damn about the trinket. Yeah, her neck was a little sore, there was a tiny abrasion, but thankfully the chain had snapped like the cheap thing it was.

Whoever the stalker was, he wasn't getting an item that meant anything to her this time.

What worried her most was that David was nowhere to be found. He'd taken the whole incident hard—even with all the precautions in the world, that guy had ripped the thing off her neck. Wasn't David's fault, though. They—she and the band—still chose to get up close and personal with fans. You couldn't keep shitheads away. They said one bad apple ruined the bunch, but Twisted Wishes had vowed not to let that happen.

Eventually she found a very grave-looking Adrian at the exit that let out to their buses. "You've seen him, haven't you?"

"Yeah." Adrian stared out at the buses. "He's kicking himself hard for this one. Thinks he was too distracted."

That roiled Mish's innards. Distracted because of her. "It's not true."

"Doesn't matter, in some ways." Adrian's voice was low and gentle. "He believes he failed at his job."

Over a stupid piece of metal with a glass bobble on the end. "Where is he?"

Adrian shoved his hands into his front pockets. "On the crew bus."

Pain, anger, and fear all laced through her, tangled into a braid that hurt every bone. Because if he was *there,* she knew what was coming.

Fucking hell.

She took a breath to steady herself, then another. Finally, she spoke. "Thanks. I'm gonna go talk to him."

Adrian nodded. "I'll let the others know."

First, though, she needed to collect something from her

berth. Because if this went the way she thought it might, she needed to be prepared.

The walk to the bus wasn't long, but each step hurt like razors, especially when the crew members—milling around the outside of the buses—stopped to watch her.

Yeah, this wasn't going to end well. Mish climbed onto the silent band bus and headed to her bunk. Marly was there, of course. David wouldn't have the heart to take him back, even if he was taking everything else with him. Her heart, her soul. She didn't understand why, but she knew what was happening. These stories always ended like this—and she was not a woman built for happy ever afters. Never had been.

Mish pressed her head against the wall that surrounded the berths, against the cool chrome strip there. There would be no tears. Not now. Maybe not ever.

Finally, she kissed Marly on the head, straightened, and headed out of the bus.

The crew members who'd been around before were nowhere to be seen now. When she neared their bus, Marcella stepped off. Before she saw Mish, she covered her face with her hands in a rare display of emotions, and that drove pain deeper into Mish's soul.

This *was* going to go the way she thought. She scuffed her boots against the gravel and Marcella jerked her head away from her palms. "Mish."

So much unhappiness in her name. When she'd chosen it, she'd never thought it would carry the same weight of sadness her previous name had. She'd been wrong about that —though what was wrapped around her name now was a life of her own making. One she was proud of, and nothing, not even David Altet, would change that.

"David on there?"

Marcella focused on Marly, then met Mish's gaze. "Yeah. He's—upset." She lowered her hands and smoothed out nonexistent wrinkles on her skirt. "I made sure everyone else is busy elsewhere."

To give him space. To give them space. "Thank you."

"Mish..." She took a breath. "Don't let him do this."

They all knew the score. All of them. "I don't keep lovers who don't want to stay. I never have."

She'd never seen Marcella look so distraught. "Sometimes you have to fight for what you want."

Mish almost laughed out of bitterness. But Marcella hadn't been there when they'd all fought for the band, or for each other. And *none* of them had been there when Mish had been a kid. "Oh, honey, you don't have to tell me that. I've fought for what I want my entire life." She drew close, pausing before she entered the bus. "But that fight can't be one-sided. Sometimes you have to let people go."

Even if she didn't want to. Wanted to wail and beg and bargain. Sure, she'd listen and hope and use logic. But if David was going to walk away, she'd let him.

When she stepped on board, David was there, in one of the crew seats, his hands gripping his hair. He looked up as Mish made her way toward him.

The heartbreak in his eyes was unfathomable. Especially when they alighted on Marly. "You..."

Mish held up a finger. "Wait. Let's talk before you make unilateral declarations."

He sat back against the seat. "Okay."

She sat sideways on the seat across the aisle from him. "What happened tonight wasn't your fault. Like the ring wasn't your fault."

A snort and a shake of his head. "I'm supposed to be your bodyguard, Mish. No one's supposed to get that close to you. Both events were entirely my fault."

"Technically, you were hired to provide security for the band."

"We both know why I was hired." His voice was flat.

"And I fucked up that job. Over and over again." He rubbed at his beard and finally looked like he had lived more than forty years. "I shouldn't have gotten so close."

There it was. "That's bullshit. All of it. First, you've done your damnedest to keep me—and us—safe. Second, we've chosen to continue interacting with fans. Doing the signings and the encounters and all of those things."

He started to argue, but she cut him off. "And third—the ring would have been stolen and that necklace would have been stolen regardless of whether we were involved or not."

He leaned his head back and looked up at the ceiling. "Maybe," he whispered. "Maybe not."

The pain in his voice and the lines in his brow were symptoms of something else—and the words came out of Mish's mouth fast and hard. "You were thinking of ending things before tonight, weren't you?"

David closed his eyes, and the truth cut through her hard and fast. She nearly dropped Marly. "Were you even going to talk to me about it?"

"I wanted to. Wanted to talk. But there was never any time. Tonight only drives home how much this isn't going to work." He gestured between the two of them. "No matter how much I want it to."

Anger finally wormed its way into Mish's veins, thank goodness. It hardened her bones and drew a shield around her fragile, shattering heart. "So, since you've got it all figured out, you wanna tell me why you're dumping me on my ass? Why this—" she repeated his gesture "—won't work?"

She was glad for David's flinch. "Because this tour's going to end. Then what? What happens?"

Mish wracked her brains. "I figured we'd keep seeing each other. I'll be in the city, you'll be in the city. Why wouldn't we see each other?

"Sometimes my jobs take me out of the city." David rubbed his hands on his thighs. "This one is a perfect example. If I take a gig with another band, or an executive who travels, or someone like that, I won't be around." He paused. "And when you go out on tour, I'm not gonna be security for you all. I'm too close now. I'd turn down the job even if Ray offered."

This didn't make sense. She held Marly a little tighter. "So?"

He rotated in his seat and stared at her. "Our lives won't intersect. You'll be off being a rock star and I'll be back working the jobs I had before I got..." He let the statement drift off, his skin blanched. "Being a rock star's significant other is...a detriment in my line of work. I'll be famous. No one's gonna hire me."

That wasn't at all what she expected and it made her blood run cold. "So you're dumping me because I'm a liability to your income?"

"God, you make me sound like a fucking asshole," he said. "How are we going to date if we never see each other? You'll be off doing your thing, and I'll be off doing mine, 'cause yeah. I still have to eat, Mish."

Except she could support him. Even as the thought slipped into her mind, she knew he'd reject it and why. She'd have done the same—they were alike in many ways. Fiercely independent. Fighters. People who'd learned to rely on no one but themselves for years and years.

She'd found Twisted Wishes, though, and learned that she needed Ray and Dom and Zavier and Adrian—and now Marcella—as much as they needed her.

Still, she felt compelled to offer the notion, at least in a roundabout way. "There's a place for you here, David."

"Doing what?" He raked a hand through his hair. "I know what you're thinking. I wouldn't have to work. It's not the money. It's—me. I need to be useful. And if I'm—If I'm not much more than a groupie because I happen to be dating you..." He shook his head. "I can't, Mish. I love every fucking second with you. You're the best woman I've ever met. But you're you and I'm me."

"I have no idea what that means." The pain slipped past the anger, dragging sadness in its wake. "There's a ton of things to do on tour. You wouldn't be a fucking groupie..." And the anger sprang back. She shoved Marly into David's hands. "Shit. I can't believe you said that."

Standing felt better, so she did, and paced a few steps down the aisle before turning and stomping back. "I get wanting to be independent. I *so* understand that. But if you hook your life up to someone, things give way. You make compromises. You do it out of love."

"You don't have to. You hold all the cards."

She froze in place, heart shattering like glass, eyes locked on his. What he said was true from a certain point of view. "Do you want me to give up the band?"

He stared back at her, his face ashen. "What?"

"Do you want me to give up the band?" she repeated. "Because it sounds an awful lot like the only reason you don't want to be with me is that I'm a rock star."

"No!" Exasperation changed his voice, tinged it higher. "I don't want you to quit the fucking band! You've worked your entire life for this!"

"Yeah, I have." She stood still, watching and waiting.

David looked away first, absently hugging Marly tighter. "I love you. It's way too soon to say that, especially since I don't know how to be with you and still be me. I fought my entire life to be me."

"I'm not asking you to change." Even as the words came out, she knew they weren't correct. Because relationships *did* change you. Partnerships changed you. Friendships.

She'd seen that with Ray and Zavier, then with Dom and Adrian. Hell, she wasn't the same person she'd been when they'd started this tour.

David didn't even have to say anything. His expression

spoke every word. And maybe—maybe he did love her. Maybe it had changed him. Maybe he didn't like who he'd become with her. That, more than anything else, sliced her open.

"Okay," she managed to push out of her mouth. "So that's it."

"Yeah," he whispered. "That's it. I'm going to suggest the band find another person for this job once you guys take your July break."

Just like that, he was leaving. "It was just a meaningless necklace."

David set Marly on the seat next to him, and rose. He took both of Mish's hands in his own, his fingers so warm against her skin.

Only then did she notice she was shaking. Trembling. Ah, fuck.

"You're right. It's not the necklace. It's not about tonight. I'm not lying when I say I loved every second with you. With the band. But we live in two different worlds, you and me."

At least he wasn't giving her the "you'll find someone better" speech. But this still felt fucking horrible. "It's the same world."

"It's not. You know it's not. I'm not built for it. I need—I don't know. Work. Simple things."

"Not to be a rock star's boy toy."

He flinched. "It's not the press, either." He squeezed her hands, then let go. "It's in here. It's me. I can't...be who you'd need me to be if we stay together."

She could taste the bitterness of her words in her mouth. "Doesn't matter what I say, does it? Even if I were to tell you how fucking much I love—" Her voice broke and the damn tears streaked down her face. "You've got all the fucking answers, don't you?"

"I'm sorry, Mish."

She wiped at her eyes. "No, I don't think you are. I think

when I walk off this bus, you're gonna be relieved that this is over. You're going to think you did the right thing." She straightened up, setting her spine and her will. "I hope that gives you some comfort, because we're not fucking talking for the rest of the tour."

Then she turned on her heels and walked off the bus.

The boys and Marcella were on the band bus when she returned there. "I don't want to talk about it." The words came out like a whip as she marched to the back of the bus and yanked the privacy curtain shut.

Then she doubled over as her lungs and heart warred with her despair and sorrow. Gasps of air, because she would not fucking break down and sob over fucking David Altet, who'd decided she was—something. Out of his league? A fairy tale? God only knew.

Yes, she was a rock star. But she was also still herself, with feelings and emotions. She was also that young woman singing in a dive bar on the Jersey Shore where Ray'd found her. She was all these things and more, and if David didn't see that, couldn't fight for that...

Well. His loss.

Except it felt like the end of the world for her.

The curtain on the entryway fluttered. "Mish, may I come in?" Zavier's voice.

"Yeah." She sounded like a cheese grater.

Zavier slipped past the curtain. In his hand he held a white mug, which he offered to her. "Not gonna ask you anything. Just wanted to bring you this, to take the edge off."

From the smell and the lovely amber color, it was a shot of Adrian's whiskey. She took the offered mug and sipped. "Thanks."

He hesitated. "Do you want company?"

She didn't know. There weren't any answers in the mug. "You don't drink much anymore, do you?"

Zavier crossed the lounge and sat down. "No, not since

Ray and I started living together. He's fine with me drinking. We sometimes even open a bottle of wine if he's in the mood. But I follow his lead on that."

"You changed for him."

Zavier cocked his head. "Yes. But also no. I'm more myself with him, more than I've ever been with anyone else, if that makes sense."

"Yeah." It did. She took another sip of the whiskey, and the tightness in her chest eased. The tears came back. But Zavier was safe. A brother and a friend. "I don't understand people, Zav."

He huffed a soft laugh. "Welcome to my world. I'm not sure I understand Ray entirely. But he lets me be who I am—and lets me figure out who I am, too."

"I'm sure you do the same for him."

"I try." He waved a hand. "I fail sometimes. I'm an asshole and overprotective and a whole host of things. I'm not sure why he puts up with me. But I want to *be* with him." Zavier folded his hands together. "No one was more surprised about that than me."

She sank down on the couch next to him and threw back the rest of the whiskey. "David doesn't know how he can be with me once the tour is over."

Zavier seemed to consider this. "Lots of answers to that."

"Mmmhmm. He had a reason why it wouldn't work for all of them."

Zavier opened his arms, and Mish accepted the hug. He didn't offer them too much, but his hugs were some of the greatest.

"I don't know what to tell you," he said. "I know you hurt. If there's anything I—or any of us—can do to ease that, you know we're here."

"I know. You guys are the best."

They were hers, and if nothing else, she'd always have them to love and watch over.

CHAPTER TWENTY-ONE

Every day hurt. There was an odd familiarity to that for David, similar to an old wound aching, though this pain was unlike all the others—physical and mental—that he'd experienced before. He was with Twisted Wishes on tour, walking the rounds at shows. Coordinating with site security. Working with Adrian and Marcella to keep the band safe. All the things he'd done before.

But the warmth was gone. That sense of belonging. He was an outsider, in a way he'd never been on day one. There was an air of pain and sadness in all his interactions, even with the other crew members.

He'd expected it, but it still hurt so fucking much. So did seeing Twisted Wishes perform in Chicago and in Detroit. Each show was phenomenal. Ray's voice was stronger than ever. Mish still sang several of the songs, and she was glorious on stage. Glowing, triumphant. Beautiful. Everything he'd wanted but couldn't have.

A true rock queen, with a heady life ahead of her.

He ached for a touch or a smile. But none was coming, not for him. That he deserved—he'd broken her heart. He'd broken his own, but that was better than pretending they could be more than a tour hookup.

Even if she had been the one person who'd understood him, both mentally and sexually. Who didn't angst about his body. Who loved him for who he was, no strings attached.

There were always strings, though. They pulled against him whenever he read another email from Mish's stalker—since the fucker had to gloat about his latest prize, stolen right from under David's nose. Or saw the way the media interacted with the band or, for that matter, the way the fans did. They worshiped the ground the band walked on.

If he wanted to be himself, he couldn't paste himself onto Mish's life. Or Twisted Wishes. He needed to live on his own.

Plus, his interaction with Mish had only fueled her stalker—David was the reason the necklace had been stolen. To show that the stalker was the better man. She didn't need to know that. Didn't need David making her life harder by being close.

At each show, he ignored the voice telling him he was making a mistake, that he was walking away from something so *good* he should be clinging to it instead. But the logical side of his brain told him this way was right. He was more focused now—seeing the things he should have seen before. People slipping line. Trying to get closer to the stage. Small things, but exactly the shit that put the band in danger.

He'd been a fool to think he could be all business and still pal around with the band. Or date Mish.

He missed her so damn much, even when he was only a couple of feet away.

They'd made it through the rest of the shows, though, and were back in New York City. There was a concert tonight, then the band were guests for a night show taping the next day, then that was it—at least for David. Twisted Wishes would take a break, and when they went on the next leg of their tour, there'd be someone else watching over Mish and the band. Someone more competent than him.

Ray'd promised David a decent referral, despite everything. "You're being too hard on yourself," Ray'd said. "You were doing a fine job." He said nothing about Mish, though every word spoken, every movement Ray made, was marred with hesitation and sadness.

Adrian was the only one who managed a smile around him, but even that was strained. He shared the texts and emails with David. Talked strategy. As expected, a photo of the necklace had been sent in. Nothing had changed.

Everything was different.

During the New York concert itself, David was on the left side of the venue, monitoring the entrance to the stage as Domino's guitar wailed over Zavier's drums and Mish's bass. Ray belted out another anthem and the crowd was dancing and screaming. David didn't blame them. Twisted Wishes was perfect tonight—a fantastic hometown show.

Mish was dressed in blood-red and white—an untouchable goddess. It hurt so much to watch her, he had to look away.

That was why he felt his phone vibrate in his front pocket—he wasn't distracted. He dug the thing out and peered at a text from Adrian. A photo. Here at the concert—but that was all he parsed out before the screen dimmed and he scrambled to unlock it.

The photograph was of David—his back—taken at an angle, but unmistakably him, standing exactly where he was now. The text was from Adrian.

> This came in email. He's here. Watch your back!

Adrenaline slammed into David, and training took over. He clicked his phone off and shoved it back into his pocket, far too aware of the noise around him. Fans jostled one another as they danced and sang. The pulsing thrum of Twisted Wishes and the movements of the lights and the band on stage cast shadows around the building.

At the same time, silence descended but for a high-pitched ring in David's ear. Everything turned sharp and slow. He stared, unseeing at the stage, all his senses tuned to his back. Then he moved to the right—the same direction the photo had been taken from.

A calculated move—the man behind the texts and emails was obsessive, but also careful. Chances were he'd have left that spot. So David glided past, then around, until he reached an emergency exit and put his back to the doors. There, he finally relaxed somewhat and the din in his ears died down. Glancing around the venue, he didn't see one damn thing that attracted his attention. No one watching him and not the stage. Yes, there were fans in a few of the aisles, hurrying back to their seats, but no one looked out of place. No one ever had. Every incident had been the same—no warning.

It was a fucking *rock concert*. This was Twisted Wishes, who skirted punk and metal and pop and were very queer. *Everyone* looked like they belonged, no matter what they wore.

Goddamn it.

David's phone buzzed again. He took it out again.

You okay?

Yes. No. He hadn't been okay since that jerk had snatched Mish's ring. He had no way to protect her. No idea who this guy was. And the man had just drawn crosshairs on David.

I'm fine. Moved near an exit.

Anything we should do?

He should suggest cancelling the signings. Refund the fans their money. He doubted the band would go for it. Still, worth a shot, even obliquely.

Short of nixing the signing event, I don't think so. Be extra vigilant. And tell the band when they come off stage.

Will do. They might agree. We'll see.

There was a pause before the next text.

Stay safe out there.

Something twisted in David's gut—a pain of his own making. These people—Mish's people—could've been family.

Don't worry about me.

Yeah, well, I do. We do.

David didn't answer that one. The twist inside stung his eyes. They understood him and they didn't. Just like Mish. Just like all of the people in his life.

A fling had been a bad idea. It had put them all in danger.

As David had predicted, the band didn't cancel the signings after the show—though only because the argument went back and forth with everyone giving pros and cons until it was far too late.

"Make a decision." Marcella looked at her watch. "We're almost out of time."

"Look," Ray said at last. "We either go out there and do this thing, or we probably end up with a riot of fans."

"Our fans have never rioted," Dominic said.

Zavier picked at his jeans and said nothing. The silence wasn't unusual, but his hesitancy was. Mish sat on a stool, arms folded around her middle, closed off.

"There's a first time for everything," Ray countered.

There was, though David doubted a riot would ensue. The fans would be sorely disappointed, which the band hated. He pressed his back against the door, still feeling the phantom eyes of the stalker on him, the lingering threat keeping his pulse up and grinding his stomach with memories of sand and fear.

Mish stirred and looked up. "David?"

His name ripped through him. She hadn't spoken it—or anything to him—since that night on the bus.

"Yes?" The word lodged in his throat and he had to cough it out like an old bone. He met her gaze.

"Can you keep me safe enough for this?"

A simple question, spoken into the now dead-silent room. Not a single other person moved. Hell, David could barely breathe. *I'm still in love with this woman. I'll always be in love with his woman.*

He cleared his throat. "I think so." His response was careful, even as his mind whirled through the logistics. "We're indoors. We can control the flow. If you don't mind being on the end of the table with me standing next to you."

Her gaze didn't waver, and that ripped him to shreds. "I don't mind," she said.

He swallowed and nodded.

Ray shifted and exhaled. "Then I guess we're doing this?"

Murmurs of agreement.

They trooped out, sat, and signed, with David hovering close to Mish and watching each fan as they passed by. Fans gushed. Mish started out somber but was soon laughing and smiling as she greeted people and listened to their stories and signed their items.

Every laugh, every smile, the way her cheeks rose and her eyes glittered—they were tiny bullets to David's soul. Mish was every inch a beautiful person. One that deserved all the hope and happiness in the world.

It took all his energy not to watch her. Instead, he scanned the lines and focused on people interacting with Ray, Zavier, and Domino. Not a damn thing was wrong. No one sparked his nerves or worried him. In fact—nothing at all happened except that Twisted Wishes made memories for a bunch of fans.

In the end, they headed backstage, cleaned up, and then—since it was New York City and their last show for a while—Marcella had a car service drive everyone home.

Before Mish left, she laid a hand on David's shoulder—briefly—but it had him swaying on his feet. "Thank you."

Her eyes were that beautiful green he remembered from nights in bed. "You're welcome. I'm glad nothing happened tonight."

"Me, too." Her smile was sad. "See you tomorrow, David." Then she was gone.

Tomorrow. Night show taping. His last gig with the band. He should have taken the train home, but he was too weary to argue with Marcella, so he took the ride she'd booked for him, closing his eyes as the car worked its way uptown. By the time he got to his apartment, his throat hurt—not from illness or overuse, but from corking up all the pain and sorrow building and building inside him. His lungs hurt. So did the scars from deployment. He took a hot shower, then collapsed into bed.

He was doing the right thing. Absolutely doing the correct and proper thing. Anything else would only bring Mish pain. He told himself that over and over, even if every part of his soul rebelled at the thought.

The night show studio was frigid—nearly cold enough that if David exhaled hard, he'd see his own breath. He was glad for the sweatshirts Marcella had thrown into a bag for the band members when they got there.

"I was warned," she said.

Apparently the audience had been as well, because a number of them sported coats even though it was in the mid-nineties outside and so humid the entire city smelled like old socks that had been left in rotting pizza.

In some ways, the cold-ass studio was a blessing.

Under the bright lights, though, the band quickly stripped off the sweatshirts, even during their warmup session. After that, they were whisked back for makeup and wardrobe, then the whole show taping happened.

Given the security of the studio, David was superfluous. He was in the way and not part of the group. His job was done, had been since the night before.

The taping itself was uneventful—the show ran through the monologue, the main guests, and then Twisted Wishes played an abbreviated version of "Finding Light" with both Ray and Mish singing. Then the band ended up on the couches, with the host bantering back and forth with snappy questions that the members answered with witty comebacks. That bit hurt to watch. This would be the last time he'd see Twisted Wishes—see Ray, Zavier, Dominic, and Mish—up close, in person, their personalities shining through.

"You could change your mind," Adrian said, standing at his right shoulder like a freaking guardian angel or his own damn subconscious.

"It's not that simple." Staying with the band and not with Mish would kill both of them in the long run.

Adrian didn't say anything, just gave a little shrug.

David kinda wanted to punch the guy. He wondered if that was what it felt like to have a brother—that mix of utter frustration, warmth, and understanding. God, he was gonna miss all of them so damn much.

After the segment with the host and the band, they taped a bit more, then the whole show wrapped up, with the studio band playing the audience out. Twisted Wishes hopped off the stage to mingle a bit with some fans, and that's when David perked up. This part—this was when he needed to be alert.

He kept an eye on the fans and the rest of the audience, moving to position himself near Mish. No idea why, but his hackles went up—the same way they had that concert where Mish's ring had been stolen. Or that night long ago in the bar.

Slipping past a few fans—they had to be in their early twenties—he scanned the rest of the crowd. Nothing.

He turned back and noted Adrian watching him, eyebrow raised. David was about to shrug when he spotted a man working his way toward the band from an odd direction. Not from where he should have been coming, and his approach would take the band by surprise.

Older guy—older than David. White. Thin face. Brown hair. Unremarkable, except for an intense look as he homed in on Mish. He had his hand in his coat pocket.

Fuck!

David was on the wrong side of the studio. No way to put himself between the fucker and Mish.

The man had passed Adrian, too. David surged forward, but the guy was maybe two arms' lengths from Mish.

"Mish!" he called. "Run!"

Mish! Run!

David's words ripped through Mish. The worry, the terror imbedded deep into his voice. She loved David. Trusted him. Believed in the danger he warned about. But she was through with running, with worrying, with being fucking *helpless*.

Instead, she turned and met the cold eyes of her tormentor. Years had passed, but she recognized him instantly.

Breath left her to be replaced by heat and anger and seething. *This* man? Of course this man. Of all of them, it would be *this* fuckhead. Coals of anger blazed beneath her skin and fire stoked in her bones.

"You." The word erupted from deep inside, from the marrow of her past, shot up through her soul into her mouth until she exhaled them like fire. "You fucking *asshole*."

She started toward the man, vaguely aware of the dismayed cries of her bandmates—they were too far away to stop her, though she understood their protectiveness.

In response, the creep dropped the jacket he'd been holding and a knife flashed in the lights of the studio. Sixteen years had passed since she'd seen those dead eyes and the glint of a blade, since this man had tried to touch her.

Everything clicked in that moment—the past and the present slowing to a near standstill, like something out of a movie. Fury and pain and rage roiled in Mish.

He'd been seeing her mother, yet another one of the shitty men who'd passed through their lives because they'd seemed so *nice* at first. One more man whose lies her mother had believed. This one, though—Mish had shoved so much about him from her mind.

His eyes. She remembered those cold, cold eyes, a shade of brown that should have been warm. The same eyes had followed her when she'd walked through the living room of the tiny apartment she'd lived in with her mother. Now she remembered that leer, that glint of metal when he'd come to her closet of a bedroom and told her to be quiet. How she'd screamed anyway before he'd even crossed the threshold.

She'd been seventeen. He'd been in his thirties. A couple of years older than her mom.

That had been the only time she'd ever seen her mother hit anyone. She'd thrown a punch to the head that had stunned him enough that he'd let go of the knife. There'd been blood, too, running down his face. Maybe that had been enough for him to fear her mom and run from the apartment.

After he'd left, they'd packed all the important things and fled, too. Stayed with friends he hadn't known until they could find another place to live.

Mish pushed past a panicked fan, intent on vanquishing this monster from her past. She didn't remember his name. Couldn't. Blotted that out.

What had come to haunt her and her mom after those events had been worse. The cancer, the struggle to keep a roof over their head. Food on the table. Then not being able to fight the demon that took her mother from her.

But this fuckwad? She was going to rip his heart out with her bare hands.

His grin was a horrible mockery of delight. "I finally found you, bitch. Took years. But I saw through your disguise."

That same voice, the one that had come over the phone at the radio station. The slickness of it. Now she remembered where she'd heard it before.

"I wasn't hiding. And you're gonna wish you hadn't found me." She slipped past someone else, and shook off their grip on her arm.

"Mish, no!"

That voice she knew, understood the horror and anguish there. David loved her, respected her, and cared for her safety. But he'd let her go because he couldn't let his job go for *her*.

That stabbed at her heart, layering sorrow on top of the rage. David would blame himself for this, just as her mother had taken the blame for this horrible man and for the cancer that claimed her.

Mish reached for this monster's throat, even as the blade

stabbed up toward her. This monster she could conquer. Fight. For her and her mom.

Except David was there, throwing himself between her and the knife, knocking her tormentor away. The blade, though—that kept moving right into David's torso.

His eyes widened and his lips turned into a knowing circle of pain. His hands moved, landing blows against the other's chest. A few grunts, but nothing more from either of them. There was blood and screaming and others rushed forward, even as David stumbled back.

The blade clattered on the floor, stickily wet, shining in a different way now.

Oh hell. Oh *fuck*. This person, this *afterthought* of a human, would not win. Not this time.

Mish's fingers caught on the monster's shirt and she yanked him to her, to his doom, and her fist landed against his face with a satisfying crunch of bone on bone. Pain lanced up her arm, but not enough to keep her from punching him a second time, for good measure. His weight falling back ripped him from her hands, and he landed hard on the floor.

Still, the monster moved, scrabbling backward and away —right into the legs and shoes of studio security, who caught him in multiple grips. He struggled until a gun appeared, held by a New York City cop.

"Stop resisting," the cop barked.

This man, this monster, wasn't a horror anymore. He slumped pathetically in the hands of security, undone.

Mish blinked, and the world swam as chaos cascaded around her without touching her at all, as if she were the eye of some terrible, awful storm.

"Are you all right, ma'am?"

Ma'am. Not seventeen anymore—far from it. She flexed her hand, and fuck, did it hurt, but nothing seemed broken.

"Yeah." That wasn't the truth, but what else could she

say? Later, she'd crumble. When it was safe, when all was settled and done.

"Mish." Ray's voice was full of worry and pain, but also her name, her truth. She'd never hidden—especially not from him. She'd just chosen to detach from her past.

She turned toward him. "Hey, kiddo."

His eyes were too dark and painful in the bright lights of the studio. "David's been stabbed."

Just like that, her calm shattered as reality caught up to her. Mish stumbled against Ray, her heart ripping, and all the horror and nausea returned. All the terror and torment. She reached for her rage to center her, even as Ray supported her, but couldn't find it anymore. The storm had caught her as well.

Zavier was there with Ray, she realized. Silent but present, concern laced into his gentle touch as he helped collect her. Kept her from falling and falling.

They were too good for words, these men, who were part of the reason she believed in the goodness of the world. Their music. Her family.

David.

"Where?" That was the only word she could manage to push out.

They took her to him, and each step was like stepping on needles with legs made of broken glass.

David lay on the floor with Adrian by his side, pressing a black T-shirt to David's torso. Drops and smears of blood littered the tiles nearby. Adrian was bare-chested, though a too-small leather jacket had been thrown over his shoulders. Domino's jacket, with all its chains and spikes, didn't look imposing on Adrian.

Dom stood nearby, no longer Domino by far, a familiar expression marring his worried face. He'd been like that with Ray, too. Eyes wide, the persona he wore completely gone. "They called 911," he said.

Ray murmured words of comfort into her ear that she didn't understand. Her vision hazed and twisted and a lump lodged in her throat, one made of regrets and sorrows and frustrations.

David had his eyes closed, his mouth twisted in pain. His breath caught every so often, but evened out right after as he obviously fought through the pain to stay calm.

He'd been a soldier. This wasn't his first wound. She'd seen a few of those scars, the ones he didn't talk about.

God, the world was wrong and awful and horrible.

Mish wanted to collapse to the floor. Would have without Ray and Zavier holding her up. Wasn't time to fall apart, not yet. Instead, they helped her kneel by David's side. She wouldn't sob, either. Wouldn't break down.

"David?" Her voice wavered, as her heart clenched and tumbled and shattered.

He flicked his eyes open. "Baby, you okay?"

Hearing him ask the question like that didn't help the ache in her lungs. "I'm fine."

"You got him?" His voice was rough, as if speaking pulled out all his strength.

"Yeah." She finally raised her hand to look at it—and it wasn't pretty. Some cuts and a lot of bruising. But all the fingers worked. "Ray's gonna chew me out again."

"Am not." Quiet, sweet words from Ray. "Love you too much."

Her sight wavered again. David coughed a laugh, then winced. "You've got a mean hook."

"I hate him." That came out as a whisper. "You were right. I knew him. Fucker dated my mom."

A small nod of understanding.

Then there was a bunch of commotion and some sort of medical personnel swarmed around David. EMTs or paramedics. God, the déjà vu was *awful,* except this time Ray was behind her. He tried to draw her away, but she could be unmovable when she wanted. He meant well, but she needed more time, so she shrugged off his touch.

Zavier spoke, but the words made no sense, because every one of her senses was tuned in to David, who pushed the hands of one of the paramedics away and reached toward her.

"Princess?" His voice was shaky and rough as they worked on him.

Mish's heart rammed against her ribs. Seeing him like that, laid out on the floor as they peeled Adrian's T-shirt away, was too much. The ache in her chest threatened to tear her apart.

"Not a princess," she said, all husk and unshed tears.

He smiled for an instant, then followed that with a deep wince. "Rock queen." His eyes were dark and wet. Despite the noise and people all around, only they existed in the world in that moment.

"Yeah." She took his hand and squeezed it, relishing the warmth and the pulse. "What do you need, David?"

He blinked a few times and blew out a breath. "Marly's gonna get lonely. Would you to look after him? He's in—" He waved in the direction of the exits.

The tears Mish didn't want came so fast, she barely had time to breathe. They ran down her cheeks and it took everything in her to keep her voice steady and not let it turn into sobs. "I can do that, sure. Keep him safe until you come home."

"Home," he murmured. "I wish..." He gritted his teeth then and grunted, low and guttural.

"Ma'am," one of the paramedics said, and gestured for her to stand back.

"Hey, come on. Gotta let them work." This time, she let Ray draw her away, because he was right. She loathed leaving David in the hands of strangers, even professional, well-meaning ones. "One of us needs to go with him."

Ray helped her to her feet and didn't let go, though his touch was gentle and unobtrusive. This man was their spine and heart. Their leader through and through. They'd all be lost without him. "Marcella's going with the ambulance. She's got David's medical history."

Of course Marcella would. She had all of their shit. "It should be me."

"Mish." A deeper voice—Zavier's. He gave her name such weight and care, as if his heart were breaking, too. She met his gaze and opened her arms—and he folded her into tight hug. A brother, a friend. "Believe me, I know. I *understand*. But Marcella will take care of him. And you and us."

"Okay." She pressed her face down onto Zavier's shoulder. "How about getting me out of here, then?"

Zavier flinched. "You're gonna have to talk to the police first."

"Shit." She'd forgotten about them. And momentarily about the monster she'd defeated. Tremors threatened to take over.

Zav must have felt them, because he melted a little. "I understand that, too." He loosened his hold. "You don't have to tell them much. We'll get the lawyer on the phone."

"But I kinda punched that shithead out."

"Yeah." He flashed a smile. "Honestly, I don't think you're gonna catch any flak for that."

In the end, she didn't, not from the police, nor from anyone else, though a paramedic did give her a cold pack for her hand and admonished her to have it checked out.

She almost wanted them to haul her away to the hospital, but the cops did have a few questions about the whole incident. She answered most of them, shaking off a few, like how she knew the man, with more vague answers. She'd have to answer more later, but when they'd gotten enough of a statement from her, she held up her hand. "Guys, I'm tired and rattled and someone I care about was stabbed. Can this wait?"

They let her go, with a business card and some murmured niceties. She found Zavier and the others waiting for her. "Now can we get the hell out of here?"

They did. Her bandmates and Adrian—her family—ushered her out, protected her, and got her into the waiting limo without so much as having one paparazzi shove anything in her face. Their ride was more of a luxury SUV than an actual limousine, which was good, because Ray directed them to the hospital.

Somewhere along the line, Adrian had acquired a new T-shirt, one with the late show's logo on it. Mish tugged at it. "They give you that?"

He nodded. "I was in the hallway after the paramedics took David, and the staff took pity on me."

"This is why we don't share clothes," Dom said. He had his jacket back on, but still looked more Dominic than Domino.

"Tell that to the sweatshirts you keep borrowing," Adrian said.

That got him a little quirk of Dom's lips, but he settled back into a frown pretty fast. "Do you think our tours are cursed?"

Mish shook her head. "This is my fault."

"No." Both Ray and Zavier echoed one another. Ray planted a hand on Zavier's knee and that was all it took for Zavier to snap his mouth shut. Worry marred his face and hooded his eyes.

"No," Ray repeated. "None of this was your fault." He shifted his gaze to Dom. "And no, our tours aren't cursed."

"Still feels like we need a cleansing ritual or something." Dom hugged himself, and Adrian pulled him close.

"Still feels like my fault." Because it did. David wouldn't

be hurt if not for her. This asshole wouldn't be disrupting their tour if not for her.

"Mish." Ray rubbed his forehead. "It's not. You know it's not."

She did logically, but emotionally was an entirely different story. Fuck it all, the tears came again. She gritted her teeth. "Doesn't make a difference, does it?"

"It does." Zavier's voice was smooth and calm. "How old were you when he dated your mother?"

"Seventeen."

He pursed her lips. "If a fan came to you and blamed themself for being attacked by someone their parent was dating, would you agree?"

She whipped her head up, the shock of that drying her tears. "Fucking hell, Zavier!"

"Would you?" Same soft voice.

"Fuck off. No. Of course not."

He nodded. "None of us would."

If something like that ever happened, she'd pull the fan aside and make sure they didn't heap the blame on themselves. Recommend people to talk to. That kind of thing. Mish closed her eyes. She hated Zav sometimes. Loved him always, the jerk.

The ache was still there, even as they pulled into the hospital. Ray spoke to the driver, maybe making sure he hung around. It was Adrian who navigated the hospital personnel and got them to the hallway outside of David's room.

Marcella was sitting in a chair in the hall, looking as bone-tired as Mish felt. She rose and held up both hands, probably to forestall and questions. "He's fine. Well, as fine as someone stabbed can be. Knife didn't go too deep and hit nothing too vital, they say. They want to keep him overnight, though, to make sure."

"Bet that went over well." Mish had a suspicion David hated hospitals as much as she did.

Marcella's weary smile was enough of an answer. "How's the hand?"

Mish had ditched the cold pack in the SUV, which might not have been the brightest idea, since her hand was still pretty swollen. "It's okay, but I should get it checked out."

"Oh good. I don't have to hound you." Marcella brushed her hair from her face. "I also called our lawyer, and she'll want to speak to you tomorrow—all of you."

There was a little collective grunt about that, but Mish nodded.

"And," Marcella continued, "that shithead is in jail for the night, so don't you worry about him. We're going to request that bail be denied in the morning—and by we, I mean our lawyer. Gonfaus already has people on it."

"That it?" All good stuff, but she really wanted to see David.

"Yeah. Go on. He's in the second room on the left."

Mish went. Behind her, Marcella spoke. "How about you guys wait a little?"

Bless that woman. She'd been the right choice for their manager after all.

Mish slowed when she closed in on the door, took a deep breath to slow her racing heart, then entered.

CHAPTER TWENTY-TWO

More than anything in the world, David fucking *hated* hospitals. Granted, he hated most medical-related things, since so many doctors generally had no fucking *clue* how to handle the fact that he was trans. At least this round of medical shit hadn't been so bad. He suspected that was largely due to Marcella handling the medical details, down to informing them about his sulfa allergy.

Everyone had used the correct pronouns, which sometimes didn't happen despite the voice and beard, and all involved in his care had been respectful, thank goodness. Still, everything about medicine rankled his last nerve and past experiences kept him constantly on vigil and so damn aware of his body that he felt every brush of the sheet and the hospital gown on his skin. He wanted out.

They wanted him to stay. He was going to have to stay. Fucking fucker with the fucking blade.

He rubbed his eyes and sighed. The pain meds had certainly diminished his vocabulary. Back in the army, he'd have come up with a much better string of expletives to call that meat-headed lug.

David had been lucky. Knives were *bad*. Puncture wounds in the chest or stomach were even worse. So much could go wrong. So much *hadn't*, which was a miracle. And Mish was safe. The stalker was in custody. Sure, David had been taken out of commission, but the danger to Mish had been removed.

She could go on with her life, and he had a reason to slip away and let her do that. Marly would keep her safe now. That was enough.

His chest ached for an entirely different reason than the stitched-up hole in his side, and he closed his eyes, wishing the drugs they'd given him would quiet his mind and soothe his soul, too.

"David?"

Mish's voice crashed into him and took away all hope of easing his heartache. He blinked open his eyes.

"Hey." He didn't know whether to use *baby* or *rock queen* or *princess* or what. No clue what he was now. No longer her bodyguard. Not her boyfriend. "How are you holding up?"

She shifted closer, walking carefully, as if unsure the floor would support her. "Me?" She grunted. "I'm fine. Little bruised." She held up her hand.

It was more than a little bruised and Mish was *not* fine. Any fool could tell that. But he knew better than to comment. "Better than me, then." That, at least, was the truth.

Her smile was wan and sad. "I'm so sorry."

"Baby." That slipped out, and he shook his head. "Mish, you have nothing to be sorry for."

Her lips twitched. "Everyone keeps saying that—but I didn't run when you told me to."

No, she hadn't. Maybe if she had, he could have taken that shitstain down without getting hurt. *Maybe*.

He took a breath. "I don't think he brought the knife for you—or not entirely for you. Dude wanted me out of the picture." So he could have Mish to himself. Hell, he'd likely have taken out Ray, Zavier, Dom, and Adrian, too, if that had meant getting her.

Something shifted in Mish, and she looked away. "He had a knife back then, too. Probably thought it would scare me into silence."

A yawning pit opened in David. "Did he hurt you then?"

Mish shook her head, a real smile gracing her lips. "Mom punched him in the face when I screamed. Like mother like daughter, I guess." She lifted her hand again.

She wasn't going to be playing bass any time soon. Good thing the tour had a break for most of July. "You should have someone look at that. Don't want those cuts infected."

"I'm sure Marcella already has someone waiting for me in the hall."

"She's good. Takes care of you all. You'll need that." Especially since he wouldn't be there anymore.

Yeah, Mish had followed his train of thought, because the anguish on her face was mirror to the twisting of his soul. "David."

"I can't." Those words came out as a harsh whisper. "You know I can't stay."

She closed her eyes, but a stray tear fell out anyway. "Fucking damn it," she muttered, and brushed it away. "It's not like you're going to be able to work for a while."

Not with this wound, no. It would take time to fully heal. He could take a few low-key jobs in a month or two, but nothing where he was expected to be very physical. None of that got to the heart of the matter.

"I will be working again. I need to. It's not the money." He'd never asked for anyone else's support. Always lived on his own dime ever since high school. Went into the military to pay for college. All of that.

"We could still—" She waved her hand, and let the rest go unsaid. It was the same argument they'd had before.

"What, with you off touring, or me off on a gig? We'd

drive each other to distraction being together but apart. You know this. We just—baby, our lives aren't the same. There's no meshing them." Not without him dropping his career and becoming another tagalong. Or a groupie. Or getting a job somewhere in their crew only because he was dating Mish.

"I nearly lost you!" Those four words, the way they poured out of her, took his breath away. "I don't *want* to lose you."

He didn't have an answer for that, not really. "You have family." He gestured out to the hallway, guessing that the rest of that little knot of people was out there. "You have them."

"You could be part of that." Mish brushed another tear off her cheek. "We thought you *were* part of that."

Knowing that opened another hole in his chest, one deeper and more awful than any knife wound. "But I'm...just a guy, Mish." He shrugged helplessly. "No one different from any other person."

"That's bullshit—you—" Exasperation seemed to take the words from her. "You were *one of us*."

"Just visiting. And besides, a queen like you deserves someone better than a bodyguard."

"Oh, fuck off with that nonsense." She was beautiful in her anger when she rose from the chair. "You know me better than to try to pull that self-deprecating shit on me." Took only a few steps for her to reach his side. "Look me in the eyes and tell me you don't love me."

He met her gaze, and tonight her eyes were hazel and wet, and so full of pain and hope. He licked his dry lips. "You know I can't do that."

Because he did love her. Truly did. She was the most amazing woman he'd ever met. But sometimes life didn't let you have what you wanted.

"Then why? Why can't we be together?"

"Because I'm not like Adrian. I can't give up my life to follow you around the country."

She blinked a few times, and he felt something slam shut inside her. "But you could for money."

"That's different. It was—"

"A job." She straightened. "Yes, I know."

"Mish."

This time, it was her shaking her head. "I don't think there's anything more to be said. Except—if you think Adrian gave up his life to follow Dom, you really don't know him at all. Or Dom, for that matter." She crossed the room and paused by the door. "Maybe you're right. Because it seems like you don't know any of us, even after all we've been through together. I guess it *was* just a job." She turned to go.

"It wasn't! It wasn't just a job, Mish! I wouldn't be dying inside if it was."

She looked back. "But you've made your choice."

He had. What else could he do? "I'd...only be unhappy. That would be unfair to you." He'd be a grouch and a bother and...everything he feared about himself. Bored. Useless.

Useless.

Mish's stance seemed to soften. "You could have a place if you wanted. Ray'd find one. For family, he does. You could find a home with us. With me."

David looked away from the inkling of hope in her. "I could tell you I'll think about it, but we'd be back here in a month. I need to be who I am, Mish. This has to end."

"Okay. Then let's end it. Goodbye, David." This time she took a step through the door.

"Mish. Keep Marly."

She stopped but didn't turn around. Her huff was full of anguish. "God, you are so fucking impossible, Altet. I'll keep your bear. Have a nice Independence Day." Then she was gone.

Fuck. He'd completely lost track of the days. That last bit stung, too. Yeah, he'd won his independence, but at what price? Part of him still was screaming *why* at the other part.

There was a murmur of voices out in the hall, but they faded away. He hoped Mish was getting that hand looked at. Wounds from mouths could get ugly pretty fast.

When he looked back at the door, he discovered Ray leaning against the frame, his expression unreadable. David could only stare back.

After a few silent moments, Ray heaved a sigh and straightened. "I'd hoped you'd change your mind."

"Sorry. I need..." What? Something. Anything but this emptiness. This feeling he'd made the biggest mistake of his life, even if it was the right choice.

"I'll have Marcella send you the paperwork and shit. Settle up and all that." He took another long look at David. "I'm not lying when I say it's been a pleasure to work with you, David. You were family."

There was that word again. Deliberately used, no doubt. Ray was a wordsmith and knew his craft. "It's been an honor," David replied. "All of you are beyond—" He reached for a word and came up empty. "I couldn't ask for a better group. I mean it."

Ray stuffed his hands into the pockets of his jeans. He looked weary and sad. "I know you do. See you around, David."

"Thanks, Ray."

Then he was gone and David was alone with unshed tears, a stitched-up knife wound and a hole in his heart that was never going to heal.

For a moment, he'd had a family, and now he was alone. He only had himself—his pride and his independence—to blame for that.

By the time Mish returned to her apartment with her bandaged hand and a bottle of antibiotics, she was done with humanity. Completely. She was even too fucking tired to cry or punch pillows or shit. She sank onto her couch and put her face in her hands, then pushed them up into her hair, feeling the curls stop and trap them there.

Her luggage was strewn about the front room. Hadn't even had a chance to unpack.

If only—

But no, she shoved that thought away, even as she slipped her fingers out of her locks. No ifs. David had made a choice, and while she hated it, didn't agree with it, didn't understand it, she had to respect it. And that meant not getting herself wound up by what she couldn't change.

She had changed the shit with her stalker, though. He was gone, and that was a damn good thing. Relief eked through the sorrow of losing David. No more comments or emails. Sure, there'd still be troll stuff, but nothing like that controlling bastard. Maybe she could get her ring back, too. She'd have to ask the police about that.

Mish stood and started her nightly routine, moving from her living room into her master suite and ignoring the hollow in her heart and focusing on the weight that had been lifted. Later, later she'd acknowledge the loss in her soul. But that was too raw and new. Too much, after everything. Did David think they wouldn't come see him in the hospital? That with this over, they wouldn't—*she* wouldn't want and need him anymore?

Mish pressed her hands down onto the cold hard marble of the bathroom counter. So much for ignoring that. *Fucking hell.* Tears welled in her eyes.

Someone buzzed her apartment. Gave her an excuse to wipe her eyes and stop looking at her horrible reflection in the mirror. She figured it was Ray, or maybe Dom. They were the most likely to come to see her after really emotional shit went down. But when she called the front desk, it was Marcella who'd come.

A couple of minutes later, she stood in Mish's apartment, Marly in her hands.

"Oh." Mish reached for the bear and pulled him into her chest. "David wanted me to have him."

"So he said." Marcella hesitated for a moment. "Do you need to talk? Do you want me to stay?"

Wasn't like Marcella at all to offer an ear, but then again, here she was. "I'm—" She wasn't fine. "Yeah, maybe." Mish gestured at the couch in the living room. "You pull the short straw or something?"

Marcella huffed. "No. I'm here because I care. And honestly, the guys have no idea what to do. Not about David, at least." She sat.

Mish joined her. She could only wince at his name and hug the bear tighter. "*I* don't know what to do about David. I want to throttle him for being so fucking dense. But I also get his need for independence. It's not that easy when you've always relied on yourself to hitch your wagon to others."

Marcella tipped her head. "You did."

Mish pressed her nose into Marly, hoping to catch some scent of David. His skin or shampoo or soap—and yes. There it was.

She lowered the bear. "I did. I bet if you ask Ray and Dom, they'll tell you I didn't rely on them. Ray was the leader and all, but I took care of those guys for a long time."

But then Zavier had joined the band during that tumultuous tour. Life had been stellar and horrible at the same time, and they'd all learned to help each other. It had propelled Ray to take care of them all—then Adrian had joined their group, too. Dom had found his own stride.

"But they don't need me anymore."

"Oh god, Mish. They need you more than you know. Those men would walk through fire for you."

"Family," Mish said. "I thought David—" Her throat seized up.

"Yeah, we all did." Marcella poked at the books Mish had left on her coffee table. "Zavier's beside himself—well, as much as he ever is."

That teased a smile from Mish. "He hates being wrong. But not, like, hate hate. It frustrates him when he doesn't understand people."

"Yeah, I noticed. People aren't always understandable, though."

Wasn't that the truth. "I loved him. Love him. David, I mean. Love Zav, too, but..."

"Not like that."

They sat in silence for a while. "I guess I should also be upset about the stalker, but honestly, I'm glad we finally got him. That he showed himself. And punching his smug face was so fucking *satisfying* I can't even put it into words. Like, that was enough."

"Well, there's still a ton of stuff you need to do there. Speak to our lawyer. Probably talk to the cops again. We're going to have to issue a press release about the whole incident. It's not going to be over for a while yet." Marcella made a face. "Plus, there's your hand."

"It's not broken. Not even sprained this time. Just swollen and cut."

"I doubt you're picking up your bass tomorrow."

"Okay, yeah. I'll be out of commission for a bit. But we have a break anyway. I don't think we're gonna have to cancel shows."

"Ray said the same." Marcella pushed at the books again. "But I have to think of all the angles, you know?"

"It's what a good manager does."

Marcella got a strange look, both sadness and joy mixed. "I'm glad I can be there for you all. I'm still pissed that you've had to go through so much." She chewed her lip. "David was stabbed. There's gonna be fallout from that."

"And our breakup, too, I guess."

Marcella shook her head. "We're not going to comment on that. I don't think the sites will pursue that angle for a while, since he was injured. There's recovery time for both of you. You guys can...disappear for a while."

"He's gonna be all right?"

"Yeah. Apparently he's had worse injuries while in the army. Take a couple of months before he can go back to work, but..."

"He can go back to work. He *will* go back to work." Mish pressed Marly against her chin. "That's what we fought about."

"Because if he's working a job, he's not going to be here with you—wherever here is."

"I suppose it's not fair to expect him to follow me around—"

"—but there's space for him. In the crew. In your—"

"Our. You're a part of this. Our family."

Marcella froze for a moment. "Oh."

Mish put Marly down and opened her arms. "I know you're not the biggest on hugs, but..."

Marcella wrapped her arms around Mish's neck. "You have no fucking clue how much both of you scared the shit out of me tonight," she murmured.

"Pfft. You'll get used to it." Mish pulled back.

Marcella laughed. "God, I hope not." She sobered. "Maybe David needs some time."

That had crossed Mish's mind. "Maybe. But I've also learned not to wait too long on another's dime. Gotta live my life, too." Tears welled. "Why the fuck do we have emotions anyway?"

Marcella choked a laugh out. "So you can write songs and sing and have fans scream in joy at you?"

The tears didn't want to stop. "He understood me. How can he leave me when he understood me?" That was the question that lurked, that kept coming back, over and over.

This time, it was Marcella that pulled her into a hug. "Oh, hon. I don't know. I don't know."

She cried then, in Marcella's arms, with David's bear between them. And the tears didn't stop for a long time.

CHAPTER TWENTY-THREE

July flew past, hot, humid, and painful. Mish had spent a good part of the first week after the attack either talking to the police, her lawyer, or some combination of the two. The next week she spent holed up in her apartment, staring at the ceiling of her bedroom until the entire band, plus Adrian and Marcella, had shown up in her lobby with various containers of takeout and three bottles of wine. Then they'd spent the day in her living room watching comedies, action movies, and cat videos until she'd laughed so hard that she'd broken down sobbing.

She'd hated them for that. Loved them, too.

The last two weeks, they started practicing again, to get ready for the next leg of their tour. This time, there was no bodyguard for her. There was security—the band hired a few guards—but they weren't David.

She wanted David. Missed him. Spent too much time clutching Marly.

There were nightmares, too. Of her stalker. Of David with a knife in him. Of her mother in the hospital. Enough that she asked Ray if he knew a good therapist.

That helped, talking to someone. Gaining some perspective. Getting some coping skills.

Once they got back onto the bus, she let herself sink into the rhythm of touring. The late nights, Adrian's fantastic coffee, and their camaraderie. Marcella joined them on the band bus. Turned out she was a natural card shark and whipped them all at any game they played with a deck, including Go Fish.

Most of the time, it was fine. Except for those late nights when Mish held Marly, listened to the rumble of the bus, and let the tears slide silently down onto her pillow.

Being on stage was the best. She lost herself in playing or singing or both. But the constant sway between the joy of the band and her own broken heart left her exhausted. Enough that Dom pulled her into the lounge one day close to the end of their touring stint. They'd sat down on the leather couch that ran along the back of the bus.

"You look like you need a shoulder. And you've been there for all of us so many times." Dom wasn't wearing any of his stage makeup, but his hair was teased up like Domino's, and he was wearing one of his ripped tanks.

"I'm fine." She wasn't, but she also wasn't going to make this tour the "fix Mish" one.

Dom looked up at the ceiling of the bus. "You know you're as bad at lying as the rest of us, right?"

She felt a spark of laughter, but it never made it out of her chest. And yeah, that was a problem. Mish rubbed her eyes. "It's hard, having him gone. It's like he should be here with us. Sometimes I turn and expect to see him. Only he's not here."

Dom nodded. "Though, even if he'd chosen to stay with you and us...he still wouldn't be on this part of the tour."

That was certainly true. Last she'd heard from Marcella, David was still recovering from the knife wound. He'd been in contact with their lawyer and the police, which made sense. When—or if—they went to trial, his account of what happened would be needed.

"I know. But it's—We don't talk. If he hadn't left me, we'd be talking."

"Yeah." Dom flopped back on the couch. "There's that. It does feel strange not having him here. Watching out for us."

"I'm just—" She gestured at the air. "I don't know how I'm supposed to get out of this funk."

"You're not." Dom spoke gently. "You don't get out of heartbreak overnight." She dropped her head into her hands and he gave her a side hug. "But I've been thinking."

"Fuck thinking." She pushed her hands into her curls.

He gave her a hollow laugh. "I know, right? But still. I needed to get my head on straight about Adrian. Zav had to figure out how to quantify the feelings he had for Ray. Maybe David needs some time."

Her therapist had said the same thing. Marcella, too. "I'm not hanging my happiness on some vague hope that he's gonna come to his senses."

"That's fair. I guess I'm trying to say not to give up hope in general? Or maybe wait until after this part of the tour and talk to him again? 'Cause you both went through a lot there..."

They had. "I don't know, sweetheart. You guys lucked out with your partners. Just wasn't in the cards for me this time."

"You two were so good together."

They had been. Mish wiped at her eyes. "I know. And maybe you're right. But I can't live in between maybe, you know? Gotta move on."

"I get it, I do." Dom bumped her with his shoulder. "We're here for you, you know. You carried us for so long. Let us carry you a bit?"

Mish bumped him back. "Let's carry each other. We're a family, right?"

He laughed and rose. "Yup. And the fam says you gotta

come and play this new game Zavier discovered at the last stop. He's trying to find something Marcella isn't good at."

"Oh, good luck there. Poor Zavier. He's found his match."

Dom offered her a hand up. She took it, because yes, sometimes she needed to let them carry her, too. So she went up and learned to play the game Zav had found.

As Mish expected, Marcella won. Every single time. But by the end of the night, Mish was laughing and grinning as much as Zavier. Ray crowned Marcella Queen of the Games, and they all crawled into their bunks happy, even Mish.

She still held Marly tight. Still missed David, but the ache was a little less harsh. She whispered into that plush fur words that barely made sound: "I still love your dad."

But life flowed onward. Tomorrow, there'd be more fans. Another show. One more day to heal as best she could, and grow. She'd make it through this. They all would.

David hadn't expected the loneliness, not while he recovered from his stab wound. There was enough to occupy his time with all the insurance shit and the rehab and exercise he did to heal and keep himself in shape until he could get back to more strenuous workouts. Plus there were all the things he'd put on hold when he'd taken the Twisted Wishes job. Shows he wanted to watch. Books he intended to read. Exhibits he wanted to go see before they left the city.

Plenty to occupy his brain and keep him busy. He should have been fine. That growing sense of isolation was just a reaction to being back in his element, that's all. He'd been off on his own most of his life, ever since high school, really. Sure, he'd been surrounded by people, but mentally, he'd relied on no one. No more than a stranger afloat in a sea of humanity, not fitting in. Everything was back to normal, or should have been.

He didn't *need* anyone. He'd had buddies on deployments and got along with people in general, but those connections had mostly drifted away. Lovers came and went. He'd had several in the army, but those had been on the downlow due to DADT—those women had moved on quickly, too.

He'd never developed feelings *so* strong and deep that they tied him up in knots about his duty versus his desires. Everything had fit neatly in his mind.

Until Twisted Wishes. Until Mish Sullivan.

He wanted to hate them all, but that was impossible. Instead, as the chaos of lawyers and physical therapy wound down, as he fell back into the life he had before he'd met that amazing group of humans, he found that he *missed* them. Mish most of all.

Life was—empty. Devoid of color and vibrancy. He ached for the sound of Mish's voice and their conversations. Her laugh and touch. The way she understood him. How she moved in bed and on stage. Her fear and anger. All of it. He wanted more time. Wanted to reach back into the past and stretch out what he'd had. Somehow make all of this better. Be the kind of person she could date and have. Who'd appreciate her and her life and not be so—selfish.

Didn't know how. Couldn't figure out a way to shake off the terror of relying on another, of not being self-sufficient. Of being useless.

Fuck if he didn't catch himself thinking about the other members of Twisted Wishes, too—of that family who'd nearly adopted him. He'd get breakfast, and Adrian's morning runs, his coffee, and his friendship burst into David's head. He'd pay bills, and Marcella's quiet, organized presence was there. Zavier's devilish grins and quips flitted through his mind when he overheard something amusing. The way Dom switched between bookworm and rock god came to David as he walked between the shelves at the bookstore.

And Ray. God, Ray, whose last words once all the paperwork had been completed still echoed in David's brain. "You know, there will always be a place for you here."

As David scrambled to find another job, Ray was there in his head. After everything that had happened, after David had broken Mish's heart. As if Ray cared about him.

They didn't need him, though. There'd been no security incidents on the latest leg of the Twisted Wishes tour. No reports of stalkers. All the photos he'd seen showed Twisted Wishes happy and smiling and whole. The show reviews were exuberant. Mish and Ray's duets were the highlight of most nights.

Maybe Ray'd been nice in saying what he'd said, but David didn't want to be shoehorned into a group out of pity. Or so he told himself over and over.

But in the months that followed the stabbing, as David tried his damnedest to ignore the ache in his heart and soul, he found himself turning everything over in his head. His unjustified frustration slid into sadness, and he couldn't help realize that maybe...maybe Ray had meant what he'd said. Maybe there could have been a place for him in the Twisted Wishes family.

He'd been a fucking fool for running out on Mish Sullivan.

Oh, he'd lie awake at night and turn that over in his head. The thought lodged itself in his brain like a hook with a barb, so deep that the more he rooted it out, the more he tugged and pulled, shit he didn't want to deal with surged to the top of his psyche. His sense of self. His pride. His unwillingness to listen when he knew what was best.

His goddamned martyr complex.

Once the doctors cleared him for it, he threw himself back into running, despite the heat in the city. Even that didn't numb away the shame that wormed up from the depths of his brain. Turned out he *was* the kind of asshole dick he hated—someone who didn't compromise. Someone who put their own fears ahead of others, without so much as a thought to working through them.

God, he wished he had someone to talk to. Not a therapist —he had one of those—but a friend.

There wasn't anyone he was close enough to. The few people from the army that still talked to him weren't the type to listen to relationship troubles. The one person David could talk to, the one whose number he still had—was one he couldn't even reach out to. He figured Adrian would have blocked his number, anyway.

But after another unfulfilling workout and run, his head and heart were enough of a mess that he did the unthinkable: he texted Adrian.

Hey. I don't suppose you'd have time to talk about something over a beer. —David

Twisted Wishes was back in the city after completing another leg of their US tour. Adrian was probably busy, though. He had a life with Dom. A house in Brooklyn. David didn't expect an answer. He didn't even know what had possessed him to reach out—other than every damn thing in his life feeling utterly wrong now that he was alone.

Maybe thirty minutes later, his phone buzzed.

Of course. Where and when?

David stared at the message. Had Adrian told Mish about the text? What about Dom? And...those were both very good questions. Part of him wanted to answer never and nowhere, but those were both lies. He chose a casual reply.

Whenever. I don't have a regular bar or anything.

He set about cleaning up his already neat kitchen. A few minutes later, his phone buzzed again.

This shit you want to talk about in public?

David snorted.

Not really.

Baring his heart in public sounded excruciating.

Okay. Address, then. I'll bring the beer.

What, now?

On the one hand, better to get this over with, on the other hand...now?

You got plans or something?

He didn't. Never had plans. Spent most nights either binging something on Netflix or reading. Or staring at the ceiling and trying not to think of Mish or the band. Hard to do when every other song on the radio was Twisted Wishes these days. He'd started listening to jazz and oldies.

No, no plans. But I don't want to disrupt your life.

Who knew what Dom thought of all this.

Dude. Just send me your fucking address.

He did, paced to his living room, set his phone down on the coffee table, then collapsed down onto the couch, his head in his hands. A tiny spark of hope ignited in his chest. Maybe...maybe what Ray had said was true. Maybe he still had a place in that family. He doubted he had a shot with Mish, but at the very least, he'd apologize for being an arrogant prick. Couldn't even blame the pain meds for that.

Pride, pride, and more pride.

An hour later, his phone buzzed again.

I'm here. Let me up?

David did, and far too few minutes later, Adrian was at his door, a six-pack of beer in one hand and a plastic bag that smelled gloriously of Chinese takeout in the other. "Figured you might be hungry, too," Adrian said.

Given the way David's stomach grumbled, yes. "I might have skipped lunch." Did, actually. He closed the door after Adrian sauntered in.

Adrian made a noncommittal grunt. "Kitchen?"

David nodded toward the door at the opposite end of the living room, then followed Adrian.

"Nice place. Decent space."

"Yeah. Been here for a while, so the rent's reasonable. Figure if I like it, why move?"

"Oh, I hear you. I own now—and that's a long story—but I lived in California, so..." Adrian set the food and beer on the counter and pulled containers out of the bag. "No idea what you like, so I got a little bit of everything."

David shrugged. "I'm fairly easy."

"No, you're not." Adrian's tone was light, but the comment still carried the weight of a gut-punch.

"I'd say I'm not picky..." But he was that, too.

A wan smile from Adrian. "Grab a beer?"

Adrian had brought a seasonal brew from a local micro-brewery. Not a bad choice. David pulled out two, stuck the rest of them in the fridge, and popped the caps off both bottles.

"Appreciate you coming." He handed the beer to Adrian.

He got another grunt that could mean anything. "Plates? Bowls?" Adrian took a drag on his bottle.

David pulled out two plates. "Fork? Or did you bring chopsticks?"

That got him a laugh. "I brought chopsticks, what do you take me for?"

"An Irish-American with a taste for guys in lipstick?"

Adrian's lips quirked up. "First part's right. Second part's close, but we're most certainly not here to talk about *my* love life."

David winced.

Once they'd taken what they wanted of the food, they settled around his tiny dining table. After a few quiet moments, Adrian regarded him. "I have a pretty good idea of where this conversation's gonna go. But how about you tell me why you reached out to me?"

Rather than answer right away, David toyed with his food and took a swig of beer. When it was obvious Adrian would wait him out, he relented. "I don't have anyone in my life I can talk to. No one I'm close with."

Adrian sat back in his chair. "No friends from the army?"

"None that I'm gonna talk about this shit with, no." He snagged a piece of broccoli with his chopsticks. "They're—We talk about the times we were in, and about current work, and avoid talking about the bad stuff. Plus, I wasn't the man I am now." Back then, he'd been seen as butch. DADT had been in effect, but no one had asked, and he had kept his deeper secret in the closet. "I'm a loner by nature."

"Gotta wonder if that's true. After all, I'm here."

"I'm desperate," David deadpanned.

Adrian cracked a smile. "Maybe you are, but I don't think that's it, either."

It wasn't. "I fucking miss you guys, all right?" David took a swig of beer to loosen the sudden knot in his throat. "First time in my life I felt like I belonged somewhere, then I had to go fuck it up, and now I have no idea how to fix it."

Adrian ate a little before replying. Those moments of silence were excruciating. "It's hard to walk into Twisted Wishes and get caught up in the community Ray built. It's doubly hard to get sucked right into the heart of the group so fast."

"You did, though."

"Not really. I was utterly taken with Dominic before I knew he was Domino Grinder. He and I had—and have—this relationship that's outside of the band." Adrian huffed. "Here we are talking about my love life after all."

This time, it was David who laughed. "It's—I wish I understood the relationships in Twisted Wishes. Maybe if I did I would understand—" He fidgeted with his beer bottle. "Understand what happened between Mish and me."

"I think you know all you need to know to understand you and Mish." Adrian set down his chopsticks. "Do you love her?"

Yes. At least he thought so. "I'm not sure I know what love is. I think about her all the damn time. I regret every word I said when I told her we couldn't be together, and I feel like a goddamned fool. Is that love?" He paused. "I feel like I walked out on my best friend."

"Sounds like love to me. Zavier would call it an intimate friendship. I'm not sure it really matters in the end. Do you want to be with Mish?"

"More than anything. But she isn't going to be taking me back. Even if she did, what the hell would I do with my life? I sure as shit couldn't be security for you all, not when my eyes are glued to the stage." He contemplated his rice dish. "You gotta know what I mean there."

"Oh yeah. That's a perk of my job. I get to ogle my own fiancé while posting about the rest of the band."

"With security, it's everyone else I should be watching. That's how I screwed up."

"You didn't screw up." Adrian held up a hand when David started to protest. "Honestly, the job bit is the least of your worries."

Once more, Adrian had homed straight in on the issue. David gave up on trying to eat his dinner. His nerves were too frayed. "I fucked up beyond belief with Mish."

Adrian nodded solemnly. "Yup. You did."

"Gee, thanks, buddy."

"I'm not gonna blow smoke up your ass, if that's what you were expecting." Adrian took a pull from his beer. "But I will tell you it's fixable."

"How?"

"All this shit you've told me? Go tell her. She damn well wants to hear it. More importantly, she fucking deserves to hear it." He paused. "If you think she's gotten over you, you really need to do a lot more soul searching, dude."

"Dude?" The way that came out was not at all New York City. "Since when do you say dude?"

Adrian shrugged. "Remember my comment about California? Spent a bunch of years out there. Sometimes it comes back."

"Shit ton I don't know about you guys." While it had been weeks and weeks on tour, and intense ones at that, that's all it had been.

"There's a solution to that problem." Adrian took up his chopsticks again and started eating in earnest.

Sure was. Talking to Adrian was both a soothing balm and a bit like ramming his hands onto spikes. Hurt so damn much to have all David knew thrown back at him in no uncertain terms. But all of this—the beer and the food and the conversation—felt like a home he never had.

All he needed to do was reach out to Mish. Tell her the jumbled mess that was in his heart and head, and hope she was willing to forgive him. "Fine. I'll call Mish."

"There you go," Adrian murmured. "Exactly." He had an expression that could only be called one thing.

"You're a fucking smug asshole, you know?" David's stomach had settled down enough to demand more lo mein, so he dug in.

"Nah. That's Zavier." He paused. "Zav wears his heart on his sleeve for his friends, but can't help trying to control the situation. I suppose I'm similar."

"Yeah, you guys are. But you're more laid-back."

Adrian's grunt was a different kind of noncommittal this time. "Maybe, maybe not. You'll need to hang with us to figure that one out."

Now that David was calmer, the food tasted pretty darn good, especially the lemon chicken. "You know, you almost sound like you're the one wooing me to come back to Twisted Wishes."

That got him a bark of laughter. "In a way, I am. We've been at loose ends with some things, and Ray'd love your advice. Hell, if I hadn't asked Dominic to keep your text and my visit tucked up nicely in his makeup box, I'm sure Ray would be here hounding you with some job offer or another."

That froze David. "Really? After fucking up the way I did?"

"You mean taking a knife while protecting Mish?"

David fell silent, and the wound in his side tingled.

"How is it, anyway?"

Beer first, then he answered. "Better. Gonna take a little more time to be fully healed." He set down his bottle. "Guy probably wouldn't have had a knife if I hadn't been in all those photos with Mish." He kept his tone even.

Adrian chose the same tone to reply. "You know that's a fucking lie, right?"

There was nothing he could say.

Adrian pushed his empty plate aside and speared David with a steady, unflinching gaze. "The fucker in question would have brought that knife, regardless. Most likely Mish, or one of the guys, or Marcella, or *me* would've ended up with a knife in our body. Don't think we don't all know this."

"My job—"

"Yeah, exactly. You put your life on the line for Mish, and for us and—" Adrian cut himself off, then pushed back from the table, stood, and gathered his plate. "You should call Mish."

Adrian retreated to the kitchen sink, and David studied the empty chair and the back of the man who'd been there. "This isn't about Mish anymore, is it?" Adrian's reactions were too personal.

Without being asked to, Adrian rinsed the dish, then placed it in the sink. "It's about you." He didn't turn around. "You left Mish. That broke her heart—and yours, too. That's what you need to fix, for both of you."

David grabbed his plate and stood, too. "But?"

"When you left Mish, you left the rest of us, too." Adrian's voice was soft. He turned around, and the tight smile he wore didn't reach his eyes. "It's not the same as with Mish, but don't think you weren't missed by the rest of us, for who you are and what you bring to our group."

Shit. Well, if he needed to feel worse about everything, that did it. He rinsed his plate as Adrian packed up the left-overs. "I think I need another beer."

"There's four left." Adrian nodded at the leftovers. "You should keep these, too. They aren't gonna make it back to Brooklyn, at least not edible."

They stacked the containers in the fridge, and David slipped another beer out of the six-pack holder. "Thank you for this. The food, the beer, the kick in the skull."

Adrian gripped his shoulder. "Any time. I'm glad you

texted." He let go. "I should get back home. I think you have some mulling and maybe a phone call to make?"

God. David didn't want to call Mish. He absolutely needed to. The only thing he could do at the moment was nod in silence. He showed Adrian to the door.

Before he headed out into the hall, Adrian gave him a shrewd look. "Regardless of anything, don't be a stranger, David. We might tour a decent amount, but we're also in the city frequently, too. Call."

"I'm not good with friendships." Obviously, given the way he'd blown it with everyone.

"Well, I am. I can give you a crash course." Adrian tapped the doorframe. "Besides, you're family now."

"Everyone keeps saying that."

"'Cause it's true." Adrian gave him a mock salute. "Night, David."

"See ya." He watched Adrian head to the stairwell, then closed his apartment door.

The talk had helped and also made everything infinitely worse. At least, though, he wasn't entirely alone.

CHAPTER TWENTY-FOUR

Despite the beautiful October day, Mish couldn't get her brain to shut up enough to enjoy it. Usually she loved their breaks in tours. A chance to relax and de-stress and eat some greens rather than the dangerous roadway cuisine they dared each other to consume. Get some sleep. Rest the hands and legs and recover from the grueling schedule that came with riding around the country and performing their hearts out.

But on the road, she didn't need to think. She could throw herself into playing her bass or singing. Ray, Zavier, Dom, and Adrian kept her busy with chatter and quips and fun. Even Marcella had kept Mish occupied with interviews and some exclusive content for this or that magazine or website about her early career.

Now back in her apartment, there wasn't anything to keep her mind from drifting to the one thing missing from her life.

David Altet.

The sadness was tempered with anger. For the way he'd left. Because of what he'd said. She didn't understand how anyone could be so damn *dense*. They *worked* as a couple. Matched in bed and outside of it. He got her humor and her need to be in control of her destiny. She understood his need to be independent, but also his desire to let go.

If only he'd realized that she wasn't asking him to give up his damn job. They could have made something work—or at least *tried*. Wasn't what they had together worth every effort to keep it going?

Apparently, no, she wasn't worth that much hassle.

Even that felt flat. It wasn't *her,* as the saying went. It was David. There was something in him, in his past or his mind or wherever—something love couldn't overcome.

That was an unfair assessment, too. The idea that love could heal all, that it could fix anything, was a fairy tale. Love—or any deep friendship between people—couldn't fix another human being. Love could support, yes. Help, yes. Contribute to the healing, be a balm, yes and yes.

Humans were messy and wonderful, and they weren't broken anyway, even when brains and hearts and bodies didn't work the way everyone said they should. People were who they were, with all their foibles and wonders and faults and greatness. Sometimes, you had to accept that. Help them, yes. But *fix* them?

She didn't know a damn thing about fixing people. She could only stumble into the future with her friends and loved ones by her side. Help them when they needed a hand. Sometimes ask for help herself. The past several months had taught her that.

She'd thought David would be one of those people—maybe *the* person—she'd stumble toward old age next to. But no. She doubted she'd ever find another human being she didn't intimidate in some way. No partner for her.

David hadn't been intimidated, though. He'd been lovely and fun and sexy and a hell of a ride. Her heart grappled with the reality of the loss. He'd been so *set* that there was no way forward together.

Mish paced around her living room, racking her brain for

something to do. She'd already practiced that morning, even breaking out her acoustic guitar to run through some pieces. She probably should work with her upright, but her limbs were itchy and music wasn't soothing her as it normally did.

Probably because she wasn't in the studio with the band. Ray was composing new material. They'd even worked through bits on the bus this last tour leg—but nothing was done enough yet to make going into the studio worthwhile.

That afternoon there wasn't a damn thing to keep her mind from wandering back, over and over again, to the hurt that seemed like a permanent part of her soul. Part of her wanted to rail at David, but she couldn't reach the fury she needed for that.

She didn't want to be angry anymore. She'd spent all her fury and fear on that waste of a man who'd stalked her. She'd need that again later—the court case was still winding through the legal system at a rate slower than molasses in the freezer—but eventually she'd have to be in the same space as him again. Hear his name. See his fucking punchable face.

Right now, though? Didn't want to pour any energy into anger. The stalking and the incident at the night show were both on the list of questions reporters and media personnel were forbidden to ask her. No one made *that* mistake anymore—not after the third time the band had walked out of an interview and the journalist had been told they'd never gain another session with the band.

Marcella had practically rubbed her hands with glee each time she'd handed down that edict.

But without the anger there to fuel Mish, most of what dwelled in her was an ache for what could have been. That was the worst kind of mourning—the constant taste of a dream that had died.

Mish paused, that phrase echoing in her head. She didn't have a notebook like Ray did, but something compelled her to dig out a scrap of paper—an old envelope from a bill—and scribble the line down.

God knew how long it had been since she'd written a song. One line—a trite one at that—didn't a composition make. But it still felt good to see the words on paper. She touched the ink. Maybe she could puzzle something together, even if it only ever lived in a drawer once she'd finished.

She sat down on the couch—the same one she'd shared with David months and months ago, at the start of this odd, wonderful, and crushing tour—and let more lines flow out of her.

The constant taste of a dying dream
Sadness on tap
How do you mend what will always be gone
Fill a hole that has no bottom
Take my hand and show me the sun
Walk along this path with me
Even in despair I am not alone
With you by my side
Fill the cracks in my soul tonight
Drink to the past and to the future
Be with me now and show me hope
Together we are now

She studied the words, then set the pen aside. Ray'd tell her to leave them. Come back later and take another look. That's what he did. He'd revise, then bring them to the group and they'd listen. Make suggestions.

This probably wouldn't get that far. But warmth spread through some of the cold places in her soul—because she *could* take these to Ray and the band, and they would take her seriously. You needed dreams and thoughts of the future to make the now bearable.

She rubbed at her forehead, the bubbles and burbles of too

many emotions making her eyes and head hurt. This needed to end—the sadness and fractured feeling. A tiny part of her said she could call David—but the greater part of her rejected that option. She'd promised herself after watching her mom chase after too many of the wrong guys, that when partners left her, she'd let them go.

If David hadn't wanted to stick around, she wasn't going to force him to. The only way relationships ever had a hope of working was when all partners worked together.

Hell, that's what made Twisted Wishes strong.

Mish closed her eyes and leaned back on her couch. She should get out of the apartment. Go for a walk. Get lost in the streets of the city for a while. Instead, she dozed off—then nearly jumped out of her skin when her phone started ringing.

On the screen was David's name.

She nearly let it go to voicemail—but that seemed worse than answering. "Hello?"

"Hey." His voice was soft, but full of all the grit she remembered, as if he were keeping his emotions in check. "If I told you I was an absolute utter fucking fool of a man, could I buy you a beer?"

She was glad he wasn't in the room, because her heart cracked and those damn tears of hers leaked out of her eyes. She answered him in a calm and steady voice. "I think we could work something out."

"Mish, baby, I'm an absolute utter fucking fool of a man." His voice broke and he cleared his throat. "I don't expect anything. I just want to apologize in person."

The tears wouldn't stop. He didn't expect anything, but this one phone call meant everything. Yes, David still had work she expected him to do, but this was a start. "How about you meet me at that bar you once came to my rescue in?"

There was a pause. "That's still a pretty touristy place, even for a Wednesday in October."

"I know." Because she had a plan, too.

"All right," he said. "I can be there in about forty-five, if the trains cooperate."

"So I'll see you in an hour or so?"

His laugh warmed her heart and did nothing to stop the cascade of tears from rolling down her cheeks. They didn't feel bad this time, even if she hated them on principle.

"Yeah," he said. "See you soon, Mish."

"Soon," she repeated. Because saying *I fucking love you, you asshole* seemed over the top.

She stared at the phone after setting it down on the coffee table, brushed the tears from her cheek, then stood and headed to her bedroom to get ready.

When Mish got to the bar, David was standing against the wall next to the door, trying to stay out of the way of the people passing on the sidewalks. He let out a breath that smoked into the cold day when his dark eyes met hers. Nervousness and tension were carved into the hard set of his shoulders and the rigid way he stood.

She'd done the same, blowing out a breath when she spied him. That combination of a gut punch and the absolute knowledge of coming home ran hard through her.

She'd missed him. More than she wanted to admit and in every way that told her this was worth fighting for—if he wanted to. He had to listen and work for their survival as well. They'd walk this path together or not at all: that was her bottom line.

She chose to step close enough that a shove or jostle from anyone passing might push them together. David met her gaze, tipping his head up a fraction.

"Come here often?" His voice was soft and broken. Full of all the things she'd wished he'd have said months ago.

"Hardly ever. But I met a guy I liked here once." Her throat stung, as did her eyes, though she could blame that on the cold. Maybe.

"Funny, I met a woman I liked here once. But I fucked it up horribly." He gave a little shrug. "Now I don't know what to do."

"Well, you did say something about buying me a beer. Let's start there?" She paused. "You okay with being seen with me in public?"

David crinkled his brow. "Why wouldn't I be?"

"Because all the rumors will start again," she said. "And this time I'll have to address them, one way or another."

More breath clouded the air. "Well, we're in public now. Might as well be in public where it's warmer and there's beer." His smile was slight, but it was the first she'd seen from him in months, and it took all her strength not to wrap her arms around him, and—hold on. Be each other's anchors in the rocky sea that was life.

But they also needed to be on the same page. She opened the door to the bar and gestured him in. That smile smoothed out when they found a booth toward the back. He peered up at the chalkboards with the list of draft beers, and that profile was everything. Hard angles, soft eyes. The well-kept beard and that smooth, golden skin.

Mish tore her gaze away to focus on the list of beers, too. "Got any recommendations?"

A little lift to his shoulder. "Depends on what you like. Lagers? Ales? Hops? Wheat? They've also got Belgians listed, though some of them are high-test."

"Well, it's not like I'm driving." She didn't even own a car, though she could afford one, even with the insurance.

"You are so in the driver's seat right now," David said.

She gave up on the board and stared at him. He'd turned,

too, and the same tension as earlier was back. "I know." All the decisions were hers to make. "But I need a good navigator. So you pick the beer."

He closed his eyes, briefly, and she couldn't read his expression at all. Pain? Hope? When their gazes met again, he nodded.

"I'd also like fries slathered in gravy." This sort of thing required comfort food.

For a moment, David's eyes danced. "I can do all that." The server chose that moment to come over, and David ordered the fries, plus two glasses of some Belgian tripel that was on tap.

When the server left, David folded his hands on top of the table. "I'm a complete and utter fuckup," he said. "You deserved a hell of a lot better than I gave you. I'm sorry."

Mish let her breath out slowly. There was truth there, and she appreciated that. But also a lie. "Not a *complete* fuckup. You're here, aren't you?"

He twisted his face, and his gaze dropped to his hands. "Should have realized a hell of a lot sooner."

There it was. "What did you realize? Will you tell me?"

Those deep brown eyes met hers, and even in the dim light of the bar, his apprehension was almost a second skin, tightening everything. He was shaking. "So many things. But mostly that you're far more important than a job or my own damn pride."

He flattened his hands onto the table. "I've been on my own for most of my life. Taken care of myself. But that doesn't mean I can't...let someone else call the shots. Especially if I love them." He paused, and his gaze never left hers. "And I love you. I do. I gotta go with that, you know?"

Mish's chest hurt and her head was a mess. But for once, her eyes didn't betray her with tears, which was good, especially since their beers appeared, in chalices, no less. Fancy.

When Mish thanked the server, she caught a woman at the

bar snapping a photo of her. The server, though, said, "Your fries'll be coming soon," before walking off.

David looked positively stricken, so Mish nudged at the coaster under his beer. "Have a drink."

A weak smile, but David did as told, which was nice. She'd always liked that about him—he didn't balk when she suggested something that was reasonable. When he put the glass down, he looked more steady.

The beer helped her as well. Loosened the knot in her chest and coated the sandpaper in her throat. "I didn't want you to leave your job. You decided that was what I wanted all on your own."

David's lips twisted again, but he nodded. "I couldn't see how anything between us would work if you were on tour and I was—I don't know. On tour with someone else. Or working some corporate gig following bigwigs, or whatever I found." He took another sip of beer. "How can we be together if we're apart?"

It was a legitimate question, and one he'd raised before. "Other people manage it. Long distance for a time, and together when schedules mesh." His expression was dubious, which she hated. "You know, when you pull that look—that one right there—you make me feel like I'm not worth the effort to even try."

That made him sit back. "Oh."

"Yeah, 'oh.'" She shook her head. "I don't want to change you or make you less than you are. I want to be with *you*."

The fries finally came. Mish grabbed two and stuffed them into her mouth. It was angry eating, but she didn't give a fuck. The fries and gravy were hot enough to burn, and as salty as her mood.

David peered into his beer. "I'm not good with long distance, but you're right. I shouldn't have discounted it. Should've tried." He turned the glass, but didn't drink. "The really fucked-up part was the answer was there. It's always been there, but my damn pride kept me from considering it."

"Keep going." It came out harsh, but she didn't regret that. Needed that. Hell, he did, too.

David's shoulders dropped. "You said it. Ray said it. I could find a place with Twisted Wishes. Be a part of your life. All your lives." He met her gaze again. "And I turned that down."

"You turned me down." The fries hadn't taken the edge off her anger at all, and the verbal blow hit David hard. He flinched, but didn't look away. His nod was a shaky mess.

Mish ate a fry, then another. Her lipstick had to be gone by now. To hell with everything. "Why?" It came out gritty and low.

"I didn't want to get a job with the band because I was your boyfriend." He worked his jaw, as if he were trying to decide if he should spit out his next words. "Didn't want to be a glorified groupie."

Part of her understood. Could even see his point. The other part wanted to toss a soggy, gravy-covered fry at his face.

Beer. Beer would help. She took a long drink, and it was cool and full of flavor and somehow soothing, even though the alcohol couldn't have gotten into her blood *that* fast.

She sat back. David was a *mess*. Sure, he was holding it together, but the fissures were there, and his remorse and sadness shown through.

"See?" His voice cracked. "My damn fucking pride." His turn to drink. He set the glass down carefully. "I'd ask for your forgiveness, but I don't deserve it."

"That's not for you to decide." Her fury was there, but it was abating. Slipping away into understanding. Frustration, too, because she felt a kinship with David's brand of dense-headedness. She could be as set in her ways and opinions, too.

But the band and the fans challenged her to be better than she was.

"There's a couple things you should know. First is that Ray would never hire *anyone* just because they're dating a band member. Don't you fucking sell yourself short like that. You've got skills. Ones we *need*. And I've got a pretty good idea where you'd fit in, 'cause the band talks about the future all the time. Second is that forgiveness isn't something you deserve. It's something you're gifted." She took a breath. "It's a lot like love, you know?"

David gripped his beer chalice around the bowl so tight Mish feared he might crack it.

"Third is that there's no way in hell I'm eating all these fries myself, so you better dig in." She pushed the plate toward him.

After a moment, he let go of the glass and took a few fries. His hands trembled. "I should tell you something."

"Yeah?" He had a weird inflection in his voice, but it didn't sound like what he was gonna say would break her heart.

"I talked to Adrian." He ate the fries and followed them with beer. "Don't have any close friends. Not much family." He shifted on the seat. "I left everyone. That's what he said." Another pause. "Being alone didn't bother me before, but I miss the band. And it's killing me to be away from you."

Another piece of understanding clicked. Yes, this was about them. But also affected everything.

"You don't have to take me back," David whispered.

"I know that." She wanted him. Wanted him back where he fit with her, in their family. "I'm going to anyway."

Those four words caused David to fumble with his beer. "Mish!" Her name came out high, but quiet. Like a prayer.

She pushed the plate of fries at him again. "Help me finish these fries, then come home with me."

David stared at her. "Just like that?" Dazed didn't even begin to describe his look.

She couldn't help but smile at him. "Yeah, just like that. 'Cause I love your troublesome ass and want you back. Took you long enough to come around."

He dug into the fries and his hands still shook. "I'm not always the best listener."

"So I've noticed." She stole a fry from the plate. "Let's not do that again, huh? We got issues, we talk about them, okay?"

The tension that had been in David leaked out. "Shit, yeah. These past few months have been hell." He shook his head as if to clear it. "Did we just get back together?"

"How about you pay, and I'll show you?"

Didn't have to ask him twice. David slipped out of the booth and headed to the bar. The fries were mostly gone. She downed the last of her beer and slid out of the booth. When David returned, she beckoned him with a finger, then did what she'd been wanting to do since she'd seen him standing there on the sidewalk—she pulled him into her arms and kissed his damn mouth. David gave a surprised grunt, but soon their tongues were tangling, his hands were on her hips and hers raked through his hair.

A flash went off, then another. Well, that would keep Adrian and Marcella busy. And happy.

Mish broke the kiss. "You think you can be a little less dense and a little more humble?"

He huffed a laugh. "Anything for you, princess."

She let that one go. Because she'd be a princess *and* a queen tonight. She grabbed his hand and tugged him toward the door. "Let's get out of here."

They went out into the cold October day, leaving a wake of social media fodder behind them. They didn't even make it back to her apartment before her phone rang. Adrian's name flashed across the screen.

"I guess the photos have gotten out." She took the call. "Hi, honey."

"Thank fucking god," Adrian said. "Ray'll be pleased."

Mish laughed loud, and it felt good, especially when David gave her hand a squeeze. "Yeah, I bet. And Zav will be smug like he planned it all along."

"Eh, but also secretly relieved."

So true. "What about your boy toy?"

"Dominic is already planning to accost you two for a double date sometime."

"Oh, do we get to be voyeurs to your teasing Dom with food?"

There was a croak on the other end. "Am I that bad?"

"Honey, you're that good." She paused. "We can talk about all of this later, though."

"Almost home, huh?"

She grinned at David. "Good*night,* Adrian. And thank you."

"Your man was smart enough to reach out to me. He's a keeper."

"Yeah," she said, "I know."

"See ya, Mish."

When she hung up, David gave her hand another squeeze, but he didn't say a word. He still seemed blown away by their whole conversation.

They reached her apartment building, and Lorenzo greeted them both. She kept holding David's hand until the doors of the elevator closed, at which point she shoved him up against the back of the car and took his mouth again. There was the moan that she so loved. The surprise and the surrender.

When she came up for air, his pupils were huge and his lips were plump. "It's a little early to ask to spend the night, isn't it?"

The elevator doors opened and she pulled him out into

the hall. "Not in my book." They tumbled into her apartment, and before David said another word, she had his coat on the floor and his shirt up and over his head. "You think you need to ask?"

They made it as far as the hall to her bedroom before she had him up against a wall again. The way he moved and squirmed when she did that was the best. She kissed her way up his neck and mouthed his beard.

"Gonna always ask." He spoke between shudders as she ran her palm down his chest to the belt of his jeans. "Never gonna take you—or this—for granted."

"Good." She silenced him with a kiss and undid his belt and jeans. "Can I jerk you off? Right here, like this?"

"Oh god, yes." He met her gaze. "Anything you want. Any time." He quirked a smile. "As long as it's not gonna get us arrested, you know?"

The next kiss she gave him was softer, more gentle. She slipped her hand into his pants and underwear, past the packer, and found his dick. The moan he made was absolutely the best thing she'd heard in ages.

She kept his mouth occupied while she stroked him off, enjoying the grip of his hands on her waist, then arms, then tangled tightly into her hair as she took him higher and higher. He thrust and moaned and practically climbed her body until he came, his groans deep and glorious.

He was beautiful like that, half-naked, drenched in sweat. His eyes were hooded and his smile was exactly what she missed so much.

"Fuck, baby." He blinked his eyes open. "And me without my bag of dicks." The smile gave way to a little sexy grin.

"I'm sure you can figure out another way to get me off." Mish kissed the end of his nose.

"Dozens of ways." The happiness dimmed for a second. "Missed you so much. Not just this. Everything."

She kissed his forehead this time, tasting salt there. "Shh.

Take me to bed and show me." He'd been in enough pain—they both had during their lives.

When she gave him room, he took her hand and led her to her bedroom. They got halfway to the bed when he stopped in his tracks. "You tucked Marly in."

"Every day." Those treacherous tears were in her eyes. "He kept me safe every night, too."

He rotated, and there was such agony in his expression. "Mish."

"I love you." She pushed a strand of hair away from his forehead. "Didn't like what you did. But I never stopped loving you." She paused. "And Marly reminded me every night that you loved me, too, even though you had your head up your ass."

David's laugh at that was part humor, part pain. "Yeah. I did. Getting better, I hope."

"Yeah, you are. And you'd be even better in bed."

This time his laughter was full of joy. He took her hand and drew her the rest of the way to the bed. Marly was set aside on the nightstand, and David proceeded to show Mish exactly how much he'd missed her.

Later, when they'd spent themselves too many times to count, she spoke against his warm neck. "We're gonna make it, you and me."

He stroked her back. "Yeah. Whatever comes, we can make it work."

She truly believed that now. "Consort to a rock queen."

"Best job in the world," David murmured, and kissed her cheek.

Yeah. Everything was gonna be okay.

CHAPTER TWENTY-FIVE

David didn't need to walk venues anymore—the security team he'd put together for Twisted Wishes did all of that work. He was a manager now, basically. Sure, he could chase after problems and add muscle if needed. It hadn't been.

But every concert, he still did a circuit of the entire place. The backstage area. The dressing and greenrooms. Loading dock. Helped free his mind. Relax him. Plus, it kept his team sharp when they saw him on the prowl.

Security hadn't been an issue at all this tour. Mish's stalker was behind bars, and no new obsessive fan had taken his place, thank god. In fact, aside from stage jumpers and some line crashers, they hadn't had any issues.

If anything, much of his time this tour—aside from coordinating and managing the security team—had been occupied with hunting down Danny, the bass player Mish's mother had dated all those years ago. Wasn't an easy task, given they had very little intel on the man, scraped out of Mish's memories. She'd even dug back into some personal items and found a single, slightly blurry photo with *Danny M.* and a phone number scrawled on the back.

Mish had shaken her head when she'd handed it over. "I

wish I remembered his last name. I think it was something Italian, but that's not really helpful."

David had kissed her cheek. "It's more than I had before. The phone number might help."

He was still chasing down those leads and turning over all the information in his head. Walking helped that, too. He headed out into the venue, a modern concert hall built specifically for rock shows. Much smaller than the arenas they'd played during the summer—but these shows were a little different. Longer sets. More intimate venues.

David strode down the aisles until a familiar voice stopped him in his tracks. "Mr. Altet!"

He turned on his heels. "Ms. Heydel." He greeted her with a grin. She was as familiar in some ways as his walks through the venues. "And how are you this fine day?"

She snorted. "You're full of charm, David. Wish you were full of an interview, though." Always hopeful, always that sharp edge. He'd gotten used to it.

They were friendly adversaries now—or maybe strange friends. He hadn't figured that out yet. "You know I don't give interviews."

"But as Mish's fiancé..."

Oh man, she really was digging. "I wasn't aware Mish and I were engaged." They'd joked about getting hitched sometime after Adrian and Dom finally married, but that was it. Both he and Mish were just happy to be dating at this point.

Heydel waved a hand. "Well, will you be? Fans want to know!"

He sighed. "Vick..."

"Okay, *I* want to know."

"No comment, Ms. Heydel." He said it with a smile.

"Can't fault me for trying, David. It's the whole bodyguard-whirlwind-romance thing. You took a knife for her, and now you two are inseparable."

He held up his hands.

"Okay, okay. Give me something, though? You guys are the hot story now."

He didn't have anything to give. Both he and Mish preferred their personal lives to stay out of the spotlight.

"Let me talk to Marcella and Mish." It was a bone without much meat, but maybe they could come up with some exclusive something or other. Photoshoot. A tiny Q and A.

"You're an okay guy, David," Heydel said.

He couldn't help laughing. "I'll be sure to put that on my résumé." He gave her a wave and continued on his route.

Marriage? Maybe. Maybe not. Really depended on what Mish wanted. David had everything he needed right now. Mish. Twisted Wishes. The loner hooked up with a partner he didn't deserve and a family that accepted him for who he was. Never thought it could happen to him.

He was so very grateful it had.

Mish had never been this nervous on stage before, even back in her early days. Hell, she'd been less of a wreck her first night stripping. Then again, that had only been her body exposed on the stage. This—this was a piece of her soul.

She covered her nervousness and how hard her heart thumped in her chest by spinning away from the screaming, cheering audience after they finished their first encore, and went for a drink from the water bottle she kept on the base of Zavier's drum kit stand.

She met his gaze before she grabbed the bottle and he spun a stick in his hand. *Breathe,* he mouthed through the space between them.

Some of the nerves fled. Zavier was being Zav and trying to control the situation, and that was so normal. She took a swig of water, grinned at him, and headed back to the front of the stage.

She met Ray and Dom halfway there. Ray slung his arm around her shoulder. "You ready for this?"

"I don't know, kiddo. You think I have the chops?" Singing, sure. Playing, yes, of course. But singing and playing a song she'd had a hand in writing? Maybe—maybe not. This was the first time they were performing it outside the practice studio. Hell, they hadn't even played it at warmups.

It was Domino who punched her in the arm. "Mish, you're in fucking Twisted Wishes. Of course you have the chops!"

Ray laughed. "Let's light 'em up." He headed back to his mic, while she and Domino danced around each other, playing little riffs.

"You'll slay them," Dom said. "They'll go home singing your song."

Maybe. No—yes. They would. They had this. *She* had this.

She danced up to the front of the stage as Ray took his mic in hand. "Hey, you ready for a brand-new song?"

Of course the crowd went wild, though she guessed most of them figured they'd sing something from the demos for the new album that had been "mysteriously" leaked onto the internet. Adrian's doing. But not *this* song. This one they'd kept under wraps until tonight, their last tour date before they recorded a new album over the winter.

She plucked at a few notes on her bass and peered out into the pit. The stage lights made it almost impossible to see past the first few rows. She shaded her eyes.

"You've never heard this before." Ray dropped his voice, and somehow the audience quieted a little.

Out beyond the pit stood David, his arms crossed over that sinful body of his. Light glinted off his face from someone's camera flash, and there was his smile, the one that crinkled his eyes and made her heart soar.

As the band's security advisor, David didn't need to be out there; he'd hired a whole team to keep the band safe. But he always watched them—her—perform from out in the audience. One fan she knew would be there.

She blew him a kiss, then stepped up to her own mic. "Ray and I got a little creative together. His music—my lyrics. My song."

The fans screamed and pounded. Behind her, the familiar clicks of Zavier beating out the rhythm, and then they launched into "Walk to the Sun," her bass line a counterpoint to Zavier's rhythm. Domino came screaming in with his guitar, and when the time was exactly right, Mish opened her mouth and sang the words that had been in her soul.

Taste a dying dream
Sadness on tap
No way to mend what is gone
Or fill a void with no end
Take my hand, show me the sun
Walk this path
I am not alone
With you by my side
Fill my soul tonight
Drink the past and future
Show me hope
Together we are one

Ray joined in on the chorus, once more tossing an arm around Mish as they sang and she played. It was perfect. Magical. Every moment of her life seemed to lead to this one, here on this stage with her voice spinning out into the crowd, mixing with Ray's, her hands playing the notes he'd laid down and they'd all perfected. Domino's guitar. Zavier's drums. The band that was her life and her family. Adrian and Marcella stood in the wings.

And David—her David—was out there to hear her sing

and play. To see that they were safe, night after night. He'd come *home*. They'd all come home.

Tears blurred her vision when she finished and the audience exploded into shouts and stomps and screams.

"Told you," Ray murmured into her ear.

She couldn't help her smile or the shove she gave him as the house lights came up. They waved to the crowd. Mish tossed her pick to a woman in the pit and they all took their bows before heading off stage. She almost took her bass with her, but one of the crew caught her.

A breathless smile from Alex, one of the newer members they'd picked up. "I can pack that for you."

She handed the bass over to them. "Last time this tour."

That got Mish a laugh. "Well, if you'll have me, I'll be on the next one, too." They paused. "We all would be, you know?"

"I know. I'm sure a lot of you will be, too." She gave Alex a little salute, then headed to the dressing rooms.

One first, lots of lasts—at least for tonight. The hallway was a blur until she reached a very familiar figure leaning up against the wall outside the dressing room door, hands shoved into the pockets of his blue jeans.

"Rock queen." David's smile was wide, his eyes so warm. Every time she saw him in a crew shirt, her heart flipped. He didn't have to wear them—he'd chosen to.

"You're never gonna let me live that down, are you?"

His laugh made her soul tumble. "Baby, there's nothing to live down. You were a queen the first day we met, and you're a queen now." He tilted his head. "Want me to stop?"

Oh, that wasn't right. She strode up, planted her hands on either side of his head and loomed over him, her leather-clad legs brushing against his. "Not on your life."

He didn't flinch, just lifted his chin a little, open, expectant. "Still want me to worship you?"

"Every fucking night." She took his mouth in a hard kiss.

His hands closed around her waist, and the space between them vanished long enough to whet her appetite for more David and less clothes.

But the night wasn't over yet. Someone cleared his throat next to them.

"I do hate to break up the party..." Adrian's voice was almost apologetic. *Almost.*

"You enjoying the view?" Mish spoke against David's lips.

For his part, David sighed, but when he opened his eyes, there was amusement dancing there.

"Yeah. You two look happy," Adrian said.

Good. It was about damn time for both of them. She pushed off the wall. "Can't argue with that."

"Don't want to argue," David said. "But you do have a horde of fans to greet, darling."

"Your man's got it in one," Adrian said, then vanished back into the dressing room.

Her man. Her very lovely man. "Later, then?"

He laughed. "Always. As long as you want."

"Always is perfect." She stole another kiss, grabbed his hand, and pulled him into the dressing room with the rest of Twisted Wishes.

Always was a promise she'd made to herself. Always this, right now.

To purchase and read more books by Anna Zabo, please visit Anna's website
at annazabo.com/books/.

ACKNOWLEDGMENTS

Second Edition: Once again, much thanks to Layla Reyne for her support and help while I worked to bring this new edition out.

First Edition: Many thanks to Angela James and the team at Carina for being supportive of all the Twisted Wishes books, but especially for this one. I owe a debt of gratitude to Mackenzie Walton for both uplifting me and also pushing me to be a stronger writer. This book wouldn't shine so bright without her. Also, thanks to Layla for the coffee and Xen for the pep talk. And always, love and friendship to Lori.

ALSO BY ANNA ZABO

TAKEOVER

Takeover

Just Business

Due Diligence

Daily Grind

ON THE BOARD (WRITTEN WITH L.A. WITT)

Rookie Mistake

Scoreless Game

Shift Change (coming soon)

TWISTED WISHES

Syncopation

Counterpoint

Reverb

CLOSE QUARTER

Close Quarter

Slow Waltz (a Close Quarter short story)

STANDALONE WORKS

CTRL Me

Outside the Lines

Weave the Dark, Weave the Light

Cinnamon Roll

Love of the Game

ABOUT THE AUTHOR

Anna Zabo writes contemporary and paranormal romance for all colors of the rainbow. They live and work in Pittsburgh, Pennsylvania, which isn't nearly as boring as most people think.

They can be easily plied with coffee or a chance to see the Pittsburgh Penguins.

Anna has an MFA in Writing Popular Fiction from Seton Hill University, where they fell in with a roving band of romance writers and never looked back. They also have a BA in Creative Writing from Carnegie Mellon University.

Anna uses they/them pronouns and prefers Mx. Zabo as an honorific. They can be found online at annazabo.com.

x.com/amergina
instagram.com/amergina
bookbub.com/authors/anna-zabo
amazon.com/Anna-Zabo/e/B00A7LA6OC

www.ingramcontent.com/pod-product-compliance
Lightning Source LLC
Chambersburg PA
CBHW021435240626
47153CB00001B/158

* 9 7 8 1 9 4 7 5 5 0 2 2 3 *